Desire
Resting Bitchface 4 late

GINGER

SPIN IT: BOOK TWO

Dance all nite!

Angera Allen

Desiree,
Testing Bithches Hoe

Dance all nite!

signature

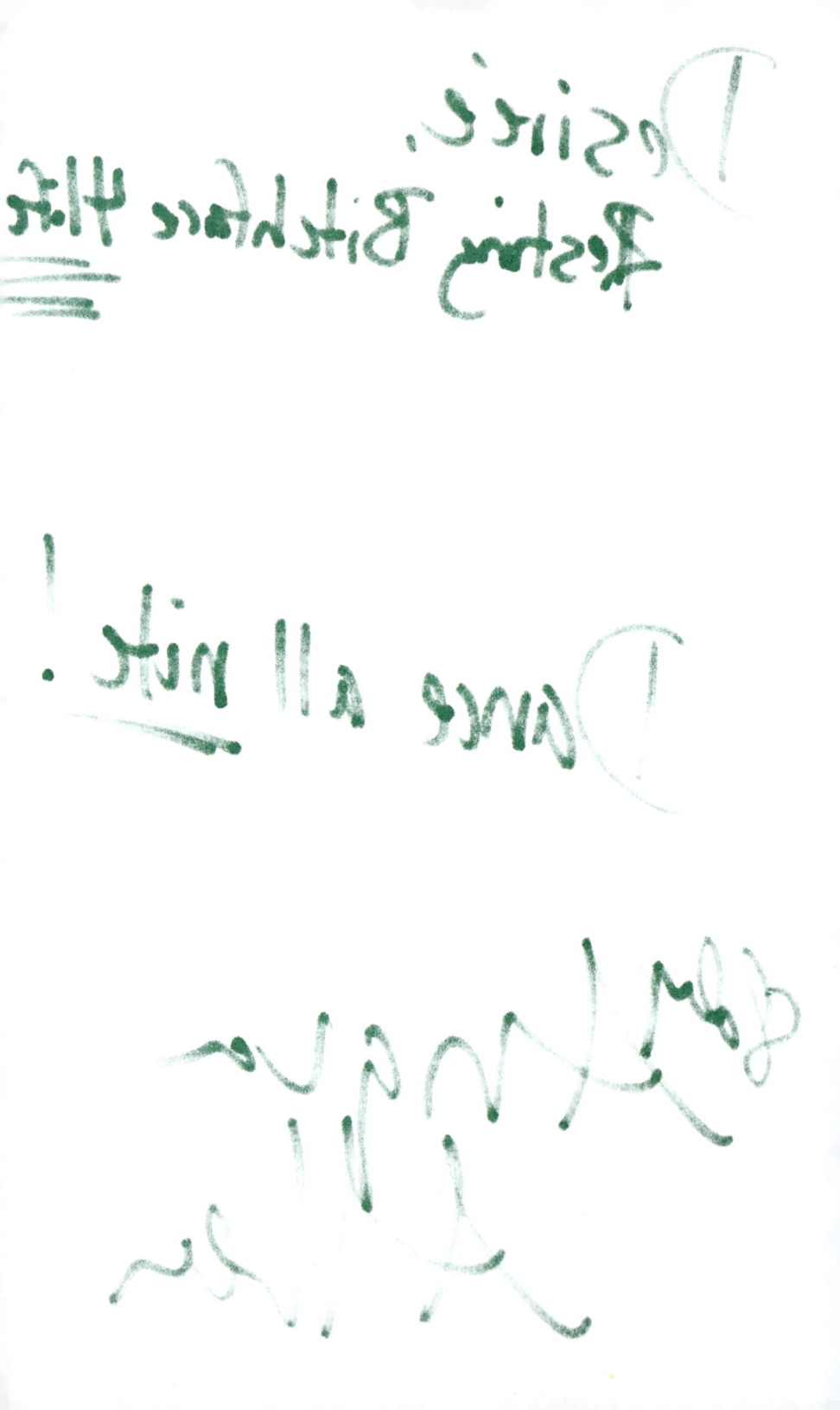

Copyright © 2017 by Angera Allen

No part of this book may be reproduced, distributed, or transmitted in any form or by any means, including photocopying, recording, or other electronic or mechanical methods, without the prior written permission of the author, except in the case of brief quotations embodied in critical reviews and certain other noncommercial uses permitted by copyright law.

All rights reserved. Except as permitted under the U.S. Copyright Act of 1976, no part of this publication may be reproduced, distributed, or transmitted in any form or by any means, or stored in a database or retrieval system, without the prior express, written consent of the author. This book is intended for mature adults only.

For questions or comments about this book, please contact the author at authorangeraallen@gmail.com.

Printed in the United States of America

Angera Allen
www.authorangeraallen.com

Publisher's Note: This is a work of fiction. Names, characters, places, and incidents are a product of the author's imagination. Locales and public names are sometimes used for atmospheric purposes. Any resemblance to actual people, living or dead, or to businesses, companies, events, institutions, or locales is completely coincidental.

Editor Ellie McLove at Love N Books
Formatted by Jessica Hildreth at Love N Books
Cover Design by Clarise Tan at CT Cover Creations
Cover Photographer by Eric David Battershell at Eric Battershell Photography
Cover Model Kaitlin Hughes
Proofreaders:
Petra with Love N Books
Dawn Birch
Jennifer Guibor
Kim Holtz

Ginger / Angera Allen. -- 1st ed.
Paperbank ISBN 978-0-9986829-3-8
Ebook ISBN 978-0-9986829-2-1

DEDICATION

This book is dedicated to my mom!
There are not enough words to describe or even express how much I love my mom. She is my everything with her undying love and unwavering support in everything I do. There has never been a time she hasn't been there for me, and I don't know where I would be today without her.

Mom,
I love you with everything I have.
Thank you for being the best mom ever!
Love, your daughter

GINGER PLAYLIST

"Barracuda" by Heart
"Pride and Joy" by Stevie Ray Vaughan
"Lucky Star" by Madonna
"Radioactive" by Imagine Dragons
"Smack That" by Akon
"My Feelings For You" by Avicii
"Dreams" by Fleetwood Mac
"Like A Wrecking Ball" by Eric Church
"Sail" by Awolnation
"Bossy" by Kelis
"Closer" by Goaplele
"It's Your Love" by Tim McGraw, Faith Hill
"If Tomorrow Never Comes" by Garth Brooks
"Bilingual" by Jose Nunez
"Wonderwall" by Oasis
"Angel" by Sarah McLachlan
"Pour Some Sugar On Me" by Def Leppard
"S&M" by Rhianna
"The Reason" by Hoobastank
"Here Without You" by 3 Doors Down
"By Your Side" by Sade
"Can't Get Enough" by Soulsearcher
"Rapture" by Nadi Ali
"Bitch, I'm Madonna" by Madonna and Nicki Minaj

Prologue

GINGER

You would think at almost twenty-three years old that I would have some kind of balance in my life since I've known what I have wanted to be ever since I was old enough to have a record player. Yeah, well I don't. Most people my age are trying to figure out what they want to be or what they want to do for the rest of their life, changing majors, blah blah blah but not me. I've always known, hell, I've been DJing professionally for the past three years, at Spin It, Inc, in New York City.

Music has always been a major factor in my life since I was a young kid, but when I lost my momma and cousin, who was my best friend at the age of ten, I threw myself into music, closing myself off to the world.

My problem isn't what I want to do for a living, but it's more the problem of who I see myself as. I left home almost three years ago completely lost with a broken heart and in search of my own identity, but I'm still torn between my two lives. I'm just as fucked up now if not more than the day I left home.

Most of my life I've been known as Ginger "Snow" Wolfe, daughter of Wolfeman MC's president John "Prez" Wolfe, whom everyone calls Wolfe. I always thought I would become an "ol' lady" or work at some local radio station. But, I've always wanted to be someone people remembered when they turned the radio on, so when I was given the opportunity, I took it, and I moved to New York.

My dad thought me moving here and learning under the famously known Lucas Mancini also known as DJ Luscious Luc, at Spin It, Inc. record label, that I would freak out being far away from home and want to move back. Yeah, that didn't work out too well for him. When I moved to New York, I became Ginger "DJ GinGin" Wolfe leaving behind Ginger "Snow" Wolfe.

In my first year here it was all business, learning and me showing Luc what I could do. He took me in and pushed me hard, helping me stay focused on my dream. With me devoting all my time and energy to the music, I pushed my heartbreak and losses behind a high wall, suppressing any negative emotions.

Luc was amazing, and he threw me out to the wolves, and by my second year, he had me on stage DJing professionally at his club, even when I wasn't of age to be in the clubs. It was the best thing in my life. I think between Luc and my father they tried to push me past my limits. Both for different reasons, Luc being that he wanted to see if I was up for the lifestyle, while my father was hoping it would scare me so I would run back to my old life but they didn't know how bad I wanted to be free. Free from what I still don't know.

A few months after my twenty-first birthday I told my father I was going on tour in Europe with another DJ a girl named DJ Izzy, along with Luc's daughter Alexandria and of course a shit load of security. I thought my father was bad, but Luc is WAY more protective than my father. My father was pissed and said no but he knew he couldn't stop me, so he put major restrictions on me, which Luc had no problem abiding by.

I thought the year away from any contact with both my lives and just being free to focus on my music would have been the best year of my life, but in all honesty, it was the worst. My heart split into two identities fighting within my own head, Snow vs. GinGin.

It all started with a boy named Micah "Shy" Jenkins who

came into my life on my sweet sixteen birthday and put my broken heart back together after the death of my momma and cousin Faith. I was broken, lost, and when my heart started beating again, he took it, never giving it back. He's the reason I left my hometown as well. I needed to get away from him so I could find myself again. The calls and texts still come, but they slowed to just text messages while I was in Europe.

I did say earlier that I'm more fucked up now than before I left well, that could be because Brant Bolton came barreling into my life. Yes, another guy for my brain to fight over. Brant is Alexandria Mancini's personal bodyguard, and when all of us girls went to Europe, he came with us. The attraction was instant as soon as he shook my hand, hence the battle of Snow vs. Gin.

Being away from my family and getting to know the girls was hard for me at first. It was another reason I'd left home. Faith was really my only girlfriend and after she was gone, I had a hard time making new ones. I was raised and hung out with men, so I don't take any shit, but being around girls made me more of an introvert, it was hard. I always felt so guilty that here I was having fun with these girls, while she was gone. Also, living with mostly all men at the clubhouse to living with just four girls was a big transition.

I had met the girls over the year leading up to us planning this tour. Alexandria, or Alex as we call her, and I became really close. We were both introverts compared to the girls that were with us, but we helped each other come out of our shells letting new girlfriends into our hearts. Izzy, the other DJ, was the hyper, crazy funny one that kept all of us on our toes and pushed us beyond our comfort zone. The emotional roller coaster in my head that year kept me pretty quiet compared to the other girls.

When we got back from Europe, I was supposed to go home for a while, but things between Brant and I started to heat up, so I stayed in New York. Then things started happening with Alex, a ghost from her past was trying to hurt her. It only made me feel

I needed to stay and be with her for support. Plus, I didn't want to stop DJing since I started to have a little bit of a following. People actually come to hear me play.

Which brings me to the here and now, with the events of the last few days that have both of my lives crashing into each other. It's time I decided between my two lives and find answers to all these damn questions running through my head. Am I going to be DJ GinGin or Snow because really I can't keep battling myself and I need to figure out if I'm ready to move on and leave behind my first and only love?

So many questions.

So many uncertainties.

Can I get out of my own head enough to be happy?

GINGER

While lying in my hospital bed, I remind myself of all the events that led up to me to be here in the first place, like DJing the music festival, and the shootout to save Alex's life, ending with me being shot. I'm safe, and Alex is safe.

Taking a deep breath in relief, I ignore the pain spiraling through my body, and I focus on trying to open my eyes. They're all waiting for me to wake up. I feel like I'm awake, I hear everyone around me. I hear everyone talking about Emmett and Jason, but it's like a dream. I try to open my eyes and can't.

Feeling the drugs start to kick in, I relax my mind and just lay there not moving or making a noise but instead just lay there waiting for something to happen. I do a mental check on my injuries. Remembering and feeling my gunshot wounds to the shoulder and thigh. When I feel a hand move within mine, I realize someone is holding it, but no one is talking.

Fuck am I dreaming? Who's holding my hand?

I try to squeeze the hand, and when I hear a gasp of air, I realize they must feel it because whoever it is moves abruptly, and I hear a chair move next to the bed.

I don't try to speak or open my eyes because the drugs keep flowing through me, pushing me deeper into sedation, so I just lay there. I feel an enormous body lean over me, pressing full lips to my forehead, and that's when I smell him. *Holy Shit. Micah!* His smell I would recognize anywhere, all the years I used to steal his sweatshirts just so I could smell him when he wasn't around. *Fuck.*

Micah "Shy" Jenkins, my father's pride and joy, the son he never had, the one he hopes will follow in his footsteps by becoming President of the Wolfeman MC. But most importantly, the pain of my existence and the one man I gave my heart to only to crush it.

All my emotions and memories start crashing in consuming me, lust- rage- desire- hurt- sadness and most of all rejection. *Why is he the one by my bed? Where is my dad?* I feel a tear run down my face because it just isn't fair.

"Angel, my light. I know you can hear me, please come back to me. Let me see those beautiful green eyes," Shy murmurs into my ear.

What the hell. He sounds like my Micah, the one that loved me.

My body heat turns up a notch and I try to calm my erratic breathing when the pain starts to rip through me only making it worse. I start to count in my head hoping it will ease my heart rate back down and release some of this rage and frustration.

Why? Why Now?

Shy leans over my body brushing his lips over mine. "Snow, please stay calm. You have a lot of injuries, Angel, so please try to relax and breathe." Another soft kiss touches my lips, sending me into a full panic and when I go to move my arm, an alarm goes off sending me back into the darkness.

When the haze lifts again, I hear yelling and then my father's voice booms over all of them, "Shut the fuck up. You're stressing her out, and I will not fucking have you two fighting over her in here. Both of you get the fuck out. I want to be alone with my daughter." Then all I hear is a bunch of grumbling and chairs moving and what I'm guessing is a door opening.

When I hear a giggle next to me, I know it's Alex. My heart relaxes hearing her, knowing I saved her life and didn't let her die. Alex touches my face moving my hair or something on my head while she speaks to my dad. "Wolfe, I guess I know where you got your nickname before you were president." She giggles.

I can feel her move around me heading toward the door with her hand gliding over my body never letting her fingers lose contact.

"She's lucky to have all of you. I never knew how much we were alike until now. She had all you big bad Wolfes protecting her, and I had all my badass brutish men too." Her voice gets raspy sounding like she is going to cry. "I'm so sorry this happened. I don't know what I would do if she…" Alex pauses. "I can't lose her, so please don't take her away from me."

I try to speak, but nothing comes out and when I move my hand I hear the beeping start, so I stop moving. I scream in my head, *Alex, wait, I'm here. I'm not going anywhere. I won't lose another best friend. I can't.*

Dad cuts her off. "Alex, none of that nonsense, you hear me. I'm sorry for the other day. I was just pissed off at your father and scared shitless of losing my princess. She's all I have besides my club. All those boys out there would go crazy if we lost her too. Promise me if those two knuckleheads start acting up in here, you'll call me."

What's going on? Who's fighting? I'm here, Daddy. I missed him so much.

Flashbacks of when I was in the accident with Momma and Faith. I was calling to them, and they never answered. *Am I dreaming?* Frustration takes over so I try moving but can't even budge. My body is floating around, but I hear everyone. I try to stay awake, but sleep consumes me again drifting off thinking about my dad and the club. My other life.

GINGER

(Sixteen years old)

I can't believe it. I turn sweet sixteen today which means I can drive myself anywhere I want to go and finally not have to ask any of the guys for a ride. Don't get me wrong, I usually don't go anywhere alone, but if I want to go to the store or maybe shopping, I can do it without having someone with me now. Having a protective father that is the president of a motorcycle club is very lonely. Well, lonely meaning no girlfriends. I have all the members who are all family to me but the kids my age are boys. Let's just say I have a lot of fucking uncles that are just as protective of me.

After my momma died, it was my dad and the club raising me. They called me Snow, like Snow White and the Seven Dwarfs but instead of seven dwarfs I have like twenty, and they're nowhere near dwarfs, more like werewolves by the way they act. I still love watching the damn cartoon. Snow White was a bad-ass. Her mom died, and she was raised by her dad, just like me. I don't see me meeting my huntsmen anytime soon, but I don't have a problem kicking some fucking ass.

A knock at my door brings me out of my fantasy dream. "Snow, you up girl? It's almost noon for God's sake."

Right on time, my auntie Storm wakes me up every year with breakfast and a motherly talk. Nikol "Storm" Harding is Dad's sister, who was Momma's best friend and she's married to one of my dad's best friends, Boyd "Bear" Harding. She pretty much took on the role of being my momma when I needed girl stuff.

Auntie and I were also in the car accident that killed Momma and Faith. They had just picked us girls up from school, and we were on our way to go shopping when a semi-truck hit our SUV, hitting Momma and Faith's side and killing them on impact. Auntie and I were hospitalized for close to a month, missing the funerals. I think missing the funeral has a lot to do with my issues. I was only ten at the time but losing them and not being able to say goodbye really fucked me up in the head.

Another knock at the door pulls me from my thoughts. "Yeah, Auntie, come on in."

I finish tying my Chucks when she strolls in. Storm is beautiful and looks amazing for having two kids. She and Momma had kids young. They were two peas in a pod back then and were pretty much inseparable. Storm could pass as my momma or my sister we looked so much alike, with our jet-black hair and green eyes. Momma had reddish brown hair. They used to call her Foxy because of her hair, and of course, Dad thought she was a fox.

"Girl, you know all those men are downstairs waiting on your ass. I had to convince your daddy not to wake you up this morning, to let you sleep and not go to school today, each year gets harder and harder for me to convince him you need your birthday off." Storm laughs leaning in the door frame.

"Auntie, I could've gone to school. It isn't a big deal. I'm either going to sit around here today or sit around at school, it makes no difference." Shrugging I turn around to grab my sweatshirt and iPod.

I don't ever really get dressed up. I'm always in jeans, Chucks, and a sweatshirt. I'm average height at five foot four inches but small boobs and a bubble butt of an ass. I don't like how my body is proportioned, so I hide it as much as I can. I think my dad loves that I'm more of a tomboy than a girlie girl.

He doesn't have to worry about me too much. I stick to myself most the time, working on music or writing. Ever since Momma died, I turned to music to escape. It helped me heal and move on, but sometimes I question if I am really moving on or just hiding from life. I started to dissect the music, learning how to count beats and I guess you can say that is where my love for music blossomed. I downloaded software to play around with tunes, reading and watching tutorials on how to mix. So, I was always either in my room or at the library most of the time.

The only person I really hang out with since I lost Faith is her brother, my cousin, Macon, but we all call him Mac. He is a senior, while I'm a sophomore and he takes me to and from school, but today hopefully that will change. Mac is totally popular, and I'm the opposite, being a loner at school, but he's always watching over me. No one messes with me thanks to him.

"Snow, what do you want to do today? Maybe go shopping for an outfit for tonight's party? We need to go get some stuff for dinner that the prospects forgot but other than that it's your day honey." Storm wraps her arms around me, giving me a big hug and kiss on the head. I hug her back knowing she is missing Momma right now, so I hold tight until her moment is over.

When she lets go she has tears in her eyes, "Your momma would be so proud of you, Snow. Maybe not your choice of clothes…" Storm laughs nudging me towards the door. She thinks I need to start dressing like a girl, but I always tell her I love my clothes. I think she wishes I was more girlie and wanted to do girlie things like getting my nails done or shopping. I hate shopping, and I never do girlie things. I love my long raven black hair, and I wouldn't think to change it, so I don't even do the salons.

Leaving my house, I hear "Barracuda" by Heart blaring in the courtyard with only a few members hanging out. The clubhouse is on twenty acres of land and was built around an old hotel. It is like a u-shape with a courtyard and big pool in the middle. They built a wall around all the buildings, so there's only one way in and one way out. You can drive all the way around our compound but if you go left it will lead you to the clubhouse and hotel parking in the back, or you can go right toward the houses, which end up close to the parking lot. Dad had three houses built on the property. Dad and I live in one house, while Storm and her family live in another, and the third house is for original members. Everyone else is pretty much in the hotel part. The hotel is between us, so we are close, but far enough away we don't hear all the parties.

The big shop is where everything happens. Dad has his meetings there, the game room, bar, kitchen and pretty much everything else you can think of. There's an office upstairs and another room. Dad usually stays up there when he parties. I guess he doesn't want to bring anyone back here or have me be around any of that. My house is pretty big itself. Dad built it before him and Momma were married. They thought they would have a lot of babies, but that plan didn't work. It's just me.

When I approach the shop, I hear one of my dad's favorite songs "Pride and Joy" by Stevie Ray Vaughan sounding through the door. It makes me smile because he would play this song on repeat if he could. Once I walk into the shop, everyone screams 'happy birthday.' Standing in front of me beside a table is my dad and a big box. He walks up grabbing my hands to dance with him while everyone cheers us on. I start laughing because he always wants to swing dance with me. Once the song is over, he hugs me tight saying, "Happy Sweet Sixteen, Princess."

A blush creeps into my cheeks. "Thank you, Daddy." After I hug him, I turn to all the rest of my family.

"Open your present, Snow."

Everyone starts cheering for me to open my gift. I look over at my dad who's smiling from ear to ear. He's a good-looking guy, I have told him he should remarry but he gets really upset when I bring up Momma.

Fidgeting with the box, before I start to open it. Everyone gets really quiet waiting for me. When I tear open the box and look in, I freeze.

No- fucking- way.

My mixing equipment that I have been saving for over a year trying to get.

"Holy. Shit. Daddy."

"Watch your language!" he barks.

I'm beaming with joy. "Oh.My.God!" I start to jump up and down then turn jumping into his arms. Everyone starts to laugh and cheer.

"Princess, you're officially our full-time DJ. Except after hours, that's still a no, but you can make one of those mix things for us." Dad kisses the top of my head. "I love you, Princess."

Tears fill my eyes I kiss him on the cheek. "I love you too, Daddy. Always have…"

He chuckles, "…always will, Princess."

He releases me, and everyone starts handing me more gifts. While I'm opening a gift, Dad's phone rings and then his smile is gone. For him to even smile is a lot because he doesn't usually do it unless it's for me.

"What the fuck" -everyone goes quiet, and all eyes are on him- "Where? Who?" he booms. Dad snaps his fingers at Cash and then the front door. Men are moving in all directions. "Well, we're on our way to the gate right now."

It's a raid. Great, on my fucking birthday we get raided.

Everyone's moving when he gets off the phone yelling, "Stitch better go get your bag, Storm we'll need the emergency kits and all ladies' hands on right now. Dallas's bringing in Mac and some kid.

"No! Please, Jesus, not my Macon," Storm cries out.

Dad turns to her with a stern face. "Sis. Dallas said he got jumped, but this kid jumped in and helped him. They were beaten up really badly but are okay. The kid got the worst of it and is in bad shape, but he will be okay from what Dallas said. Now I need you to get the supplies, darling."

All the ladies are running around, some comforting Storm while others are making room for them to bring the boys in and I just stand there watching. *Always something in this life, never a fucking dull moment.*

They are carrying Mac and the other kid into the shop, and they lay them on the pool tables where the ladies covered them with plastic. I make my way over to see if Mac's okay. He's more like a brother than a cousin to me. Everyone is screaming or yelling, but when I look down, I gasp when I see this kid. His face is swollen, black and blue all over with his clothes drenched in blood from multiple stab wounds.

I react instantly pulling my sweatshirt off and applying pressure to his arms. I jump right in, cleaning him so we can assess his wounds. Everyone is freaking out about Mac, but this kid is really hurt. I push his blood filled hair out of his face.

"I need a lot of ice, and I needed it two minutes ago," I yell out as I start patching his arm. They're all superficial cuts but bleeding a lot. I order one of the club girls to cut his shirt off so we can see what else is wrong with him.

Fuck, is he even alive? Please be alive, kid, please. Dallas comes back with ice, and I tell him to put it on his face but make sure to put a towel on his face first, so he doesn't get burned. Dallas just looks at me like I'm crazy.

"Ice. Fucking. Burn. Dumb. Ass. You know, like freezer burn." I hear laughter behind me.

I'm starting to bandage one of his cuts up when I feel someone grab my hip. I jump back but keep holding his arm. He doesn't let go of my shirt. I move the ice from his face to see if I can see his eyes yet but they are still swollen shut.

I lean down to his ear. "Don't worry kid, you're going to be okay. My name is Snow, and I got you, just relax." When he tugs on my shirt again, I know he understood. He still doesn't let go of my shirt, but he relaxes.

I'm working on his hip when my dad comes over to check on him, putting a hand on my shoulder. "How is he doing, princess?"

Still working, I respond, "We need Stitch to come look at him, maybe even take him to the hospital. He's so swollen, bloody, cut up all over and I'm pretty sure he has broken ribs from the looks of it. He has several lacerations, but the one on his leg is the worst. All these other ones are just minor." I face my dad with tears filling my eyes. "Who did this to them? Is Mac okay?" I feel a hand on my hip, and we both look down. When my dad sees the kid has ahold of me, he goes to move it, but I stop him. "Daddy, he doesn't know where he is, he can't see, and I'm pretty positive he's in a lot of pain. I'm the only comfort he has. Let him hold my shirt." My dad is so protective of me that he doesn't like people touching me unless it's a member and that is usually just a hug.

Dad grunts. "Mac is going to be okay. He has a pretty big gash on his head and will probably have a concussion from getting hit from behind with a crowbar, which they said is what took him down. His ribs are probably broken as well, some minor cuts, and a broken nose."

"I guess from what everyone's saying Mac was on the phone with Dallas when he got jumped. Dallas heard it over the phone and rushed to get to him but when he arrived this kid was fighting four guys off while covering Mac with his body. Some kids Dallas knows said the kid came out of nowhere and started kicking ass but when they pulled out the knives is when he went down but didn't stop fighting. Even when Dallas showed up, he was still trying to get up. Once the guys saw Dallas they took off."

We both turn to look at the kid. "Do we know who he is or his name?"

Dad shakes his head. "No, but I'm going to find out. This kid has our protection for life if he wants it for what he just did for Mac."

He walks off, and I turn back to the kid and slip my hand into his and squeezed. When he squeezes back, I smile going back to work on patching up our mystery kid.

GINGER

    I feel a hand squeeze mine and I just know it's him letting me know he's here. Tears escape out the side of my closed eyes, running down the sides of my face from just thinking about the day I met him and here we are now, with me laid up and him comforting me.
    Get-a-grip, Ginger, he doesn't love you. He's just being a friend as you were all those years ago. Fuck it hurts, though. I still love him. But I can't. He let me go. But he is here. No way... My heart's broken and no motherfucker's getting near it again.
    My subconscious fighting itself only builds a rage inside of me, and my fingers must twitch because Shy is up out of his chair squeezing my hand. When he moves over me, I can feel his leather cut brush against my chest before getting another whiff of his... Motherfucking. Mouth-watering. Panty-dropping, scent.
    Sonovabitch. He smells fucking good. My body just comes alive when he is near me. Stop! He rejected *me.*
    "Don't worry Snow you're okay, and I got you, just relax, Angel," Shy whispers in my ear. The same fucking words I said to him like he wants me to remember that day and our connection. I wish that day never happened, but the day I met him was the day my life changed.

Why did he love me back then but not when I needed him to? My body starts to heat with anger and most of all frustration. I want to get out of this fucking bed and back to my life. *Where is Brant?* It feels like I've been sleeping for months. I'm tired of this fucking pain in my head. If it's not the pain in my head, it's all the pain running throughout my body. If I'm not in pain, I'm high as a kite. I try to control my heart rate, which feels like it's going to explode. Then I hear the fucking beeping. *God, I'm so tired.* Sleep consumes me once again.

I hear a big commotion, which pulls me from my dream. Dad is speaking to the doctor and is obviously getting upset.

"Well, how much longer do you need to keep feeding her the drugs to keep her sedated? I mean it's been a couple days don't you think you can lower it so we can get some kind of response from her?"

Please God, let them lower it. I need to be able to function and move a little. HELP...

When the doctor responds, Alex speaks up quieting down the other people that are in the room, but I can't make out their voices. "She is healing nicely, and we'll lower her dosage, but every time we try to lower it, she gets upset. I think we need to limit the number of visitors in here with her. Let her wake up and not be overwhelmed with so many people staring at her. I'm limiting it to two people, and once she's awake, we will stabilize her and then she can have more visitors." I hear a door open with cussing from my dad and I hear Shy.

"I agree, when I sing, she tries to open her eyes, I think it soothes her. No offense, but all this fighting and commotion is probably too much for her. I will stay with her and you all can take turns coming in. Sound good?" Alex says.

More men speak up and when I hear Brant speak about staying with me they all start talking at once. My head starts pounding with pain making it feel heavy. Shit. Brant's here with my family and Shy. I feel the anxiety start to form in my chest and my heart

starts beating uncontrollably before the beeping. The room goes quiet then all I hear is the fucking beeping.
Goddammit, not again.
Sleep takes me back to dreamland.

GINGER

(Four years ago)
I can't believe I left and I'm here in New York. My nerves are shot and I try to keep calm when I follow Beau Bagwell into the building. I'm getting ready to meet the famous international DJ, Luscious Luc. Lucas Mancini is also the owner of the record label, Spin It, Inc. where I will be working. I'm so fucking nervous. When my phone vibrates in my back pocket of my jeans, I slowly pull it out and see that it's a message from Shy.

SHY
Lucky Star -143

I turn off my cell and put it back in my pocket. One-four-three, meaning he loves me, yeah my ass. Shy and his fucking songs- "Lucky Star" by Madonna" -telling me, he loves me, and good luck is only going to piss me off.
Goddamn him.
Beau stops and turns around to look at me. "You ready to meet him? Don't be nervous, Snow. He's totally a low-key guy."
Don't be nervous- HA! Easy for him to say, it's not one of his idols.
"Beau, can we just stick with Ginger or Gin? I don't want anyone to know about my nickname. I'm trying to start fresh here and make a name for myself, and yes, I'm ready. Thank you again for helping me," I reply, smiling to hide my nerves.
Beau nods his head agreeing with me and opens the door to

what I'm assuming is Lucas's office. I follow Beau inside and come face to face with Lucas Mancini one of my favorite DJ/producers. I'm star struck.

Lucas stands up and extends his hand. "Hel-lo Ginger, I'm Luc, welcome, why don't you sit down so we can start." Jesus Christ, he's even more gorgeous in person. Beau clears his throat snapping me out of my star struck gaze.

"Nice to meet you, Lucas, I'm a little bit star struck, sorry. I've been listening to you DJ for years," I reply laughing.

Lucas laughs, taking a seat. "*Grazie*, and please call me Luc. I'm glad you decided to join our team here. Now both Beau and I have spoken with your father, and we all have agreed that you'll be stayin' in our buildin' where there's high security, and we'll all be around you. I know you want to start a new life here and become your own person, but New York is a dangerous city. I have sessions set up for us this coming week so I can see what you have so far. I'll have you workin' with some other seasoned DJs once I know where you are with experience. I own a club, so when you're ready, even though you're not of drinking age, I can get you on the stage to mix."

On stage, meaning DJ in a club? Holy Shit.

My brows rise in shock while butterflies erupt in my belly along with panic but I quickly mask my inner turmoil, and thankfully Luc doesn't even notice but keeps talking.

"You'll have a bodyguard with you most of the time, meanin' when you go to my club or an event but not your day-to-day stuff. We will want you to check in with us, kind of like we're your guardians even though you're over the age of eighteen, we just want you to be safe."

Holy mother of hotness, his accent has my nipples hard.

There's a knock at the door and before Luc can say 'come in' the door opens and in walks two more huge men. Beau clears his throat again and Luc starts speaking, bringing me back to look at him. "These are a couple of our security guys that also live in the building. This is Gus and Eli, guys, this is one of our new girls, Ginger Wolfe."

Yeah, I think I'm going to like my new life here in New York, fuck Shy.

GINGER

This time when I wake it's to complete silence. No one is talking, but I feel a hand on my stomach, resting next to my arm that is in a cast. I don't move, and I try not to change my breathing because I want to stay awake.

When I hear singing, I know Alex is in the room. Her voice soothes me and calms my inner turmoil. I try to open my eyes, but the pain hurts too badly. The hand on my belly moves to smooth the blankets over me, when they lean over, I inhale letting me know who it is - Brant. He's here with Alex, so I try to move my arm toward his on my stomach.

Brant must see it move or twitch because he says, "Alex, I think she moved."

Instantly Alex stops singing and I hear her move to my other side. She glides her hand down my arm before gripping my hand. Once they both have my hands, I try to return their squeezes back.

Brant leans over me placing a quick kiss on my cheek before whispering, "Baby, I'm here. Open your eyes for me. I need to see my emeralds sparkle."

I'm trying but fuck it hurts...

My head starts pounding near the temple, and a moan escapes me, which they both must hear because Alex gasps, "Santa Maria."

"Gin, we're here for you, just relax," she says in her angelic voice.

My breathing becomes labored with each breath, pain ignites all over my body, and a machine starts making noise next to the bed.

Sonovabitch, not the fucking beeping.

I try to move my arm, but it's too heavy. Brant squeezes my hand stopping my motion. "Don't try to move too much, baby. You need to relax and stay calm."

Frustration builds inside me wanting to get out of this fucking bed. The beeping doesn't stop, and I start to feel myself slipping back into the fog of memories. Dammit…

GINGER

(Three years earlier)

Feeling exhausted from a much-needed workout, I head toward the exit door wiping the sweat off my face with a towel while listening to "Radioactive" by Imagine Dragons. The place is empty since it's two-thirty in the morning. Thank goodness Luc and Beau set up our very own gym in the building so we can come at any hour. Wiping the sweat from around my neck, I reach for the door, only for it to fly open smacking me right in the face.

"Fuck!" I cry out in pain.

I bend over rubbing my head only to see stars along with a tanned, muscular leg that comes into view. Once I stand back up still rubbing my head, I come face to face with Mr. Holy-Shit-

Hot guy.

Realizing he's talking, I pull one of my ear buds out so I can hear him mid-sentence, "…seriously didn't think anyone was here. Are you all right? Shit, I'm sorry."

I must have a stupid ass look on my face since my mouth is open, my eyes are bugged out, and I'm frozen in place just staring at him.

Damn, this man is fine as fuck. Is he real? I must have hit my head too hard. Sonovabitch.

His hazel eyes are hypnotic, putting me in a haze. When I don't say anything or move, the gorgeous man takes a step toward me. I instantly hold my breath.

Shit. Fuck. Shit. He's going to touch me.

He reaches up touching my forehead where there is now a bump forming. "It's starting to swell. Let's get some ice on that. Come over here and let me help you," he says.

He's put a spell on me. I can't seem to form any words or move. Looking concerned, he places his hand on my shoulder bending down and looking into my eyes.

"My name is Brant, but everyone calls me B. Can you walk? I can carry you if you want me to."

When he smiles down at me, I let all the air out that I was holding inside, giving my brain the oxygen it needed to snap me out of the lust induced haze I was in.

I clear my throat. "No, I mean yes and no."

What the fuck was that?

Rubbing my forehead, I close my eyes and try to pull myself together. When I open my eyes again, Brant has his arms folded across his chest with a smirk on his face. My face heats up with me getting angry. *Obviously*, he thinks this is amusing, and *obviously*, he knows what he is doing to my insides.

Good gawd, snap out of it, Ginger.

Standing straight up, I clear my throat again. "What I meant was… yes, I'm okay, and no, I don't need you to carry me," I say in a snarky voice.

Rubbing my forehead, I hiss when I feel the bump getting bigger. My face feels like it's on fire and I'm irritated with myself for how this man affects me. When he doesn't say anything, I move to take a step only to falter, feeling dizzy as pain shoots through my head, I cry out feeling like my head is cracking open.

Brant is there in an instant catching me in an embrace and in one swift motion has me in his arms carrying me over to the bench. Once he sets me down, he moves to the fridge pulling out an ice pack. Trying not to get caught staring at his ass, I look away before he turns back.

Brant breaks the ice pack rubbing it together before speaking.

"This looks bad. Maybe we should take you to the ER? You might have a concussion. That bump keeps getting bigger."

Moving my hand over the swollen lump, I just stare at him trying to get myself together. Taking my sweet ass time to answer him only stresses him out more. Brant pulls his phone out and presses a number connecting to someone who answers on the first ring with a barking sound.

"I got a situation in the gym, get down here, I need your help," Brant barks back.

Brant hangs up without even letting the other person answer, which snaps me out of my confused state and I say, "I'm fine. It's late, and I'm just really tired. I've hit my head before, and I'm sure it won't be the-" The door to the gym flys open again with Gus running through like a crazed man.

Great, now I have two hot-as-fuck men to deal with. Aengus, whom we all call Gus, is a very tall, very massive, and very red-headed Irishman. Half the time I never understand a word out of his mouth with his thick accent.

I'm about to say something, but Gus sees my forehead and stops in his tracks.

"Jaysus, wat happened? A nice bump you got there on your noodle," Gus says, pointing his finger at his own head.

Brant answers first since my brain is in slow motion. "I threw open the door, just like you did, I might add, and she was on the other side of it."

I speak, but it's more like a squeak. "I'm fine."

Only to be silenced when Gus puts his hand up to stop me. "Bollocks, you're goin' to ER, or you're goin' to let this whanker stay with you tonight because it looks bad."

Thinking Brant is going to protest to what Gus just said; I look up at him only to see him looking down at me with a smirk. I try to stand up to protest that no one is going to stay with me tonight, but I lose my balance feeling nauseous and out of sorts only to be swept up into Brant's massive arms, again.

My head's hurting so bad I feel like it is being split open so I just relax into him when we walk up next to Gus, who is holding the door open.

Gus stops us by touching my forehead. "Gin, boi's one of my head security. I trust him, or I would be doing it myself, plus he fukin' did it."

"It was an accident. Let everyone know what happened and why I'm carrying her into her place," Brant grunts out.

My head gets dizzy from all the moving, and I feel sick all of a sudden.

GINGER

The last few times I have started gaining consciousness, I feel the pain start to lessen and with Alex singing or humming I feel myself healing. Breathing is probably the hardest with my injured ribs. This time when I come to though, I hear her singing the words to a song I remembered her working on. Each time I have tried to open my eyes but have been unsuccessful, so when I try to open my eyes, and they crack open I want to scream out but I know I can't. When they blink open again, everything is blurry, so I blink a few more times looking in the direction of her voice.

She must see me open them because I see her jump off the windowsill holding her shoulder but still singing or more like half humming. Then I feel movement next to me and he grabs my hand.

Smelling him before I see him I know it's Shy next to me. Both are looking down at me not saying a word. I blink a few more times then close them. When I feel Alex grab my other hand, I try to hold it, but it's hard with the cast in the way, so I open my eyes again.

Alex gasps, "Santa Maria."

"Angel, you here, baby?" Shy murmurs.

I hold both of their hands, and when I actually can squeeze it, they look at each other and smile before looking back down to me.

"Welcome back, girl. We've missed you," Alex whispers.

They both give me another squeeze. I blink my eyes a few more times trying to get my eyes to focus. Alex smiles. "I'm going to give you a few minutes to adjust before I push the nurse's button."

She looks up at Shy before continuing, "God knows we don't need a shit storm rushing in here overwhelming her."

When Shy doesn't answer but just nods, I understand, squeezing both their hands. Alex starts to hum, but when Shy reaches up, moving my hair away from my face, caressing my cheek, I turn my head toward him.

When our eyes meet, my heart goes into a frenzy. Oh, my God. He looks so, so different. I know it's been over a year, but fuck me, he looks rougher, more dangerous. He has a baseball cap on backward holding his hair back, but I can see it's longer, still shaggy with light curls but it's the goatee that has me glued to him.

Jesus, he's so goddamn beautiful but in a bad-ass biker way. He looks so much older with wrinkles around his light chocolate brown eyes, and his eyebrows are drawn together in worry. Fuck my heart hurts and I want to comfort him. *Stop Gin, stop.* Then all the emotions start to flood me. I want to yell at him, punch him, kiss him, hate him, love him…my thoughts are in overdrive.

My Micah, he is so fucking fine.

Tears fall from my eyes, blinking before I turn away from him to look at Alex to calm myself. Alex smiles but I can see she is worried. "Are you ready? I'm going to push the button." I squeeze her hand and blink, letting her know I'm ready.

Once she pushes the nurse's button, within minutes a nurse rushes in followed by my dad, Beau, Cash, and Brant.

Fuck. Me.

When everyone sees my eyes open, they all smile, but no one speaks. Everyone is at the foot of my bed with Alex and Shy next to me.

Right about now I am thanking God I can't speak because I don't know what I would say. I am so torn between my two lives, and with both of them here, I just don't know what to say. Exhaustion starts to take over and I feel my eyes getting heavy.

While everyone is talking about me, I just keep glancing around the room watching everyone watch me. My dad is looking run down with a few day's beard growth, and his hair is wild like he has been running his hands through it, which only tells me he is stressed out.

Brant isn't looking too hot himself like he has been living here at the hospital in his usually pressed shirt which is now wrinkled. When my dad calls my name, I turn to face him.

"Snow, did you hear the doctor?"

Looking to the doctor and back to him, I just shake my head, turning back to the doctor giving him my undivided attention. He goes into telling me about where I am, and how they are going to start taking me off all medicines and see how I do, also something about more tests, blah, blah, blah…

I just nod my head and try to focus on him but am losing the battle with exhaustion as my eyes get heavier and heavier. When he tells everyone that I still need my rest and only two people can be in the room, he ushers everyone out except my dad.

Leaning over the bed, he kisses me on the forehead before saying, "Princess, I have been going crazy, I don't know what I would have done if I lost you too. I can't keep doing this, worrying about you and if you're safe. Baby girl, I can't lose you too. I want you to come home with me. Please." Leaning over me he kisses my forehead, and I try to grab onto him letting him know I am okay.

Telling myself and wishing I could tell him…*I can't go back, Daddy. I just can't. Not yet.*

I try to smile up at him as he moves away and exhaustion finally takes over. The last thing I hear is him telling me he loves me and to get some rest.

BRANT

When they tell us she is awake, I rush in with everyone else, not taking no for an answer. I know I shouldn't be here and that her family is all here, but I can't seem to stay away. We aren't together, shit she tells me every fucking day how we are not anything but friends.

HA! Friends my ass, maybe friends with benefits. Friends that mess around all the time and stay at each other's place are definitely more than just friends. I have been trying to get her to commit to me for the last six months. One night on our tour we had a few too many drinks, and when the other girls passed out, we hooked up. It wasn't until a few weeks ago that we had sex for the first time and I thought we were moving forward.

Watching everyone in the room staring at her, listening to the doctor, I just stand back with my focus on her.

Damn, she is beautiful.

She truly is a princess like they all say, when they call her Snow White. When she glances over at me, I just smile at her, letting her know I am here for her. That's all I want is for her to know I am here if she needs me. I will always be here for her.

She's so damn stubborn and has built a wall bigger than the Great Wall of China. I know she was hurt pretty bad by the dumb fuck over there in the corner. I know she is still in love with him but fuck me I won't go down without a fight. She is so worth the fight.

I knew that from the first day when I smashed the door into her face giving her a concussion. Holding her hair while she threw up and watching her while she slept. I fell for her petite

little body all hard and sweaty from working out.
Damn, I need to quit thinking about her body, I'm getting hard.
Shifting my weight, I try to calm the big guy down before I embarrass myself in front of everyone. When the doctor tells us pretty much to get the fuck out, I glance once more, trying to make eye contact, only to get shoved by the dumb motherfucker himself.
Once we are out the door, I turn on him. "Look, motherfucker, don't touch me. I get you need to feel bad-ass and shit around her but quit fucking with me because I'm not going anywhere until she tells me to leave."
Crossing my arms over my chest, I stand toe to toe with Ginger's first love, the stupid fuck who let her go- Shy Jenkins.
"Bitch, you best get ready because I have a feeling once she finds out that I never let her go and have been around this whole time she will be saying bye bye *B*."
My blood boils when he uses my nickname, but I don't reply, it would only antagonize him more, so I just stand there nose to nose. When Shy starts to laugh, it only pisses me off more. He's a couple inches shorter than me and is pretty well built, but I'm bigger than him up top. It would be a good fight, but I am more than confident I could take him.
We just stare at each other with neither one of us backing down. Alex walks up tapping us both on the shoulder, laughing, "Down boys, down. Seriously, you two need to get over this shit. Ginger is going to flip the fuck out on both of you if you two don't stop having a pissing match over her."
Fuck him. I'm not standing down.
Shy keeps laughing but turns to walk away when Ginger's father walks out of the room, telling us she is passed out again. Obviously, he saw us toe to toe because he calls out to Shy as he's walking away.
"Shy get back here, I want to talk to both of you...*and*... both

of you are going to listen to me."

When Shy comes to stand next to her dad folding his arms mimicking my stance, which I still haven't changed, he continues, "Look, I understand both of you have feelings for my daughter, and I respect both of you, but this is *my baby*, and I don't want anything, and I mean *any-thing* upsetting her. *Both* of you will get time with her, but this fighting shit needs to stop."

Neither one of us says anything back, but we both nod our understanding. I know my place and when I should shut the fuck up, and I'm guessing, so does fuck-face over there.

Still, no one is saying anything when Beau walks around the corner. He places a hand on my shoulder saying, "We all good here, Wolfe?"

Wolfe nods his head grabbing Shy's shoulder turning them to walk away.

Once they are out of sight, I drop my arms and relax. I know Beau must feel my tension ease in my shoulder when he releases me. I take a deep breath turning to face my boss and good friend, "Yeah, we're good."

SHY

"Fuck, No! I'm not good." I grumble once we are out of earshot of the stupid son of a bitch.

"I am not okay with that fucker here and up her ass all the time. I'm done watching from afar and I sure as fuck am done waiting for her to figure shit out. Prez, I'm sorry, but I'm done."

Wolfe chuckles. "Kid, you and me both. It is most definitely time for our princess to come home but-" he turns to face me grabbing both my shoulders, looking me in the eyes- "you need to play it cool. Don't go spouting off our plans and shit. I need to see where my girl's at once she is out of here and until then you don't say a fucking word. She is my baby, and I need to make sure what is best for her. That's an order, Shy."

I nod my head, clenching my jaw, holding back my rage. When he turns away pulling out and barking into his phone, I mentally flip out, *Fuck that- Hell no- She is* my *girl and always has been,* but of course, I would never say those things to him out loud, at least not yet.

I am always telling him off in my head. I have fought within myself over the years about what I'm doing about getting her back, or should I say *not* doing about it. I have always loved her, but back then I was young, lost, no family, so I put our feelings on the back burner for the club. The club that got me off the streets - the club I now call family. He told me it was what's best for her, and she needed to live a little before becoming my ol' lady, so I have been waiting, and the waiting is fucking over.

This club is my life, but she is my air – she is our MC's princess, but to me, she is my queen. I need her to make my life complete. These last few years I have busted my ass working my way up the ranks, being the best to win over her father's approval.

I have loved my Angel from the very first day I heard her voice and that smell – jasmine mist. Fuck, she had me before I even saw her. I was in so much pain that day, but I didn't care as long as she kept taking care of me. I thought I was going to die that day, but she and her club saved me. Every day since, I have been paying my dues to this club and making a name for myself proving to everyone I am worthy of her. I had her in my arms only to let her go for the bigger picture. Well, that bigger picture is now, and I am ready to fight for her.

There has never been anyone else that could fill her shoes in my life. The first couple of years I was so consumed by club business or running off to see her that I never thought of another girl. This last year with her being gone in Europe, I lost it and became my own enemy. A few times I said fuck it and let a patch chaser suck me off, or I'd bend one over to get a quick release, but then I would get so depressed and upset with myself for letting anyone touch me beside her, it drove me even crazier. But no matter what, all those bitches knew there was no kissing, no touching, no anything but a quickie and they were out. I don't want anyone but my angel. One taste of her and I was forever ruined.

Her going to Europe was my breaking point. I knew I couldn't live without her. I lost it when I found out she was going on her European tour. It took five brothers to hold me down, keeping me from jumping on my bike and going after my girl. Her dad told me she needed to get it out of her system and I had a job to do and that it was the perfect timing because I didn't need any distractions or my quick trips to go check on her. I needed to focus on club business.

That day I promised myself when she got back home I was done, no more waiting around, no more playing fucking games. I told her dad that day, she was my girl, and I was going to claim her when she got back. She was going to be my ol' lady no matter what anyone said. Almost four years is enough time for her to find herself and for me to finish building our future.

For a year, her father and I have been butting heads about her, and what is good for her, he told me if she wants me and this life, he will give me his blessing but only when she tells him that is what she wants. I think it's time she pulls her head out of her ass and comes back to me. I can't lose her again, and she needs to know the truth. It started out as a plan for *our* future but if she isn't in it, then how can it be *our* future.

GINGER

(Eighteen years old)

"Micah," I moan his name into the crevice of his neck, letting the orgasm course through me.

We are lying in the back of Shy's truck at the creek, where we always go to get away from the club and watchful eyes. I know my dad knows we like each other but I don't think he knows we are doing this kind of shit, or Shy would be castrated.

"Fuck me, Angel. Your pussy is so fucking tight. It clamps down on my fingers sucking them back in."

Slowing his thrusting fingers, I nuzzle my face into his neck letting the aftershocks make their way through me, kissing him under his ear, knowing it drives him crazy.

"Baby, I can't keep doing this, I need to be deep inside of you. We need to get a hotel room and soon."

With us, both lying on our sides, one of his hands is up my skirt finger-fucking me, while the other one is supporting my neck sucking and biting my collarbone. I lay back looking up into his golden brown eyes that are like a light milky swirl filled with lust and desire. He smiles down at me letting me see his boy next door smile. He has a baby face that all the girls swoon over, and when he smiles showing off his dimples, it knocks you on your ass.

"Shy, why do you keep putting it off? We don't need a hotel room. Why can't we just do it right here and now? I love you, and your truck, plus looking up at the stars is so much better than any hotel. Anywhere you are, is good enough for me. We are never going to be alone for it to happen besides here. I mean, I am okay with it."

Seeing the lust filled storm brewing in his eyes, fighting the urge to fuck me and take my virginity. I have tried pushing him over the edge several times, but he had stood his ground telling me we had to wait till I turned eighteen and it wouldn't be in the back of his truck.

Withdrawing his fingers, he puts them into his mouth sucking my cum off of them before gliding them over my lips and then sliding them slowly into my mouth. He says in a hungry but needy voice, "Angel, I will not take your virginity in the back of a truck with people to see. I want to claim you and fuck you all night long. You deserve the best."

Sucking his fingers, I reach between us gripping his massive erection, and when he pulls his fingers from my mouth, I lean up crashing our mouths together pushing him to his back.

Fuck, he can kiss! I want him so fucking bad.

The way he devours me like he can't get enough of me. With one hand I unbutton his jeans releasing his *very* huge, *very* thick cock. Shy growls deep in his throat. Wanting more lubrication to jack him off I slip my hand between my legs fingering myself, making myself whimper.

Oh, God. Yes.

Once my hand is covered with my own arousal I use it to stroke his cock, making Shy break our kiss with a hiss of approval leaving us both panting with pleasured moans.

"Son of a bitch. I'm so fucking hard. You always make me so goddamn hard - all the time."

Stroking him faster, I pick up the pace with each stroke.

"Yes, Angel."

Stroke.

"Does that feel good?" I ask seductively.

Stroke.

Moving over him positioning myself to straddle his calves, I bend down to suck the tip into my mouth while I stroke again.

Shy cries out arching his back. "Fuck, yes."

Stroke.

Suck.

Popping off his dick, licking around the shaft making it even slicker down to the base. I move my other hand between my legs rubbing my aching clit.

"Micah," I whimper.

Moving my body up toward his mouth while still stroking him. Leaning forward crushing our mouths together placing his cock between our bodies. I start to dry hump him only it's not dry from all the wetness between my legs, coating his cock making it slip easily between our bodies.

When he's close, he starts to thrust faster, gripping my hips to rub harder against my pelvic bone. Reaching between us like I'm going to palm his dick for the final thrust only to guide his enormous length straight into my dripping entrance. We both cry out, but I move up his body letting it come out a bit before sliding back down a little further, making us both hiss. I close my eyes, so he doesn't see the pain.

Please don't be mad. God, I want this.

Still gripping my hips, he freezes. I look down into his eyes and say, "I took my own virginity. I want this. I want you. I love you." I move slowly up and down his throbbing cock. It hurts bad, and I'm holding back the cries. I know it will feel good sooner or later.

Shy closes his eyes taking a deep breath tightening his grip on my hips but still doesn't say anything while I work him slowly into my tightness until he is seated fully inside of me.

I lean down taking his mouth. I suck in his lower lip before slipping my tongue into his mouth and sucking his tongue like it's his cock, Shy growls.

"Please. Say something." *Pl-ease.*

After another deep breath, Shy opens his eyes. Lust and desire shine back at me. In a blink of an eye, he has me flipped over onto my back.

"You sure? This is how you want our first time?" he finally speaks in a raspy voice.

Before he can finish, I am panting 'yes' over and over while moving my hips for him to move.

Shy slips his hand under my shirt lifting it above my head. My bra was already off from our earlier makeout session. He leans over me taking one of my breasts into his mouth. I cry out arching my back wanting more so I move my hips.

Shy lifts his head from my breast with a pop and starts to thrust into me, so I push back meeting him thrust for thrust. Both of us grunting and moaning chasing our high, pushing it to the brink with the anticipation of what will explode any minute.

"Yes! Micah…"

When he slows his pumping, he leans back onto his heels, slipping his fingers between us flicking my clit. "Angel, your pussy… fuck your pussy is everything I dreamt it would be, so fucking tight. I won't last much longer, baby. Fuck!"

Lost in the euphoric feeling my body starts to spasm. *Yes, I'm so close.*

Shy must feel me clench because he picks up his pace, along with his assault on my clit.

"Micah, oh, God." Shy drives harder, going deeper each time sending me into ecstasy.

"Yee-sss!"

"Fuck. Snow…Jesus, I'm gonna come, baby."

Shy starts grunting saying, "Yes!" repeatedly with each thrust. I open my legs wider and let him go deeper with each drive.

Waves of prickles erupt throughout my body with the orgasm rippling through me. I reach up, pinching his nipple making him lose it, and he moans his release with one final pump. "Angel. Fuucck-yeees."

After a few more pumps draining his seed inside me, he lays back down next to me letting us both catch our breath, coming off our orgasmic high.

Yes, finally. I'm not a virgin.

"Goddamn, that was so fucking amazing. I couldn't last any longer." Micah leans up on an elbow turning to cover half my body with an ear to ear grin plastered across his face. "I'm sorry, but you took me by surprise. And fuck baby, I knew it was going to be tight but damn, Angel this" -moving his hand to cup my sex- "is divine and all mine!" I start laughing, but he keeps going. "I was nowhere near ready and almost came when you slammed it in. God, what were you thinking? I could have hurt you. Did I hurt you?"

Before he ruins this by freaking out, I reach my hand up and around his neck pulling him down to kiss me, shutting him up. When we break the kiss and are only inches away from each other, Shy pushes the hair away from my face becoming serious. "Seriously babe, are you sure you're okay with this? You're not going to flip out and blame me that we did it here in the truck?"

What the fuck - Seriously?

I start to laugh seeing he *is* serious, *deadly* serious.

"Micah" -using his real name, so he knows I'm serious- "I have lived around bikers all my life and have seen way too much. I love you for wanting to wait for a bed and sex all night long, but I would rather have a hotel room for a night full of sex not taking my virginity and lasting only minutes before we pass out. Seriously Shy, I am fine. Fuck, I have been on the pill and been begging you for over a year, and I understood that you wanted to wait until I was eighteen, but it has been over a month, so the Wolfeman blood in me took what I wanted."

Shy rolls off me onto his back laughing. "Angel, you surprise me every day. Fuck, I love you so much, but you are your father's daughter."

We both continue laughing. "What? I was tired of waiting. You might be my first trying things on a man, but you definitely are not my first orgasm experience. Believe me, I have played and practiced on myself plenty of times. AND - I have wanted you for two fucking years." Tilting my head toward him, I smile. "It was damn time I claimed my man!"

Pulling me on top of him, he kisses me before saying, "Damn, you can claim me, fuck me, or practice on me but whatever you do, it better be with only me."

Reaching up to push his hair out of his face I say dead serious and with all my heart. "It has only been you and will always be just you, Micah. I love you, baby."

Feeling his dick harden under me I move up slightly slipping him back inside me. Moaning, I close my eyes loving the feeling of him filling me.

Sonovabitch, I am addicted.

GINGER

I have been a chicken shit lately. It has been almost twenty-four hours since I opened my eyes. Alex caught me halfway speaking to the nurse, so she knows I am talking now. I just keep quiet when anyone comes in, letting them do the talking. I just smile and nod my head but the jig is up, and Alex wants answers. Thank God, Brant and Shy haven't been back in here, but I'm guessing that has to do with my father and Alex keeping them away.

"Spill it. Seriously, Gin, you need to tell me what is going on with you and these two men" -waving her hand to the door behind her- "I mean- what the fuck? Shy is hot and obviously in love with you." Folding her hands over her chest, she waits. "We have time, so take your time and tell me the whole truth." Alex sits back waiting for my response.

How am I supposed to respond to this? *I love him but hate him? I'm so lost!*

"Where should I start?"

My voice comes out hoarse and dry, so Alex grabs some water before she answers me.

"Start from the beginning. Let me see if I can help you figure this shit out. That is what friends are for, so start when you're ready."

I start by telling her about after Momma and my best friend dying that I threw myself into music and isolated myself from everyone for a few years and how I felt broken without my best friend or Momma to confide in. I always felt alone even though the club was always full of people, and everyone loved me, but it wasn't the same. I felt a hole in my heart, but I pushed through and dove into my music.

That was until I met Shy. I go on to tell her how I met Shy on my sixteenth birthday and how we were attached at the hip from that point on. Our club found out he was a kid in the system but being that he was nineteen he pretty much was on the streets.

My dad, being the man he is, took him in and treated him like his own. We all called him Kid, but he later got his name Shy from always being so quiet. We bonded and became super close, two broken people finding comfort in one another. Mac, Shy and I became inseparable. Shy was always with me, and we had this connection that I can't explain. When we touched, both of us would react to the shock or feelings it brought on.

When Alex stands up to grab some tissue, I pause giving her time. After she wipes her eyes, she falls back into the chair before saying, "Gin, this is crazy. Why haven't we talked about this before? My God, we are so much alike." Tears pool in her eyes again.

Feeling guilty for not sharing all my secrets and only giving her the bare minimum. I try to explain. "I just wanted a fresh start here. I didn't want to be the girl that lost her Momma and cousin. Then to top it off to lose my best friend/first true love. That is pretty pathetic, so I didn't tell you everything. I am sorry for that."

Alex gets up and comes to sit on my bed grabbing my hand. "Gin, you are one of my best friends, and I will always be here for you. You can tell me anything, and I will always be by your side. Now…go on."

I tell her how time went on and how Shy's and my relationship grew into something so much more, but we were young and afraid of my father, so we acted like friends around the club, and when we were alone, we couldn't keep our hands off each other. He was my first for everything, and I wanted more.

I always thought I would be his ol' lady and would work at the local radio station. Shy threw himself into the club, trying to prove to my dad he was worthy of me.

Alex interrupts me. "Well, fuck it sounds to me like you two are perfect for each other, what happened?"

I feel the tears coming but push them back. No more crying for him.

Shy, and I had been going at it for a couple months, if we weren't fucking, we were fighting about my father. He wanted to tell my father about us and make me his ol' lady. I kept saying fuck no! It was an ongoing argument, and he kept feeling something bad was going to happen, but I told him he was being paranoid.

When my father called both Shy and I into his office telling us he needed to talk to both of us. I should have known or felt it, but I didn't. It was a few months after my graduation.

Taking a deep breath, I tell her about the worse day of my life. I remember it like it was yesterday.

Once we were both in the office, my dad shut the door telling us to sit down. He asked us if we were in love. We both said yes at the same time. He asked me if I was sure I was ready for this life giving up all my dreams of music. I told him I was still pursuing my music, and I have lived the lifestyle all my life so why wouldn't I be ready.

When he turned to Shy, he said are you ready for this lifestyle full time? Are you ready for her to give up her dreams to stay here with you? Shy got pissed and said you know I am ready to be full time and I have been putting all my effort into this club. What do you mean giving up her dreams?

My father leaned back in his chair. "Well, let me ask you this... If I told you right now, Snow has been given a chance to move to New York, work for Spin It, Inc. under Lucas Mancini and give her music a shot, would she go? And if I asked you, Shy, to let her go would you be able to do that? Would your love stand the distance? Shy, would you be able to give the club your full attention, as a member of this club?"

Shy was still a prospect, but I knew they were getting ready to make him a member. After hanging around everyone and getting a bike, and with the push from Mac, he became a prospect.

I'm in shock, still not registering Lucas Mancini, let alone what Shy was thinking. Shy jumps up pissed off. "Do you question my loyalty and commitment to this club? I have been working my ass off trying to prove to you that I have what it takes to become a brother."

My dad leaned forward resting his elbows on the desk. "To become a brother or to claim my daughter? Because there's a difference," he replied calmly.

I am still just sitting there not saying a word with the two men of my life staring each other down. "Both, this club is my family, and I have proven to you and every one of them out there I would die for them and even more so for her. Your daughter is everything to me, and you know that too. She might be your princess but she is my queen, and nothing will change that," Shy responded.

My father gets up putting his hands up in surrender. "I'm not questioning your loyalty, what I am questioning is, are you both ready for the long haul. Will you let her go or hold her back? Will you go with her and leave the club behind or stick it out and become an official Wolfeman for life? I'm going to give you both some time to talk about it."

When my dad walked out of the office, we were both in shock. He was pretty much asking us to pick between what we have always wanted in life over being together forever.

Alex is crying again when the hospital door swings open and in walks Brant.
Fuck my life!

GINGER

I see Alex trying to pull herself together, but Brant knows her probably better than she knows herself and by the look of her and me, we both look wrecked. Brant immediately moves to the side of the bed. "What's wrong? Are you in pain? I heard you talking, so I rushed in here. What's wrong with you? Why are you crying? What happened?" he asks with concern, turning to Alex.

Looking from Alex to me and then back again he is about to freak out when Alex comes to my rescue. "Relax, B. I was just thanking her for saving my life. We were having a moment until you barged in like a mad man."

Alex wipes her eyes and she shifts off the bed giving me a swift hug before moving away and heading toward the mirror hanging on the wall near the bathroom to check her makeup, giving us some time but not leaving me.

God, I love her!

Brant pulls up a chair, and once he is settled up close to the side of the bed, he reaches for my hand. I smile not really knowing what to say. I have always told him from the beginning we were just going to be friends. That I would never let another man near my heart again and I would never say he was my boyfriend. But,

here he is still by my side trying to fix the world.
Fuck he is too good to be true.
When I hear my name being called, I snap out of my thoughts and focus on his beautiful eyes beaming at me. My heart jumps remembering all the good times we've had over the last year while in Europe. I squeeze his hand, closing my eyes while taking a deep breath.

"Ginger. Hello? Gin…"

When I open my eyes, I see concern sketched across his unshaven face. I reach up to touch his scruffy face and say with a crackly voice, "What is this? I have to almost die for you to grow hair on your face?"

Brant laughed leaning into my touch and kissing my hand. "If I knew it was this important I would have grown it out a long time ago darlin'. How are you feeling?"

Confused as fuck!

I wince trying to take a deep breath but say, "Good. Better, but still in some pain."

We both grow silent, and just as Brant looks at me and is about to say something, Alex jumps back in the conversation. "Well, you will be back to yourself after some much-needed R&R. I guess this is the best time if any, to tell you all the news and let it all sink in before your papá or anyone else tells you, I need you to get better, not flip your shit and reinjure yourself."

Fuck, now what?

I don't reply but instead just look at her, and when Brant squeezes my hand, I start to get mad. I have never been one to stall or beat around the bush. I rush out, "What!"

Alex sits back on the bed reaching for my other hand. "Gin, your injuries are pretty severe, and you will need a few months to recover."

Getting impatient I huff out, "Soooo."

"Sooo, we're going to have Sasha do the first three months of the US tour, and when you're better, you will join us. I will be leaving once Maddy is done with his gigs this week. We are going to see his mamá in Italy for a month until we have to leave for the tour. Izzy had to go back to California suddenly to her family, she said something happened with her mom, but I think something is going on with her and Dominic. He was just cleared of any associations with Emmett but has to stay local until investigations are done."

"Wait-What?" -cutting her off- "Dominic was involved?

"No, when the police found out where Emmett lived they realized that he lived with Dominic. So they thought he might have been involved, but he was cleared."

What the fuck? When I don't say anything, she continues.

"Sasha was scheduled back in Spain right after the festival but canceled until she knew you were okay but had to leave to get her affairs in order before leaving. Soooo that leaves you and Brant!

She smiles like she didn't just dump a huge amount of shit into my lap and looked to Brant. So I turn away looking straight ahead at the white wall before closing my eyes, taking a deep breath.

Fuck my life. Gawd-damn-motherfuck. Investigation. I can't DJ...

I want to cry, scream, hit something and then do it all over again. My emotions are all over the place with all these questions building up. I can barely move I'm in so much pain, so I just lay there and take deep breaths.

I can deal with this, be strong. I got this, don't cry!

Saying my little chant to myself, I build up that wall of mine, and when I open my eyes, Alex has tears in her eyes again. But it's Brant that speaks, turning my attention to him.

"Ginger, everything is going to be fine. I know how much this tour means to you. I will take care of you, and we will meet up with them when you are feeling better. I promise."

Just when I'm about to say, "Really," the door swings open

and in walks another storm, my auntie Storm, crying and cussing my father out while she enters the room with him hot on her tail. Seeing I'm awake, she throws her hands together and cries some more moving her way over to me. Brant jumps up, squeezing my hand. "Like I said don't worry. I will take care of you."

My auntie must have heard him because she smacks him to move aside and says, "Like hell you will. Her auntie" -pointing her finger at herself- "*Me* - will be the only one taking care of my girl."

I am a Wolfeman. I will not cry. I am a...

𝄞

After kicking everyone out of my room, even my father, I know Auntie is pissed, and when she is pissed, everyone listens or gets out of her way, hence her name, Storm. I lay there and wait for it to happen because I can't get out of the way or prevent it from happening so I just watch her move around my room.

She is like a tornado swirling around waiting to touch down, moving from one side of the hospital room to the other, putting her purse down, taking her jacket off, moving chairs around, all the while talking to herself but I hear her say, "I swear to God, Fox..." I know she is talking to my momma. Just hearing her name brings me comfort knowing if anyone can calm Auntie down it will be my dead momma's spirit.

When she finally turns to me at the foot of my bed, I look up and straight into her eyes. I try to hold back the tears, but I feel them pooling up. Taking a deep breath, I hold her stare.

"Ginger" -fuck she never calls me by my given name- "I have sat back long enough, but I need to get some shit out. Please, I need to get this out. I love you like you were my own, always have, always will." Gripping the railing, I see her knuckles turn white. "I have sat back and watched you grow up and become a very beautiful, independent and talented woman. You are following your dreams, but at the same time you are not really living."

What the fuck?

"I know you call me religiously every week, but not coming home to see me in almost a year, and a half is *not okay*." Turning she starts pacing the room before continuing. "I know I am not your momma but damn you, girl, I need you in my life too. Did you ever think about when you left that you left more than just your daddy and Micah?"

Micah? He left me...

"Now, I haven't said anything to you because you were learning and off in Europe doing your thing, but I can't keep my tongue anymore." She stops again at the foot of my bed looking me straight in the eyes, and we both see tears coming down our faces, but I don't say a word.

"*And* when *your* daddy - or any of those gawd damn men - don't tell *me* that *my* baby girl is in the hospital-" stopping she looks up at the ceiling clenching the railing "I will flip the fuck out! Now I have been in the truck with Mac for the last" -throwing her hands up- "fuck, I don't even know because all I saw was black, and baby girl you know when us Wolfe women see black you best get the fuck out of our way. And, so help me God if any of those Wolfeman need something from me they can eat shit and die!"

She goes back to pacing. "I can *not* believe they kept you being in the hospital from me. All these fucking days, they didn't tell me. They are lucky I didn't have a gun, and that it was Sissy who told me. All those chicken shits, they sent Mac to come get me - bunch of pussies."

Wow. I haven't seen Auntie this mad, like ever.

I let her ramble for a few minutes more, and when she is on my side of the bed, I try to reach for her and say, "I love you,

Auntie, and I'm sorry."

She turns with a gasp. "Snow, you can talk? They told me you hadn't spoken yet. Oh, baby girl, here I've been rambling!" She rushes to my side grabbing my hand "I was so mad at you and at them that I didn't take a second to check on you really. I'm sorry."

We both start to cry, and I squeeze her hand, trying to pull her in for a hug, but the pain hurts too much. I try to relax back into the bed. Auntie sees I'm in pain and calls for the nurse.

The nurse comes in a second later followed by Mac, Shy, Cash, Bear and my father. I hear Auntie start to mumble obscenities at the men, and none of them move in her direction. Instead, they are all focused on me.

Great, just what I fucking need. Can this day ever end? Please let her give me good drugs to knock me the fuck out.

God must be on my side somewhat because one look at the nurse and she kicks everyone out but my auntie. I don't think anyone will get her to leave my side at this point. The nurse gives me the good shit, and finally, sleep consumes me.

I wake up hearing Auntie telling someone "over my dead body." I don't open my eyes hoping whoever she is threatening will go away, but when I hear Alex say to her, "She wants to join us on tour as soon as she is well."

I open my eyes, letting them know I'm awake. I muddle out, "What did you say about the tour?"

Alex laughs, moving over to the bed. "I was telling your aunt that you will be joining us on the tour once you are all rested and better."

Auntie moves to the opposite side of the bed across from

Alex. "And, I was telling this young man here that in no way in hell am I leaving you here. That you will be coming home with me to rest and get better."

What? Hell no.

"Um, Auntie, I agree with them. I want to stay here and get better. I need to work on music. I have a deadline to release one of my original songs in Miami."

Brant moves to the foot of the bed making his presence known but my auntie doesn't back down. She turns to me. "Ginger, did you hear any of the shit I said yesterday? You have been away from home for far too long, and you need to rest. You will be coming home with me, and once you are okay you can go meet them on tour, but until you are recovered, and I see it with my own eyes, you are stuck with me. Now if you want me to move here for a few months I can do that too but baby girl, I am not leaving your side for a while. So you decide, here or back home but either way you have me by your side."

Seriously? Come on God, help me out again.

"Can you two give us a few minutes alone?"

Both Alex and Brant reply yes and excuse themselves. Once they're gone, I focus my attention back on my auntie. When she raises her hand, I pause. "Look, Snow, if you and that nice looking gentleman are seeing each other that's fine. I have no problem moving here for a few months. Shit, I'm so pissed off at the men it would be good to be away for a while but knowing your uncle, he won't allow it. I'm serious about this and not taking no for an answer. I need…no actually we all need you to come home for a visit. Let us take care of you, and then you can run off to your rockstar lifestyle, but for a few months, you are my Snow. Please."

I don't say anything but just smile. I can't tell her no, not yet at least but I can't go back.

Goddamnit!

BRANT

When Alex and I walk out of the room, we are confronted by Shy and Mac. I instantly go on alert, ready for the fight. Alex being her ever so loving self-speaks first, "Boys no fighting today. Gin-" she stops talking when she turns toward Mac "-hey aren't you the guy who reserve booth thirty in the back every few weeks?"

Mac smiles. "I don't know what you're talking about, darlin'."

Shit! Fuck.

Alex can't know about this, or she'll run off and tell Ginger that the ex-love of her life has been coming and watching her DJ since she moved here. Because then she would know, I know, and that is all bad, so I turn to Alex. "Um, bikers don't go to clubs, they only do dive bars."

I know they have a strict rule that no-one is to tell Ginger about the MC having a VIP booth in the back. They are to be hidden at all times, no cuts and no contact. I knew this from the beginning, but I always thought it was because her dad is just as crazy protective as Alex's dad. When I got to know Ginger and noticed it was always these two, I put two and two together.

Shy steps forward smiling at Alex. "Actually, yes it has been the two of us renting that booth out-"

Alex gasps cutting him off. "Santa Maria…for like a few years now." Alex takes a few minutes, but you can see the light go on in her head. "Obviously, Ginger doesn't know, and I'm starting to see her papá is as bad as mine…" she pauses to look at me, " and you've known the whole time haven't you?" When I don't say anything, she turns back to Shy. "So are you following orders by renting it or did you never really give her up like she says you did?"

Fuck. Here we go. Goddamnit!

Crossing her arms over her chest, she waits for an answer. We all look to Shy who is smiling big at Alex, but it's Mac who speaks up sounding surprised. "I'm Mac, by the way, Snow's cousin and I now know why Maddox is so bat shit crazy for you, brains and looks, goddamn I need to find someone like that. All the pussy around where we live are fucking dumb as fuck."

I can see Alex getting ready to mouth off when Maddox appears next to me, coming up behind and grabbing Alex around the waist, making her squeal. He leans down kissing her on the side of the head with a "What's up, Mi Amor?"

Mac must have seen him coming up behind us because he chuckles watching them interact. Maddox looks up giving me a head nod, and I nod back but don't say anything, letting this all play out. Then he looks to the guys saying, "How's it going Mac, Shy? Did Ethan get ahold of you?"

"Whaddup," Mac replies.

"Been better. Not yet but Wolfe told me he was going to contact me tonight. I'll let you know what happens," Shy actually answers him.

What the fuck?

Maddox is oblivious to what he walked up on or that his girl is about ready to flip a fucking switch in his arms. I look down to Alex who is staring at Shy, and I can feel her brain working, so when Shy is done speaking she turns to Maddox, and here we go with her tantrum.

Always a fucking princess.
"What are you talking about and how the fuck do you know them? I mean you have only been here at the hospital a few times, and I just met Mac for the first time."
Good point.
Laughter erupts from Shy and Mac making Alex look back to them, but Maddox slides his hand from around her waist down to the globes of her ass. "Alexandria-"
But Mac jumps in looking at Alex with a laughing remark, "It's been fun but..." he chuckles looking to Maddox, "Maddog, we'll be in touch."
When Shy moves to Ginger's room I'm about to tell him he can't go in there but I remember the state her aunt was in and she will probably kick him out as well. I turn my attention back to Maddox and Alex, also wanting to hear how he knows them and what they are working on together.
Folding my arms over my chest, I watch Alex get testy with him folding her arms like she is mad at him, when all the while he is fondling her ass trying to get her to let it go. When neither of them is going to say anything I decide I don't have time for this. "What's going on with them? What is he finding out?" I ask Maddox
God, I sound like a fucking pussy right now.
They both look over at me with Alex smiling huge and Maddox shooting daggers. Alex turns back to him arms still crossed over her chest, not budging. "Yeah, Mad-Dog, What's going on?" dragging out his name.
Maddox lets out a deep breath releasing her ass, standing back up, fully towering over her. "My team has been in touch with them since the incident, and we've been working with them and the police to see if there was anyone else working with Emmett."
What the fuck! Why didn't we know this?
Alex is one step ahead of me rattling off shit. "Why doesn't Papá's team know this? What do they know that we don't know?

Spill it, Maddy."

Damn, I love this girl.

I just stand there watching them, hoping he answers, so I don't have to be a pussy again asking questions. Maddox replies, "Your father and Beau are involved in the investigation as well. You know all that, but I guess you didn't know Ginger's father is involved too."

Crossing his arms mimicking her, he laughs. "Do you really think her father is going to let this go? Of course, he is involved and his guys" -pointing to the door where Shy and Mac walked through and still haven't come out of- "are helping, so of course, I know them."

Fuck! He is still in there. Motherfucker.

Jealously boils up inside me making me clench my fist. "Fuck!" I grunt

When I turn to head for Gingers room, Alex grabs my arm. "B, let them visit with her. Storm is Mac's mom, and I'm sure they're all visiting. He gets time with her too, and if you barge in there, it will only make things worse. Plus we can't have her getting upset. We need her to recover not get worse."

Goddamn it!

I let out a deep breath turning to my best friend. "I have to get the fuck out of here then. I can't sit here while they are all in there. Call me when they're gone."

Not waiting for their reply, I turn and walk away. Leaving behind my girl and it feels like my heart is breaking. If she finds out he never let her go and was always there watching I might lose her.

"FUCK!"

SHY

Walking into Ginger's hospital room, I get butterflies in my stomach. I haven't been alone with her since she woke up and started speaking. Shit, she hasn't physically seen me in over a year, a year that I've changed so much without having her in my life. I've tried to stay away, but I can't do it. I need to get my lady back.

When we hear Storm jibber jabbering about coming home or something, we walk in knowing Ginger can't be sleeping. Mac enters first. "Whaddup, cuz! Welcome back to the living."

He laughs walking over to her, kissing her forehead. Storm speaks up next. "Boy leave her alone." She leans down kissing Ginger on the forehead as well. "I'll be back in a few minutes. I am still so pissed off with these boys I can't be around them." Storm turns and walks out not even giving me a glance.

Shit!

"Shit! I haven't seen her this pissed in a while. And I'm the one who brought her here," Mac says what I am thinking.

Ginger laughs pulling me out of my daze. "She'll get over it. She always does with you two."

When she looks over Mac's shoulders giving me her attention, I move out from behind him. Mac is a couple inches taller than I am but we're both built the same, seeing as we both work out every day together, sometimes a couple times a day to release some stress.

"Glad to hear you got your voice back, Angel." Seeing the pain cross her face with me calling her by her pet name, I smile.

Her face changes from pained to something like shock and her eyes move up and down my body as if she has never seen me before.

Yeah, Angel, I've changed.

I let her study me because I don't look anything like I did over a year ago when she last visited. I have put on a good twenty-five pounds of muscle. When she was on tour, I lost my mind, and the only release was beating the shit out of a heavy bag or lifting weights. But by the look on her face, which she is trying to hide but doing a shit job of, it's telling me she likes what she sees.

Take a good look Angel because I am here to stay.

I say what I'm sure she wants to but won't allow herself to. "You look good," I pause and wait for her eyes to reach my face before continuing, but it's Mac's muffled laugh that jolts her hankering eyes from engulfing me.

When she closes her eyes, I continue, "What did the doctor say about releasing you and your injuries?"

Ginger takes a slow deep breath, and I know she is trying to mask her emotions and pain when she speaks. "Well, the doctor told me that my left side was injured by my fall when I put my bike down leaving me with road rash on my leg. I have a sprained ankle, but they said it also showed a hairline fracture in my upper tibia. When I fell, I must have put my left arm out to break my fall because I broke my wrist and dislocated my shoulder at the same time when I landed."

She moves her right arm, which is bandaged where she got shot but it's at least mobile to move around, grabbing the cast on her left forearm. I notice Mac tense up, no doubt thinking the same thing I am, thank God this fucker is dead.

Moving her hand down over her ribs, wincing painfully she takes a couple short breaths. "Emmett shot me in the right side hitting my chest, leg, and right shoulder. The doctor said those would take the longest to heal." Ginger reaches up to touch her head but can't move it up that far with her bandages, and it probably hurts like a bitch, so she just points to her head.

I let out a deep groan, causing Ginger to look my way, so I mask my rage, knowing damn well I am going to fuck something up when I leave this room. "I remember falling, but I guess when I fell to the ground I hit my head on something pretty good, but the doctor said my head injuries could be from both the crash and the fall but we don't really know," she continues.

Ginger takes a few more short breaths before looking up at

both of us with a smile. "I should be released tomorrow and hopefully healed up soon to hit the road with Alex for the end of the tour. I won't let this keep me down. Mac, you need to help me talk to your momma. She wants to stay with me here while I recover and Dad thinks I'm going home with you guys. I can't go back - I won't go back."

I feel my blood start to boil, clenching my hands in my pockets, I try to hold it together, but it's Mac who loses it.

"What the fuck, Snow? Did you forget who raised you and where you came from? This is killing my *ma*, and you know it. You act like this high and mighty fucking rock star, but really you're just our Snow. Don't change who you are inside and out because we all know the Wolfeman blood will always break through any facade that you put up."

When he steps away from the wall, Mac moves to the foot of the bed grabbing her good foot that isn't in a boot. "Your life wasn't bad, we all lost someone, but we are and will always be family. Quit trying to run from us."

Mac turns and walks out the door, giving me a head nod before exiting. I know he's just as pissed off as me with this new 'I'm a DJ and don't have time for my family' shit. She has only been home a handful of times these past few years.

I look down at my steel toed boots gathering my thoughts, so I don't blow up myself. I want to try to get it through that pretty little head that she is my queen and will always be my girl. Fuck the club. I'm talking about her and me.

Before I look up, Ginger speaks up in a broken voice, which has me snapping my head up.

Nothing breaks this girl, well besides me.

"No one understands. I needed to find myself and become someone other than the Wolfeman's little princess."

Goddamn, it hurts like hell to see her looking so fucking broken. She is like a beautiful, wounded angel. A knot forms in my throat with a pain in my chest.

Fuck, where is my shining Angel?
"Angel, I have always understood what you need, and I have given you more than enough time. Remember I was just as broken as you until your family took me in and I know how lost you were but running from your life and what family you have that loves you beyond words, to become some superstar is not the answer. You can be both, our princess and live this lifestyle."
Ginger snaps her head up staring daggers at me.
There's my Angel.
"I am *not* running from my family to become some superstar, and I would *never* forget my family."
Bullshit!
"Then why haven't you come home since your tour? I know you've grown into this amazing woman but what are you really running from if not your family?"
Say it. Just say it!
I paused waiting for a reaction, but when she doesn't reply I go for the big question. "You running from me?"
I finally get the reaction I was looking for because her face turns beet red. "Fuck you, Shy! We have been over for a long fucking time. Remember *you* let *me* go." Folding her good arm over her stomach trying to comfort herself.
If only you knew.
I move off the wall, taking two steps to reach the side of her bed. She doesn't move or react but only stares into my eyes challenging me.
Keeping my hands in my pockets for control, I bend at the waist leaning over her, getting inches from her face. I say in a calm and smooth, even voice, "Angel, you need to get this through that thick little head of yours. I never left you, and you will *always* be *my* girl. I am done with you finger fucking around. It's time I have my woman back. We're not fucking teenagers anymore Snow, and I am damn sure not some little boy you can push around. So" -standing back up I smile a wicked smile-

"things are going to change around here. Best you get on board with it because I know you still love me and I am ready to fight for you."

Ginger's face, red as blood, glares back at me. Folding my arms over my chest waiting for her to lash back out at me, I keep smiling. "Why fight now? Is it because of Brant? You should have fought back then when it meant something," Ginger grits out.

Just then, Storm waltz's through the door interrupting our little standoff.

I have been fighting and here the whole time. If she could just get past her ego, think about it and not hide behind that wall, she would see I never left her.

Leaning down again, I kiss her forehead, and whisper, "I have always been here fighting for *us*, but in all due time you will understand and know everything. I promise you that, my Angel."

Turning to leave, I move to give Storm a hug, but she puts her hand up halting me. "Sorry, Micah but I am still super fucking pissed off at you boys." Smiling at her, I nod my understanding and walk out the door without looking back at my girl. She will be mine again soon.

Very fucking soon, indeed.

9

GINGER

Fuck him!
He can't just come in here, looking all bad-ass biker and tell me it's time to come home. Give up all that I have done these past few years. I want to cry with all the different emotions running through me. I hate that I can't get myself under control.
Sonovabitch!
He looked so damn good and so much bigger. I couldn't believe my eyes when he moved from behind Mac. He looks so much older and badass. Fuck, my pussy spasmed just seeing his biceps bulging out of his cut and that fucking goatee. Fucking hell I need to stop thinking like that. What am I supposed to do, just fall at his feet now that he finally wants me back? I am so done with his games and all these hidden messages with texting me daily with a song. One would think he would of let me go after we broke up, but no, every day I get a message with a song or part of a lyric. Making me feel he is always around me. I have to let him go. I need to let him go.
"Ginger!" Auntie yells at me snapping me out of my fit.
Looking up I try to focus on her, and when I see the worried look on her face, I break. I start sobbing, and my auntie sits on the bed and holds me. I haven't cried like a baby in years but just

having her here, added to all the pain I'm in, along with all my inner turmoil going on due to all the events that have occurred these last few months, I can't keep my wall up anymore. So I let go...
Why can't I hate him!
"Baby girl, it's going to be okay. I don't know what is going on between you two, or even you and this new guy but I am here for you. Let it go. I got you."
I don't know how long I cry in her arms, but I feel like I heard the door open a time or two. It's not until Alex walks in and gasps that I pull away, instantly feeling pain shoot out from my ribcage. Auntie says to Alex, "Maybe come back in a few minutes, sweetie-"
But I cut her off. "No, Auntie I want her here."
Seeing me crying Alex starts getting teary-eyed. Moving to the other side of the bed, she too sits on the bed. Auntie on one side and my best friend on the other. Like the old days but it was Faith, not Alex. All my thoughts and feelings that I have pushed away or stored up just come flooding out, and I start to cry again. I move my good arm up as far as I can, trying to cover my eyes.
Fuck, I miss her. I am running. I am running from my family, Micah, and mostly from that little girl that wants her momma and best friend back.
Both of them are quiet, opening my eyes I see they're crying too.
I break the ice. "Well, I guess I shattered your whole, 'Ginger is a badass' image."
"It makes me happy to know you are actually human," Alex replies softly.
Yeah, look at me now, I am a fake.
Everyone starts to laugh. I hold my ribs, feeling so much pain mentally and physically.
God help me.
Taking a few short breaths, knowing I need to get it all out, I

start talking. "I can't seem to let anything go. I put this wall up and tuck all the bad stuff away and think I can handle it." I look to Auntie with a sad smile. "I'm a Wolfeman, we can handle anything but in reality, I can't. Faith is gone, Momma is gone, Micah let me go, and I don't know who I am-" cutting myself off I start to sob again.

It hurts so fucking bad. I can't breathe. Oh, God.

Storm speaks up. "Sweetie, you are Ginger Wolfe, daughter of my brother and president of the Wolfeman MC, the princess of more than a dozen men, one amazing DJ, and besides what you may think, Micah has never let you go, baby. Your momma and my baby girl are with us every God given minute of every day and don't you forget that." Lifting her hand to her mouth trying to hold back her own sobs but failing.

Alex takes that opportunity to jump in with, "Why do you have to decide between one or the other? Why can't you have both lives? You can be the princess of the Wolfeman and be the best fucking DJ out there. Look at my papá and mamá. They lived in different countries for God's sake. The only thing I see you need to figure out is which fucking hot guy you're going to pick because they both love you. I don't know what happened between you and Shy but if he-"

Commotion at the door interrupts Alex, and we all look to see what new storm will blaze through and of course my luck it's Brant and Maddox followed by Shy and Mac.

Why God. Why, me. Fuck!

We all wipe our faces, and they both get off the bed turning to face the boys. I smile seeing they're both in a protective stance next to me, not letting anything come near me. *I love my girls.*

Maddox and Mac are discussing bikes while Brant and Shy both have their sight set on me. When Maddox sees the look on our faces, he shuts up and moves to Alex. "You okay? Why are all of you crying? What happened?"

Alex hits him in the arm. "Relax Maddy. We were having a

moment with our girl."

Maddox wraps his arm around her waist. "Well, are you ready to head home? We need to change before the club tonight."

The mention of the club has me taking small breaths trying to keep the tears away.

Do not cry. Stay strong.

When Auntie moves to sit in the chair next to the bed, Alex looks to me seeing if I am okay. I smile at her with a nod, not wanting to sound emotional. I glance toward my aunt, and once Alex is satisfied that I will be okay, she says to Maddox, "Okay, we can leave now."

Brant speaks to Alex drawing everyone's attention. "I'm going to hang out here tonight, so you will have Maddox's team with you."

Shy steps forward with a growl. "The fuck you will. I will be staying the night here. You don't need to be watching over Ginger anymore. *We*" -Shy points to Mac but never breaks eye contact with Brant- "will watch over her now. She won't be needing your services anymore."

Oh, my God. Seriously!

They stand toe to toe, and I tune them out watching them bicker back and forth. They are like night and day. My brain is on overdrive, and I can't handle this shit right now, so rage consumes me again, and the feisty Ginger is back, I snap.

"Get the fuck out! All of you get the fuck out!" My voice comes out loud and strong, surprising even myself but I feel pain shoot from my ribs. Everyone stops to look at me, and I don't back down. In a softer but still pissed off voice, I look at both of them. "Get. The. Fuck. Out." Punctuating each word making sure they understand. "I don't want to see either of you."

Just at that moment, the nurse comes in, so I say again, "Please would everyone leave."

Brant looks at me and huffs out, "Fuck this," and walks out.

Alex kisses me on the forehead and says in a whisper, "There's my badass," and walks away with Maddox in tow, along with Mac.

Shy rounds on me. "Angel, you need to think again if you think I'm going leave your side."

When I threaten to call my dad, Shy leaves but only to stand guard outside.

Damn, he is pissed.

Once everyone is out, the nurse looks at me, then to my aunt and then back to me before saying, "Damn girl what did I miss?"

I relax back into the bed not answering her question but instead tell her, "Please give me the good shit and make it all go away."

She laughs. "Now *that* I can do."

I look toward my aunt, but she doesn't say anything, only smiles at me while she reaches for her book.

Yep, I have my watchdog now. I can rest easy.

SHY

(Club Spin before European tour)

"Bro, what the fuck, man?" I hear Quick, a prospect, yell at Mac across the booth.

"Nut up bitch, this little trip isn't so you can get your dick wet, fucker, I don't care how *Quick* you are, put the drink and the bitch down because you have the first watch right now."

The prospect, which we'll be making a member next week, does what he is told giving the girl a smack on the ass, motioning for her to leave, but you can tell he isn't too happy about it. Only making Mac madder. "You better wipe that fucking frown off your face and smile, bitch. We're here for a job, not to fucking party."

I have to laugh. *Yeah, it's our* job *to come watch my lady.*

We have been watching my girl every chance we get while

we have been checking out members of the Scorpion MC seeing who is trustworthy and who is going rogue along with making our own moves for this takeover. The club made a deal with Luc before Ginger even came out to New York City, and we've stuck with that deal.

One stipulation was that we would always have one of the secluded VIP booths in the back of Club Spin. The DJs were always up front and in a VIP booth right next to the stage, while ours was off to the other side completely in the back but no matter what we could see the stage. Wolfe knew once his daughter started DJing here on a regular basis I needed to be able to see her, plus he had no problem with this because it was me.

The only rules were we were not to engage or become noticed by her at all. Like no contact even when fights broke out in the club. Luc said his security team was more than enough to keep her safe. We are not to wear our MC cuts, no bikes in sight and most of all we couldn't cause any trouble. We could only have four men at the most inside the club and not more than six around the nightclub. All the men needed to be new prospects and people she didn't know except of course Mac and myself. Wolfe just wanted eyes on her and a way for me to be able to see her. It was part of his and my deal from the beginning.

"Shy!" Mac waving his hands in front of me snaps me from my daze. Mac "MacDaddy" Harding is my best friend and saving his life was the best decision I had ever made. I look over to him answering him with a head nod while finishing my beer. I don't speak much and when I do it's only to a select few.

"Bro, what the fuck? Are you in la-la-land? I've been sitting here talking to you, and you've got your head up your ass, and my cousin isn't even here yet. What's got your panties in a bunch? You need to nut-the-fuck-up, man."

Shrugging, I say, "Nothing, just got a lot of shit on my mind, and you know how I fucking hate this" -throwing my hand out toward the club- "not being able to have any contact with my girl. It's fucking killing me."

I need my Angel, that's what the fuck is wrong.

"Fuck bro, I know this is hard but just keep looking at the bigger picture. You and I both know she loves you." Just as he finishes his sentence, we both get the text from Quick that she is entering the club and my heart starts pounding.

Fuck, I need her like I need my next breath.

Grabbing a new beer from out of the bucket I sit back and just pray to God I can make it through this night without breaking the rules. Every time I come to the club where she's at I pray I can hold up my end of the deal because if I can't, Wolfe will pull the plug and I could lose everything. I need to stay focused.

Seeing her walk in with a group of girls, my cock jumps to life becoming instantly hard. *Fuck me.*

She has changed, but I still see my Angel. She has lost weight since she left home, but fuck she has filled out in all the right places, even her ass looks plumper, probably from those fucking tight ass clothes she now wears. This new image she has going on is so fucking sexy that I jack off to her at least twice a day from pictures on my phone that I have taken from afar. She will always be perfect to me.

Mac breaks my daze by waving his hands in front of me again. "Goddamn Shy, I need to bring Quick back over here with those girls because you're boring as fuck. I know you got it bad, but you're looking at my cousin like some meth addict and she is your next fix, bro."

Watching her move toward the stage I know she is getting ready to go on, so I ignore Mac, never taking my eyes off of her as I flip him off.

I need my fix that is for sure, fuck.

I feel like we have always had this spiritual connection that neither one of us could explain. Our mutual love of music made our relationship move faster than anyone would have thought.

You could say it was love at first sight, but I didn't actually see her for almost two days with how badly I had gotten beat. That first night when they moved me to her place, all was quiet until I heard her music. Fucking had me crying, or at least I felt like I was crying, I couldn't really tell with my eyes swollen shut. She became my Angel and I became her Shy.

Everyone called me Kid for the longest time, but she started calling me Shy a week after I was up and moving around. Probably because I didn't talk much, I'm more of a thinker and a do-er. Fuck talking, but she gets me because she was the same way, only she talks way more than I do. We used music to express our emotions. It's what I love most about her, that I can tell her how I feel through a song. I have always used my hands to speak, and it was never for love but instead survival. When she came into my life, I never felt anything like it, and I know I can't live without it. She is my Angel, my light.

When I see her look around, I wonder if she senses I am watching her. She doesn't ask if I'm ever around, but I get this feeling when she scans the crowd that she is looking for me. I so badly want to go to her and make her my girl again.

Fuck that. She is my girl.

I pull my phone out, and I stake my claim the only way I can right now by texting her.

SHY
Be good my Angel – "Smack That" – by Akon. I feel you creeping, I can see you from my shadow.

Once I push the send button, I wait for her reaction. Her reaction that I crave each and every time I see her is the look of longing, desire and most of all love. I know she still loves me when I see her read my texts. That's why I text her every single day at least once and no matter what, that one text will always have a song for her. I usually text her when songs come on that remind me of her or when I need her to know how I feel about her.

Quick walks up to the group with four girls in tow. I down my beer and don't even acknowledge them. "It's about fucking time. I have people to talk to. Fuck!" Mac yells.

Come on, Angel, read the fucking text.

The group starts to talk with the girls bouncing around dancing. I stand up moving to the edge of the booth, knowing I won't stop staring until she reads the text and gives me that smile. Watching her bounce around on stage, shaking her hips to the music, my cock stands rock solid against my briefs. I dream every night about sinking my dick deep in her again.

Fuck!

Just when I'm about to flip out and text her again from growing inpatient, Ginger reaches down picking up her cell phone looking at my text, and then I see it - she smiles - but it isn't for long. She looks around probably feeling I am around her but knows it would be impossible for me to be here in the city. My dick instantly reacts to her facial expression to my text. She always reacts with a smile before she can put that wall back up and tell herself anything different. That right there is still love, and I know I haven't lost her.

When my phone vibrates, I know it's her replying.

GINGER
I'm always good as I'm sure you remember, but I'll ask the guy I'm with tonight after he smacks it and see what he thinks! Now fuck off Shy!

Oh, I'll fuck off, for now.
I turn to my boys. "Let's fucking party!"
Mac hands me another beer. "It's about fucking time, bro."
Slamming the beer back laughing to myself because she has no idea that I know damn well she will be home alone tonight

like she is every night. *My queen.*

By the time I finish my beer, I hear the next song she plays, "My Feelings For You" by Avicii. I smile, that's my girl confirming she still loves me. Knowing she doesn't know I am here she is playing from her heart, what she can't and won't tell me. My heart picks up knowing my Angel is still, *my* Angel.

GINGER

The next few days get a bit stressful, but luckily for me, I have my auntie and Alex by my side, so I didn't have to make too many decisions. I did make the decision to head home with my family to recover. Plus having the break down with my auntie and Alex, I knew I needed to get my shit together. I needed to quit running.

I am due back in three weeks to get a check-up of the hairline fracture of my tibia and in six weeks to have my cast removed from my arm, and if I don't have any complications with healing, I would be back on the decks. Having both my arms and shoulders bandaged up I couldn't really DJ anyway.

Once Shy heard I was coming home, he took off with the guys only to come back today when we were headed home. I told my auntie I was going to be riding home with Brant and Alex.

Alex was leaving with Maddox once she got back but she wanted to make sure I was home and good. I also think she wanted to be with me for moral support. We never did finish our conversation, but I know we will once everything settles down and everyone isn't up my ass.

I needed to talk to Brant, so it made sense to have them drive me home, plus I knew it would piss Shy off. I don't want him thinking because I am coming home, that I am his. *I belong to no one.*

The ride home was going well, like old times with us three just shooting the shit, laughing and talking music. Brant was driving with Alex in the front seat, while I spread out in the back seat of the SUV. Brant hasn't been himself around me since I told him to get out. It hasn't stopped him from being around, but I can feel the tension.

Thinking I should say sorry or something I look up to the rearview mirror only to see him staring back at me, so I give him a smile.

Brant cuts Alex off who is rambling about something that obviously neither one of us were listening to.

"Are you getting back with him?"

Brant holds my gaze while Alex goes quiet.

What the fuck? Where did that come from?

"Hell no!" I reply without hesitation.

Brant looks straight ahead driving, and Alex turns to look out the window giving us our privacy. Well as much as she can, since we're in an SUV. I become disgruntled, and I snap.

"Just because I'm going home doesn't mean I'm running back to him. He broke my heart, and I left a long time ago. It's my family that I am going home to see, and so I can rest. I haven't been home in over a year."

I stop ranting when I realize, why the fuck am I explaining this to him. I have told him from the beginning we are not together.

But you let him in...

"You and I have been together every fucking day for over a year. I know you said we're not together but it's kind of hard to just be okay with you going home to your ex-first love."

Oh, my God.

"Brant, I'm not going to be home long. I'm not getting back with my ex, and you are correct, I am not ready to be with anyone. That is what I have told you from the beginning. I haven't kept anything from you and all I'm doing is going home to rest. I just need some time to recover."

In her seat, I watch Alex squirm, knowing she wants to jump in, but hoping she doesn't.

Brant groans making me look from Alex over to him locking eyes with his in the rearview mirror again.

"So what do you want from me, Gin? Do you want me to wait around these few months while you are home with your ex" -he puts his hand up silencing me- "because I know him and he will be all in your space trying to get you back. So again, what do you want from me, Ginger? I want to be with you. I have given you enough time and space. I need to know what you want out of this?"

Shit. Breathe. Don't freak out.

I feel my face turn red and I can feel my temper rising. I take a couple short breaths before answering him.

"B, we have been friends for a few years now. Yes, we have messed around. Yes, I have feelings for you. But, like I have told you, *numerous times*, I am seriously fucked up in the head regarding abandonment and commitment issues. I'm nowhere near ready to be tied down. I'm going to be twenty-three soon, and I want to be me."

"What the fuck does that even mean? You want to be you? You're saying that you're not you with me? I'm not asking you to marry me, but I would like to know you're not going to fuck him while you're home and that we'll have something when you come back. I thought we were together, that we were moving forward," Brant fires back.

Alex turns facing both of us. "Okay, that's enough. B, I understand you-"

I cut her off not letting her finish her sentence. "B, I care about you, but I can't give you what you want. I can't give myself over to anyone again, at least not until I am mentally ready. Going home is going to give me closure on a lot of things."

Brant stares daggers into the rearview mirror. "So what you're saying is he has your heart, and until you get over him you can't move on." He looks away lifting his shoulders twisting his neck trying to loosen the tension. He continues in a dead voice. "Don't you worry about me, Gin, I'll be fine. I hear you loud and clear. Friends with benefits right, gotcha."

"B, that's not cool," Alex huffs out before turning back to look out the window.

Wanting to cry and punch someone at the same time has me looking away out the window. What am I supposed to say to him because he is correct? We have been friends with benefits. I do need to move on and let go of my past. Not just Shy but my momma and Faith. I need to close those doors before I can move on. Even my friendships have been on hold because I haven't wanted to give up Faith. I am seriously fucked up in the head.

One more hour. I can do this.

BRANT

(Week before Ginger gets shot)

After meeting with everyone at Alex's place, we all disburse heading to our own places. Ginger better be at my place or I will have her ass. Walking back to my apartment, I give myself a pep talk, knowing I need to pin her down and have "the talk" with her. We have been messing around since we were on tour in Europe but nothing too heavy because we were never alone unless the girls were asleep and even then she would push me away. It wasn't until we were back here in New York that this started getting more serious but we were still hiding it from everyone. We are together all the time, but she is hot and cold, I never know if I am going to get sweet and sexy Ginger or biker Ginger. She says she doesn't want anything serious. I know it has to do with her ex-boyfriend, but she says she is over him.

When I open my door noticing her sprawled out on the couch, I almost come in my pants. Her pajama shorts that barely cover anything showing me her sexy as sin fucking legs. *Fuck me!* I lick my lips scanning her body with my eyes until they lock with her emerald ones. I shut the door, taking a couple of steps into my apartment never breaking eye contact with her.

Jesus, I probably look like a crazed man.

"What's up? What happened?" Ginger asks, sitting up.

I move to take my jacket off while I scan over her little string top cami which now shows her hardened nipples, giving away that I affect her as much as she does me. When I still haven't answered her, she jumps off the couch letting her temper take over.

"What the fuck, B? What happened?"

A smile creeps across my face. Goddamn, I love when her temper flares, so fucking hot. I chuckle coming to stand toe-to-toe with her placing my hands on her hips.

"We found bugs and videos. This guy hacked into our security system and has been watching her. There was a camera in her office under her desk."

Ginger gasps taking a step back. "Are you fucking serious? How is Alex? Should I go check on her?"

"Fuck no! You are staying right here with me. Maddox is with her, and she is fine."

I try not to think about Alex's rapist trying to get her again. We all are overworked and stressed the fuck out. I need to relax. Goddamn, I want to consume Ginger, but I have been letting her run the show, not wanting to scare her off. I slip my hands up her arms and over her shoulders hooking fingers into the strings of her cami only to bring them back down, exposing her mouth watering breasts.

Easy big guy, go slow.

"I need this." Seeing her nipples harden into small little raisins have my dick so hard it's busting at the seams.

"But-"

Cutting her off, I lean down engulfing one of her breasts into my mouth.

Ginger moans arching her back, pushing her breast further into my mouth.

Slipping my hands around her tiny waist I lift her up, and she instantly wraps her arms and legs around me. Being almost a foot taller than her when I wrap my arms around her, I feel like I swallow her up. Grabbing the globes of her tight little ass, I move her up and down grinding her against me, while I assault her breasts.

Jesus, I need to slow down.

Hearing Ginger's sultry sounds have me losing control, getting more aggressive, I bite and tug on her tits, moving up her chest to her neck. Ginger moans, "yes, God yes."

It's my undoing. I march us into my room tossing her in the air. Ginger squeals landing with a bounce on the bed, giving me time to undo my belt and drop my jeans, leaving my boxer briefs on. Pulling my shirt off, I see Ginger is up on her knees moving toward me like a tiger with her tits bouncing.

"Fuck baby, I'm going to come just watching you do that. I'm going to have some serious blue balls tomorrow unless we do something about this." Pointing to my throbbing cock begging to be let loose.

I don't push having sex with her since she told me that she wasn't ready but fuck it's hard as hell not to dominate her and try to persuade her. It's been a while, and I've had to masturbate the last few times we hung out just to relieve some pressure.

Ginger crawls to the end of the bed grabbing my dick through my briefs, making me hiss. "Fuck, baby."

I grab her shoulders, thrusting my cock toward her while staring into her sparkling greens but when I see her brows pinch together, I freeze.

Oh, shit!

Ginger palms my cock. "Are you sure she is okay? If I find out you are trying to distract me when something big is happening, I will cut your dick off. She is my best friend, so don't lie to me."

Jesus Christ.

I take a breath, leaning toward her but leaving inches between our faces. "I promise you. She is fine, and I will let you know the plan later." Keeping my momentum moving forward, leaning over her making her fall back onto the mattress with her feet dangling off the bed. "But right now I need *you* to help *me* relax."

Pulling her shorts off, sliding them down her body leaving a trail of kisses, yanking them off her feet, she sits up.

Standing in front of her with only my briefs and socks on, I take a second to see what she will do. Waiting to see if I will get the sexy or the bitch version of her. Ginger pulls her cami completely over her head throwing it to the side and stands up, and we wrap our arms around each other. I lean down to take her mouth, but she moves her head, kissing my chest while she hooks her fingers in my briefs sliding them down my body.

Thank fuck. I get sexy Gin!

Wrapping her small hands around my cock, I almost come instantly. It has been a while since she has touched me.

When she licks the rim of my dick, I can't keep quiet. "God. That feels so fucking good."

Ginger slips a small amount into her mouth and sucks coming back up letting it pop out saying, "You like that?" Before sliding back down taking me fully into her mouth.

I moan like a bitch. "Fuck. Yes."

With her hair in a bun on the top of her head, I slip my hands on the side of her face palming her head, hooking my thumbs over her ears bracing her head for my assault, increasing my rhythm. When I look down locking eyes with her letting me know she is okay, I bite my lower lip with a moan.

Fuck, me. Don't come yet. Hold on.

Ginger cups my balls with one hand and grips my hips to steady herself, moaning, her eyes start to water. I close my eyes imagining it's her tight little pussy. *Fuck!*

Ginger moans, making it vibrate along my cock, while saliva starts to run out the sides of her mouth, making a sloshing sound each time I enter her. When my grunts get louder, and I feel my nuts tightening up. "I'm close. Fuck baby, I'm going to come so fucking hard." *Motherfucker!*

I pull out grabbing my cock, knowing she won't swallow, and push her back onto the bed. She instantly moves back, wiping her face.

Fuck.

With Ginger laying on her back, she spreads her legs showing me she is just as ready as she slides her fingers over her clit. I jack my cock harder, squirting cum everywhere grunting my release. "Oh, God. Yes."

Still feeling euphoric from my orgasm and needing more, I reach over grabbing ahold of Ginger's legs pulling her ass to the edge of the bed, I drop down to my knees throwing her legs over my shoulders and dive in. Flicking her hand away with a growl like I am jealous of them touching what I have come to crave. I slowly lick up her already wet folds.

"Oh, fuck," Ginger gasps.

She arches her back off the mattress, moving her hand up her tight abs, over her ribcage, gripping her perfectly erect nipples. "More. I *need* more."

Fuck yeah. Baby.

Not wanting to move too fast and have her deny me, I keep sucking her clit and tongue fucking her pussy. It only makes her thrash around on the bed. Ginger grabs my head holding me in place and starts to grind against my face. "Please. Please. I *need* more."

She has never asked for more, only moans and thrusts against my face. I slip two fingers into the tightest pussy I've ever felt. Her begging mixed with her pussy suctioning around my fingers has my dick rock solid again. I start to rub my cock up against the bed while sucking her nub and finger fucking her.

Jesus, I want to be inside her.

Ginger's eyes are closed while she moans with each pump of my fingers. She moves in sync with me, meeting each thrust and I feel them go deeper with each stroke. Finding her g-spot, she cries out, "Oh, God, right there. Fuck."

I press up and move faster. "Fuck baby, I want you so fucking bad. My dick is already hard again, just watching you. Come for me, baby,"

"Faster. Fuck yes," she replies.

I suck on her clit and release it. I move my free hand over it to start circling in the rhythm with my fingers.

Ginger claws at the comforter. "Fuck me. I *need* you to fuck me."

My whole body stills except my fingers that keep moving in and out of her. "What do you need, baby?"

Holy shit. Please say it again.

"Fuck. Me. Please," Ginger replies out of breath, drawing out each word.

Removing my fingers from her clit, I move up her body, crashing our lips together only for her to move her head, so I suck on her neck. I tell her to move up the bed while I keep moving my fingers in and out of her.

Once in place, I cover her body capturing her mouth again, but she breaks free begging, "Please. Harder." Grabbing a condom from the bedside table I finally take my fingers out of her, I sit back to roll the condom on, and I see that her eyes are closed.

"Gin, baby open your eyes. Tell me this is what you want?"

She opens her eyes. "Quit screwing around and fuck me for God's sake."

Good enough for me.

I want to ask her why all of a sudden but fuck it. Once the condom is seated all the way on, I place my cock at her entrance, and I try to slip it in slowly feeling how tight she is. I slide back before I inch in a bit more, but Ginger gets frustrated pulling me over so she can flip me onto my back.

"Fuck, B, I'm not a fucking virgin." She straddles me lining up my cock and takes over lowering herself down onto my shaft till she is almost fully seated.

"Oh, God. Yes," she moans out.

"Motherfucker. You're so fucking tight."

Ginger leans forward letting my cock slide almost out before moving slowly back down into a sitting position on top of me. Ginger moans, tilting her head back and starts to ride me, starting out slow. I try to calm myself, so I don't nut in seconds.

God, she is perfect. So fucking tight, fuck yes.

Ginger leans forward picking up the pace moving her hips faster and faster while gripping my chest, she groans, "Yes."

When I feel her walls clamping down around my dick, I grab her hips meeting her thrust. "Yeah, baby, ride my cock. Fucking take it."

Ginger screams her release, letting the orgasm consume her, falling forward, her pussy contracts around my cock. Holding her hips, I pump into her faster chasing my own release.

Fuck yes.
Thrust.
Almost.
Thrust.
Fuck. Me.
Thrust.

Ginger's pussy spasms with another orgasm that ripples through her, clenching my cock and sending me over the edge. "Yes. Yes. Ahhhhhh."

Both of us are out of breath and she's sprawled out over my body. Ginger's black straight hair is spread across my chest hanging over her face. I don't move, not wanting this to end. Hearing her soft moans have my dick already twitching again, so I slide out of her while caressing her back. When her breathing evens out, I slip out from under her, leaving her naked and fully satisfied. I go to discard my condom but hurry back not wanting this night to end.

I need to get my head in the game and off Gin's pussy. I hated leaving her laying in my bed naked this morning. If it wasn't for this sick fuck after Alex, I would have called in sick and stayed inside her all day. Fuck yeah!

Finally, after all these years of flirting and these past six months of blue balls, it finally fucking paid off. Shy was one dumb motherfucker for leaving her. I just don't understand why he comes to the club and watches her but never engages. Oh well, his loss and my gain because I will not let her go. Sinking my cock inside her last night and again early this morning was over the top, and I don't think I can give her up.

Maddox walks by me leaving Alex's office but hesitates while he texts someone before giving me a head nod.

Fucking get it together.

I adjust myself and hope no one notices the slight bulge in my pants.

My phone ringing distracts me until I see it's Ginger calling. Knowing I'm not alone and I'm in the office with Alex being nosey as ever, I try to keep my voice even and not sound too excited.

"Hello," I say.

Ginger huffs out, "B, you didn't wake me up when you left." I chuckle, and Ginger keeps talking, "I know you're at the office-"

I cut her off when I hear a car horn, saying, "Yeah, I'm here in Alex's office. Where are you?"

Ginger huffs again, "I'm downstairs parking my bike, relax." I watch Alex stare at me obviously trying to figure out who I am talking to.

I talk into the phone. "Okay, you remember what I told you last night, though."

"I was fucked last night, not deaf, of course, I remember," Ginger snaps back, getting more irritated.

Chuckling again, I try to keep from exposing our relationship. "Yes, so just remember," I reply.

I hear an elevator ding before she replies, "I'm on my way up."

"Right, see you in a few minutes." Once I hang up the phone, I expect Alex, being my best friend, to drill me about who was on the phone but to my surprise, she doesn't. Taking a seat in front of Alex's desk I go through my emails and check text messages trying to keep myself busy and counting down the minutes until she gets here. And on cue, Ginger bounces through the door looking stunning as usual in jeans, t-shirt and Chucks with her helmet tucked under her arm.

My badass little biker. Fuck me.

My dick stirs to life, and I thank God I am sitting down in a chair. Otherwise, I wouldn't be able to hide this bugle.

She looks from me to Alex and then says, "Hi!"

Jesus, we are so caught, Alex is going to see right through us. I look down to my phone like I am ignoring them while they start rambling about something but all I can think about is bending her over and fucking her.

Hold it together big guy. Later.

I look up trying to concentrate on whatever the fuck they are talking about but failing terribly, so I just look up and smile at Ginger when she looks over at me. "You're riding with us tonight, right?" I ask.

Ginger laughs, looking back over to Alex before she replies, "Um, yeah. Don't I always ride with you?"

I don't care if Alex is listening or not. "No, you don't always ride with us. Lately, you have been running off doing stuff for your dad and meeting us places," I fire back.

Ginger folds her arms. "And? What's the big deal about riding in the car with you or meeting you there? I still end up where you're at."

Alex interrupts, pointing her finger at us. "Am I missing

something here?"

Before either of us can reply her phone rings, followed by my phone ringing.

Great something must be going on.

I look down at my cell and see a message from Beau letting us know they found two more cameras in the offices. We better find this guy soon, or we're all going to start freaking out on each other.

Alex hangs up the phone. "Do either of you know what the fuck is going on? Why am I being called to my papá's office?"

Ginger replies but I get up from my chair heading for the door, saying over my shoulder, "I don't know shit, ladies. Let's go find out."

I should have stayed in bed today.

The meeting in Luc's office didn't go any better. Ginger and Alex started to flip the fuck out over reports being made on them. They have bodyguards on them twenty-four seven what the fuck do they expect, and we've had to write reports from the beginning. Heading downstairs Maddox and I follow the girls just waiting for the tantrums to erupt into full swing, all the while trying not to laugh at how ridiculous they are being.

Ginger storms outside and once she is clear of all the video cameras that this motherfucker has placed throughout the building, she turns on me.

Great, let the biker bitch come out and play.

For the next few minutes, Ginger goes off about me writing reports to her father. I try to explain to her I have to write a report on all of them but I know she is more upset that her father is getting reports on her making me suspicious of why she is really mad. Is she worried her father is getting the reports or Shy? Trying to hold in my anger, I look up to the sky, trying to calm myself down.

"Um, are you two dating? What the fuck?" Alex asks.

Ginger and I both snap at her at the same time, "Fuck no."

The girls finish their tantrums but I can tell Ginger is not over being pissed off and once we're all in the elevator, Ginger's phone chirps alerting her of a text. She looks at it and then huffs out, "I've got some stuff to take care of today. I have my bike down in the garage, and it looks like I'll have to meet you all at the club tonight after all."

What the fuck? Hell no.

I tell Maddox and Alex that I am going to walk Ginger to her bike ignoring her outburst. Once the elevator doors shut, I turn on her pushing her up against the elevator wall pinning her.

"I don't know what the fuck has your panties in a bunch, but you need to figure it out. If you have a problem with your dad getting reports, talk to him. You know I would never put anything about us in those reports so what's really got you all worked up? Is it because Shy will know what you're doing?"

I'm tired of being tame with her, and she needs to know I won't take any shit from her.

"Fuck you B. I'm pissed because he doesn't need to be getting reports on me in Europe or here and seriously are you really bringing up Shy?" Ginger spits out.

The elevator doors open and I turn to walk out heading to her bike. Her cell phone rings and I hear yelling from behind me.

"What Shy?"

Pause.

"I said I fucking would do it so deal with him. I gotta go."

Turning around I see she's still in a mood, so I just stand there with my arms folded across my chest waiting for her to say something.

When she throws her leg over her Kawasaki Ninja 300, my dick jumps to life. Jesus, her and this bike have been my wet dream since the day she got it.

Fuck. Not now big boy. Not now.

Ginger places her helmet on top of the tank. I can tell she is thinking of what she is going to say and knowing her it will be something to try and push me away only pissing me off more. It always is after she deals with her father or Shy, but she needs to understand it doesn't work that way.

You're mine, baby!

I take a step toward her. "Look Gin, I understand you got shit going on in that head of yours, and I have given you time, but after dipping my cock into that sweet pussy of yours I am not going to let you push me away. So deal with whatever the fuck you need to, but I will be the one in your bed tonight."

Before she can open her mouth, I cover it with mine in a swift kiss, and before she can move her head like she always does, I turn to go back upstairs calling over my shoulder, "You better be at the club on time, or it will be your ass."

Fuck letting her run the show. I know what the fuck I want.

GINGER

My welcome home party was better than I thought, besides the tension between Brant and myself I loved it. When we arrived, all the members were there waiting for me like I never left. It was hard for me to maneuver around with both my legs messed up, so I was being carried around. I got pretty emotional with all the love they showed me. Alex had the best time meeting my other family. She never left my side and helped me mentally overcome my nervousness at coming home. Brant stayed in the courtyard talking to Mac and Dallas most of the time but always watching me. Shy hadn't returned yet from New York, and Mac said he had club business to attend to, but it was fine by me. Made things easier for me with him gone and not watching over me.

When it was time for them to leave, Alex hugged me crying, telling me she would call me every day. After she let go of me, Brant squatted down in front of me, placing his hands on my thighs. I'm freaking out because this will be the first time in a little over a year that I won't see either of them every day. Especially Brant, he has been a part of my every day, even before we started hanging out on our personal time. He has been protecting me for so long, that it will be hard not to miss seeing him daily.

Breathe. You got this.

Brant reaches up, cupping my face. "Baby, don't be upset. If you need me for anything, I will be right back here. It will only be a few weeks, and then you will be back with us."

I feel my father and the club move up behind me when my dad embraces Alex telling her goodbye. Brant stands up placing his hands on the sides of my chair bracing himself when he leans into me giving me a quick kiss and then I do something I never do; I try to deepen the kiss by swiping my tongue across his lips. I never really kiss him, I mean not like a long deep kiss. I think I always feel like I am betraying Shy when in reality we aren't together. I guess I feel it's so much more intimate compared to touching. I want him to know he does mean something to me, so I reach up again trying to deepen the kiss but wince in pain.

Brant moves to the side of my face. "I will be back. I will *never* give up on you, and I *will* fight for you, baby. I am sorry for being a dick, but I just got you, and I don't want to lose you," he whispers in my ear.

I turn my head to him, whispering back, "Thank you. No one else has fought for me. I will be back."

When he looks me in the eyes something passes before he smiles at me. I want to ask him what, but he moves away from me telling me he will call and they are gone. Everyone disburses leaving me and a few members and girls I don't recognize sitting around the firepit, which is in the middle of the courtyard with a bunch of tables and benches surrounding it. I haven't been able to move around, so they placed me here once I arrived, only moving me if I had to pee. I sit there and watch everyone. It still feels like home. Mac throws himself down into the chair next to me handing me a cup full of beer and then takes a drink of his own.

"So how does it feel to be back?" Mac lifts his sunglasses to the top of his head giving me his full attention.

Damn, my cousin has always been popular and good looking but I can say he has definitely filled out since I've been gone. He has wavy dark brown hair that falls around his face with a nicely trimmed beard and of course his chocolaty brown eyes that twinkle whenever he smiles. His bulging biceps stretch his white t-shirt showing off his olive skin, the girls used to go nuts over him, and I am sure they still do. I see how much he and Shy have filled out since I've been gone, making them look that much older and of course more dangerous.

After leaning down to take a big gulp, I reply, "It's not like I've been gone all my life. I did come back a few times before I went to Europe. It's not my fault y'all were on runs..."

Mac chuckles taking another swig of beer. "I'm glad you're home. We've all missed you."

Watching him lean forward putting his elbows on his thighs, he becomes serious. "Just be prepared... It's not like it used to be around here, and I am sure you can handle it, but I just don't want you running off again if things get tough."

What the fuck?

I don't say anything because I am sure he is talking about his best friend and my ex-lover. I just nod with a smile, trying to lift my beer as high as I can.

Then all of a sudden I hear Cash bellow from behind me, "Mac, go get her a straw so she can drink her beer." The crowd that I didn't know was behind me starts to laugh. "We don't want her lifting her arm too high, or her pops will have all our asses."

Mac stands up towering over me at six foot two inches the same height as Brant.

Damn, I already miss him.

The sound of Harley Davidson's pulling up to the gate pulls me from my thoughts of Brant, and of course, it's Shy. It's like he has a sixth sense when I am either involved with Brant or thinking of him. Shy will text, call or show up distracting me. For years I thought he was following me, but when I called home, he was here. I never could figure it out, but I guess it was my subconscious wanting to believe he would come for me but that never happened.

When I see him pull in, my heart speeds up and my body ignites, fuck I haven't seen him ride in years and right now with five guys flanking him he looks so fucking delicious. My chest starts to hurt, and I take deep breaths, but my ribs scream at me. My panties instantly moisten and I think my clit just grew a heartbeat with how hard it's throbbing.

Shit, and him in leathers, sweet baby Jesus. He only had his cut on in the hospital, but good Lord, him in full leathers has me shifting in my seat. I still can't believe how much bigger he is than before. His cut hangs perfectly on him. He maneuvers his bike like it's nothing, showing off tanned arms and muscular forearms.

He parks in front, and when he takes his helmet off, I can see he is wearing the bandana that I gave him for his twentieth birthday. His golden brown hair hangs out the back curling up over the bandana from the wind. He doesn't take his sunglasses off, when he looks around, I know he is looking for me, and when he finds me, he smirks. I feel the wetness in my crotch pooling up between my legs.

Sonovabitch. Little fucker is playing dirty.

I hear Cash and Bear behind me talking, but I ignore their bullshit talk about soulmates. This whole club couldn't believe we broke up and when I left everyone was betting I would be back within a month. Yeah, that didn't go too well for some. I knew they didn't like Brant but Shy let me go, he dumped me and never came to get me. Staking claim on me now is a little too late in my book.

Watching him stalk over to me I try to drink more of my beer but damn them, they were right with my shoulders taped, and without a straw, I can't lift my glass up high enough to finish my beer. Which I probably shouldn't even be drinking with all the medication I'm on. I guess Mac knew I was going to need some liquid courage to stay strong.

He's almost to me when this redheaded woman that I don't know strolls up to him, touching him on his shoulder trying to tell him something but when he looks over to her, he says something that makes her back away.

That's right bitch, back away.

When he walks away, the whore turns looking straight at me, not him walking away but instead, she just glares at me. So I do what comes natural, I just smile at her, lifting my good hand and wave. I don't know where this possessiveness comes from, but I'm sure it's just automatic. I try to tell myself he isn't mine, but I still find myself clenching my fist even with one of them in a cast.

Mac hands me a full beer with a straw, so before Shy is standing in front of me, I try to suck as much beer through the straw as I can.

Shy takes my drink. "What the fuck? You're on a shit ton of medication."

The guys all yell out at the same time to give me back my beer but when he doesn't, Bear growls, "Give her back that drink. It's her welcome home party. She can drink-" but he is cut off when he hears my dad yell, "The fuck she can. Take that fucking drink from her. What the fuck is wrong with y'all. She can't walk without help, arm in a cast with both shoulders wrapped. Who the fuck is going to take care of her if she falls or throws up."

Everyone including Shy all says at the same time, "I will."

It makes everyone laugh but me. I just lean forward and snatch the beer out of Shy's hand. When Shy turns to face me, I laugh and tell him to fuck off, only getting more laughs from the peanut gallery behind me. Shy clenches his jaw but I can tell he's holding his tongue.

Take that bitch!

Shy moves to sit across from me in the only open chair and when they light the fire more people flock to the surrounding benches. When "Dreams" by Fleetwood Mac starts to play over the courtyard, I smile remembering this song. It was the very first song that I learned to remix. I look around seeing so many new faces, but the ones that aren't new are family, making me warm inside seeing them smile and have fun. My heart aches feeling the love and closeness of everyone that I've missed, but won't let myself think about. Always pushing it to the back of my mind telling myself I'm following my dream.

Just like the song.

Cash and Bear are still behind me, but I haven't been able to turn around, I only hear them talking shit as usual with my dad stopping in here and there to put his two cents in only to take off again. I'm sure he's hanging out inside the club where more people are. Everyone keeps checking on me and it's mostly small talk, but my focus is on the little fucker across from me.

Don't let him get to you – but fuck he is fine.

Mac sat next to me most of the night only getting up to refill our glasses. I was on my fourth beer, and I could totally feel it making me tipsy. When my phone chirps I pull it out of my pocket to see I have two texts.

ALEX
Miss you already. I hope you are doing okay, just know I am here for you if you need to vent or need an alibi. j/k well not really. Love you girl. I'll call tomorrow, and let you know what our travel plans are.

GINGER
I miss you both so much already. I might need that alibi, but I will keep you posted. I will be here doing nothing but watching people so call when you can.

I scroll down to the next text, and it's from Brant.

> **BRANT**
> Almost home baby. My bed is going to be empty and smell like you. Fuck, I miss you. Hope you are doing okay.
> **GINGER**
> Sorry, guess you will have to take care of it yourself until I am back. =)
> **BRANT**
> I am sure we will figure something out. Nite babe. Chat tomorrow.

I must have a huge grin on my face because when I look up, I see murderous eyes staring straight at me and my phone chirps again. Thinking it's Brant, I hurry to open it only to find it's Shy.

> **SHY**
> Having a nice chat? I'm back. "Like A Wrecking Ball"- Eric Church

I think about the song, knowing it's about a guy coming home and fucking his girl or I should say taking back what is his, so I reply quoting from the song but add my twist on it of course, like I always do when he texts me.

> **GINGER**
> The whole damn place will fall but WITHOUT ME. Yes, It was a nice chat.
> **SHY**
> Soon Angel, soon you will know all.

Fuck him and all his songs with all these secret meanings.

Getting pissed off, I look up to meet his eyes across the fire and yell, "What does that even fucking mean? You keep saying that shit to me, but I've been waiting years and nothing. I don't know shit."

Shy is up out of his chair, but Mac stands up blocking him from me. "Not today, bro, not today. It's her first day."

Pissed off at both men and wanting to fight. I go to stand up, but it's too fast, feeling the alcohol rushing to my pounding head. I feel off balance until two strong arms grab me by the waist, and when I go to protest, I see it's Cash and my uncle Bear flanking me. Feeling more confident I'm determined to find out what the fuck Shy means.

"What the fuck, Mac? What is everyone talking about? Not today, like I should know what the fuck y'all are talking about."

Mac who is facing Shy says, "Not today, cousin. This will be discussed another day."

What the fuck. I am so sick of all this secret shit.

Feeling my temper rise, I'm ready to throw a major tantrum if I have to. "Discuss what? I am so fucking confused by all of you like I should know something! Just fucking tell me!" I'm yelling which makes everyone stop talking and watch this cluster fuck unfold.

Shy is clenching his fists together looking like he wants to murder my cousin. My aunt's voice rings out over everyone. "Snow, it's time to head in. You need to take your meds, and I have all your stuff set up." My auntie comes from behind me to stand in front of me blocking both the guys.

Seriously!

"I'm not some kid you all can make go to bed before shit gets real," I grit out.

"That's enough!" comes a boom from my father somewhere behind me.

"Fine. Whatever," I gruff.

Standing there glaring at my auntie, I don't want to be the

first one to move, but I am swooped up by my dad like I weigh nothing.

"Daddy!"

"I said that's enough, Snow."

And just like that, I'm back to being treated like a kid again with him carrying me across the grass courtyard. I look over his shoulder noticing everyone going back to their own thing but one person…Shy. It is always Shy watching me.

Just like I never left. I'm still that little girl. I turn away and start to cry.

GINGER

The few days go by and I don't leave my room, well not my old childhood room, but one of the spare rooms. It's the room that has a bed like a hospital. It's a Sleep Number bed, so it was easier for me to sit up and maneuver around.

I'm glad that I'm not in my old room, it has too many memories of the past. With everyone gone and not flipping out over me I finally let go, exhaustion takes over, and I sleep. If I'm not sleeping, I'm on my laptop listening to music or downloading new music for when I go on tour. As usual, I lose myself in music so I can process what is going on in my life. I am only bothered when I need food and medication, but it is usually my auntie who comes up. I see my dad once or twice but never Shy or anyone else.

Knowing my dad, he is keeping everyone away from me since I lost it crying that first night when he carried me into the house. I cried myself to sleep in his arms, and like always he held me, letting me know everything will be okay.

Sleep consumed me, and I have ignored all texts from everyone the last two days, but today when I am eating cereal that my auntie just brought me, I glance over and notice my phone light up, receiving either a text or email.

I pick up my phone and see that I have twenty texts and five missed calls.

"Sonovabitch."

Pulling up my text messages I see half of them are from Shy and the other half are from Brant, Alex, and Izzy.

Ignoring everyone else I pull up Izzy's text since I haven't heard from her since waking up in the hospital. I know she went to California to see her family but from what Alex was saying she thinks her and her boyfriend Dominic had a huge fight.

IZZY
Hey girl, sorry I've been MIA. Once I knew you would be okay, I had to take off to see my family before the tour. Lots of shit went down after you got shot. I've missed you so much and was hoping to stop in to see you on my way back to New York. I left a message too, so call me when you can.

I look at my missed calls and see that she is one of them and I call my voicemail to hear her message. The first one is Shy, and I hit save before he even can finish his first word. As well as the next two messages.

On the fourth message, I hear Izzy's voice. "Gin girl, I hope you are doing better. I need to see you and soon. Call me, please."

I hang up right after and call her. She doesn't sound like the same perky Izzy, and I hope that she's okay.

The phone rings a couple times before she answers, sounding like she was sleeping. "H-Hello?"

"Izzy, it's Gin. I just got your text and voicemail. How are you?" I say whispering.

Izzy replies, her voice more alert. "Gin, Jesus girl what time is it? Why are you whispering?"

Shit, I didn't think about the time difference. I look at the clock and see it is eleven in the morning here so it must be like eight in the morning in California.

"Shit, I totally forgot the time difference. Do you want to call me back?"

Feeling bad I totally just woke her up. I wonder if she had a gig last night.

Izzy laughs. "Naw, girl. You're fine. Whatcha doin'? How are you? Alex says you are healing really well."

I laugh at my hyper friend, feeling better hearing her talk like her old self again.

"I'm fine. Just got a bunch of bullet holes and a broken arm."

I try to make a joke of it, but Izzy doesn't laugh.

"Jesus, Gin. I can't believe that happened to you and thank God you saw them take her but it sucks you got shot."

"Yeah, I was in the right spot at the right time I guess, but enough about me. When are you coming to see me? How are you?"

She huffs. "I'm bored as fuck! I am headed back to New York soon so I will swing by your place so I can see you before heading out. Alex told me you would be joining us soon, but I still need to see you."

I miss my girls.

"Yes, come visit me. I am going nuts here too, and I have only been here what, three days? Two of them I haven't even left my room. I'm still in bad shape, but I should be moving around by the time you get here," I reply with excitement.

Making a mental note, I need to get my ass up today and start mending so I can get the hell out of here. Being around Shy brings back way too many memories and feelings.

Thinking of Shy and ex's, I ask Izzy about Dominic but her only reply is, "Fuck him. Long story that will need lots of alcohol. So we will have that convo when I get there."

After saying our goodbyes, I text her my address telling her to let me know her plan when she finalizes it.

With the excitement of knowing Izzy is coming, I try to get

out of bed. I push the button to move my bed into position for me to get up. I lift the back of the bed all the way up and lower my legs so it is easier to slide off the bed. Yesterday we took off the Ace bandage and sling on my shoulders so I could sleep better and I could move them around letting me eat and drink without help. I still have the cast on my left arm and bandages over my gunshot wounds, along with the broken ribs which I think are the worst. My legs are both messed up, but my left leg with the walking boot is pretty bad since I can't put any weight on it. I try to stand up, but pain shoots through my left foot making me fall back onto the bed.

"Goddamnit!" *I can fucking do this.*

On my third attempt, I get myself up holding onto the head part of the mattress on my bed putting all my weight on my right foot.

I am a fucking mess!

Out of breath, I try to put weight on my left foot and hold onto the crutch with my left hand, which is in a cast but when the pain shoots through my foot I try to use my hand to brace myself steady on the crutch only to feel pain shoot through my arm and leg again, losing my balance I fall forward on the floor crying out in pain.

Shit. Fuck. Goddamn. Motherfucker.

I hear the sound of loud pounding boots coming up the stairs. I know my dad is coming to rescue me as always. "Daddy, help me," I cry out.

Lying in the fetal position in pain, I hold my ribs and arm crying, waiting for him to come help me. When I notice black steel toed boots come into view, I try to roll and look up, but when I do, I come face to face with Shy.

"Jesus Christ, Snow. What the fuck." Shy reaches down and in one motion picks me up off the floor, cradling me to his chest.

No. No. Not Shy. Oh, God.

"Angel, what were you thinking?"

I can't even get the words out, so I reach for my side because I'm in so much pain. I manage to squeak out, "I gotta pee" letting him know I have to use the bathroom.

"Why didn't you use your wheelchair?"

I'm a dumb ass.

Placing me on the bathroom counter, he starts to look me over. "Where does it hurt? Did you open any wounds?"

I don't say anything but instead just stare at him, watching him worry over me. His facial features are so much more masculine showing he isn't a kid anymore.

He let me go. God help me.

He must have just showered, his wet long shaggy hair falling around his face with curls that bend around his neck and ears. I want to run my hands through the loose strands falling into his eyes. His stormy brown eyes lock with mine. My heart stops, and I stop breathing.

Why me. "Fuck!"

The fullness of my bladder makes me squirm, and I tear my eyes from him. Taking a few short breaths trying to fight the pain in my ribs while I catch my breath. I look down and see that he is standing between my legs and so many memories flood my mind of us, here in this same spot so many years ago. I start to cry again. I can't hold it together and keep this fucking wall up.

Shy lifts his hands up to my face pushing my hair back away from my face before making me look at him again.

"Angel, talk to me. How can I make it better."

Tell me why! Why now? Fuck it hurts.

When I don't say anything and just cry, he pulls me into his enormous chest hugging me. God, he feels so good. His arms engulf me, and he expands his large hands out over my back gripping me tighter. He has always made me feel safe, but now he tries to cocoon my body with his big body, trying to take away all my worries, holding me tight. If only he knew he was my problem. After what seems like forever, I feel my bladder screaming for release. I pull my hands from around his waist pushing him back. "I have to pee. Can you put me down and get my wheelchair?"

Shy just looks at me but doesn't say anything. I look away from his milk chocolate eyes hoping he just lets me go. He takes a closer step in between my legs, and I intake more air holding my breath. Shy smiles before he reaches around me grabbing the globes of my ass lifting me up against his body.

Tell him to let you go. I don't say anything.

My hands are on his chest and I try to push him away, but I can't with my injuries.

Don't grab him. Don't feel him up. Oh, but I do with my good hand, and he is rock solid, making me bite my lip to keep a moan from escaping.

Snap out of it, Gin!

I am stuck in the memory of him holding me, but when my legs slide down his body while he turns us placing me in front of the toilet, I snap out of it.

I clear my throat that is dry from holding my breath. He lowers himself down my body sliding his hands down from my ass along my legs only to go back up to my waist grabbing my pajama shorts. I look down and stop him before he pulls them down.

"Shy. I can do this part," I say, placing my hands on his shoulders.

Shy looks up sliding his hands up and down my legs, igniting goosebumps across my body and causing my clit to throb. His hands stop over my bandage where I was shot. I close my eyes, trying to take a deep breath but I feel my ribs scream at me for doing it. I need to get my body under control. I open my eyes to say something, but he stands up and turns away shutting the door behind him.

Goddamnit! I'm so fucked.

I sit on the toilet and try to get myself together. I can't let him get to me. I can't let him hurt me anymore, and I need to stand up to him. I need to move on and get over what we used to have.

After taking care of business and having a good pep talk with myself, I stand up but don't try to walk, only pull my shorts up. Once I flush the toilet the door flies open and in stalks Shy. I put my hand up stopping him. "Shy, get my wheelchair."

He stops in front of me close enough my hand is now touching his abs. Again. His very large, very muscular chest just inches away, but I can't get my arm to move any further up from where I am standing.

God, help me.

"Please," I beg.

Shy still doesn't move, and when I look up at him towering over me, I want to cry but hold my ground. My body remembers his touch, his smell, and wants him but my mind is fighting.

Shy leans toward me placing his hands on my waist. "Angel, I think we need to talk."

When I try to say something, one of his hands shoots up pushing a finger to my lips, shutting me up.

"Shhh, Angel, like I said you are very much like your father and very stubborn. You have been all these years, and I've let you, but things are going to change, and you're going to listen to me."

When I feel my courage return, added with the rage that is boiling back up, I push him away. "You're right. I am like my father. If it has to do with us, I don't think there is really anything that needs to be said."

"Jesus Christ, Snow!" Shy roars, looking up to the ceiling to gain patience as I just stand there, watching his muscles flex and try with everything in my body to not give into him. I have never been able to say no to him. That is why I left. The power he has over me is undeniable and furious.

"Shy, please get my wheelchair or put me in bed but I can't stand here all day." I try to cross my arms but with a cast it is hard, so I just put one hand on my hip and try to look irritated instead of turned on.

I need to get the fuck away from him.

Once Shy calms down, he turns his stare to me from the ceiling with a smile. "I will put you in your bed if you would just listen to me for one second and really listen," he pauses, but I don't say anything because I'm fighting the internal battle going on in my head. Shy pleads with me, saying one word. "Please." My shoulders slump in defeat knowing I will give in to him.

Blowing out air frustrated with myself, I look into his gorgeous eyes, and I nod my head in agreement.

Shy's whole face lights up giving me his full smile making my knees go weak and my nipples hard.

Fucking great.

Shy looks automatically to my chest, which is only covered by a small tank top, so my nipples are on full display, but he smiles stepping into me. I automatically put my hands up between us, but Shy grabs my ass again lifting me up onto the counter again.

"Shy, what the fuck."

"Easy, Angel. I am just helping you out. While I talk, you can brush your teeth and comb your hair. See I am compromising with you. That way you have something in your mouth while I talk and you won't interrupt me."

I do need to brush my teeth. Goddamn him and his sweetness. Fight it, Gin. Fight him off.

When I don't say anything but instead grab my toothbrush with my good hand, I start to brush my teeth.

"Snow, there is so much to tell you, but I can't tell you everything. I think it would be best if your father tells you the majority of the story since he is the one who's orchestrating it."

My eyes shoot up when he says, 'my dad.' What the fuck is he talking about? I lean to the side and spit. Shy turns the water on giving me a glass of water before continuing.

"I just need you to know that I have always loved you and I

didn't let you go."

Again, rage fills me. I start to see black, which is never good. I pull my toothbrush out of my mouth again and spit before turning to face him. "I remember that day and the days that followed it like it was yesterday. I know for a fact that you told me numerous times we should break up, that you were letting me go and I should forget about you and move to New York."

He didn't want me anymore.

"Angel, again you need to believe me and trust me when I say that I have *never* loved anyone else but you, and I have never wanted anyone but you. I love you. I have told you every day since then that I love you. That I've wanted you and needed you."

My temper is almost at breaking point. "Texting me songs and lyrics *is not* telling me that you wanted me back. *Being* with me and *loving* me in person is what you should have done."

Shy places his hands on my thighs. "Angel, I did everything in my power, that I was allowed to do, to let you know, I never left you or stopped loving you. You gave up on me so easily. You let me go too."

Is he fucking crazy? I never gave up on him.

I am beyond the point of pissed, so I cry out in frustration before I speak. "Shy, get the fuck out. You have had more than three fucking years to have me. Get. The. Fuck. Out." My face is red, and my wall is up so fucking high I want to punch him.

I never gave up on him.

Shy clenches his fists. "Goddamn it, Ginger. I have never stopped loving you, and I have never let you go. You just don't see it. Open your eyes. I have told you *every fucking day* that I love you and miss you. Yes, through text but I never stopped telling you. FUCK!"

When I hear footsteps coming up the stairs I yell, "Please make Shy leave. PLEASE." I don't even care who the fuck it is but whoever it is, needs to get Shy the fuck away from me.

Seeing I'm done listening, he only gets more pissed off.

"Ginger, so help me, God. You need to get this through your head. I. Did. Not. Give. You. Up."

At that, he turns and walks right into my dad who puts a hand up stopping him, but Shy is the one who snaps. "You have until the end of the week to tell her everything. I'm not fucking around and losing her again. I swear to God I will blow this whole fucking thing to keep her."

When I see my father give him a nod releasing him to go, I grit my teeth and narrow my eyes on my father.

"What the fuck is going on? What is everyone talking about."

"Watch your language!" he barks back entering the bathroom all the way.

"I am not some little girl anymore, Daddy."

"I don't give a fuck, you are *my little girl,* and I don't want you cursing like a goddamn sailor."

"Well, then you shouldn't have raised me to be a biker brat."

Running his hands over his face, up through his hair, he tries to calm down. But I'm so worked up I can't relax.

"Princess, let me help you to your wheelchair, and I will send Storm up here to help you get dressed. Then we are going to have you come downstairs and get you outside today. You need to start the therapy exercises on your shoulders," he says after taking a deep breath.

Fuck this. He is avoiding the questions.

I don't give up. "What is he talking about? What does everyone mean when they say I will know in good time? I'm going to fucking explode. You need to tell me what the fuck is going on."

My father groans, more than likely from me cussing but when he swooped me up, I cry out, "Daddy. Stop."

Putting me in my chair, he leans down in front of me looking me straight in the face. "Ginger, a lot of shit has happened these past few years. I've had to make some hard decisions, and I've had to do some things to ensure your future. I know you will be mad at me and will probably still be mad at Shy, but we did all this for you. Now, get dressed and come outside, you need to get out of this room. Okay?"

Oh, God.

My dad is using my full name, I knew he was serious, and it must be something big if he is this leery of telling me. I just nod my head letting him leave me to my thoughts.

GINGER

When I came downstairs to have this chat with my father, I find out him, and the guys had taken off. It has been over two weeks and still no guys. Shy has been texting me every day like he always does but with only a song or that he loves me. My father won't even reply to me, but Shy just told me today that they're busy with club stuff and they would be home soon.

I've reunited with some of the girls that used to hang around and meeting the new ones. Gigi's the new girl that's here everyday bartending and helps Sissy with cleaning and stuff. Seeing all these ladies and catching up has me feeling torn. I have missed so much not being around, but then again I miss being back in New York.

Izzy is coming in a few days, I've been doing my therapy with Bear every day, and I'm walking around without crutches. My headaches are getting less painful and fewer every day. My incisions are healing well, but my ribs still hurt if I move too fast. I am just happy I'm moving around by myself now. Without the guys here it is boring but Bear and Hawk, who I found out were left behind to watch over things at Felicia's, are here trying to entertain me. Hawk's ol' lady Felicia owns a strip bar, so the guys took me to the club the other day while they were closed to see the girls.

I got on the decks and mixed for the first time even with my hand in the cast. It wasn't awful but it sure as shit wasn't good. It was hard, but nothing was going to stop me from getting in that booth. It just felt so fucking good. I have been trying to mix with my old equipment in my room, but it isn't the same as being in the booth, something about the club and the atmosphere gives you such a high. Even if the crowd was only prospects and the girls, it was better than nothing.

Each day I learn something new or notice things that have changed. The Wolfeman became partners with Felicia, and they remodeled the club. It looks really good, and they are bumping with business, making the girls and guys busy. No wonder they wanted new music for the girls, and for the last few days, I have been working on a couple of songs for them.

I still feel like they are keeping a lot from me but how can I be mad when I was the one who left and didn't come back. It still hurts though to know you talk to these people weekly and they don't tell you what is going on around them.

Why would they tell me when I never ask.

I have been going back and forth between being upset and mad, but the end result is I am the one who pulled away and haven't been there for them.

Bear and I are sitting at the bar watching TV when the door to the club swings open and the woman who came up to Shy that first day walks in. And she doesn't look happy. Bear turns on his stool. "What are you doing here, Rave?"

Her long red hair flows wildly around her face when she comes to a halt next to us.

"Where are they?"

I watch Bear crosses his arms over his chest. "Not here. So you can go."

This Rave chick crosses her arms mimicking Bear. "If she is here why are they still gone? Neither of them has gotten back to me."

"Are you talking about me?" I fire back.

"Rave, you need to leave," Bear groans, giving me the impression he doesn't care for this lady.

Rave obviously doesn't care because she squares on me. "Yes, you. The princess-"

Bear cuts her off standing up. "Raven, I suggest you shut the fuck up and leave now before you are banned for life."

I stand up feeling my bitch radar click on and stand my ground. "Yes, I am Snow. If you want to call me princess too, by all means, go ahead."

When I feel someone come up behind me, I freak for a minute but realize it's Gigi coming from around the bar. Thanking the gods because I was taught never to take your eyes off your enemy and right now I can totally feel this chick doesn't like me. For what reason, I have no idea, but I think it has to do with Shy.

"Bitch, what the fuck are you doing here?" I jump when I hear my auntie Storm yell something fierce.

Rave turns to face my auntie. "Why the fuck are they still gone when she" -she points to me- "is here?"

Fuck this! I'm so sick of this shit. What the fuck is she talking about?

"Raven, you best get your ass out of here before I beat the shit out of you again. You know you are not supposed to be here. They all made that clear to you a few months ago."

This girl is the one that started the fight with my auntie. I get more defensive toward the girl, "What the fuck does them being gone have to do with me?"

Bear steps closer to us, giving Raven a look but I counter him. "Don't look at him. I want to know right fucking now what you're talking about."

Rave, whatever the fuck they call her, looks me straight in the eye and grits out, "Bitch, they've been going and watching you for years. Maybe if you pulled your spoiled little head out of your ass, you would know." And with that, she turns around and stomps off not even turning around when I yell at her, "What the fuck did you just say?"

I know something's up and I'm fucking sick and tired of everyone trying to keep it from me.

Once she is gone, I turn on my family, hot as all hell and will stop at nothing to get answers.

My auntie, Uncle Bear and Gigi just stand there looking at me like the secret has just been let out, but I still don't understand.

"One of you better tell me who the fuck that was? Why she is banned from here and what the ever loving fuck she's talking about?"

Bear sits down on his stool, grabbing his beer and draining it. Gigi goes back behind the bar grabbing drinks, and my auntie Storm stands in front of me just staring.

Sonovabitch.

"And I swear to God if any of you give me the line it's my father's story or some other line of bullshit I will walk out of here and never come back. Something is going on, and I want to know what the fuck it is, and now."

Bear speaks first. "Both of you sit down, Gigi grab the girls a beer and give me the Jack. It's going to be a long fucking day." Leaning on the bar, he rubs his face like he is waking up from a bad dream.

Fuck, it's that bad. Be strong. I am a Wolfeman.

SHY

Walking into the Scorpion's clubhouse, I hear "Sail" by Awolnation soar through the club, and I think of Snow. She always makes me think through music, dissecting it. This song reminds me of going mad, letting go and ending things. Well, today things end for sure but hopefully not for me.

Wolfe is beside me with Mac and Cash flanking us showing no fear. My brothers for life, I was blessed the day they were all put in my life. I don't think people know the power you feel when you have so many people behind you. Walking into the Scorpions, I feel like a motherfucking king with my boys beside me.

The Wolfeman have known the Scorpions for a long time and have always had an alliance with them. Wolfe has been friends a long time with Striker the President and has respected him but he is dying of cancer with no kid to hand the gavel down too, and the VP has become so corrupt that he has lost control of his club. For years the Wolfeman have been watching over the Scorpions and using them in certain dealings, but with the division of the club, things have only gone downhill.

Over the last few years they have tried to deal with their issues within the club, but it started to conflict with our own business. We warned them if they didn't deal with the issues we would strip them of their colors and end the Scorpions. They're a small one chapter club with roughly twenty men while we have ten chapters, a couple of them bordering New York.

We've always let them be due to the alliance Wolfe had with Striker, but when we got wind that Crow, Scorpions VP, was double crossing them and dealing behind their back, we decided to step in.

Striker coming to Wolfe all those years ago only saves him and the ones that were loyal. I have been infiltrating their club and dissecting who is loyal and who isn't. Crow and his son Snake have joined forces with the Devil Duos MC to overrun the Scorpions and take over their territory. Now with Striker's cancer being terminal and the fight within the club, our decision has been made, and we are here to take over.

Wolfe had a sit down with our other chapters, taking a mass vote on what to do with them a while back and came up with a plan and ever since they started running their illegal dealings throughout our territory we have been implementing that plan. Wolfe then had a sit down with Striker and made more plans for him to infiltrate them within his own club, to see who was loyal and who needed to be cast out. They have a division in the club, less than half want to keep dealing in illegal activities, and the other half want nothing to do with it. The last few years we have planned and picked this club apart.

Tonight, it all ends.

We have a meeting set up with Striker and it won't be pretty, but hopefully, not too many will get killed. I only know of one who will die tonight. Walking into the clubhouse with half a dozen Wolfeman and another dozen outside would scare any normal person, but some of these Scorpions are pretty damn scary themselves. They're down to a handful of them left.

Striker stands up greeting all of us, but we can see and feel they all don't welcome us as their president does. Striker reaches out grabbing Wolfe's hand. "Wolfe, so good to see you, my friend. Sorry to hear about your daughter. How is she?"

I tense when they mention Snow. Knowing it was all over the news and that they would know but still, it makes me uneasy them acknowledging it.

Worm their Secretary and Tiny their Sergeant at Arms get up to greet Wolfe, but when I glance over at Crow, their VP, he doesn't move to greet any of us. I notice he looks bored but his son behind him, Snake, looks all amped up on something. Scanning the rest of the room, I notice that the room is divided, so I turn toward the problem facing off with Snake giving him a nod with a smart ass smirk.

"Thanks, she is doing good and healing back at our clubhouse," Wolfe says.

Crow stands up taking a step forward and making his presence known. "Glad she is doing better, but I would like to know what was so urgent to need this meeting. Are you here to tell me what happened to Timbo?"

Timbo, being the guy we took down this week when we caught him raping a girl at one of the bars nearby that we frequently visit when in town - which is all the time nowadays.

"No, we're here on other business, but for your information, we don't know what happened to Timbo after he raped that girl. I guess he must've gone nomad thinking we were after him. Who the fuck knows, but if I do see him, I will let you know," Wolfe fires back in a modulated voice.

Snake bounces from foot to foot. "Fuck that. This motherfucker right here took him." Pointing at me as I just smile.

Striker hits the gavel making everyone quiet. "Timbo was a piece of shit and one of your minions, not a Scorpion. He's no loss to me. Let's start this fucking meeting and get it over with. Now I have asked the Wolfeman here because it has been a long time coming and I'm fucking tired of dealing with all this bullshit."

Crow turns toward his own president and old friend. "Are you finally fucking handing the gavel down to Snake?" Looking surprised and excited at the same time.

My smile gets even bigger. *Nope, motherfucker. Try again.*

I can already tell how this is going to end. We have planned it all along, but it's still hard to know the outcome. All our guys are armed and ready. They know who is with us and who isn't, but I pray it doesn't come to us losing a brother.

"Crow, there will be a vote tonight. I doubt you will like it but since we have had a division in the club for a while now, and after hearing the news that some of you have joined forces with the Devil Duos, I have asked the Wolfeman here to make sure this vote is overseen and goes as it should. Tonight, we vote on ending the Scorpions and patching over as Wolfeman."

Crow roars, "You stupid fucking pussy. I should have killed-"

I fire my gun, and Crow falls to the ground. Snake cries out pulling his gun on me, but when he sees all the guns pointed back at him, he stops. He has four guys behind him with guns drawn as well. All of us to four of them is a big difference. Everyone's guns are drawn but Striker, who turns his attention to Snake. "Today you become a nomad. If we see you around here - any of you," he points to the four men standing behind Snake, "wearing your colors you will be killed. Scorpions are now Wolfeman. Everyone in agreement, say aye." The group all yells aye except the five men that have guns drawn on them.

"Fuck you, Striker. This isn't over, but you're right Scorpions are over. Let me take my pops out of here, and we will be gone," Snake grunts out.

Striker steps forward. "For respect that I once held for your father, you may leave here with your life and his body. You have six hours, you can use our van to remove his body, and two of your boys can come back to get his bike and theirs. Six hours but if *you* ever return here again you will be killed."

None of us move but instead watch the two men move to pick up Crow's dead body and follow Snake out of the clubhouse. Once they're out the door, everyone puts their guns down. Wolfe motions for a few guys to follow them to make sure they are gone.

After Striker nods his gratitude to us, he turns to the six remaining Scorpions standing. "As we all have discussed and you know, I will be stepping down as your president. I only have a few more months, and I want to live my life stress-free and not looking over my shoulder every second. Each of you has been voted in as a Wolfeman. The six men we knew were cancerous to our club left, one being dead. So, if any of you want out, this is your chance to go without any repercussion, but you will be stripped of your cut. Tonight we will all become Wolfeman. Whoever we pick tonight as the president it will be for the Wolfeman, New York Chapter."

I know each and everyone one of these men. I have been researching and making sure they're all worthy of the Wolfeman patch. I knew no one would leave and when all we hear is whistles and cheers, he continues.

"I know these past few years have been hard but just know it all changes now. Wolfe it's your floor," Striker's voice comes out even more strained.

Striker sits down with a coughing spell, holding his chest. Wolfe turns to all the men. "Most of you know me and know what I represent, what my club represents. Loyalty and respect are the most important. In a few minutes, we're going to vote Shy Jenkins in as your new president. If you don't think you can pledge your loyalty to him as your president as a Wolfeman, you should leave now."

No one moves or makes a sound, so Wolfe keeps speaking, "Well then I nominate Shy as your president, if you agree, say aye."

The whole place erupts in ayes.

"Anyone disagrees, say nay," Wolfe yells.

No one speaks.

Wolfe turns to Mac, "I nominate my nephew Mac as your VP if you agree- say aye."

Again, the room filled with ayes.

"Anyone disagrees- say nay," Wolfe bellows out.

Silence.

When I turn around, I notice all the Wolfeman that were outside from the other chapters have joined us and are now filling the room.

Wolfe turns to Worm and Tiny standing next to Striker. "I nominate to patch over and keep Worm as Secretary and Tiny as Sergeant at Arms, if you agree, say aye."

The room explodes with all the Wolfeman responding. These two men have been the backbone of the Scorpions club, keeping it from being taken over by the Devil Duos. Everyone is getting riled up with the excitement of the new chapter leaders. Striker hits the gavel drawing everyone's attention back to Wolfe.

Wolfe who is laughing at the excitement. "Anyone disagrees,

say nay."

When no one speaks he continues, "Without this next guy I don't see how you will be able to last." Wolfe becomes serious turning to Dallas. "Brother, you will be missed, but I nominate Dallas as Treasurer."

But before Wolfe can finish his sentence the whole place explodes with ayes.

"Any nays motherfuckers?" Wolfe smiles and yells.

Wolfe turns to me smiling ear to ear, and then he looks to my side. "My last but definitely not least, I nominate Quick as your Road Captain."

Again everyone says aye with no nays. When Striker walks up to me, he hands me the gavel. "Congratulations Ride or die, brother."

Fucking finally!

When I slam the gavel down for the first time the room amplifies with the noise of whistles and shouts of approval. The brothers move around congratulating and giving respect to all the members. I make my way over to Quick and when he sees me, he gives me a full embrace. I sponsored this little fucker two years ago, patched him in last year, and he's done nothing but been by my side and loyal to a fault.

"Congrats my brother!" I say to him while we hug.

"Thank you. I owe you my life brother, and I will never forget it," Quick replies while pulling away.

"Damn are you two going to fucking kiss now or what?" Mac laughs next to us before slapping both of us on our backs.

In sync, we both spit out, "Fuck off."

"I think he's jealous," Dallas says before shaking my hand and pulling me into a man hug congratulating me again before doing the same to Quick.

"Well fuckers, it's the four amigos, and we did it!" I say to the men that have been my closest brothers and family. We finally did it, and now I needed to focus on my girl.

"Fuck ya. Now I need to get some pussy, it's nut up time, bitches," Mac says headed toward the door. We all laugh saying in unison behind him, "nut up" before we go to follow him, but Wolfe's voice calling my name stops me in my tracks. All the other members head out toward the bar.

Turning to Wolfe, I see the huge smile on his face and return the smile. I extend my hand and say, "Thank you, Prez! I hope I don't let you down. Now it's time I get my girl."

He laughs. "Kid, you haven't let me down so far, and I don't see it happening anytime soon. As for my daughter, let's just hope she will forgive us both for keeping this from her. I'm proud of you, son."

My insides tighten when I hear him call me son. I have always looked up to him as a father figure, and I have tried so hard to make him proud so to hear him call me son, there are no words.

GINGER

I'm so overwhelmed with all the information they just told me, I couldn't think straight. I'm so hurt and mad at both my father and Shy. All these years they just let me think Shy didn't care when it was my father who orchestrated this whole thing. Making Shy push me away thinking he didn't want me, only for him to have to watch me from afar. And everyone knew they were there watching me, but no one told me, not Alex and sure as fuck, not Brant.

Everyone lied to me.

I keep going back and forth between being enraged and questioning who I needed to hate. I went into shock when my uncle Bear told me. Not reacting but instead taking it all in, trying to understand why my father would do this to me. When my uncle was done explaining what was going on, I just stood up and wobbled to my father's house and have been there ever since.

Going over and over what he said trying to put the pieces together.

"Snow, what I'm about to tell you, please take in and try to process it. You need to understand your father did this for you and your future. Please let me just get all this out, and if you

have questions I will try to answer them, but I won't go into details, that you will need to get from them. I will not fight with you, and I will not let you disrespect your father or Shy in front of me. If you want to know what is going on, you need to sit here and listen to all of it and really listen to me. Can you do that?"

I give him a nod.

"Okay, your father's friend Striker came to him a few years back needing our help with his club. He found out he had cancer and his club was divided. We've been helping him clean up his club ever since. His club is in New York.

"When your father saw you and Shy together, it reminded him of how he was with your momma. You two have this connection that we all see. He wanted more for you though. You have so much talent, and he wanted you to go after your dreams and live a little before you settled down as an ol' lady. You were only eighteen years old. He knew you would never leave Shy and we knew Shy would never leave the club or you. We didn't want you to settle.

"When we were in NY on one of our runs helping out Striker, your father met with Beau Bagwell, knowing he worked for Luc Mancini. He gave him a few of your mixed tapes. We've helped Beau over the years with sticky situations. We have a good relationship with them. Your father believed it would be a perfect place for you. Also, the Scorpions clubhouse is located in New York so we could keep eyes on you but from a distance, so you could have the freedom to do what you wanted.

"Your father approached Shy a few days before he pulled you and him in for that meeting that set everything off. Your father told Shy if he loved you he needed to let you go. He promised him a club of his own and you if he let you go to follow your dreams in music and live a little before he made you his ol' lady. Shy loved you and didn't want you to settle so he agreed, but over the years he and your father have battled. Shy wanted to tell you, especially when he saw how amazing you were doing and with him in New York all the time to deal with the Scorpions. He wanted to tell you so you two could be together but your father said no, that he needed to keep his head in the game. He needed him to focus. He has been with you from the beginning. He focused on the Scorpions while you focused on your music. The year you were gone was probably the darkest I have seen your boy look. It wasn't a good year.

"They left this week to finalize the patch over, and Shy is becoming president of the Wolfeman, New York Chapter with Mac being his VP. He was coming for you regardless. You getting shot just gave him an early in really and he won't let you go now."

"And the girl?"

"Raven is a whore and has never belonged to the club. I think you can figure it out. She hated when the guys would take off to look after you. She has been causing drama here for a while, and your auntie took care of that."

I scream out my anger throwing my hands over my face to muffle the sound. *Fuck.* I have so many questions, and the main one is why not tell me. God, I am so mad. I don't want to think about it anymore. My head and heart hurt so much. I cried myself to sleep and turned off my phone not wanting to hear from anyone. I feel like my whole life has been a lie. My auntie has checked on me, but I tell her to leave me alone and that I will be okay. My door is locked, my music is loud, and I just want to be alone to process all this.

How can my life go from DJing in front of thousands of people to me crying in my childhood house? My life has been turned upside down within one month. When my stomach growls, I know I need to head downstairs to get some food. I need to get my shit together before the guys come home. I need to put that wall back up and be the bitch I was raised to be. It's just so hard because it's my father that I will have to defend myself against. Hitting the controls for the bed to sit myself up,

I grab my phone debating whether to turn it back on. I asked my uncle and auntie not to contact the guys and tell them that I knew because I needed time to absorb all the information.

A soft knock on the door has me turning to sit on the edge of the bed. When I hear Sissy's soft voice calling my name through the door, I stand up grabbing my crutches. I open the door and turn back to the bed, letting her come in.

"Sweetie, you need to eat. It has been almost twenty-four hours you have been in here. Everyone is freaking out, and we've had to take Bear's phone away from him. He wants to call your father."

"Fuck it. Let him."

Sissy walks over crouching down in front of me. "I understand you feel betrayed and hurt but just try to see where they were coming from."

I look her in the eyes saying in a vicious rage, "They took away love and happiness from me, leaving me broken even more than I was. I was already broken, and he saved me only to break my heart again." My words have her moving back, and I instantly feel bad for how I came across to her, and I go to apologize, but she replies before I can say anything.

"Snow, I get it. I really do, but sitting up here getting even madder is only going to hurt you more. Fuck them. Don't let them have control of your feelings anymore. Come with me to the club. Let's have fun and when they come back act like who the fuck cares that they've lied to you. Hurt them back by not giving a shit and not letting them run your life. Get better and go back to your life, if that's really what you want."

Jesus, she has changed so much.

Knowing she's right, I need to quit feeling sorry for myself and be the bad-ass I was in New York. I didn't take any shit, and I didn't let anyone near my heart. I get up from the bed, and I try to put a smile on my face. "Let's go have some fun."

Fake it. Wolfeman up. Wall is back up. Hide from everyone.

An hour later I am sitting at the strip club watching Coco dance to "Bossy" by Kelis featuring Too Short. Coco is beautiful with her light milk chocolate skin glistening on stage. She starts to move her body while she descends down to sitting on her heels with her knees in front of the group of guys in front of the stage.

When she starts to bounce, she widens her legs, eventually spreading them, showing her crotch while the guys throw dollar bills at her. Once she stands back up, she heads over to the pole, and I know right then she will do her pole act when Too Short's solo part comes up in the song. Sissy walks up with another drink pulling my attention from Coco.

"Heads up, the guys are all trickling back in today. Quick just arrived with Cash, and he said your dad and Shy were leaving tomorrow so just a heads-up, sweetie."

Fucking great! Be strong.

I smile at her taking another swig of my beer. "Thanks, Sissy."

Just like she said, the guy I'm guessing is Quick, and Cash saunter up to the bar next to me where I've asked everyone to leave me alone. Hawk has been just that *Hawk-eyeing* me from the other side of the bar, making sure I don't do anything wrong but really what can I do wrong at a fucking strip club?

Cash leans into me. "You doing okay?" I take another swig of my beer before turning to him with a smile.

"Of course, what could be wrong?"

"Fuck Snow, I've missed you so much," Cash laughs.

I have always loved Cash. He's always pushing me and making me laugh. I give him a smile hoping he knows that I missed him too. My heart melts but only for a second.

They all knew. They all lied to me.

Quick looks over nervously but I smile a sinister smile reaching across Cash to introduce myself. "Hi, I'm Snow, but I'm sure you already know this, being that you've been watching me for two years now."

Cash chokes on his beer, laughing as he leans back giving me room so I can talk to the prospect. I lean in closer, knowing I'm probably giving him a heart attack, but he takes my hand and leans in to kiss the top of it. "Actually, Snow I have only been watching you for a year, but it has been my pleasure. They call me, Quick, and anything you need, you just let me know."

Taking me off guard, I pull my hand back, which only makes Cash continue his laughter.

Fucking prick!

Quick looks to Cash, smiling. "Can I go get some pussy now or am I on the first watch?"

My piss poor attitude is in full swing, so I fire back, "Go get some pussy, Quick. I'm sure it will be just that *real Quick!* I won't move."

Cash bends over laughing holding his stomach. When Quick gets up and walks by me, he leans in whispering, "Princess, I'm *anything* but Quick, but if you want to know where I got my name just ask. I'm not Shy, and I don't hide. As I said, I'm right here if you need me."

Before I can say anything to him, he's gone.

Where the fuck did he... I guess, he got his name because he is fast as fuck.

Emptying the rest of my beer, I slam it down harder than I meant to, making Cash turn to face me, which only makes me madder and setting me off.

"Cash, I'm fine. I'm not going anywhere, and Hawk has been my bodyguard since I walked in, so can you please leave me alone."

When I hear "Smack That," by Akon start to blare out of the speakers; I cringe thinking of Shy.

You have got to be kidding me...

I can't do it. I can't hang out and act like nothing is wrong. I need answers, and I need answers now. I will start with Alex and Brant before I deal with my father and Shy. I nod to Hawk that

I need him, and he moves down the bar coming to stand next to me. "What's up?"

I turn around to face him. "Can you give me a ride home."

"Snow, I can give you a ride home," Cash replies first.

But Hawk grabs my arm. "Naw, I got her. You've been on the road all day. Stay here and watch out for any problems. I'll be right back."

Once we are outside, I realize Hawk is on his bike. I haven't ridden on the back of a bike since Shy all those years ago. I hesitate, making Hawk turn toward me. "Are you okay?"

"I haven't been on the back of someone's bike in a really long time," I whisper.

Hawk chuckles. "Snow it's fine. You'll be fine."

I chuckle now. "I know *I* will be fine, but it's just *weird*."

I flip my boot over slipping onto the back of his bike and wrapping one arm around his waist. Once we are on the road, I close my eyes and let the wind whirl around me, praying it will take all of my negative shit away. I forgot how free I feel sitting on the back letting the air cleanse me. By the time we get to the compound, I feel so much better, so much lighter and when I get off the bike, I give Hawk a big hug thanking him for the ride. He only laughs but hugs me back before taking off, heading back to the club.

Once inside my house, I grab my cell phone that I left here on purpose. I turn it on taking a seat on my bed. Hearing all the message alerts, I take a deep breath when I see fifteen messages and eight voicemails. I pull up my text messages first.

Jesus. Here we go.

ALEX
Where are you? Haven't heard from you.
ALEX
Okay, Where are you?
BRANT
Babe, did you get my voicemail? Call me.

A pain forms in my stomach. *He has known all along.*

IZZY
Girl, couple more days! Can't wait to see you.
SHY
"Closer" by Goapele... be home soon. Love you, Angel.

All the texts. All the secret messages. He should have just told me instead of pushing me away.

BRANT
Alex called and said she hasn't heard from you all day. Where are you?
ALEX
I just called your aunt. Call me.
ALEX
Just so you know, I didn't know until I met Mac in the hospital and I put it all together but didn't know for sure. I'm sorry I didn't tell you.
BRANT
Babe, you need to call me. Alex just called me.
SHY
What, no reply?

IZZY
Alex just called me and told me what happened with your family. I'm leaving a day early so I can be there for you. I'm not taking no for an answer. I'm coming. Call if you need me sooner.
SHY
Quick just called and informed me of what went down with Raven.

Yes, Raven your whore.

BRANT
Gin, you better call me back today, or I will come there. I don't give a fuck if you're mad but not replying to my text or calls is only making me pissed off and worried. ANSWER YOUR PHONE...
DADDY
Snow, I know you are mad and hurt right now but just let me explain when I get home. I love you, princess.
SHY
Be ready. I'm back, and I will not let you go. Like I said the other night - Like A Wrecking Ball... I've been gone for way too long. I'm coming home, and I don't give a damn. I am here for my girl, so be ready.

Before I can call my voicemail, my phone rings displaying Brant's name across my phone. Making it easier on me deciding who to call first. I answer trying to keep my voice normal, "Hello."

"Fucking finally. Ginger, I was about to drive all the way there. I was so worried about you when your phone was off."

"I'm fine. My phone was off while I was at the strip club," I reply emotionless.

Hearing him take a deep breath. "What the fuck were you doing at a strip club? Talk to me. Don't put that fucking wall back up."

"You should have thought of that before you decided to keep from me that my club and *my ex* were watching me *since I moved there*." Yelling the last part, I take a deep breath.

Don't give them my emotions.

"Gin, I couldn't tell you. It was written in the contract with Luc. There were stipulations for you moving to New York."

What the fuck!

"What contract and what stipulations?"

"Fucking hell. What did they tell you?" Brant huffs out.

"Ah, not that! Tell me now, Brant."

Hearing him sigh. "I can't tell you everything. I will lose my job. You need to ask your father about the contracts with Luc, the rules, and stipulations. The reports were one of them, no contact, no awareness. Just know that I wanted to tell you but I couldn't lose my job, and it really isn't for me to tell you. Shy and your father should have told you. I understand you need some time to process all of this and to deal with your family, but I am not giving you up. This is something you need to deal with your father about. I was doing my job."

"Was it your job to fuck me?" I grit out.

"No, what the fuck!" Brant roars through the phone.

"Was it your job to keep vital information from me. The reports were one thing but knowing my club, and *my ex* - were literally watching me for years. That is fucking bullshit, and you know it. I need some time, a lot of time," I continue ranting.

"I will give it to you, but this isn't over."

"Thanks," I smart.

I hang up on him before he can say anything else. I know it's not his fault, but the betrayal hurts. No one trusted me to just talk to me and know I would know what was best for me.

Contracts? Rules? What the fuck...

GINGER

The next morning I listen to all my voicemails, and I text Izzy and Alex back, I am just so exhausted from thinking. I need to clear my head. I leave my crutches behind and wobble out of the house. A few more members have returned, so the clubhouse is a bit busier with Gigi behind the bar. I just keep walking, only giving head nods and smiles. I beeline it straight for the garage and go to her knowing exactly where I put her before leaving. Pulling the cover off of her, I dust off my Harley Davidson, Freedom. God, I missed being on her while in New York. I bought my Ninja 300 six months after I moved to New York. I was tired of Luc's men driving me everywhere. It was fun to ride but the feel of a Harley between your legs, vibrating through you went straight to your soul. I sit on her and lean forward laying over the tank, hugging my bike. I can remember it like it was yesterday.

All the members form a half circle in front of me - closest to the gate, while everyone else forms a circle behind me, encircling my dad and myself.

They all start to whistle and holler. I hear the gates open, but I can't see with the men forming a wall in front of me. When they all split in the middle, that's when I see it...

The guys always talk about it, but I truly never understood until now. Dallas rides in on a beautiful Harley Davidson Sportster with a white tank, and it has a custom paint job with Snow White and the seven dwarfs, or at least you would think that from afar but it says Princess Snow and her Wolfeman. I start to cry, and all the men are whistling and hollering Snow. My dad comes up behind me wrapping his arms around me. "Surprise, Princess. Happy Sweet Sixteen from all your Wolfeman. We love you."

I'm sobbing now, there are no words for the love I have for all these men. I would die for any one of them. I'm passed to each member for a big hug and kiss then I'm handed back to my dad.

"Daddy, I don't know what to say. I love it."

Still, with an ear-to-ear grin, he walks me to my bike handing me a helmet. I have been riding bikes since I could walk. Mac still lets me ride with him if we have an extra bike around that he is working on, so I know how to ride.

"Well, you need to thank Mac. He was the one that did most the work and had it custom painted, and you need to name it."

Before he even finishes, I say, "Freedom."

Everyone is looking at me like I'm crazy when I get on the bike and I look over at everyone laughing, "Her name is Freedom because I am free *to go where I want and when I want, she is my Freedom…"*

Everyone starts to laugh except my dad who looks pissed.

"Don't get any ideas. You still have to ask to ride her and you will always have someone with you. Freedom. My. Ass. Now let's ride."

When I hear a noise, it snaps me from my memories, and I look up to see Mac leaning on the door frame watching me. I sit there and don't say anything. I just stare at him. He isn't smiling which is not like him. Mac is always smiling and happy. It takes a lot for him to get mad. Sensing I'm not going to talk, he pushes off the door frame walking toward the big roller doors where all the bikes are parked out back.

Seriously! He's going to leave and not say anything.
I stay seated on Freedom waiting to see what he is doing. When he stops I hold my breath hoping for something, I don't know what but I need something from him. He has been my rock all these years. Always holding me up when I needed him.

Mac turns slightly around and he's still not smiling, which scares the shit out of me. Did something happen? Where is Shy and my father? Weren't they all together? When he speaks, I pray it's not going to be bad. "Let's go. I got you."

Um. What?

Stunned and confused I stay seated until he yells over his shoulder, "Grab your helmet."

I let out the breath I was holding. He's giving me what I've been deprived of and what I need. I haven't been able to drive a bike in weeks, and I need to clear my head. Besides that short ride Hawk gave me home, I haven't felt the wind on my face or had the freedom to think in a while. Mac knows what I need- to ride. I jump off Freedom grabbing my helmet and wobble after him with a smile spread across my face.

"Where are the others?" I ask, jumping on the back of his bike.

Mac still hasn't spoken or smiled, and it is bugging me because even when we fight, he doesn't shut up or stop smiling. When he answers me the feeling I have in my gut grows bigger.

"Something came up, and they'll be a few more days."

I want to ask him what came up but his bike comes to life, and he tells me to hold on.

I guess he needs to clear his head too because we ride not speaking again. Holding on to his cut the best I can with one good hand before leaning back looking up to the sky. I pray that Momma and Faith will watch over Shy and my dad. I close my eyes and just let the wind swirl my long hair around whipping my face.

God, I miss this.

Mac turns onto the highway, and I lean into his back putting both hands around him because I know him, and he loves to ride fast. He taps my good hand, giving me the sign to hold tighter before he takes off opening up and letting her roar to life. The love for a bike is such a spiritual thing if you really think about it. It is part of you, and you become one while riding. The freedom you have out in the open with God's creations all around you. I forgot about all of this living in the city. The open road with nothing around you, no one to bother you, it's just you and your thoughts.

I take a deep breath hugging my cousin harder. He grabs my hand squeezing it and holds it for a few minutes before letting go. We have been through so much. I can't believe he didn't tell me. All those times I cried to him about Shy. Why didn't anyone tell me? I just don't understand. I start to cry letting all my anger and resentment go. I need to cleanse myself and move on.

That's what this whole trip was for, and I need to figure out what I'm doing. I can't choose between the two lives, so I need to be able to be around this life without hiding myself. I need to figure out who I am, and I need to find balance.

I know Mac can see my face since I don't have on sunglasses with my shell helmet, he can see me crying. Putting my head on his back, I just let go of everything and pray Momma can hear me and help me heal.

I don't know how long we ride for, but when we slow, pulling off the road, I open my eyes to see we are at the creek where we used to go to all the time as kids. The same creek where I lost my virginity to Shy. Stopping I jump off pulling my helmet off and hand it to Mac. We still haven't spoken. I can't read his face, so I turn around and start walking toward the rocks by the water that we always hang out on.

I sit down hanging my feet off the rocks wondering what is going through Mac's head. When he sits next to me, we both just look out over the water.

Mac breaks the silence. "Gin, I know you are really pissed off right now, and I get it, truly I do. When your dad came to the club and told us his plan, I was pissed. Shit, half of us were going to blow the whole thing and tell you, but the first time we all went to see you perform at Club Spin we were all in awe of you. You looked like you belonged up there, and I knew right then he was right for pushing you away from us so you could pursue your dream."

What! They all came and saw me?

I start to cry but don't say anything. My heart hurts that I didn't get to see them or feel their love and support. Instead, I felt elated by my success alone.

"I know this isn't going to change anything, but you need to know Shy has never stopped loving you. We have been there every step of the way, watching you grow and become the most amazing woman ever. You two were so young and Shy loved you so much that he let you fly so you could reach your potential not cage you. He never let you go, and it was all because your father believed in your love for each other. He wanted to build a future for you, not hurt you. When he saw the talent you had, he knew you didn't need to be living in some back country town. He knew you needed to be in the big city with your man beside you. That's why he did what he did. He gave Shy a club of his own where you could be who you want to be."

I am sobbing now with my hands over my face. Mac pulls me into his chest holding me.

"I know this is a lot to process, but you needed to hear all this before you put that wall up and let your stubbornness take over. Who do you think this has been worse on, you or him? Do you really think it was you? Yes, you were hurt but don't you think he hurt too? Would you be able to just sit back and watch the love of your life, grow and live a life without you, *and* be happy for them? It hasn't been easy, and I know because I am the one with him, holding him back from going to you. He is my best friend, and you are my family. He did what he thought was the only way to express his love for you and that was through music and texting you. If I can ask anything of you, it would be to please let all this sink in without all the resentment and anger. Think about all the text messages, all the times you thought you felt someone watching you and just knew we were your guardian angels making sure you had the best life ever, and it's only going to get better. Your life is just starting, cousin. You're going to be twenty-three soon, and most people don't even know what the fuck they want to do and are still in college. You need to get out of your head and just live."

I pull away from him, wiping my eyes and take a deep breath getting myself together. "Why not just tell me? Why not tell me the plan?"

Mac laughs and smiles the first time since being here. "Snow, seriously? You would have thrown a fit. You and Shy would have fought all the time, and neither of you would have been focused on what you really needed to be doing. Probably breaking up and getting back together. He needed to be focused on club business and you on your music. You wouldn't have done half the shit you did single if you had Shy as your man. You went to Europe for a year for God's sake. If we had told you, none of that would have happened. I know that for a fact. It has pushed Shy to become the man he needed to be to move forward. He has been so focused on the prize at the end of the road, and that is you and his own club. He is going to be a great president, that's why I'm going to be his VP. He's a leader, and he has shown that these last few years, especially with you and his patience. Your father knew exactly what he was doing when he made this plan. He saw the love you two have and knew if Shy could pull this off he deserved you because he loves you enough to give you what you really deserve, and that is the world."

Tears are still streaming down my face, and I keep looking in my lap fidgeting with my hands. I have so many feelings going through my body I can't handle it. Mac rubs my back trying to soothe me.

"I feel so lost. I don't know how you do it. He made me feel again, and then he was taken from me, and now everyone is telling me, he was there the whole time. Well, he wasn't there *with* me, helping me cope and deal with life. I needed him."

Mac drops his hand from my back down to his lap. "Snow, you are not going to like this, but I have never lied to you. I might not have told you stuff, but I never lied to you. What you need is to depend on yourself. You need to be strong. Faith and Foxy died. They are with us everywhere, and we see your momma in you every day. Your dad had tears in his eye when he saw you on that stage. You are strong enough. You just need to believe in yourself. You are one bad-ass girl. I see it, shit everyone sees it but you. Quit living in the past and live for right now, they would want you to. Let them go and celebrate their life by living and being the best you can be. Shy knew you needed to grow and spread those wings. If he didn't let you go, I don't think you ever would have really lived. You need to let go."

Fuck, it hurts so bad!

"It hurts - my heart hurts so bad," I blubber out, sobbing again.

Mac cuts me off grabbing my shoulders turning me to face him. "What do you want? Right now, what will make you happy?" he asks forcefully.

Wiping my tear filled hands on my jeans, I try to think.

"I don't know. My momma and Faith back."

"Wrong, they are with you every day. What do you want right now? What makes you happy?" Mac says, shaking me.

"My music..." I say, looking my cousin in the face.

"Yes! What else?" Mac yells, throwing his hands up in the air.

"My friends." I smile knowing that without them I would have moved home a long time ago.

Mac smiles throwing his hands in the air again. "Hallelujah.

What else makes your day."

I sit there thinking about my days in the city. They included my friends, music, the guys and… Shy's texts or phone calls, if I was having a bad day. "Fuck." He always knew when to call or text me.

Mac crosses his arms over his chest smiling. "See. Now you get it. Decide what makes you happy and do it. Don't dwell on things you can't change, focus on the things you can."

I launch forward taking him off guard and hugging him with all I have. "I love you Mac, and I have missed you so much. I have missed everyone." I pull away from him feeling whole for the first time in a very long time. My phone chirps in my back pocket, when I reach to get it Mac's cell beeps.

There goes my happy bubble.

I open up the text messages and see it is from Shy.

SHY
"It's Your Love"- by Tim McGraw & Faith Hill. It just does something to me. Better than I was and more than I am.

Damn, I never saw it. I was always thinking he was just fucking with me or keeping me hooked. I'm still so mad, but my cousin is right, I need to let go and live each day for what makes me happy.

Mac cussing next to me pulls me from my thoughts of Shy and when I see his face I know something is wrong but before I can ask Mac is up on his feet yelling we got to go while jogging back to his bike with me on his tail.

Please let everyone be okay.

SHY

Finally, I get to go home and claim my girl. I just hope she doesn't fight me for long. I know she is going to be hurt and upset, but I will make her see reason. I just need to break down that wall of hers again. Wolfe, Striker, and I are finishing up with the paperwork and club stuff. We sent most of the club back except Dallas, Stitch, Wolfe and me. Wolfe told me to start calling him Wolfe now that I am president of my own club but that is going to be hard since I've been calling him Prez for years now.

Coming out of the bathroom, I start to text Snow, making my way down the hall toward the front of the clubhouse. We are getting ready for our drive back when my phone rings, interrupting my text but displaying Ethan, Maddox's guy.

"Whaddup?" Thinking we need to find him a good nickname, Ethan just sucks.

"We might have a problem. You need to get over to Beau's office and now."

Before I can say anything, he hangs up on me. "Fuck!"

When I come out of the hallway Wolfe is on the phone, and I can see by the look on his face, he is getting a call similar to the one I just got.

I place my hands on my hips watching and waiting for him to get off the phone. He hangs up without saying a word. "Well, did you get the same call to meet at Beau's?"

Wolfe looks more on edge and Dallas walks up after seeing our faces, and he becomes alert as well.

Wolfe shakes his head. "Yeah, they have some information, and they want us there. Let's go."

"What?" I ask him.

"Let's go," is the only reply he gives me.

I pull my phone out and send my text to Snow and then shoot a text off to Mac asking if he is with her and if so to keep her in sight since she might be in danger. I'll explain when I know more. Jumping on my bike Wolfe is already taking off with Dallas and Stitch behind us.

Once we get to the building where Spin It, Inc. and the Security teams offices are located, we notice Chad. This building is one of the safest places around or at least one of the most secure buildings. When the four of us jump off our bikes, we are greeted at the door by Chad, Maddox's head security guy.

"Thanks for coming. We are all up in the security office."

We all nod hello while filing into the elevator. Wolfe speaks up first, "Is this regarding Emmett?"

Chad, head of Maddox security, looks like shit. He looks like he hasn't slept in days, which tells me they have been sitting on this, making me madder.

The door to the elevator opens, and we all follow Chad out who still hasn't answered. Opening the door to the security office, we all walk into the room only to find it full of all of Beau's and Maddox's team standing around.

Goddamn, this isn't good.

When we enter, everyone turns giving us their attention. Beau moves toward Wolfe extending his hand followed by Luc. Beau extends a hand to me before talking. "Thank you guys for coming. It looks like maybe Emmett was working with someone after all, who we don't know yet. As you know after the shooting, we have been looking for the girls that were taken the same night but with no luck. Every lead has been a dead end. We've had no new incidents until this last weekend. One girl was drugged, but luckily she had a sober friend with her who got her to a hospital. The next Saturday one girl went missing from Club Touch. We don't know if it is related or just someone trying to get laid, but we wanted to touch base with you before you left."

Motherfucker!

Wolfe moves toward me putting his hand on my shoulder, knowing what I'm thinking but says looking at Beau, "What do we know?"

Beau throws on the table two pictures of two different girls and fuck me if they didn't look just like Alex and Ginger. One with black shoulder length hair and bangs while the other has dark brown long wavy hair.

Both Wolfe and I say in unison, "Fuck!"

"Which one is missing?" I asked.

"I'm sure you're thinkin' what we all think, that they look a lot like our girls, yeah? Well, they do, and this one was taken." Luc points to the one that looks like Ginger before continuing. "No leads, just that she disappeared from the club. It all sounds like before, so we want everyone in on this. *Capisci?*" Luc speaks up.

"We might want to look into this but last week Shy and a few of the boys took down a guy outside a bar raping a girl in the alley. The guy was linked to Scorpions but not a member. Do we have eyes on all the girls? It could be related but if not do we have trackers and has there been any tampering of the video systems again?" Wolfe asked.

My Angel isn't safe. I can finally protect her. I need to get home.

Beau points to Ethan, who moves forward taking over the conversation. "I have trackers on all the girls' phones. I have eyes on almost all of the girls except Ginger, but she's within the compound, so I am sure she's safe. Maddox is with Alex and a team of security. He doesn't know about this yet but he will tonight once we finish this meeting. Izzy, I have her cell tracked but no eyes on her. We hacked her cell today, and she will be at your compound in the next few days so she should be safe. Sasha is the only one I have no links to but can try."

Luc moves forward taking the floor. "Let's give it a week just in case the girl's found, but before the girls go on tour we need to have a plan. We'll brief most of them next week before they leave on tour. No keepin' secrets but let's not scare them, and they'll need to have more than one tracker on them. We still don't know if this has anythin' to do with us and most of the girls have been gone the past few weeks so I don't see it bein' linked, but we're not takin' any chances, *yeah*."

Luc's a big man with a thick Jersey-Italian accent. He's usually so calm and controlled but seeing him right now with so much anger in his voice. He isn't fucking around.

"We'll be workin' with the police and all the night clubs so everyone can up their security. We can't take any chances this time. If this is related to Emmett, then it was bigger than we thought, so we need everyone to know and be on alert until we figure out who we are dealin' with. *Capisci?* The good thin' is no one knows where they'll be and that they'll all be together, easier to look after," Luc continues.

"Except Ginger, who will be with us but we need to be in the loop with what is being planned and done. If or when Ginger joins them, one of my men or myself will be with her at all times. She knows everything now, and we won't be hiding anymore,"

I shout out.

Beau nods his head. "Good, I'm glad we don't have to keep any more secrets from our girls. We will need everyone on this one, and we all need to be on the same page. The girls are smart and can handle themselves, and we need to trust them, as they do us. Let's get our IT guys busting ass to see what we can find, but until this fucker shows his face again, we are kind of in the dark."

I get pissed when he calls Ginger his girl even though I know he is calling all the girls his girls.

"We took down the Scorpions but a hand full of them went nomad, we will be watching and dealing with them but just so you know not all of them patched over. We're headed home now, and I'll have Hawk and Dallas linking into whatever we can and let you know what we find. I will hook Izzy up with another tracker and inform her of what's going on. When she leaves to head here, we will have men on her. If we can track her now, I will send my scout Quick out to meet her. I would rather be safe than sorry," Wolfe speaks up.

Beau's second in command, Gus, whom we have nicknamed Redman, steps forward. "I got Iz. I'll call her and make it happen."

Everyone nods. I need this meeting to be over with, so I can get home and hold my girl. I need my girl in my arms again. Fuck.

Ethan jumps up grabbing his computer, yelling, "Gus give me five, and I'll let you know if she's driving or flying."

My phone rings, both Wolfe and I step back. I see it's Mac and answer it. "Hold on a sec."

I turn to Wolfe. "Do you want Mac to have everyone at the compound on lockdown till we get back?"

"No, but get everyone to the clubhouse and just be on alert. Keep eyes on all the women and mandatory church when we get back," he replies.

I put the phone back to my ear walking away to the corner while they keep discussing shit. "Okay, you there?"

"What the fuck is going on, brother?" Mac sounds stressed out, which I can understand with the little information that I gave him.

"Sorry, we're going to take precautions, so get everyone to the compound. We need eyes on all the girls. Got a call from Mad Dog's guy telling us we needed to meet. Can't explain it over the phone but just keep Snow close and her girl Izzy is coming so we need to protect her as well. Dallas is working with Ethan right now, so I got to go but be on alert and keep eyes on Snow at all times."

"You got it, Prez," Mac replies. Him saying that shocks the shit out of me. That's the first time he's called me Prez. I guess that was my first order to him and even though it wasn't for the New York chapter it was still my order.

Goddamn, that feels good.

GINGER

The ride back to the clubhouse was good, giving me time to let go and try to sort all that was running through my mind. I just wanted to get back to my room and go to sleep. I feel vulnerable out around people. I don't want anyone to see me cry or be weak and after what my uncle and cousin just told me, I need to be alone to get my head sorted. I'm grateful that once we parked Mac gave me a hug and said he would see me later. I wanted to ask him what was wrong but I knew better and really if it was bad he would tell me. Watching him walk away while taking his phone out, I know he's calling Shy.

I pull my phone out of my back pocket pulling up his last text and re-read it. *It's your love...* without thinking, I reply with the only thing that has been on my mind since.

GINGER
You should have told me!

I swipe my phone off and make my way through the parking lot to walk the long way around the back side of the hotel not wanting to see anyone in the courtyard by the fire. I just want to get to my house and sleep. I'm wobbling up the stairs when my phone chirps, I know it's Shy, so I wait until I am back in my room sitting on my bed before I pull up his text.

> **SHY**
> I need you to do something for me. Go to your old room and pull up this song. Lay down on the bed and really listen. It's my thoughts. I need you to listen to it like we used to do back in the day when we would just lay there listening to music - dissecting it – and you would tell me what you thought it meant. I need you to do that, and when I get there tomorrow, we will sit down and talk about EVERYTHING. I will not keep anything from you again. I promise on my life, Angel. I just need you to give me a chance to explain.

I think of the days we used to spend in my room listening to music, me laughing at him for the crazy ideas he would have about songs and what they meant. We always used to laugh so much. We were happy. I reply to him.

> **GINGER**
> You didn't tell me what song.

Raising my hand to my lips, I smile at the memory of our first kiss. It was in my room while we were listening to "Closer" by Goapele. Talking about our dreams, I can remember it like it was yesterday. I can see me lying on my bed with my back to the mattress, while Shy lays on his side looking down at me, watching me talk about music. When I looked over at him, he just moved over my body taking my mouth without asking, but he didn't need to. I was more than willing and so thankful he did. His kiss - my very first kiss - was so soft. I was scared out of my mind that I would do it wrong, but he took his time with me, slowly engaging his tongue, guiding me along the way.

I bite my lip, holding my phone and thinking about his kiss when my phone rings, making me jump. It's Shy calling me.

Oh, God. He is calling me and not texting. I don't want to talk to him.

I stare at my phone and hit the green button instead of the red. *Fuck me.*

I don't say anything but just listen, and when I don't say anything, Shy's thick husky voice comes through the phone. "Angel, I didn't tell you the song because I wanted to make sure that you *wanted* to know the song *and* that you were listening."

I take a breath, and I know he can hear me, but I still don't say anything, so he continues. "I just hope you are thinking of us in your room listening to music and that it brings back good memories. All the talks about your dreams and your love for music. Well, I heard what you were saying. I need you to listen to my song now and really listen. But, the other reason I am calling is that I wanted to tell you what is going on. I told you I wouldn't lie to you, so I'm calling you before anyone else can call or text you."

Shit! Something has happened. I knew I could see in Mac's face.

"What happened?" I snap sounding bitchy instead of scared and nervous.

"The clubhouse is going to be on alert. Your dad and I are on our way back once I get off the phone. We should be home in the morning, and if you want me to come straight to you I will, or I will wait for you to wake up but some shit went down over here, and none of it's good. I need you to stay in the compound and don't leave for anything. Some of the shit is in regards to the club. But Snow, some of it has to do with you and the situation that was going on before Emmett was killed. I can't give you or anyone details over the phone, but I will fill you in once I get there."

Just hearing Emmett's name makes me quietly gasp, trying to keep my panic to myself. Flashes of that night run through my brain distracting me from what Shy is saying until he shouts, "Snow. You there?"

"Yes. I'm here. Don't go anywhere. Got it," I answer, shaking the bad thoughts from my head.

Hearing Shy take a deep breath, I wait for him to bitch at me for being a smartass and for whatever it was I missed but when he talks his voice is filled with worry only making the knots in my stomach tighten.

"Angel, I'm coming home, baby, and we can talk then. Just know you're safe. I love you. Now go listen to my song and really listen to it. Don't think of anything else but us. Okay?"

"Yes," I answer automatically.

"The song is, 'If Tomorrow Never Comes' by Garth Brooks. I gotta go, Angel."

The phone goes dead, and I didn't even get to say goodbye.

Great. Real fucking great.

Since I have been back and out of the hospital all I have been thinking about is Brant and Shy, only a few times did I ever really think about Emmett. I have been so consumed by Shy that I really haven't had much time to think about that night, about Jason getting killed and me shooting Emmett to save Alex. The doctors and Alex had filled me in on all the details of what happened after I passed out. Alex was the one who eventually put the last bullet in Emmett, killing him.

I've had a few nights where I have woken up in sweat soaked pajamas thinking Emmett had killed Alex or Faith. A lot of my dreams have Faith in them. I know she died in a car crash, but my subconscious switches Alex and Faith in my dreams, making them horrific.

I just don't understand what could be happening right now with Emmett that would make everyone freak out. The investigation went dead, and they ended up closing the case with the theory Emmett was working alone, kidnapping all those girls. They never did find the bodies of the other girls that went missing the same night Emmett snatched Alex. Maybe they found more information about the girls?

My mind starts going in all different directions with so many questions and what-ifs, that I can't fall asleep. Then I finally remember Shy's song and I head to my old room. Once the song is pulled up, I lie down on my bed and just stare up at the ceiling, closing off my mind, taking in each word.

Okay, Shy. I'm listening.

I wake to the covers being pulled up over my body, and half asleep, I murmur, "Hmmm, B."

"What the fuck did you just say?"

I freeze.

Oh, shit. Shy!

Fully awake now, I try to get my bearings and go into defensive mode. "What the fuck, Shy!"

The light next to the bed flips on, and Shy is over me in seconds, looking like he is about ready to murder someone.

"Brant? You just called me by his fucking name, Ginger."

Dammit. This is really bad.

"You are tripping out, Shy. Get the fuck off of me and why are you in here?" I reply, still trying to play it off.

I try to deflect and change the subject but Shy doesn't budge. "Have you slept with him? – Like slept with him?"

Oh, God - Oh, God.

Keeping my emotions hidden, I try to hold it together by defending myself. "Fuck you, Shy. That is none of your business, and it isn't like you are some fucking saint not getting laid all these years!"

Yelling the last part, I try to push him off me again, but he is rock solid and naked except for shorts. My body is now aware of his massive form lying on top of me. *Fuck, he is gorgeous.* So many memories. God, I loved when we used to fight and then fuck. My lady parts start to throb in memory, moistening my panties. My body is defying me, making my mind lose the battle of staying mad at him.

Fuck it. I'll be mad tomorrow. I need this.

Shy moves his face down only inches from my face, staring me straight in the eyes. "Angel, I may have fucked or gotten sucked off, but *no one* and I mean *no one* has been in my bed except you. NEVER. My rules - NO kissing, NO touching, and NO overnight. It has only been you, and *everyone* knows it."

No kissing. No touching. Oh, God.

I gasp and without warning Shy takes my mouth violently. Fuck, I missed his passion. I forget everything. I forget the past, the present, everything except him devouring me. Letting myself feel what I have always felt but without denying it anymore. I've missed him so much. My good hand goes instantly to his hair gripping a handful pulling him closer, deepening the kiss.

A deep throaty growl erupts from within Shy, sending a zing straight through my body down to my toes, making them curl. I am so lost in his touch. I don't even notice he has my nightgown halfway off, exposing my breasts.

Shy breaks our kiss, gripping my breasts forcefully, sucking one into his mouth with a moan. I arch my back off the bed. God, I love when he dominates me. I crave it. I love it. Being taken forcefully has always been our thing. Something I've missed.

I moan, thinking of being fucked by Shy. He kneels back on his shins pulling my panties down one leg, leaving them hanging on my boot. He spreads my legs open and just stares at me.

"Angel, I can't even think about someone else having you

without feeling like murdering someone. This" -entering a finger into my wet entrance- "this pussy is and will always be my property, regardless if you acknowledge it or not."

Closing my eyes, I move my body trying to speed up his strokes, but he leans down slicking his tongue through my folds before licking over my clit. Doing this a few times and doing it so slowly it has me losing my mind. "Please Shy. Please fuck me," I beg.

"Tell me what I want to know."

Shy enters two fingers into my sex only making me lose concentration all over again. I try to think about what he asked but can't remember. All I want is to feel him again. It's been so long.

"Have you been with Brant?" he asks while moving his fingers in and out of me.

"Yes," I answer without hesitation.

Goddamn it. I can't lie to him when he's touching me and he knows it.

I keep my eyes closed, not wanting to see Shy's reaction. I just want to come. I pump my hips faster building my climax.

Shy keeps up his assault on me while getting all the information he wants, knowing I can't deny him.

"How many others?"

I can hear the anger in his voice but answer breathlessly, "Only Brant."

Shy leans over my body pulling his fingers from me. He places both hands on the bed next to my head caging me in. I'm about to protest him withdrawing his fingers but don't say anything when I see the look on his face, so I snap my mouth shut. I see the pain and anger within his eyes before he closes them taking a deep breath. When he opens them, he states, "It kills me that someone else has had you. I don't ever want to talk about this again, but I need to know. Do you want to be with him?"

I feel tears pooling, and I close my eyes, not knowing what to say. "Micah, you have always been the one holding my heart and I have tried to let you go. Brant finally broke through my wall. Both of you held information from me that could have stopped me from hurting. Neither one of you told me. Right now I don't know what I want. I am so upset with both of you. I love you, but I do care about him."

Shy leans his forehead to mine giving me a soft kiss on the lips, moving around my face placing soft kisses everywhere. "I will tell you everything and promise you this, I will never lie to you or leave your side again, and I will never let you go. You are my queen and will forever be my girl," he says.

Tears slide down my face, thinking of the song he asked me to listen to last night. I need to feel him inside of me again. I move my head up taking his mouth, whispering, "Take me."

Shy groans. "Angel, If I take you right now, there is no going back. I will be claiming you, and you will be my ol' lady."

Moving between my legs grinding his shaft into my wetness, I whimper, "yes" letting him know I want him. I need to feel him. It's been too long. I reach around his waist with my good hand, slipping it under his shorts and gripping his ass.

Shy growls, smashing his mouth to mine while slipping his shorts down, freeing himself. Placing himself at my entrance rubbing between the slick folds lubing his cock and I break the kiss. "Shy, a condom."

"Angel, I have only been with one woman bare, and that was you. Your pussy has always been mine, and I've dreamt of being inside you again. I'm clean so I will not wear a sleeve while fucking my girl."

Before I can say anything, he surges into me, and I lose all concentration. I cry out in a pleasurable pain. "Fuck!"

Shy leans over my body placing one hand on my hip and the other around my neck holding me in place while he slides out and back in only to repeat a few more times until he is seated fully inside of me.

"Jesus Christ. This-this is fucking heaven. So fucking tight, Angel."

Oh, God. He is bigger than I remember. "Yes, faster, Micah."

"Fuck, I've missed hearing you call me that," Shy groans.

"I need more," I plead.

"I know what you need. I got you, Angel. I don't want to hurt your injuries, so we'll have to be somewhat easy though."

Shy lifts my leg that's still in a boot over his shoulder, leaving my leg that was shot, flat on the bed. He moves his hips in a circular motion moving deeper inside me, making me moan with pleasure.

Shy leans over and starts pumping into me with long deep thrusts. "So fucking beautiful."

"Yes. Harder." *Holy Mother of God, he feels so amazingly good.*

Leaning back on his shins, Shy spreads my legs, reaching around my waist lifting my ass off the bed, he places a pillow under me before grabbing my hips, holding me in place as he starts thrusting harder and faster. It's like our bodies remember each other with each thrust, pump, touch, grip because I can't deny it anymore - he is my other half.

Fuck, I'm close. "Yes, Micah. Right there."

Shy keeps fucking me, grunting with each thrust. I grab my tits, tugging my hardened nipples and I'm almost ready to explode. I chant, "yes" over and over again. My voice gets higher and higher with each drive, while I try to grasp my release. I'm so close that my body starts to shake.

When Shy moves one of his hands between my legs he slips the pad of his thumb over my clit, saying, "Fuck, Angel. You are so fucking beautiful. Come for me…come for me now."

His circling around my clit a few more times sends me over the edge, and I scream my release bucking around. My orgasm keeps going, and it feels too much like I have to pee, and I start to panic. "Shy, it's too much. Oh, God."

Shy speeds up slamming into me over and over again, while continuing his assault on my clit. Sending all my senses into a frenzy. "Keep going, baby. Ride your orgasm. I've got you, Angel. I will never let you go again."

It's too much. I've never had multiple orgasms. *Oh. My. God.* Bucking around, Shy holds me down with one hand on my hip, while the other one keeps circling my nub while pounding his enormous cock into me. Another orgasm crashes through me, and I lose it. Screaming again, "Yes, Micah. Yes."

"That's it... Angel. Fucking feel me. Are you my girl?"

"Yes," I answer without hesitation.

I've known all these years that it's been him. I'll deal with everything else tomorrow. Right now I can't think of anything but this fucking mind blowing orgasm that is never ending.

"Yes. You. Are... Always," Shy answers.

While Shy rams his cock deeper with each word. I look up seeing all his muscles tense, with my pussy convulsing around his cock sending him over, grunting his release, "Fu-uck. Y-yes."

My body still feels like it's floating when Shy moves to clean us both up before he lays behind me, holding me. The last thing I remember is him telling me something about having a lot to talk about and that he loves me.

GINGER

Waking up in Shy's arms was like a dream. I felt him move around but I was so tired and sore I just laid there drifting in and out of sleep, not wanting to wake up and deal with life. I feel his warm body and when his hand moving my hair out of my face, smoothing it down over my back. And then the smell of coffee assaults my nose. I open one eye to see Shy staring down at me, completely clothed. He breaks the silence telling me we needed to get up and handle business. I still don't say anything because to be honest; I don't want to deal with reality. I know my father wasn't in the house and knew if we didn't get up that he would come barging through the doors sooner than later. I know my father wants to talk to me and I have a shit ton of questions for the both of them, but right at this moment I don't want to think of anything but Shy and him next to me.

I want him so bad. I want to be with him but can I?

We were so young back then, and now that we don't have to hide our relationship, being older, it just feels so different. Waking up to him, having him hold me has always been a dream of mine. Back then he would always have to sneak in and out before my father would wake or come home.

When I still don't say anything Shy turns me to face him in bed with both of us laying on our sides.

"Angel, talk to me. I know you have something to say. Questions?"

Silence. *I'm scared. I'm pissed. I'm happy. I'm sad...*

"Baby, you're freaking me out. Say something, anything, fuck yell at me or something."

Silence. *Goddamnit, I love you, Micah Jenkins.*

"If you don't say something and soon, I am going to call your father over."

Fuck!

"I'm so overwhelmed I don't know what to say. It has been so long that I have tried to hate you and now finding all this out I just don't know what to think or feel." I say in a low voice trying to keep my bad girl image but knowing I'm on the brink of crying.

Shy reaches up pushing strands of hair away from my face, and I close my eyes taking in the feeling of him touching me.

God, I love his touch.

"I know Angel, and I have so much I want to share with you too, but we have a lot of other things we all need to discuss today. I'm not going anywhere, and now that the cat is out of the bag, I will never let anyone get in the way of you and me again. I promise you that."

I feel my eyes pooling up. The love and passion in his eyes has never faltered, and if only I could have looked past all my hatred and hurt to see the truth. The text and voice messages all make sense now. He never let me go all those years ago.

Looking at his beautiful face, I move forward placing a soft kiss on his lips.

"Okay, let's get up and get ready. I need to get this day over with, so I can process all this." I move to get up, but Shy pulls me down on top of him.

"Angel, one thing *you* need to understand and process right now, is that *we* are together. I will not be leaving your side again. If *you* have a problem with *us,* *we* need to talk about it right now."

"Micah, we have *a lot* to talk about regarding *us*. I have *a lot* of things that I need to process, and I need to handle things with Brant," I state letting out a deep breath.

"The fuck you will! I will handle Brant," Shy growls.

I try to push him off but fail only pissing me off more.

"No, you won't. He's my friend, Shy. One that was there for me all these years, even before we hooked up. I have told him we are only friends and I care about him. I need to handle this, and in my way."

Shy closes his eyes taking a deep breath himself. "Angel, this is something we can discuss later. Like I said we have a shit ton of more important things to discuss, but I am telling you right now - I put my dick in you last night – meaning you are mine and no one else. I will not let you go. WE will figure everything out together."

Before I can answer, he tosses me onto my back kissing me before he pops off the bed pulling me with him.

"Now go shower."

Sonovabitch!

Walking into the clubhouse, I'm so lost in my own thoughts, that I don't even realize that Shy has grabbed my hand until Uncle Bear says, "It's about fucking time you two quit fucking around."

When I see he is smiling and looking at our hands together, I try to pull away, but Shy grips my hand tighter, not letting go. Shy replies over his shoulder when we pass him, "Yes, it is."

Everyone's eyes are on us as we walk through the clubhouse heading toward my father's office. When we reach the stairs, heading up to his office, Shy goes first still not letting my hand go. We stop a few feet in front of my father's office and he pulls me to him. "Angel, you need to get used to this. You are my girl, and I am not going to keep my hands off of you - ever again."

Looking into his eyes, I know he is dead serious, but this is all just too much for me to handle right now. Shy kisses me on my forehead before taking the last few steps to my father's office, knocking on the door and I hear my father tell us to come in.

Here we go, deep breath, I've got this.

Shy enters first and once I am through the door I can see my father, who is staring at our hands still together. I instantly try to pull away again but like last time, he holds on tight. It's a force of habit, not wanting my father to know about our relationship, since we used to hide everything, and it just felt so wrong doing it in front of him now. He is still looking at our hands together. His expression is blank, and I don't say anything until he gets up from his chair and moves around the desk.

I finally say, "Hello," but it's quiet.

God, I'm like a little kid who just got caught cutting class.

When he comes to stand in front of me, I see the worried look on his face, and I instantly start to panic that it has to do with Shy and me but then he hugs me. Shy lets go of my hand finally so I can hug him back.

"Princess, I am sorry for all of this, but at the same time, I'm not."

Pulling back so we can see the each other's faces, he keeps embracing me as he continues. "Everything I do, I do for you. You are my life, more than this club and more than my own life. You are my everything. I hope you can understand and listen to what I have to say."

Just seeing my father's eyes and seeing the love along with the sad look on his face, has me giving in to him even before he speaks. My father is a very scary man most of the time. He reeks of authority, and for him to look like this, makes me want to make it all better. I can't seem to say no to these two men when faced with a problem.

They are my weakness.

When my father lets go and gestures for me to sit down, I feel a sense of déjà vu come over me with Shy and myself sitting in the same seats. The seats we sat in all those years ago when my father ultimately changed our lives forever. I just pray this time it won't end with my heart broken again.

After we are all seated, my father looks back and forth between the two of us landing on me when he finally speaks. "Snow, I know we have a lot to talk about, but I want to start off with the two of you. I don't know what everyone told you, so I will just start from the beginning and tell my side of everything."

He takes a deep breath before speaking again. "After your momma passed, I sheltered you making you into a biker brat. But I wanted you to become more than this" -throwing his hand out towards the door- "I knew you had talent with music and when Shy came into the picture, I wanted more for you, than to just become an ol' lady."

He looked to Shy. "Sorry and you know it had nothing to do with you. I thought of you as a son from the get go, and you know it."

Be pissed. Don't cry.

Turning back to me, he continues, "Again, it had nothing to do with the club or Shy, it had to do with me being a father wanting his daughter to pursue her dreams."

My father leans forward on his desk, clasping his hands together, taking a deep breath, and when he looks back up, he says, "When Striker approached me about needing help with his club that's when the plan immediately formed in my head.

"I approached Shy and explained what I wanted for the both of you. I hoped if Shy was in love with you like I thought he was, he would go along with the plan. I knew you probably wouldn't have gone along with the plan or may have even left if it wasn't for us pushing you away. You have always taken care of everyone else, always putting their needs before yourself, and you were only eighteen years old."

Be pissed. Don't cry.

I can't let them see me upset. My body is tense, so I try to sit back into the chair and relax. I glance over to look at Shy who is relaxed in his chair and just staring at me with his beautiful God given eyes. When our eyes meet, he smiles letting me know he is here for me. I look back to my father but don't say anything because I know he is right. I would do anything for this club and my family.

But I left them – But he left me.

When I don't say anything my father continues, "Snow, I know you love Shy and the way you two looked at each other, it was undeniable. I wanted you to live a little and figure out who you wanted to be. If you choose this life and want to become Shy's ol' lady, then I won't stop you, but at least now you can say you lived and followed your dreams.

"We have new chapters forming, and Shy here is the same age I was when we started this club. He has proven to me and this club, he is a leader. With all that he has done for the club and the way he has handled you and this situation, I know without a doubt, he loves you and deserves you."

"Believe me, there were days I wanted him to grab you and bring you home but all of us" -pointing to the club- "we all have held it together for you to become the women your momma wanted you to become. This club and Shy has been, and will always be here for you, even if you don't know it. Princess, after your momma died, I saw how the music helped bring you back, giving you peace and I just couldn't let you give it up. I know all this information has been a lot for you to process but I wanted to tell you my side. What questions do you have for me?"

I start to fidget with my fingers. Not really knowing where to start, I just start with explaining my side before hitting them with the questions. "I am more hurt by everyone's secrecy, that no one trusted me to know or believe I would do the right thing."

When my dad starts to protest, I put my hand up stopping him. "Let me finish, please. When Mac explained it to me yesterday, it finally sunk in but you still waited so long to tell me, when in fact, you could have told me after I left, even a year later instead of waiting this long."

I look down to my fidgeting hands pushing back the tears that are fighting to fall. I take a deep breath and look back up before continuing.

"You raised me not to take any shit and I know I'm a biker brat who's stubborn, even a bitch at times but you took him and this club from me. The only things that kept me going after Momma died and you took that from me without even giving me a chance. I know I was young, and you thought you were doing the right thing but like you said I was a lot older for my age."

I look to Shy and then back to my father who looks sad and tired, so I keep going. "I understand. I truly do, but it's going to take me some time. Shy and I have a lot to discuss. To be honest, things are finally making sense with everyone's behavior. which only makes me mad again because all this could have been avoided if you'd just told me."

I pause to take a deep breath and calm the rage inside. "Who knew in New York that you all were watching me even if from a distance? What contract or rules were made with Luc? I want to know everything."

When I stop speaking, my father starts right off the bat telling me about his meetings with Luc, the guys following me from the beginning, and for an hour he and Shy pretty much tell me every little detail. We went back and forth with all the questions and answers, but in the end, I was still upset. I knew they meant well, but it was so much to process. Shy got a phone call, and had to excuse himself, leaving my father and me to finish the conversation alone.

Once Shy was gone, my father came around the desk bending down in front of me, taking my hands into his own. "I know all of this is a lot to take in, and I am sorry for the pain we have caused you, but I believed it was the best for you. Shy proved himself to be worthy of you. The year you were gone on the tour was not a good year, but he still held it together. I pray to God you forgive Shy because he does deserve you and I'd trust him with my own life, so I know he will protect you always."

Sonovabitch.

I have held it together throughout this meeting only getting teary eyed a few times, and at this moment, I stare into his eyes letting him know I understand. When I don't say anything, he stands up pulling me with him embracing me in a bear hug.

"I love you so much, princess. Let's go have some lunch and get all the guys together for our next talk. This one will not be any more pleasant but you need to know, and as we said, we will not leave you out of any decision that has to do with you. We will not keep secrets from you anymore."

Knots form in my stomach. "Does this have to do with Emmett?" I ask looking up at my father.

Seeing his jaw clench I know I am right, but before he can say anything my phone rings, so I pull away to answer it. I see it's Izzy and answer right away, "Hello."

"What the fuck is going on?" Izzy's high pitch voice echoes through the phone.

I am already so high strung from having this conversation that I try not to overreact.

"What?" Trying to sound cool, knowing she couldn't have known about the meeting we all just had.

"Um, exactly what I just said, What- the- fuck- is going on? Gus is on his way to meet me and says he will be staying with me from now on until I get back to New York."

Holy shit!

It must be bad then if Luc sent Gus to watch out for Izzy. I turn to look at my father and say to Izzy, "I don't know much, but my father is getting ready to brief me and everyone else on what is going on. How much longer until you get here?"

I try to sound more pissed off than concerned hoping to relieve her of any worry.

"Well, something has happened because Gus called me freaked out and is on his way. He said the same shit that he would tell me once he saw me. I'll be there tomorrow morning now."

"Okay, let me talk to my dad, and I'll get back with you. I am so glad you will be here tomorrow." I try to sound happy and get her mind off whatever is going on and focus on us seeing each other.

"Gus is calling me again. Call me back." She hangs up before I can reply.

An hour later we are sitting around listening to my father tell everyone about the meeting with Luc and how a girl went missing and another one was drugged. They don't think it's linked, but we are going to be on alert just in case. When he tells us, I don't react because Emmett is dead. Auntie and I are allowed to be in here for the first part since it had to deal with us and the security of the women. Through all of it, I keep quiet just trying to take it all in. No reaction. No questions. No nothing...

When Emmett's name was brought up, I flinched, just thinking of how much I hated him.

"Do we know the girls? What their names are? What does-" I stop mid-sentence and look over to Shy. I know what I'm about to say will piss him off, but I ask anyway. "What do Beau and Brant say? Are they getting in touch with all the girls?" I ask thinking he is close to being done.

I'm looking at my father when I say it and Shy snaps, "I don't give a fuck what *they* say." He points around the room. "*We* will be protecting you now. *We* will not be hiding anymore. *We* are going to keep you safe. Are *you* okay with that?"

Each of his words are dripping with anger but I don't back down.

Here we go with Mr. Biker bad-ass.

"*I* understand but do *you* understand that *they* have been there for *me*. *And* yes *I* care what *they* think, I care what you both think," I fire back just as angry.

Shy pushes his chair out and turns toward me saying with a clenched jaw. "Well, there was always an *us* watching you too. *And* there will *only* be an *us* now, so get used to it."

The sound of the gavel hitting the table has both of us looking to my father. "Enough, both of you."

I notice everyone is smiling at us when I turn my chair away from Shy, facing the table.

When my father speaks, it gains everyone's attention. "Look we just want everyone to be alert and safe until we know if it has anything to do with Emmett. We also need to be on alert because of the patch over. Izzy will be here tomorrow along with Gus, Beau's second in command. We will be working with him until Izzy takes off to New York."

He turns to face his sister. "Storm, before you and Snow head out I want you to round up the girls, and we need to have a sit down with Felicia, so we can go over the game plan and details for the next week."

Storm gets up and speaks for the first time. "The girls aren't going to be happy. I will deal with them, but we need to figure out a deal so they can still work. Snow let's go, I need your help."

I lean forward placing my hands on the table. "I want to stay and listen to what else they have to say. What we are going to do about this threat?"

Shy leans toward me to speak, but my father replies first, "Princess, I know you are mad, upset, and scared but you know we don't discuss club business around anyone that isn't a member. We have a lot to discuss with the takeover, the move and yes this threat, but I will, or Shy will brief you when the meeting is over. Once you and Storm leave we will be in church, and you know the rules."

Storm is standing at the door when I kick my chair out shooting daggers at everyone before leaving.

GINGER

The whole day was like a blurry dream, one I dreamt about when I was younger. One where Shy and I were a couple living the biker lifestyle. When Auntie and I left the meeting, we left with a couple of prospects and headed to Felicia's where we had a meeting with her and all the girls. I don't think I was supposed to leave the compound, but when Auntie told me we were fine, I believed her and didn't think anything of it.

Once we met with Felicia and the girls, setting up shifts and who was going to cover them. They weren't happy, but they knew the lifestyle, and what it comes with it, so they deal with it. When we come back to the compound, we have Felicia, Peaches, and Gigi with us and what we are greeted with is a bunch of seething men.

My father and Uncle Bear flipped their shit on my auntie for taking me off the compound grounds since they wanted the girls to come here not us go there. My auntie didn't take their shit and fired back with Felicia having her back. I was greeted with Shy fuming as well, but he only grabbed me pulling me into a tight hug.

The rest of the day went well though, and you wouldn't

think we had a threat or a worry in the world with all the people and partying that was going on. Shy never left my side he only took some calls and even then he only stepped a few feet away. Holding my hand, putting his hand on the small of my back, wrapping his arms around my waist, kissing my head or cheek.

It was all surreal for me and I felt like I needed to wake up, that it was all a dream. Having Shy within such close proximity to me all day did things to me, did things to my insides, making me feel all kinds of stuff. Shit, I have masked my feelings for so many years, that I forgot what they felt like.

During the day I talked to Luc, and he asked me not to tell Alex about the missing girl until he had the chance to talk to her when she got back from Italy. He assured me that she was safe, and he didn't want to ruin her trip by telling her the news only for her to run back worried. He wanted her to have a good vacation before coming back to more drama. I agreed with him and told him that Izzy was going to be here tomorrow and that I wouldn't lie to her and he agreed that she needed to know but asked again if we could try to keep it from Alex for another week until she came home.

I thought about her keeping the secret about Shy watching me and knew this was probably how she felt. It sucked.

Alex texted me a little while after her father called, asking how I was doing and I said I was fine that I was just dealing with Shy and my father. Once she got back, we could play catch up. I left my answers short and sweet. I had too many other things on my plate at the moment, one of them being Shy sitting next to me at the bonfire with his hand resting on my thigh.

I look out across the fire, and my heart swells just seeing my father, Cash, and Uncle Bear laughing about something one of them said. Felicia sits on Hawk's lap wiggling her ass and laughing while chatting with my aunt. I look to my left and see Mac kissing some red head, and my body stiffens only to realize it's not Rave and my body relaxes.

I hope Shy didn't feel my body tense and I don't look his direction but instead keep scanning the group of people I call my family.

My family.

People that love me and I love them. My heart swells with happiness and pain. Pain caused by me being so stupid and staying away because I was afraid of my feelings for Shy. If I'm being honest with myself, I think I was afraid he would want to keep me, and I wouldn't get to continue with my music anymore. I could have come home years ago, but my feelings for Shy kept me away, knowing when I'm around him I would not be able to deny him. I love him too much.

Tears pool in my eyes, and I take another sip of my beer hiding my face behind the cup until I can get it together. When I pull the cup away, I feel his stare before I feel him squeeze my thigh. Sitting on a bench together side by side, I turn to face him.

Fuck, he's so goddamn fine it's breathtaking.

I smile trying to hold in all the emotions running through me. Shy moves his hand from my thigh to around my back pulling me into his side, and leaning down he whispers, "Can we go somewhere to be alone? I have shared you all day, and I don't think I can take it anymore."

Not trusting my words, I just nod my head yes with a smile. Shy stands up, downing his drink. I do the same, but once I stand up, Shy bends down grabbing me around the knees, lifting me up, and throwing me over his shoulder.

"Shy, put me down," I scream. Everyone around us cries out laughing, only making me laugh harder while slapping his back. When I look up, I see all the smiles from my family. People are whistling, and some are calling out, "It's about fucking time," while others cheer, "Get her, Prez."

Prez...

Wow, that is so weird to hear people call him that. I think of my father when I hear Prez, but all day people have been congratulating him and calling him Prez. Again my heart swells.

Shy carries me into my house, up the stairs, and into a bedroom. Not my childhood bedroom, but instead the room I've been staying in with the hospital bed. Curious to why not my old room, I ask, "Um, my room is the other door."

Shy puts a knee on the bed, putting me down softly before he moves over me eventually pinning me to the bed.

"Angel, seeing you in this bed, all I could think of was how many different positions I could get you into. Fuck, my dick is so fucking hard just thinking about it, I can't stand it."

Shy leans down placing a soft kiss on my lips. When I open for him, he slowly and torturously slips his tongue into my mouth.

Fucking glorious.

He tastes like Honey Jack, and it only makes my mouth water, wanting more.

Shy breaks the sensual kiss moving over to my neck, sucking and kissing up to my ear saying, "Why do you think I didn't come check on you the first few days. All I thought about was putting the bed into different positions and having my way with you. Like the first day, you had your legs elevated up high, and all I wanted to do was flip you around and bend you over."

My pussy starts pulsing like a heartbeat demanding attention, so I buck my hips up grinding into his steel-like erection restrained by his pants, hoping the friction will ease the throb. The contact has me moaning and squirming under him even more.

Shy laughs but pulls back and straddles me only to reach over to grab the remote to the bed.

Oh, my God. He wasn't joking!

When the bed starts to raise, Shy grabs my hand pulling me up to stand, and I just stand there in awe watching the bed move.

"Are you serious?" I get no response, so I keep watching the bed.

When the bed stops, I laugh because he is totally serious and he has the bed in the Zero G position, meaning zero gravity. I love this position with my legs up and head elevated slightly, so when you are laying there, you feel like you're floating.

I'm still laughing when I turn around but stop dead when Shy's back comes into view. His back is bare, but his skin is anything but bare anymore, it is filled with tattoos. I gasp, making him turn around.

The last few days I have only seen him shirtless from the front.

Holy Mother of God. It is so fucking breathtaking.

"Turn around," I say breathlessly.

Shy does what I ask and I take the two steps between us reaching out touching the intricate design. The Wolfeman insignia, which is a wolf head howling, is in the middle of his back, and it reads above the picture Wolfeman MC, but that isn't what has my attention. It's the woman who's holding the wolf. It's a picture of my face and I'm dressed like Snow White, but you can only see the top part of my body and my arm. My arm holds the wolf and reads underneath, "Snow White and her Wolfeman." I trace my fingers over the tattoo.

Oh, my God. He branded me on his body.

I start to get teary eyed, and then I see the small words place strategically throughout the picture that unless you are close and are really looking for them, you would miss. They read; My family. My brothers. My queen. My life. One percenter. Wolfeman for life.

I still haven't spoken, and when Shy turns around, I drop the wall that has been shielding my heart and launch myself at him. He catches me easily and holds me to him while I throw my hands around his neck.

Fucking cast.

I'm limited to clawing at him, but I need to feel him. Our tongues frantically dual with each other, while Shy cups my ass lifting me up, I kick my legs up and around him, but my booted foot stops me from linking them together.

"Goddamnit," I cry out frustrated.

Shy chuckles, putting me down, moving his hands to my waist. He slips his fingers under my shirt pulling it up over my head, and throwing it aside. I let out a deep breath wanting more, needing more. Shy swipes my hair back over each shoulder leaning down kissing each one after slipping my bra strap off them. I just stand there not moving or touching him. Shy grabs one of my breasts, popping it out of my bra, engulfing it in his mouth. I moan at his wet tongue circling my ripe nipple, and I arch into him. I feel him slip his free hand around my back unclasping my bra pulling it from around me.

"Micah, please."

Shy squeezes both breasts while he sucks and tortures each one of them. My panties dampen instantly, and I feel the wetness forming between my legs. I wore a skirt today since it was easier to put on with the boot on my foot. Shy slides his hands down my torso to my skirt and tugs it down. Once it's over my hips, it falls to the ground.

"Don't move." His voice is thick and filled with lust.

When he steps away from me, I already miss his touch and when he unzips his pants, and his jeans hit the floor along with his boots, my pussy clenches in anticipation of his next move.

Shy never takes his eyes off mine, but I can't help but break the contact to enjoy the view of him in all his glory, and glorious he is. I can see his defined muscles ripple across his stomach. He has no excess fat on his body. It's all tightly formed against his well-built muscles. I'm still standing there in my panties not moving, as he instructed, and a second later Shy moves toward me with his protruding cock. His cock slides up my belly leaving behind a wet trail, and I whimper with desire.

Shy slides my panties down, placing soft wet kisses down my neck, my chest, ending on my belly where he licks his trail of pleasure before standing.

"Angel, I need to be inside of you. I need to make up for all the lost time. I need it like I need my next breath." Closing my eyes, I go to touch him but he clasps hands with me, and he moves us toward the bed.

Slowly, he picks me up, placing me in the center of the bed before crawling up after me. I lay back onto the bed and immediately feel the pressure of my lower back ease with the bed set to zero gravity. My body relaxes with my legs lifted higher and Shy moves between them, using his hands to spread me wider.

"Fuck me, you're so goddamn beautiful," Shy whispers

My heart swells while my body lights up sending waves of heat through me just from his words. He pauses for a moment, and I see he has another remote in his hand. I'm about ready to ask him what it's for when I hear the music start to play, "Like A Wrecking Ball" by Eric Church blares through the speaker. I close my eyes letting the music consume me.

"This song has been on repeat every day for the last few weeks. I can't get it out of my mind..." Shy speaks softly.

Shy moves to kiss my inner thighs moving back and forth between both legs, moving closer to my entrance. He kisses and nips at me, saying, "Angel, I've wanted to break down your door so many fucking nights…"

Shy gently places his hands on the cusp of my knees, slowly gliding them up bending them spreading me open and when his tongue laps at my folds, I moan, begging for more.

My hands are palming his head, gripping his hair. Shy slowly, and gloriously builds my climax. Hearing the song say that old house is going to be shaking Shy slips a finger in and I explode, shaking uncontrollably. He fingers me and licks around my puckered hole.

"Oh, God. Yes," I cry out.

Shy slides up my body positioning his cock at my dripping

entrance and like everything tonight he slowly enters me. Shy covers my body, leaving his chest in my face for me to suck his nipple into my mouth. Shy places his hands above me, gripping the bed's edge and thrusting hard into me, seating himself deep within me. I twirl my tongue around sucking and before releasing his nipple, I softly bite it.

"Fuck yes." Shy's thickened voice has my walls contracting against him, and he starts to move slowly but with force.

With the bed this way and my legs bent I use the bed as leverage to meet his thrust. He starts to slam against me moving me slightly up the bed, and I grab under his arms clawing with my good hand against his back.

Shy bites my shoulder making me cry out in a pleasurable pain. "Yes."

"This-This right here is our future. You are my future," Shy vows.

Our bodies are glued together my chest pressed to his, and each thrust has me moaning and grunting for more.

"Angel, I have jacked off so many times thinking of you..."

Shy leans back and grabs my knees pushing them out widening me. "...spread open for me, I want to watch my cock consume you..." Licking his lips, he slowly slips into my pussy before he begins pumping faster and deeper.

"Micah, yes."

He responds by placing his hands on my hips, getting a better grip saying, "Fuck yeah."

I love when he dominates me, devours me, and we become one. This position is perfect for my injuries not putting them in a position where they'll hurt. Shy can fuck me hard, and I'm protected by the mattress.

I'm close to coming again when the next song starts "Bilingual" by Jose Nunez, and if I wasn't so close to coming, I would laugh. He has been listening to my sets because I play this song a lot and usually after he has texted me. Now, I know he was there and heard my sets. I buck my hips, meeting him thrust for thrust.

"Fuck me," he growls slipping a hand in front of me, using the pad of his thumb, he circles over my clit, sending my orgasm rippling through me.

The music mixed with him fucking me consumes me. I feel like I'm floating.

"You know my body like the back of your hand... send me into ecstasy. Please, Micah."

Shy growls, hearing me singing part of the song, he picks up the pace hammering into me. My tits are swaying in sync with his pounding, and our bodies are slick with sweat.

"Fuck, I'm so close. Yes." I start to chant, "Oh, God" with my voice raising higher the closer I get to my next orgasm.

Shy grunts breathless, "Angel, come for me, baby." He pumps faster - feeling his cock swell inside me, my pussy convulses around him, and we both explode. Shy groans his release while I cry out.

I relax into the mattress letting the orgasm spiral through me with tingles spiking from my head to my toes.

Shy falls back on top of me gripping the bed above my head. He slows his thrust into slow, long and deep ones, not pulling out but instead staying inside me, even when his cock starts to soften. Pressing his face into my neck, his labored breathing gives me goose bumps. Feeling a gush of wetness start to drip down onto my ass, I wiggle, and his cock slips out, but he still doesn't move.

When the song "Wonderwall" by Oasis starts to play, Shy falls to the side pulling me with him, laying us face to face before he kisses me, deep and passionately. Our bodies are entangled, feeling each other up while we kiss.

Hearing the words play... anybody feels the way I do about you now. My mind drifts off to all the songs he ever sent to me and thinking about the meaning behind them.

I pull away looking him in the eyes. The eyes that used to haunt me. The eyes that I loved so much and then hated. The eyes that all along have been watching me.

"The songs. The texts and all the messages. It was you trying to get through to me, and I was so stubborn and mad I didn't see it. I'm sorry." The last two words are a whisper, but he heard me.

"Angel, don't be sorry. I love you and if we didn't do what we did you would have probably ended up pregnant, working some job you didn't love. Yes, we would have been happy but baby, seeing you DJ is a high all on its own, for you and for me. I know you hated me, but I knew and could see deep down you still loved me too. I would have stepped in if I thought different. That's why the year you were gone was the hardest because I couldn't see you. I couldn't see the look in your eyes when you read my texts or hear your sets. I knew after texting you that the next song you played was for me, even though you didn't know I was there listening. I would have never let you leave me."

He moves my bangs aside kissing me softly on the lips. "I will never let you leave me. You are my queen - my girl. Always and forever. I needed you to hate me to leave me and the wall you put up, I knew would save our love. It sounds crazy, but the more I texted you and the more you got mad, let me know I still had your heart. I'm sorry. It's all over now, and I hope you forgive me."

Gripping his hip with my good hand, I lean into him kissing him with more force.

Breathless from the kiss I answer him, "I'm trying. It's just so much to process."

Shy's cock twitches between us and I giggle into his mouth. When he pulls back I giggle more, "I have an idea of my own."

One of Shy's eyebrows lifts letting me know he is listening. I push up grabbing the bed remote and sit next to him. His cock bobs growing bigger every second, eager for our next exercise. Shy is smirking, and I know what he is thinking.

"What? You don't think I haven't been thinking of positions in this bed while I laid here?"

It's Shy's turn to laugh a deep hearty laugh. Shy's eyebrows rise though when I place the head of the bed a little bit below a normal leveled bed. I move the legs all the way up. I get up on my knees and move to straddle him, but when I turn away, I must shock him.

"Fuck yes. Give me that ass, Angel." Shy grips the globes of my ass spreading them to watch as I lower myself down over his cock. I know in this position his head is at the perfect level for him to watch his cock move in and out of me.

"Goddamn, I can see everything," he exclaims.

I giggle.

With the end of the bed raised all the way up I can grip the bed easier, giving me leverage to ride him like a jockey rides a horse.

I close my eyes in ecstasy. I rock my hips simultaneously with him starting out slow and increasing with each thrust. Shy's hands are so large, and when he spreads them wide, he palms both of my ass cheeks guiding them up and down onto his cock.

"Fuck. Angel." He grunts from behind me.

While I'm riding him hard and fast, I slip a hand down to play with my clit, and I cry out his name. Shy grips the base of his cock using our wetness to lube my ass before slipping a thumb in.

"That's it, Angel. I love watching you ride my cock. Fuck yeah." I moan, liking the feeling of him milking my ass. I keep riding, bouncing faster and faster. My pussy clenches down, and my orgasm hits me hard with a painfully pleasurable release.

"Micah." I start to moan his name with each thrust. My body is shaking, and I'm about to collapse when Shy leans up grabbing me around my chest and pulling me back onto his chest.

"Kick your legs out," Shy demands.

I do as he says and we fall back to the mattress together.

Shy grips each breast while spreading his legs and then starts to jackhammer into my pussy. He's breathing hard against my ear. "Fuck yes. You're - my girl. Yeah. Oh, God."

I grip his hands over my tits and squeeze harder, pinching my nipples between his fingers. Feeling another orgasm about to crash over me, I cry out yes repeatedly. I tilt my head back toward him taking his mouth, muffling our moans while we both come together.

We're both exhausted when Shy pivots up so we're on our sides. He grabs the bed remote putting it back to normal before he gets up to clean himself off and return with a hot wet towel to clean me. I can't move or think of anything but him and the song that starts to play next, "Angel" by Sarah McLachlan.

GINGER

I wake the next morning to an empty bed. I sort of panic and try to decide if last night was a dream or not. I roll over to get up, and my body aches to let me know it wasn't a dream. A smile creeps across my lips thinking of last night, of him holding me. I roll over onto my stomach smelling his pillow and wondering where he went. Did he leave? I get out of bed and hobble over to use the bathroom, throwing on a pair of boy shorts and a tee.

When I start down the stairs I hear men's voices in the kitchen; I slow trying to figure out who is with Shy. When I hear my father's voice, I descend the rest of the way and enter the kitchen. What I find is a shirtless Shy and a very angry father.

I pause at the door weighing my options, and I try to figure out why my father is mad. I hope it's not because Shy is half naked in our kitchen and when my father says good morning I know it's not that.

Shy's back is to me, and I say good morning back but don't take my eyes off Shy's tattoo until he turns towards me.

Goddamn, he isn't a little boy anymore.

Butterflies take flight in my stomach only to be overpowered by hunger when my stomach rumbles. Shy comes to me wrapping his arms around me. "Did we wake you?"

I shake my head no, and by the look on my father's face, I know something happened.

"What happened?" I say.

Shy speaks first, but my eyes are locked with my father's.

"I came down here when I heard the front door, and I was about to make some breakfast. Your father was just telling me about what happened this morning."

Moving away from Shy, I ask my father directly knowing I can tell if he is lying or not. "Daddy, what is going on?"

My father is leaning against the counter with his arms folded. "Gus and Izzy had some car trouble on the way here, but everything is fine. They should be here any minute."

"What do you mean car trouble?" I fire back.

I look at the two men standing in my kitchen when the doorbell rings. My father moves out of the kitchen, so I turn my stare to Shy and repeat myself. "What kind of car trouble?

Before Shy can answer, I hear a gasp and then. "Fuck me till Tuesday."

I turn to see Izzy walking into the kitchen with her strawberry blonde hair piled on top of her head in a wild bun. She is wearing yoga pants showing her slender model-like legs. She's always full of piss and vinegar. I smile at her, but her eyes are glued on Shy, who is still behind me.

"God was generous the day he made you, my friend. Fuck!"

Gus who is right behind her, warns, "Iz."

I laugh, "Hey Iz!"

She breaks her stare for a minute to embrace me with a beautiful wide smile on her face.

God, I've missed her.

Shy must move behind me again because she keeps going. "Please tell me you are fucking this fine piece of godliness."

When I hear throats being cleared, I know more men have entered the room. I pull away from Izzy realizing I'm in boy shorts, when I turn around to face not just Gus, but my father and Mac.

Sonovabitch!

Yeah, this isn't good. No bra and in my panties. Fuck me. Shy moves to stand next to me and Izzy doesn't take her eyes off of him.

"Put some fuckin' clothes on." Gus is always serious, so I don't move, but instead, cross my arm over my chest, holding my arm with the cast to kind of hide my hardening nipples.

"What the fuck happened with your car?" I rant.

Gus moves to stand next to Izzy and says, "We had two flat tires, this morning. We think it was just some random act of vandalism since we were at a hotel and no one knew where we were staying. Now can you both go put some fuckin' clothes on yer arses."

I look to Izzy, but her eyes are still on Shy when she says "Why do they need to put clothes on? I think they look great."

Gus smacks her ass hard and swiftly, making Izzy yelp and her face turn beet red. Gus groans, saying something in Gaelic while rubbing his hands over his unshaven stubbled face.

Holy Shit. Two flat tires and something is up with these two.

Mac starts laughing, and Shy grabs me around the waist, pulling me towards the stairs. Shy grabs his shirt and we both hurry to get changed. "Is she always this crazy?" Shy asks before we head back down.

I laugh making my descent down the stairs, "Yes, she doesn't hold back what she's thinking. That is what I love about her."

When we enter the kitchen, Izzy is sitting on the counter with Gus standing next to her while Mac and my father lean up against the counters across the room. Our kitchen is big with a four person table in the middle. Cabinets line all four walls with two ways to enter. One from the front of the house and one from the back.

I take a seat at the table and Shy stands to the side of me. Izzy watches us with a smile. "Gin, how are you feeling today? You look good, kinda like you're glowing."

When she says, glowing really slow, I know she is fishing, wondering if I got laid.

"Hm, crazy I was going to say the same about you. It must be the West Virginia air," I fire back.

She keeps her smile but I see her cheeks turn slightly pink and I make a mental note to ask about what is going on with her and Gus later.

Shy starts to make breakfast while we catch up on what everyone knows. Gus heads out to get their stuff and my father and Mac head back over to the clubhouse leaving Izzy, Shy and myself in the kitchen. Izzy had moved down to the table to sit with me, and we watch Shy move around the kitchen cooking.

Izzy tries to be quiet, but I know Shy can hear her. "Uh, hello GinGin. Me likey. What the fuck girl? You need to spill, and you need to spill now."

I laugh fidgetting with my hands, explaining, "Remember you telling me, you need a lot of alcohol to tell me about you and Dom? Well, let's just say we can swap stories that night."

Izzy throws her head back laughing, "Well fuck me, pull out the Patron and let's get this party started."

Gus walks in just at that moment. "The fuck you say?"

Shy turns around with a plate of food for me laughing. "I would love to be a fly on the wall that night."

"I'm sure you would," Izzy snaps.

Shy folds his arms over his chest, squaring off with her. "You're damn straight I would since she is *my girl* and all."

Izzy turns to me. "What the fuck happened since I was gone? Lordy-lordy."

My face turns red and Shy leans down to kiss my head, "Eat. We got places to be today."

"What? Where? I thought the club was on alert and I couldn't leave."

Shy smiles. "Angel, I said *you* couldn't leave without me

with you. We have to go to Felicia's for a bit. I thought you would want to show Izzy the place."

Shy knows something or is up to something. I can see it in his face, but I just go with it and nod.

"What's Felicia's?" Izzy asks.

I smile turning to my friend. "A strip club."

Izzy's face lights up. "Fuck yes!"

Gus groans followed by a string of words in Gaelic, so we don't know what the fuck he is saying, but I know it isn't good. I'm sure he's having flashbacks to when we all went to a strip club in Spain.

The boys went into one of the side rooms where we have big group parties. Obviously, they needed to have privacy and didn't want us to hear. There were also a few men I didn't recognize that were brought in by a prospect to the room. They left us a while ago and told us they would be out in a bit, leaving a couple of prospects out here with us, and since the place is closed, they really don't have to worry about anything happening to us.

I introduce Izzy to the girls who are all practicing. Tawnya, who goes by Lolli since she is always sucking on a damn lollipop, is dancing to one of the songs I remixed for them, "Pour Some Sugar On Me" by Def Leppard, and we are all watching.

Izzy and I sit at a table, and we've both had three shots of Patron. So far all we've been talking about is stripper moves and how they could use some pointers to update their stuff. She leans towards me, and says, "So how are you really doing? I mean with all this" -she waves a hand in the air while pouring us another shot- "Shy and Brant shit, that is?"

I've been nervously waiting for the questions to start, but

now that I have liquor in my system I don't seem to mind.

I reply, "I was a fucking mess, but the more I think about it, the more it makes sense. I'd get all these messages and they always seemed to come at the craziest times. I sometimes wondered if he was around or how he knew to text or call me right at a moment I needed someone."

I swallow another shot making this my fifth, and know damn well I'm going to be trashed soon since I am still on medication and haven't really been drinking.

Izzy laughs. "Girl, it's like the fucking fairy tale."

I am about to ask her what the fuck she is talking about when she continues.

Izzy lifts one of her fingers to point at me before using it to count and says, "First, Snow White lost her mother."

She raises another finger.

"She was put under an evil spell."

Her third finger goes up.

"Then the prince's kiss awakens her."

Izzy laughs placing both hands on the table, leaning in closer to me so she can explain it better. "The dwarfs you already know are the MC."

I nod my head.

"The Huntsman is Brant who saves you from being killed. In your story, it's more like he saves you from your own misery."

Jesus, I never thought of this. I don't say anything or acknowledge her, so she keeps going, "You eat the fucking apple. In your story, you believe what your father and Shy tell you, which breaks your heart, kills your spirit, and throws you into a dream-like state."

I nod getting where she is going with this. "The prince's kiss awakens you. But in your story Shy comes and fucks the shit out of you, making you realize the truth, that he never gave you up."

Izzy takes another shot before leaning back in her chair. "See, total- fucking- fairy- tale."

Oh, my fucking God.
I start to bust up laughing, and she joins in making us both laugh even harder.

Izzy stops laughing first. "Seriously girl. You look and sound different. Just being around these guys and these girls, you look complete. Don't get me wrong, you are still my Gin, but that thing that was missing inside you was your biker roots. Something I knew was inside you but were too scared or just didn't want anyone to see. I know music is your world, but damn girl, don't hide who you are, and that is a fucking biker. I can see it's in your soul. Shit, we all can see it, I mean you ride a fucking Ninja for Christ's sake."

I sit back in my chair, tears welling in my eyes and look over to see Lolli descending the pole. I can't believe everyone around me understands me more than I do. Maybe I have been too deep into my own self-misery to see what was really going on around me.

"Iz, you're so fucking right." My voice coming off shaky. I cough trying to clear it giving Izzy time to interrupt in her sassy voice.

"I know. I am pretty fucking awesome." She takes another shot as I continue.

"Girl, I have always felt that I couldn't be both and live both lifestyles, but these last few weeks I see that I can. I can be both people. I just need to make time for each and balance everything in my life."

"Well, Gin it all comes with life experiences. You moved to New York at the age of fucking what, eighteen-nineteen years old? Who fucking does that? Not many, but you did, and you did it for something you love- music. You just thought you had to leave behind the biker, but damn girl, we all saw that bitch wanting to come out and play," Izzy replies.

Izzy laughs, and we both take another shot. Lolli's song ends and the girls all whistle and holler at her. Izzy clears her throat grabbing my attention, and when I look over at her, I see the crazy idea forming in her head.

"So... before the boys come out, I need to have some fun. Do you think I can have the stage for one song and show these girls a thing or two?"

I laugh knowing damn well this girl can dance and definitely can show these West Virginia girls a thing or two, so I reply, "Fuck yes, you can."

We both take another shot and get up moving toward the stage. I feel light headed from the shots and know Izzy is buzzed as well since she wants to dance.

I scan the girls and see Lolli. She's Izzy's size, tall, long legs and I ask, "Tawnya, can you show my girl Izzy some of your stuff? I think my girl here wants to show your girls a thi-" a hiccup escapes me "...ing or-" hiccup "...two."

All the girls laugh but when Izzy steps forward they quiet. "If not, I don't really need them. I just won't do the dead drop."

All the girls are looking at her wondering what the fuck she is even talking about but Tawnya moves forward telling Izzy to follow her. I move toward the DJ booth knowing I'll be able to find one of her songs.

A few minutes later, Izzy walks out on stage still in her shorts and a tank top but she's now wearing thigh high black pleather platform boots with her long strawberry blonde hair flowing down her back.

I laugh, excited to see all the looks on these girls' faces. Once I start the song, I exit the booth taking a seat in front of the stage along with the rest of the girls, even Felicia and Sissy have come from behind the bar.

Izzy giggled, stretching her arms, rubbing the pole with her hands and bends at the waist stretching her legs. Once the song "S&M" by Rihanna comes on, she smiles down at me and instantly switches into stripper mode.

Izzy starts out grabbing the pole moving side to side, flicking her hair around and with both arms, she holds herself up while she kicks her legs up into what looks like a karate style kick while she twirls around the pole. She continues to move around reaching higher up the pole and with one hand windmills her body around the pole with her legs spread wide before hooking them around the pole.

She is very beautiful with her strawberry blonde hair flying around in the air. Izzy's body is lean and fit, and when she pulls herself up the pole, you can see her muscles flex.

Half way up the pole she wraps her legs around the pole and into a sitting position higher up.

Izzy then leans her upper body back extending her arms out before she drops about a foot down the pole leaving her hanging upside down. She slides down a bit more when her hands are touching the ground looking like she is doing a headstand against the pole. She unhooks one leg outstretching it leaving the other foot hooked around the pole sliding herself into the splits. Izzy's legs are so long it looks fucking amazing.

All the girls are going crazy, and when I hear a couple of cat calls from behind me, I look to see we have a bigger crowd now with all the men back. Shy, Mac, Quick, Dallas and Gus make their way over to us girls while most of the others stay at the bar where Hawk is handing out drinks. The guys take a seat with us, but all eyes are on Izzy except Shy's who is smiling at me. I smile back but turn around to watch Izzy.

Izzy is on the stage tossing her hair around. She has the perfect size tits, and her legs go on for miles. She grabs the pole slipping it between her legs by thrusting up and down against it. Pretty much fucking it, when I hear Gus say, "Iz, bloody hell."

I don't know if she heard him or not but she turns her body with the pole behind her and slowly uses it to lower herself into a squat. She's looking straight at Gus and signs the chorus of the song about liking whips and chains. She moves her hand up her body and over her tits antagonizing him. Gus growls a string of words we don't understand, but you can tell he is trying not to react to her. Izzy breaks their challenging stare-off to move back up to a standing position before turning to face the pole.

"Fuck me. She's good," Mac says from behind me. She starts to twirl around it faster getting enough motion to fling herself up around it, going around the pole while she reaches up higher with each twirl. She extends her body from the pole only holding herself up by her hands making her body look like a fucking flag.

Shy leans forward and says in a whisper, "Tell me she gave you lessons because fuck I want to see your ass up there next."

I turn laughing. "I know a thing or two but you will have to wait till I'm all healed."

Shy smiles but curses under his breath, leaning back in his chair. When I turn back to watch Izzy, she is at the top of the pole all the way up at the ceiling, and the pole is between her legs, which are bent and her feet are wrapped around it as well. She leans to the left moving her upper body in front of the pole so she can stretch her arms out like she is bowing to us. Izzy smiles down flicking her hair behind her and then she does it. She does a dead drop, with her arms spread out she drops half way down the pole before she clenches the pole with only her legs and everyone goes fucking crazy.

The guys are yelling, and I can only laugh. I love this crazy girl. She reaches behind her, gripping the pole, releasing her legs, and sliding down the remainder of the pole landing on the ground. It's like she is breakdancing with the pole. She gyrates around a couple more times, flipping her body before she lands. Izzy walks around the pole flipping her hair back out of her face, and she starts to laugh.

Everyone is up off their feet clapping and whistling.

Shy moves up behind me wrapping an arm around my waist pulling me into him.

"Angel, she had to have been a stripper before."

I keep facing forward, my eyes on Izzy who is heading back

to the changing rooms when I answer. "No, she used to teach pole dancing back home in Calfornia at her gym, and she's really good."

Shy laughs replying, "No shit?"

I sit back down with Shy next to me when Felicia starts up, "Christ almighty that girl can dance."

I take another shot. "She's pretty much good at anything she puts her mind to. She loves to dance and definitely loves pole dancing."

Gus gets up and heads toward Izzy, who is now back in her flip-flops heading toward us. Gus stops her and moves to her side, cupping her neck. Izzy's face goes blank. Gus leans down, pulling her to him, and I can see him whisper something into her ear. Izzy's eyes close, inhaling a big breath but she doesn't say anything or even look at him. He releases his hold on her moving toward the bar to get another drink. Izzy stands there a beat, and when her smile spreads across her face, I let out the breath that I didn't realize I was holding. I would have flipped out if Gus made her upset for dancing. He's possessive of her I know, but he shouldn't get upset with her for dancing.

Izzy takes her chair on the other side of me, and all the girls start in asking question's, while we all just sat around bullshitting. About thirty minutes later with the bottle of Patron gone, Felicia's yelling for everyone to get back to work, it's almost time for the club to open. Izzy and I are pretty shit-faced and Shy says it's time for us to head back.

GINGER

It's a week later, Izzy and Gus left four days ago but today is the day they leave on tour, and I'm sad. I had the best time with Izzy here. Having her here just made it so much better. I liked having both worlds together and know it will all be okay. We had a lot of heart to heart talks, and I think it was good for both of us. We've never really just hung out, the two of us, without Alex or someone with us. I enjoyed her visit more than words could express, and she said the same thing.

Izzy explained to me about her and Dominic fighting all the time. I knew she was into kinky shit. I just didn't know all that it entailed. She told me about him being a dominant person, but when he started trying to change her, bossing her around and even getting a bit more forceful during sex, she got upset. They are still together, and they talk every day. But she took a break and headed home to her parents to have some time to think. She's meeting him back in New York before they all go on tour. She said everything was fine now and she's happy, so I didn't push.

I like to be dominated, but when I want something, I don't hesitate to take it either. Shy gave me space to be with my friend, but he was never far off with Gus right next to him. I got shit faced drunk every day with her and was fucked into submission by Shy every night, passing out only to wake the next day to do it all over again.

 I asked her about her and Gus, but all she said was they had become close, and he gets her. When I pushed for more, she told me it was hard to explain but just that he understood her and they were friends. I let it go, but anyone could see they were more than friends, even if they didn't know it themselves. Anyone around them could tell they had feelings for each other.

 The last day they were here was the best day, we all went on a ride. We didn't go far, only to the creek, but it was a good ride. Gus borrowed a club bike. Everyone sat around in the sun drinking beer while a few of the others got into the creek. Izzy and I just hung out and talked.

 I'm thankful that Gus nor Izzy judged me for being with Shy. I still haven't spoken with Brant. He texted me saying he will be out of the country but would text when he got back. I replied for him to be safe and that we needed to talk when he got back. I found out he had to go to Spain to help Sasha bring her stuff back over and get ready for the tour. Izzy slipped up one day telling me about what was planned for the tour. I need to make that call but would rather do it in person.

 When I asked Gus about Brant, his answer was, "It's yer own business, las." Gus doesn't say much as it is, so I took that as a good sign. Shy and I haven't spoken about it either. Every day Shy makes time for me, and we have our little moments. He loves to set me off and see my hellion side come out only to tame it by fucking me or kissing me stupid.

 My father has been in and out of the compound leaving us to have fun, but he too checks in with me seeing how I am feeling. I guess there is a lot of club business to be dealt with in our other chapters taking him away.

 Since Izzy left, I've been working on music, trying to keep myself busy. Luc sent me his changes to my original song that

I have been working on. Music always seems to keep me in a good mood. The girls from the club have been stopping by every day as well. There have been no more incidents in New York, and they haven't heard of any blowback from them taking over the Scorpions.

Shy and I are heading back to New York next week. I have a doctor's appointment for a check up on all my injuries. I am hoping I get to take my boot off, but I still have another few weeks before my cast is removed.

Tonight we are setting up to have a party since I'll be headed back to New York for a while. I am sitting by the fire with Sissy and Gigi drinking a beer when I see out of the corner of my eye a head full of red hair. I don't think anything about it, thinking it's Trina, the girl my cousin has had around a few times, but when I see her come into full view, I see it's Raven. She is headed straight toward Shy and Mac standing over by the bikes. I stand up and when Gigi sees who I have my sights on she says, "Stupid fucking bitch just doesn't get it."

I move toward them with Gigi on my tail. When Shy sees her headed his way, he immediately looks to me, seeing I'm on my way toward them. Shy smiles at me and turns his body toward me ignoring Raven when she comes to stand in front of them. His shoulder is turned to her, and that is when I hear her yelling, "What the fuck? I'm banned from here because you two fuckers don't want to get your dick wet anymore?"

Mac steps forward looking murderous. "You are banned from here because you're a bitch. You complained more than you sucked dick. You need to leave, Rave."

Shy is still smiling at me, and when I walk up, he kisses me, pulling me into his side but I push off to face Raven. "I never did thank you," I say in a matter of fact voice.

When she squares on me, she folds her arms over her chest pressing her tits up over her already low cut tank top. "Thank me for what?" she replies bitchily.

I laugh at her and take a step toward her. "For letting me know my man here was watching me for all these years. I had no idea and just think if you didn't say anything I would have never known."

"The fuck you wouldn't have. I was going to tell you," Shy grits out coming to stand behind me. Knowing damn well to keep clear of me.

I reply facing her with a fake smile across my face. "Well, whatever, I just thought I'd tell her thanks."

Rave's face scrunches together looking even more pissed off with Shy behind me putting his arms around me. She looks over my shoulder at Shy. "All these years for this? She must have a magical pussy because she isn't that special."

"Bitch, you better leave now before I have you removed, *again*," Shy snarls from behind me.

Rave laughs looking straight at me now. "What she can't stand up for herself?"

I feel everyone start to crowd around me and I know I'm safe, but the whore obviously doesn't know me. I take two more steps, standing face to face, only inches away. I have to give this whore credit she never hesitates or backs away. She just stands there with her arms crossed.

"Rave, you need to leave. I don't think you want your ass beat and it is obvious you're not wanted here anymore. I'm pretty sure Trina and myself can handle it from here."

Rave's face turns beet red turning her head towards Mac, and I see her jaw clenching. She is seething, and I laugh at her. "Oh, you didn't know. My bad."

Rave turns back to face me. "Well, Princess I'll be back, and I bet when you're off in New York, your man here will still be sinking his-" I don't give her chance to finish the sentence when I push her, and she stumbles back.

I hear Shy say something but I move forward, and when Raven comes back with her fist I move to the side and bring my right hand up connecting with her face. Shy has me up over his shoulder before she can recover. Raven's nose is bleeding, and I love it.

I'm hanging over Shy's shoulder, while I scream at Raven holding her nose. "Fuck you!" Mac is pulling Raven toward her car, but I keep yelling. "Bitch, now you know. Don't fuck with me or what's mine."

Shy smacks my ass telling me to shut up and I lean down smacking his ass back.

When I see my auntie storming over to where they have Raven I know she will handle it from there.

Holy shit that felt so good. I feel alive!

Shy places me down onto the picnic table, grabbing my hand to inspect it when my father comes rushing up with Cash. "What in the hell happened?"

Shy is trying to hold back the laughter when he says, "Well, I think our lone wolf just made her claim and became the alpha female around here."

"She was talking shit, and I just lost it," I defend myself.

My father looks over to see Raven being placed in her car with a bloody nose screaming at Mac and my auntie. I am waiting for my father to say something, but Shy kissing my right hand, has me turning to lock eyes with him.

My father chuckles. "Well, it's about fucking time someone put that skank whore in her place. Storm has run her off a handful of times, maybe this time the bitch will stay gone."

That bitch will be gone for good. I promise.

GINGER

Today I had my doctor appointment in New York. Shy and about six of his guys rode out with us yesterday. I was worried it was going to be hard to ride for seven plus hours with my cast and boot, but it wasn't bad. We left early and stopped a few extra times. It felt good to go on a long ride instead of the short ones Shy has been taking me on. When I get cranky lately Shy would tell me to get on the bike and he would take me for a ride. He knows either music, riding, or sex are the only things to calm my craziness.

I was worried I would run into some of the guys at the apartment, but Izzy told me on the phone that everyone was gone but maybe Beau and Luc. She told me Brant has not been happy these past few weeks on the road. I have messaged him a few times but haven't heard anything back. I'm sure Alex or Izzy told him I'm back with Shy. A couple nights ago I got a call at three AM from a blocked caller, but no one was there when I answered it. Shy flipped out wanting to know who it was and the next morning he told Dallas to track the call, which caused me to flip the fuck out.

Last night was weird, having Shy in my apartment instead of

Brant, and coming back here has me pretty emotional. I had such a different life here but like Izzy said, I was missing something. That something was Shy, but my heart hurts for Brant too. He was like my best friend, and now he's gone. I know things will never be the same and it's hard to swallow. I'm also worried if Shy will be able to handle my lifestyle here. My life here in New York is so busy and fast paced compared to living in West Virginia where everything is *not* busy or fast. Being a biker and living the lifestyle is a whole different world and I hope he can handle both. Shit, I don't even know if I can live both lifestyles.

My doctor's appointment went well. They took off my boot, but my cast will remain for two more weeks. My ribs are healing well but are still sore when I move a certain way. My gun shot wounds are healing nicely, and my head scan looks clear. So overall, I'm almost completely healed.

After my appointment, Shy takes me over to see the clubhouse. I gasp when we walk in. They have done so much to it or at least what Shy explains they changed. Shy introduces me to all his guys, a lot of them are patched over from the Scorpions. Striker and a few of the elder men are still wearing their Scorpion cuts. Striker greeted us when we arrived but left soon after having a doctor's appointment himself.

The place is coming along nicely but is still under construction. Shy says they will be up and running in a month. I can't believe he's been doing this all remotely from West Virginia. I know he should be here with them, but instead, he's been staying with me. I wonder what is going to happen when I go on tour and if he'll have to stay behind.

Shy takes me over to my apartment so I can rest and work on music while he heads out to take care of some club business. I'm more than happy to have some time alone in my apartment so I can regroup. I know Shy has a lot on his plate seeing all the men and the construction going on. He's dealing with the patch over and all the men from both clubs becoming one unit. He hasn't discussed with me too much of what's happened with the takeover, but I know there is still a threat out there because he's been getting phone calls that I've overheard.

Later that day I'm laying on my bed, alone just listening to music looking up at the ceiling. I love to listen to music and hear all the sounds and beats to the song. I love dissecting it and thinking of how I can make it different.

I've been home for a couple hours now, and I've spoken with Izzy who is in Detroit. They seem to be having a great time, and I can't wait to meet up with them in Los Angeles. Izzy was telling me she and Dominic are still fighting but other than that they're having fun. She told me watching Alex and Maddox perform is like another level of good. She couldn't stop talking about it. She says it's like they've been doing it for years not months.

I spoke with Luc after asking him if I could come into the studio, but he told me I could just use his studio at the house that way I didn't have to leave the building. He said most of his men were with the girls on tour or with some of the other DJs. I told him it was okay, that I just wanted a studio and it didn't matter where, so I planned to be at his house tomorrow morning.

I know Shy had a bunch of club business and I needed to get back into my usual routine. I prayed we could work something out and make this work between us. My heart hurts every time I think of Brant. I needed to speak to him and see him face to face. I asked Luc if he could tell Brant to call me, but he hasn't returned any of my calls. Luc laughed and said he'd relay the message. I wonder if he knows about us, but I didn't ask.

Shy texts me that he will be home soon, so I get up and start cooking dinner. When I hear the front door unlock, I freeze, knowing I only gave a key to Brant.

NO! He can't be back.

I panic and run to the door but when the door opens and in walks Shy, I relax, but I'm still confused. Shy sees the look on my face and drops his bag. "What the fuck? Are you okay? What happened?"

Knowing I look freaked but not wanting him to know why I recover by snapping, "Fuck Shy, how did you get a key. I was freaked out wondering who the fuck was opening my door."

Shy laughs. "Angel, I've had a key to your place since the day you moved in and don't think we didn't put cameras in here too." Shy bends down to pick up his bag, shutting the door and giving me a kiss before walking by me.

What the ever loving fuck! Fuck!

I stand there frozen, staring at the door. I start to go over all the times Brant and me were together, trying to remember if we were ever in my place or was it at his. When I remember we were always at his house, I become enraged, for two reasons - one because Brant knew they had cameras on me and two they had mother fucking cameras on me. When I turn around, I can't see Shy, so I move slowly becoming more enraged with each step I take. When Shy emerges from my room, I unleashed my wrath.

"What the fuck did you say? You have cameras in my apartment?" My voice is laced with so much anger that Shy steps back in his tracks, realizing he slipped up but recovers by saying.

"Yes, you didn't really think your father would let his princess move away without having eyes on you at all times."

Shy takes two steps in my direction, and I hold my stare on him thinking to myself of all the ways I could hurt him.

I know I can't physically hurt him with my injuries, but at least with my boot off I am quicker, so when he goes to grab me, I slip by him.

"Hell no! I am pissed off. Where are these cameras at, I want them removed."

Shy laughs. "I'll remove them. They're only at the front door and living room. We gave you some privacy."

I have my hands on my hips, not believing him. "All of them,

Shy, I'm serious. I know you, and you probably put a camera in each room."

Shy pounces on me, and we both drop to the couch with him landing on me. I squeal out his name before his mouth crashes over mine making me forget what we were talking about.

SHY

Our mouths dance, growing more demanding with each swipe of the tongue. I grip her waist bringing her up with me only to switch positions with me sitting on the couch. I have her straddling me, with her boot off I don't have to worry about hurting her.

I break the kiss, leaning my head forward, touching our foreheads together I look her in the eyes. Those gems are swirling with desire, and need, and I know she wants to take me.

"Angel, I want you to ride my cock."

Taking her here in her apartment is something I want, no I need. Last night when we got here, I knew she was having a hard time with coming back to her old life, and I wanted to be there for her, so I just held her and talked all night.

Ginger leans back gripping her shirt, and I move to help her lift it over her head. When she throws it to the side, I reach behind her unclasping her bra.

Fucking Heaven.

My mouth waters looking at her raised nipples just begging me to take them. I slide my tongue out barely flicking one of them.

"Shy, please!" Ginger whines while thrusting her heated center against my hardening cock.

I grab the waistband of her boy shorts and slide them over her ass gripping her globes when I thrust up against her. I muffle her cry with my mouth. Ginger leans up so I can slide her shorts down and once she is naked she pushes me back deepening our kiss, placing her hands on either side of my head.

I undo my jeans, barely sliding them past my ass, just enough to free my cock. I stroke it letting out a deep growl from within. I break the kiss. "I need you to smother my cock with that beautiful pussy of yours."

Ginger smiles while lowering herself down onto my cock. Her pussy is so wet and ready I take her fully in one shot.

"God, yes. Micah," she breathes.

Ginger wraps her arms around my head, and I hug her close to me while she moves her hips back and forth, riding my cock.

She feels so fucking good.

"Fuck Angel. Faster," I grunt.

I suck one of her tits into my mouth and grab her ass lifting her and pounding my dick up into her. She screams my name over and over, while she prays to God that I fuck her faster - which I do.

I feel her release and want us to come together, but need to be deeper. In one motion I flip us, placing her on the couch. I have one leg on the couch, but the other is stretched out to the ground. I lift her legs up over her head with her knees touching her shoulders, and I fuck deep and hard as hell.

No boot - equals deeper fucking.

"Yes. fuck me," she screams.

"Yeah, Angel. I got you."

The couch is pounding against the wall, and if she has neighbors on this adjoining wall, they definitely knew what we were doing.

"Love your tight pussy," I praise.

Another orgasm rips through her with her walls clamping down around my cock and with a couple more thrusts I see stars with my own release.

"Fu-ck y-ess!"

I release her legs but don't move from inside her. I lower

myself, taking her mouth with a moan, while I slowly pump in and out of her, spilling my last drop of cum into her.

Motherfucken heaven.

23

SHY

My phone vibrating on the nightstand wakes me, and being the president of a club means you can never ignore your phone. After our sexcapade on the couch, we ended up having dinner and then went straight to bed where I fucked her senseless again. With our limbs entangled, I don't want to move, but I need to grab my phone, so I stretch out hoping I don't wake her.

Mac's number blinks across my screen.

"Whaddup," I say in the lowest voice I can.

"Prez, you're needed at the clubhouse, we got issues," Mac replies rushed.

I know his voice, and he wouldn't be calling me if he didn't have to, so I don't even question him but reply, "Give me ten."

"Five if you can," Mac fires back.

Goddamn it.

I am moving off the bed before I can even hang up and once I pull my arm out from under Ginger, she's awake.

"Something wrong?" she asks, wiping her eyes.

Pulling my jeans on, I sit back down on the bed grabbing my boots.

"Yeah, Angel, I have to run to the clubhouse. Go back to

sleep. I should be back before long. If I can't be back before you wake up, I'll text you."

I lean over giving her a quick kiss and then I'm out the door.

Parking my bike at the clubhouse, I notice the parking lot is full of bikes. That can only mean something bad happened if we got other chapters here.

I walk into the clubhouse, and I see Wolfe, Bear, Mac, Cash, and Hawk. Wolfe sees me and motions for me to follow him. I say hello and give my head nod following Wolfe into my office. Once I shut the door, I turn to face Wolfe

"What the fuck is going on?" I sound more irritated than concerned.

"We got a problem. Snake and a few of his boys were sighted thirty miles North of here at a bar. They were starting fights and took two girls from the bar. We don't know if the girls went willingly or not, but they were throwing around our name causing havoc."

Motherfucker. I knew I should've just shot his ass.

Wolfe says what I am thinking. "We should've shot the mother fucker when we had the chance. Now we need to head out and try to find them. They'll only keep causing shit."

I nod my head. "Let's get everyone on board and split up so we can cover more ground."

Wolfe agrees and before he can open the door, I ask, "We need to get Snow back to your clubhouse where I know she'll be safe. Luc doesn't have enough men here to watch her, and until the construction is done here and I know she'll be safe I want her at your clubhouse. Let's leave a couple of prospects at the building, but we need to have everyone on alert."

Wolfe nods his head and answers, "I already spoke with Luc earlier, and he said she has studio time tomorrow and after she is done, he would get her back to my place safe. I think her in one of his SUVs compared to being on the back of a bike is safer for her. I trust him, so he'll make sure she is safe."

Knowing Brant is gone I agree too, and once Wolfe leaves the office, I pull out my cell phone.

Ginger answers after the first ring but sounds like she was still sleeping. "Is everything okay?"

"Angel, we have some club business that is going to take me out of town for a day or two. I know we were going to head back to your dad's, but I need for you to head back without me. Luc is going to take care of you and get you back home safe after you are done with studio time."

She cuts me off sounding fully awake now. "Is everyone okay? I can wait here for you, I have my song that needs to be finished, so we can release it."

"No, you need to spend as much time there as you can because soon you'll be coming back for your cast removal. Then you'll be heading out on tour so go get some more rest and let Storm baby you. I will meet you there as soon as I can."

When I hear her sigh, I know I have won and she will do what I say. "Okay Shy. Please just text or call to let me know you are okay."

I smile to myself, knowing she cares and is worried. It feels so good to have her back, it's like the years apart never happened.

"I gotta go Angel, but I love you and will call when I can."

"I love you too and be safe," she says in a low voice.

I answer reassuring her I'll be back, "Angel, nothing is going to take me away from you. I just got you back. See you in a couple days."

When she replies with a yawn, I laugh and hang up.

Three hours later my club and I head northeast, while Wolfe and his club head north and our other chapters head west and south.

GINGER

The next morning I wake up to my phone ringing, and I jump to answer it thinking it could be Shy letting me know he's on his way back. After we hung up last night, I couldn't fall back to sleep, so I am exhausted and answer without even looking to see who is calling.

I answer half asleep. "He-hello."

"Shit, you asleep Gin?" Brant's voice echoes through the phone.

I bolt up in bed, becoming alert at hearing his voice.

"B, is that you?" I croak out.

Hearing him laugh eases the tension I feel from hearing his voice.

"Yeah, babe it's me. Luc sent me a text yesterday after you talked to him, saying you needed me to call you. Is everything okay?"

Yesterday?

My head starts to clear and I remember I did speak with Luc and asked him to get ahold of Brant. Then I remember Luc is supposed to get me home safe and before I know it I am blurting out, "I need you to come home."

Sonovabitch. Why...

Instantly Brant goes into defense mode. "Why, what happened? Are you okay?"

I feel bad and know it's wrong to ask him, but I want to see him and make it better between us, so I do what I know I shouldn't.

"Nothing is wrong, and I'm fine. I..." I pause taking a minute to make sure I should do this, but my heart tells me I need to do this, and with Shy gone, he won't make things worse, so I continue with confidence. "I just need a ride back to my dads and Luc is supposed to send one of his guys to make sure I'm okay. I just miss you and think we need to talk."

I hear Brant take a deep breath. "Where is Shy, Ginger?"

Feeling like shit, I explain, "Brant, I want to see you because I miss you. I'm worried about you. I know I asked for space-"

Brant interrupts me. "Ginger, I know you're back with him. You don't have to worry about me. I get it. I'm not happy, but I get it. You needed me to leave you alone so you could reconnect with him."

I get pissed off with his dick ass reply, and I lash back. "I needed space from both of you. *Both* of you, who lied to me."

"Ginger, I did my job, and *I am* sorry you feel the way you do, but I'm not the one you should be mad at. I loved you and did all that I could to make you happy, but it wasn't enough. I get it." He sounds hurt.

Does he love me? Shit. Easy girl. Don't freak out.

Taking a deep breath, I let it out, calming myself so I don't say something I will regret later.

"B, I'm sorry if I hurt you. That was the last thing I wanted to do, you're my best friend, and I miss you."

I hear commotion on the other end of his phone before he sighs. "Let me talk to Luc, and I'll give you a callback. I gotta go."

He hangs up before I can reply.

Goddamnit.

𝄞

The rest of the day goes by without incident. I get a text from Shy telling me he loves me. Then I get one from Luc telling me Mia is home and would let me in so I can use the studio. I spend most of the day in the studio trying to finish my song that is going to be released soon, but with my hand still in a cast, it's hard to maneuver. After I finish, Mia has dinner ready for me, and I stay to hang out with her since Luc isn't home.

When I am back at my apartment, I get another text from Shy with a link.

SHY
Angel I miss you. "The Reason" by Hoobastank

I smile clicking on the song while I read his text and reply with my own song link back.

GINGER
I miss you too. "Here Without You" by 3 Doors Down

Proud of myself I giggle putting my phone down on the nightstand thinking he probably wouldn't be replying right away, but when my phone vibrates I get giddy reaching for it.

SHY
Now you get it. I'm always near. "By Your Side" Sade

I reply with a quick love you and lay back on the bed listening to his songs. When my phone vibrates again, I laugh, picking it up thinking it would be Shy again, but it's Luc.

> **LUC**
> Be ready to head home tomorrow at noon. Your ride will be downstairs. See you in a couple of weeks.

I reply with a quick, okay and thank you. Exhaustion takes over and I end up passing out listening to music.

I wake up to someone pounding on my front door. I panic at first wondering who could be at the door since we have a bellman and no one can get up here unless they call or are on the list. I jump out of bed and run to the door. When I look out the peephole, I see Brant.

Holy fucking shit!

I make sure I am covered and then I panic remembering the cameras that Shy has up. When Brant yells to open up, I snap out of it and open the door.

"What the fuck, Gin?" Brant says, sounding pissed off, barreling through the door.

I shut the door. "What the fuck, B. Why are you here, beating on my door so early?" I reply.

Brant stands in my hallway with his hands clenched at his hips. "Gin its fucking twelve thirty in the afternoon. You were supposed to be downstairs a half hour ago, and you haven't replied to anyone's text or calls, so again what the fuck?"

Oh, my God.

I look around the room to my clock hanging on the wall and see he is telling the truth. Shaking my head, I think to last night and remember I didn't do anything but listen to music.

When I still don't reply, Brant moves towards me, and his facial expression goes from pissed off to worry. "Babe, you okay?"

When I take a step back, I immediately regret it the moment I see the hurt cross over Brant's face before he masks it.

"I'm sorry, I must have overslept, let me get ready." I start to move toward the bedroom when Brant grabs my arm pulling me to him.

"Gin, you sure you're okay? No one could get ahold of you." He brushes my bangs from my face, and I tilt my head into his touch. He smells so good and damn if he doesn't look amazing, but Shy's face flashes across my mind like he always does. This time I know I love him, without a doubt.

Brant must notice my gaze change too because he lets me go. "I'll be waiting in the car."

I grab his arm to stop him from going. "No, don't go. Please wait. Why are you here? I'm just seriously tired and not awake yet. You know how I get in the morning. Just give me a minute." I give him a smile hoping he believes me.

He nods, moving toward the couch. "I felt bad with the way we left things, and after talking to Luc I decided to come back so I could take you to your dad's and we could talk. Go get dressed and get your stuff ready to go while I call everyone and let them know you are okay," he explains.

"Everyone?" I question.

Brant nods. "Yeah, Luc, Wolfe, and Shy have been trying to get ahold of you, but you never replied, and when you didn't come down, I thought something was wrong."

What! Oh, God.

Before I can reply, Brant is headed toward my kitchen. I swing around and head toward my room, and when I grab my phone, I see it's dead. I didn't plug it in to charge last night. No wonder I didn't wake up. Plugging my phone in, I rush to get ready.

After a quick shower, I call Shy from the bathroom where I am getting ready. He answers on after the first ring.

"Angel, what the fuck happened." Shy's voice is even and calm, which surprises me.

"I was listening to music last night and forgot to plug my phone in, and it was dead this morning. I'm sorry for worrying everyone. I am getting ready to leave soon to head back to Dad's. How are you?" I try to change the subject, knowing he is going to bring up Brant.

"Is Brant with you?" Shy asks, his voice still coming off as calm.

Him sounding so calm gives me the nerve to speak out, nipping this convo in the bud so I can get on the road. "Shy, I didn't know Luc was going to have Brant take me home. You are the one that wanted me to go home and not wait here for you. He's here in the kitchen. He knows we're together and you have nothing to worry about. I need to get going so we can get on the road."

Shy doesn't reply, all I hear is silence. I can hear his breathing, so I know he didn't hang up, and just when I'm about to ask him if he is there, he replies, "Angel, I can't discuss this right now, but I'm far from fucking happy." Commotion in the background of men yelling cuts him off.

" Shy-"

But he cuts me off. "Keep your phone on *and charged*. I gotta go."

When the phone goes dead, I pull it away from my ear and look at it.

Motherfucker just hung up on me.

An hour later Brant and I are in his SUV headed toward my father's. After Shy hangs up on me, I looked at all my text messages. I replied to everyone that I was fine and explained that my phone died. I also messaged Shy letting him know I wasn't too happy with him hanging up on me only to follow it up with a text telling him I hoped he was okay and to text me.

Brant has been quiet so far letting me deal with everyone and getting us on the road, but now that all is well with everyone and we are settled I feel the empty silence killing me.

We used to always have things to talk about, so I turn in my seat to face him. His hair is cut short again, but I notice it's longer on top with a clean shave showing his strong jaw line. His skin isn't as tan, probably because he hasn't been in Spain much since Alex moved back to New York.

I've missed Brant, but I know now that we will only ever be friends and I need him to see that too. He has been my one constant all these years, but my heart has always been with Shy. I know that, and I think I always have, which is why I've always told Brant we could never be anything more than friends.

When his hand gripping the steering wheel flexes, I know he feels me looking at him. I lick my lips watching his biceps coil, expanding his shirt to the max.

Fuck me, he is fine. Why does he have to be so fucking cute?

"You need to quit looking at me like that, babe," Brant says with a tight mouth.

I snap out of my inner debate to fire back, "How are the girls? How is the tour so far? I hear Alex and Maddox are on fire with their performance. I also hear Dominic and Izzy's fighting is the same if not more annoying." I stop rambling and just sit there.

I don't move, and I definitely don't take my eyes off of him. I smile because I know he hates people staring at him. He's been my friend for so long it's hard to be anything else.

Taking a deep breath, he goes into detail about the girls, where they've been so far and how much they miss me all the while keeping his eyes on the road ahead of us. We go back and forth with ease falling back into our old friendly shit talking.

We are a few hours away from my father's, only stopping for gas and food, so we are making good time. Alex and Izzy have already called and shot the shit with us, so we are back to dead silence with just music playing. It's almost ten o'clock, so it's dark outside, but I'm still staring out the window into the darkness, thinking of Shy, who I still haven't heard from. When I look down at my phone, only to see there are still no messages,

I sigh.

"Why don't you just call him?" Brant's voice booms next to me, making me jump.

I glance over at him and smile. "You scared the shit out of me."

Brant turns the music down to a whisper. "Sorry, the music was loud."

Looking down to my phone in my lap, I lift it up, and I check it again. "He's busy with club business. He'll call when he has time."

Silence.

Glancing over I see Brant looking straight ahead, so I do the same, not knowing what else to say.

Silence.

"I've always known you loved him. I just thought if I could break that wall down and show you…" Brant doesn't finish, and I don't look over. Instead, I just stare out at the open road.

Silence.

"B, I can't lose you as my friend. I'm sorry if I led you on, I care so much for you. I just don't…" It's my turn to cut off my sentence not finishing. Words are stuck in my throat, and I blink the tears back.

I can't lose him too.

Silence.

"Babe, I knew going into this you didn't want anything serious. I knew and pushed for more, for that I am sorry. I'm not sorry for the time we had together, and yes, I am selfish and want more. But I also want you to be happy," he ends with a smile.

Goddamnit. Why does he have to be so perfect? Fuck!

Silence.

With tears in my eyes and a lump in my throat, I turn to him. "B, what'll make me happy is if you don't take your friendship from me. You know my abandonment issues, and if you leave, it will break me. You mean a lot to me and I don't want to lose you as a friend. If you need time I understand but please don't give up on me," I say.

Not Brant. I can't lose any more friends or family.

Brant makes eye contact with me. "Babe, I want to be with you. It'll be hard for me to be around you and him together but I'll try to deal with it the best I can. I can't say it'll be fun, but I will try. Until I know for sure you and him will last in both your worlds I will not give up on you," he replies.

"B, I don't want you to give up on our friendship. Regardless if Shy and I make it or not, my heart is taken."

Brant smiles, breaking eye contact first to look out the window. "Babe, don't you worry about me. I'll be here for you when you need me, like right now. Just keep being you, and we'll be fine. I promise."

"Okay, B."

We both stare out the window at the darkness flowing by on the open road.

25

BRANT

    I can't give her up and I will not stop trying until I know in my heart it's over. I can't lie and say it doesn't hurt like hell, her being with him, but I have thought long and hard about this. Shy has been watching her with me for years now. Granted he didn't know we were fucking around. I knew about his camera and knew about all his hiding places. We only flirted, but she has always been so closed off, not letting anyone past her wall.
    When her walls went down in Europe, I thought God had answered all my prayers. Just being around her makes me feel alive. Her shit-talking, bad-ass biker attitude just sets me on fire. I have been following that flame for years. Now that I got a taste I can't give it up yet.
    I'm going to let the roles be reversed and sit back and watch. I don't see Shy being able to live the music and fame lifestyle. Plus, he just became president of the Wolfeman's New York Chapter. I'll just be here for her when she needs me and bide my time.
    Glancing back over at her, I feel my dick twitch, and I try to calm myself. When I called Luc to see what was going on with her and he told me about the guys headed out to take care of a

threat to the club I jumped on a plane back to New York so I could be the one to drive her back.

These are the times I will have to steal with her to keep my foot in the door. I've never really been in love before, with Alex being the only girl I have ever cared about, but only as a sister. Ginger is the second woman I have ever wanted to spend all my time with. She is the only woman I have ever wanted to be monogamous with, and I jack off at least twice a day to pictures of her sleeping in my bed. I can't get her out of my mind, and I will not give up.

Headlights and the roar of motorcycles coming up behind us snaps me from my lustful thoughts of Ginger naked in my bed.

Ginger hears them too because she turns in her seat towards me. "Is that Shy and my dad?"

Looking into my rearview mirror, I answer, "From what I know, they were a day or two day's ride away. Call them."

Ginger grabs her phone and dials.

Let's pray it's Wolfe's club.

"Shy, are you behind us?"

Pause.

"Is my dad?"

Pause.

"We have-" Ginger turns to look behind us trying to count the bikes, but I answer.

"We have five maybe eight guys behind us. There are a couple cars back there so it could be a truck in the rear too, but I'm not sure."

"Did you hear that? Is it our guys?" she asks.

Pause.

Ginger answers okay before turning her phone on speaker. "You're on speaker now, Shy."

Shy's voice echoes through the speaker. "Brant, that is *not* our guys. Do not stop or let them get next to you."

Motherfucker.

"What do we have coming up our ass, *Shy* and how fast can your guys get to us? We are about thirty minutes away from the clubhouse on I-68," I bellow.

"Fuck! Give me a second." We hear Shy yelling at Mac to make a call but the bikes gaining on us has me forgetting the call and focusing on what I'm doing. I start to speed up and grab under my seat for my semi-automatic Sig 44 magnum.

When I pull it out, Ginger finally speaks up, also ignoring the guys on the phone. "Let me have that or do you have another one?"

My brow rises. "What you didn't bring yours?" I say disbelievingly.

"Motherfucker. Don't let anything happen to her Brant," Shy shouts

Ginger grimaces. "It's in the back, packed away. Would you like me to climb back there and get it?"

She reaches out to grab my gun, but I pull it back. "Babe, this is my gun and no one uses it but me. There's a Beretta M9 in the glove compartment."

Shy is yelling at someone, and the bikes behind us rumble, getting louder with them closing in on us.

Ginger doesn't look scared which only turns me on more, and when she cocks the gun, I feel my boxers dampen from how aroused I am watching her.

Goddamn, I want to fuck her so badly.

Shy's voice interrupts my eye fucking her. "Mac says Bear, Hawk, and Stitch are headed toward you with a couple of prospects. They're on Cheat Road so you should run into them, just hang tight and keep hauling ass. We're all on our way."

When my own phone rings I toss it to Ginger. "Babe, answer that for me."

"Who the fuck you calling babe?" Shy yells.

"We'll call you back, it's Beau," I say and hang up before he gets the chance to reply.

I wince but keep my eyes on the road.

Ginger answers my phone and explains to Beau what's happening, but a gunshot hitting the car has her crying out. The bikes are about fifty yards or so behind us.

Ginger speaks in an uneasy voice letting me know she's scared. "Beau's on his way too. I might have hung up on him."

Two more gunshots fire off shattering the back window and driver side mirror.

"Get down," I order her, while trying to reassure her we'll be fine. "We're going to be fine, babe. Just stay low."

I increase my speed to well over a hundred miles per hour and just pray they don't shoot a tire out. Another shot rings out but doesn't hit the SUV

"Goddamnit," I roar.

They have to be fucking with us because they haven't tried to pass us and their aim is horrible.

When I see the sign for Cheat Road, I feel a shred of relief. When we take the exit, the bikers must decide the chase is over because they keep hauling ass down the interstate. When we turn onto Cheat Road, we see bike headlights coming toward us.

"Flash your lights twice and if it's our guys one of them will flash three times," Ginger explains.

When I do, and they return with three flashes, I slow to a stop letting them come up next to us. Two guys ride up to either side of the SUV, and we both roll our windows down.

"Bear is on your side and Hawk is coming to my side," Ginger says.

When the guys come up, I yell to Bear that they kept going on the interstate. He throws his hand up motioning something I can't see, but when a van pulls around the bikes he yells orders and it takes off toward the interstate entrance. When he turns back to me, he tells me they'll be following us home. When I look back over to Ginger, she's releasing Hawk's hand giving me the nod to take off.

I didn't even pay attention to her and Hawk's conversation because I was too engaged in my conversation with Bear to notice them. We speed off and within twenty minutes we were getting out of the car with all the bikes parking around us. None of them get off their bikes though except Bear who comes up to Ginger and grabs her for a hug.

"Snow, you okay?" I can only hear her muffled yes. When his eyes land on me he says, "Thank you. Did you happen to see if they were wearing colors or anything about them that will help us figure out who it was?"

He's speaking to me, but Ginger pulls away from him and answers, "They're in all black. No colors, full helmets and there was five of them. I couldn't see anything that I recognized."

Placing my gun I still have in my hand, behind my back in my jean's waistband, Bear steps forward shaking my hand. "Thank you again, Brant. I'm so glad we didn't have some rookie bringing her home. Stay here tonight. We have extra rooms in the hotel, and everyone should be here by tomorrow morning. We'll figure shit out from there. We're going to head back out and meet up with our scout." I nod my head before he turns to Ginger. "Get some rest. You're safe now."

"I was always safe. Brant would never let anything happen to me," Ginger replies

My heart swells, and I still see a chance. Slim but I'll take it, and I just smile.

Goddamn right, I will protect her till the day I die.

GINGER

Once the guys leave to meet up with the others, Brant and I went down to the clubhouse and sat at the bar. Gigi and Storm were there to greet us with a drink. Storm had come running out thanking the Lord I was okay. She helped me get the room ready for Brant, and now we're all just sitting around bullshitting and talking about who it could have been. Brant slipped away a couple of times taking calls from Beau and Luc. I texted Shy, letting him know I was okay but knew he would probably be riding and wouldn't return the text or call till he was either home or stopped.

A couple hours later we're all tired, and there's still no sign of the guys, so I announce I'm headed to bed. Brant walks with me, and I stop halfway to the hotel entrance.

"I can walk you to your door," he states.

"It's okay. I'm just right there," I reply, pointing to the house just a few feet away. "B, thank you for everything, just you being here to help makes me feel so much safer," I say, smiling.

He takes a step toward me grabbing ahold of me, pulling me into a hug. I know I shouldn't be doing this but fuck he feels good, making me feel even safer.

I give him a tight squeeze before I pull away.

"Goodnight, B. I'll see you in the morning."

"Goodnight, babe. See you in the morning."

When I reach my father's front door I turn to see him still watching me, so I wave.

I wake up when warm arms wrap around my waist pulling me into a massive chest. I freeze, and this time I don't say anything until I get my bearings. The instant I smell him I relax into him - Shy. The smell of leather, oil, and smoke lets me know he must have just gotten here.

"Hmm, Micah, you're here," I cooed.

Shy slides his hand down my body slipping my boy shorts down, and I kick them off turning my body, so my back is to the mattress. Shy leans up on his side sliding his hand between my legs before taking my mouth with a low groan. "Fuck, Angel. I need to be inside you," he says.

Wrapping my hands around his neck, I pull him on top of me, spreading my legs and welcoming him inside. Our tongues dance the starving dance of need and wanting more, with our animalistic sounds intensifying our desire for each other.

"Fuck me, Micah."

Shy slams into me with one hard push seating himself deep within me. Shy slides his arms under my shoulder blades and up, gripping my shoulders before powering into me again and again, holding me still in his embrace.

I grab my knees pulling them up allowing him to go deeper.

"Yes, Angel."

Sucking my neck, he starts to move...

In and out.

Oh, God. Yes.

Slow and Deep.

Holy Shit.

His pelvic bone rubbing against my clit and the rhythm he's moving in has my orgasm exploding. I moan his name repeatedly, wanting more.

Shy pulls back so our faces are inches away from each other. He kisses me, licking my lips. "Say you're my girl!"

"Yes," I answer breathlessly.

Shy starts hammering his cock into my pussy. "You're my girl. Say it again," he chants.

He picks up his pace, and I feel like I'm going to come out of my skin. I just orgasmed, and I'm already feeling the next one with the pressure building. I can't focus on anything but our bodies slamming together.

"More. Oh, God. It's too much. Oh, God."

Shy flexes his hips, thrusting sharp and fast, hitting my clit and g-spot perfectly. "Oh, God. The pressure. Fuck," I scream.

I freak out when I feel myself come and it squirts out, my walls spasming around his cock. Shy growls. "That's it, Angel. Let go… Yeah."

Shy places his hands above my head, gripping the headboard and fucks me harder than he ever has, grunting out his own release. I feel his cum dripping from my pussy, and I feel another wave of spasms swirl through me.

Shy slows his movements, grabbing my hips and shifting back on his shins while still pumping soft thrusts until his cock softens, pulling out of me. He tilts his head back, taking in deep breaths before falling to my side. We are both breathing hard, and my body is limp like a noodle. I couldn't move even if I wanted to. Shy rolls over to face me. "Angel, I can't be away from you that long again."

He moves my bangs to the side so he has a clear view of my eyes. "You were fucking unbelievable. You finally let go completely. Fuck," he continues.

I can't even form words, so instead, I just lean forward and kiss him.

I moan into his mouth hoping he'll understand how much it meant to me to surrender control to him as well.

When we break the kiss I whisper, "I love you, Micah Jenkins."

Shy stands up and before I can ask what he's doing. He has me in his arms carrying me out the door.

"What are you doing?" I ask.

"Our bed is soaked, Angel. I'm taking us to your old room."

I giggle.

The next morning I wake up to yelling voices. I sit up in bed listening, trying to make out the voices, knowing one of them is Shy and when I hear Brant growl "fuck you," I'm flying out of bed.

Throwing on clothes, making sure I am not showing too much, I take the stairs two at a time, and when I enter the kitchen, I'm glad I got fully dressed because the kitchen is full of men. This is rare because usually meetings like this are in the clubhouse.

Shy notices me first and strides his no shirt, barefoot, jean wearing God-like body over to me, as I try to contain myself. I know my nipples are hard and I try to mask my inner desire. When my father speaks, my flame is distinguished.

Problem solved.

"Snow, come in. We were all just discussing you."

Oh shit.

Shy has an arm around me as we walk all the way into the kitchen where I see Bear, Cash, Hawk, Beau, Mac, Dallas, along with my dad and Brant. Everyone either says hi or nods hello.

"Good morning everyone. What's being discussed that y'all are yelling at each other about?" I ask calmly.

Brant steps forward. "They want to cancel your tour, and I said hell no you're meeting us in LA."

I push out of Shy's grasp only to have him pull me back.

"Hell no, you're not canceling my tour. Whoever that was last night didn't want me."

My father steps forward. "They're going to come after you to hurt us. You're safe here where we can protect you."

"We can protect her too and have been for years now," Brant yells.

Mac steps forward. "Yeah, but you didn't have a rival club after you either. This is serious, and we need to keep Snow safe. They know she is our prized possession."

Anger, along with love, fight within me and builds, but anger wins. "I am not going to hide. I didn't hide back when Emmett was a threat, and I won't do it now. I know how to take care of myself and like Brant said, they can protect me."

Shy speaks up for the first time. "The fuck he will. If you go on tour, Angel, I'm going with you."

"How the fuck can you do that, chase after Snake and get the club up and running?" Beau finally speaks up.

"I'll make it work." Shy pauses. "We will make it work," Shy vows.

When my father speaks, everyone turns to him. "Let's all discuss this in the clubhouse. We will figure this all out. We still don't even know if that was Snake and his men last night."

GINGER

It's been almost a week since we were chased and I'm headed back to New York tomorrow to get my cast removed. The MC has been out looking for Snake and his men with no luck. There was a sighting of him up North. I haven't been able to leave the compound, so I've been mostly working on producing my new song. It's been hard with my hand and not having the state of the art equipment that I'm used to. But working on music is the only thing besides riding that can ease my mind. Shy is gone most of the day, returning in the evenings. He's only left me over night once, but he woke me up, taking me. We've been making up for lost time having sex multiple times a day. Even though I see him every day, he still sends me texts with songs or to tell me he loves me.

Brant left with Beau the next day, heading back to be with the girls on tour. We have messaged each other back and forth but nothing serious. I feel relieved I haven't lost his friendship. I just hope when we go to meet up with them, that we can all stay friends. Shy never brought up the ride or anything about Brant after he left. He just said he trusts me and knows my heart is with him.

I pray things will be the same when we are on the road. I know Shy is under a lot of pressure with the new clubhouse being remodeled, looking for Snake, and just trying to build our relationship again. I haven't given him or my father any sass since the chase. Instead, I focus on my music.

It's late afternoon and I'm about to head over to the clubhouse to meet Gigi and Sissy, who are here today to clean the hotel and suites. While I am walking towards the main building, I notice there are several more bikes here today. When I work on my music, I never hear bikes come or go. It has been pretty quiet here lately with everyone out searching for Snake. Hawk, Bear, and Stitch have been the main men who stayed behind, taking turns going on runs with the others but today there are more than a dozen.

Once I'm through the door, I notice everyone is crowded around the door to the meeting room where they have church but with the door open I can see there are quite a few men piled inside looking at something.

I start to move towards them, but Gigi yelling my name has the place going quiet and everyone turning around.

O-kay, what the fuck is going on.

I turn around to see if anyone is behind me, but no one's there. It's my father who emerges from the group of men, and when I see his face, I know something bad has happened. My first thought is that something happened to Shy.

"Is it Shy?" I croak out with a lump in my throat.

My father's face relaxes for a second. "No, Princess, but it's something bad."

My insides start to tighten, and my heart speeds up. He grabs me for a tight embrace not saying anything. When he starts to let me go, I see Luc emerge from the group.

Oh, God. No.

"It's not Alex or Izzy is it?"

"Nah. They're fine, why don't you come in and sit down,"

Luc speaks softly

All the men part, giving me room to walk by, and when my father says to give us the room, all the men leave the room, leaving Luc, my father and myself alone. On the table sits a box and my stomach turns, as dread fills my body.

"What is that? Just fucking tell me. I can't take all this silence shit." I'm trying not to freak out, so my defense is to get pissed off.

Luc walks around the table standing directly across from me, and when our eyes lock, he speaks, "It's a girl's hand. Your father received it this mornin'. He didn't tell anyone because he was waitin' for me to confirm it wasn't any of our girls. We're all here to figure out what our next move is and to try and figure out who sent this to you. *Capisci?*"

What!

"Me?" I question. "Why me?"

I turn to my father standing next to me. "Is this Snake? Why would he send me a hand?"

When my father speaks, it comes out hard. "We don't think it has to do with Snake or the MC, but that's not being taken off the table." When he looks over to me, I see the worried look in his eyes. "We think it has to do with Emmett."

I gasp, grabbing my chest.

Luc starts to speak getting my attention. "There was a letter…" handing me the letter, I reach out to grab the Ziploc bag with the letter inside.

> Ginger – Snow – Gin – DJ Gin
> So many names – so many faces
> You take from us - we take from you
> Your guys took from us - we take from them
> You kill my guy – I kill you
> Be ready – We're coming

I freeze.

This can't be happening. Emmett is dead. He was working alone. I just stand there re-reading the letter.

When I don't say anything, Luc continues. "We think the hand is from one of the girls that went missin' a few weeks back. The girls, *do not* know about this yet, no one does. *Capisci?*"

He waits for me to nod my head in understanding before continuing. "We wanted to get a game plan together before the madness erupts from this new discovery. We also think you goin' on tour will be good."

My head snaps up. "What do you mean? I thought you said it would be bad?"

My father sighs placing his hands on the table, locking his arms, his head falling between them. I know he is having a hard time with all of this and his not speaking only proves he's trying to keep his shit together.

Luc speaks again. "Your father and I've been talkin', again, we think you bein' on tour in different states each week will make it harder for this person to find you. No one knows your schedule or where you'll be next. With Maddox's men, my men and the MC guardin' you it would be hard for anyone to get near you girls."

Holy Shit!

I take a couple deep breaths, look back down at the letter and my mind starts running a mile a minute with miscellaneous thoughts.

"It says, 'I killed their guy,' but I didn't kill Emmett, Alex did! Has she gotten any threats? Why are they targeting me? My boys took from them? Who the MC - or your guys? Took what?" I am rambling off questions, never taking my eyes off the letter.

My father stands up. "That's what we were just discussing when you came into the room. We were trying to piece this letter together. In the papers, it never said who shot Emmett, just that he was killed. We think maybe the guys finding the other girls in the warehouse, that's what they meant by taking from them, and they will take you girls, to get back at us. We don't know, but what we do know, is you will need to have a man on you at all times, even when Shy's with you."

My first thought is Brant, but I don't say anything because us three together all the time would end in a disaster.

"I want to see the hand," I demand as the door flys open and in storms a crazed looking Shy with Mac, Dallas, and Quick on his heels.

"What the fuck happened," he bellows.

Sonovabitch.

I go to him automatically, and once I'm in his arms, I feel safer. I stay there clenching his cut, trying to hold back the tears pooling in my eyes while Luc and my father explain what's going on. I hear growls, curses, and someone punching the wall, but I never move my face out from Shy's chest. I need to calm down and get myself together.

I am a Wolfeman. I can handle this.

I pull away to look up at Shy when he starts to speak. "I agree. She needs to be on tour moving around, with all three of our groups watching over them, they will be safe." Shy finishes his sentence looking down at me. "Angel, I will keep you safe. *All of us* will keep you and your girls safe. We *will* find out who is doing this, I promise."

I lean up and kiss him briefly. "Micah, I know."

My father tells Mac to bring all the men in so they can finish talking.

I turn around looking at Luc across the table. "I want to see the hand."

Luc leans forward and I feel Shy behind me giving me comfort, but when I see the petite hand in the box, I close my eyes. I take a deep breath and hold it. Tears are falling from my eyes when I open them to see Luc staring at me with sympathetic eyes. He's such an amazing man and has given me so much.

I nod my head, and he closes the box. When I'm about ready to leave the room, Luc speaks up, "Ginger, *do not* tell anyone about this. I need to prepare my men, and you can see the girls soon. Don't talk about this over your phone or anythin'. For everyone's safety, this needs to be kept quiet, *yeah*?"

I turn around and nod again before saying, "Yeah, I understand. Just keep them safe."

All the men return to the room while I exit so they can meet and go over all the details with Luc. I go to the bar where Gigi, Sissy, Felicia, and Storm are waiting for me, with hugs of support. Gigi hands me a shot of Patron right off the bat, and they all work to try and erase what I just saw and heard by getting me drunk.

GINGER

Early the next morning, I ride back to New York with Luc in his SUV. Shy, my father, Mac and the boys ride next to us, boxing us in, making sure we're surrounded. Luc and I have always been close, being my other father figure since moving here. He's very handsome and young, but I feel these past few years have taken a toll on him, seeing more stress wrinkles around his eyes and forehead. He is always so polite but I've seen his Italian temper, and it's scary as shit. I look up to him and trust him, so I believe him when he said everything will be okay.

We talk about the new song I am making with Alex's vocals. Once I get this cast off, I will be able to finish working on it.

Luc brings me to the apartment after my doctor's appointment. I threw a fit at the doctor's telling them we didn't need fifteen guys hanging around while I got my cast taken off. I told my father and Shy to let the guys go to the clubhouse. Thankfully they agreed, and just Luc, my father, Mac, and Shy stayed with me at the appointment.

The boys headed to the clubhouse after the appointment and Shy was going to meet me at the apartment in a few hours, so Luc walked me up to my place before heading to his own place to see Mia. I know I'm safe in this building with it being monitored twenty-four-seven. After what happened with Alex, they installed even more security precautions. Also, the security office is on the same floor as my apartment, just on the other side.

I try to get my head around everything now that I'm alone and have time to process it all. I try to keep up the bad-ass biker persona most of the time, but behind closed doors, I can let it all out. I think I'm still in shock from seeing the hand. Why me? My heart hurts that some girl lost her life because of me.

I want to call my girls and Brant to make sure they're okay but I know they are and Luc will take care of them. I'm supposed to have studio time at Luc's place tomorrow. Now that my hand is out of a cast I want to get back on the decks mixing. I've been going nonstop since early this morning. I lay down to rest and listen to music but the exhaustion takes over and my mind finally shuts down.

When I feel the bed dip down, and a warm body move up against my back I know Shy's home and safe, so I can fall back into my deep slumber. Sleep that only brings good memories and takes away all this bad stuff going on around me. I squeeze Shy's arms around me. "Love you, Micah Jenkins," I murmur before drifting off again.

I wake with a startle and movement from the doorway has me jumping with a scream. Shy's voice calls out letting me know it's him. I bend over grabbing my heart, feeling like it's going to explode.

"Fuck, Shy, you scared the shit out of me." I stand up. "What are you doing just standing there."

Shy chuckles, moving around the bed towards me. "I was just checking to see if you were alive and was watching you sleep. You looked so peaceful that I didn't want to wake you."

I look over at the clock. It reads three in the afternoon.
Holy shit! I slept for over twelve hours.
"Shit, I slept all day! Why didn't you wake me?"

I kiss him, give him a brief embrace and move to get ready. "I'm late. I was supposed to be in the studio today at Luc's before having dinner with Mia," I explain.

Shy pulls me back into his chest, and with a hand on my chin, he lifts my gaze locking eyes with him.

"Angel, I tried to wake you this morning before I left but you were out. So I closed up the house, turned your phone off and talked to Luc. I told him no studio time, that you needed to sleep and that we would be over for dinner. *We* are having dinner with both of them."

Looking into his deep brown eyes, I see the desire and love shining back at me. I soften into him. "I really wanted to get back in the studio, I'm behind on my song, and since my arm is out of the cast, I can finish," I say.

Shy kisses my forehead. "Angel, you'll have all the time in the world to be in the studio. Tomorrow I'll be out running errands to get stuff handled before we leave for LA. I thought I would spend tonight with you. I want to make sure you're really okay with everything. I know you have this hard ass wall you keep up, but I need to know what you are thinking. I need to have my *Angel* time before all this madness and traveling starts. I need my special time with you. I told Luc we would have dinner but right after, you are going to let me spoil you," he replies with a chuckle.

My pussy clenches pooling with wetness and dampening my panties. I lick my lips just thinking about what we can do to each other later.

Shy throws his head back laughing a deep heart filled laugh. "That look right there says it all, Angel, so get dressed and let's get this dinner over with so I can have some dessert."

Shy kisses me before letting go and heading out of the bedroom. I watch him leave and I salivate just thinking of having him in my mouth for dessert.

Thank you, baby Jesus.

When Shy walks out of the bathroom, I freeze. Fuck, he is mouth watering. Jeans, black steel toed boots, and white tank top with a light green short sleeve button-up shirt. His wet hair from showering falls around his face in curls. He is freshly shaved and his goatee - fuck that goatee does things to my body. My pussy starts to throb with its own heartbeat, making me wet instantly.

"Holy mother of God, you are gorgeous," I exclaim.

Shy smiles. "Oh yeah, you haven't seen me in" -he uses his hands to make quotes- "club attire."

He keeps laughing, buttoning up the rest of his shirt as he continues, "When we would go watch you at the club, we couldn't wear our cuts and had to dress up, so bam."

I laugh with him but move towards him, needing to touch him, and once I'm within reach, I slip both hands up his chest and around his neck, pulling him down for a kiss. Not just any kiss but a wet, deep, starved kiss. I moan, wanting more of his deliciousness. I push my body up against him feeling his hard body against my soft, needy one. Shy's hands instantly grab my ass, lifting me up, turning to walk towards the front door.

I break the kiss and say with a pout. "Just a quickie."

Shy groans. "Soon Angel, but in no way will it be a quickie. What I have planned for you will take all night long."

Dinner with Luc and Mia was truly amazing but couldn't end fast enough. Listening to Shy interact with them was breathtaking. It made me want him more. My heart hurts from being so happy. Seeing Shy in this different element away from the MC life, was so surreal. I got choked up a few times.

The whole dinner Shy has toyed with me, keeping me aroused.

I squirmed trying to tame it, but each time I did, Shy would slip his hand under the table caressing me between my legs, igniting it all over again.

Damn him.

Shy, I think, surprised Luc and Mia with how much he knew about music and he definitely shocked all of us with how much he talked. It just showed me that these past few years he changed a lot, becoming more of a man than a kid.

We didn't discuss anything negative but instead focused on all the positives about the future. Including my song that I made with Alex's vocals that the label will be releasing, and Shy discussed the club remodel. But, right at the end of dinner, Shy slipped up revealing yet another secret. One he had yet to tell me and obviously had been sitting on because he was talking to Luc about clubs and lounges. When Luc mentioned a small lounge downtown near the clubhouse, Shy slipped up saying, "Yeah, I actually just bought it."

He said it like it was nothing, but must've realized he said it because he paused when the table went silent. It's more of a lounge than a club, but it has live music there. Luc speaks first, sounding surprised, "You- you bought it?"

Thanking Luc in my mind for asking what I was thinking. I wanted to make sure I heard him right and when he answers my blood starts to boil.

"Yeah. Last year, while Snow was gone on tour, we went there frequently. The owner and I got close since we would help out with security or whenever we would see stuff go down. We looked out for him. He told me he was going under and was probably going to have to sell his business soon. Mac and I told him we would buy it from him, pay him to manage it and that's how it all came about."

Luc looked shocked and impressed. "*Yeah,* so you guys own it now?"

I sit back and cross my arms trying to calm down and not

make a scene here in front of them.

"We are closing escrow this week or next." When he's done talking, I'm in shock. Luc and Mia become excited, explaining how they know the lounge and how he could do so much with it.

Shy continues talking with them, but when he looks over at me, I can't hold my tongue anymore.

"When were you going to tell me? What other secrets do you have that I don't know about?"

I shouldn't be mad but damn him for keeping more secrets. I mean, him buying a fucking lounge hasn't come up once since we have been back together these last few fucking months.

The table gets quiet again, and Shy just stares at me, so I continue my rant. "You know *ev-ery-thing* about *me* since you have been *watching me* all these years but what about you? What else don't I know?"

I sit back folding my arms over my chest not caring that we have an audience. Luc and Mia just sit there and wait for Shy to reply.

Shy takes a deep breath. "Angel, I have been planning from the day I met you, how to make you happy. I have studied you, listened to you, and I have built us a life that will be safe and fulfill both of our dreams. We have been so caught up in drama, and I have been trying to make sure I have won you over before laying all these *extra* things on you. Things I thought would make you happy."

Sonovabitch.

I look over to Mia, who's looking at Shy like he's the sweetest thing ever, and Luc, who's looking at him with pride. I should be looking at him like all those things and more, but I'm mad he kept another secret from me. I push my empty plate away and finish my glass of wine.

"Mia, Luc, thank you for dinner. I think I need to head home. I'm still exhausted from the last few days, but I will be over around noon tomorrow if that is okay."

Luc stands up with a soft smile. "Of course, I hope you had enough to eat."

I hug and kiss both of them, giving each of them a thank you and goodbye. Shy follows suit hugging and shaking Luc's hand. I hear Mia whisper to Shy before we leave, "Hold her tight, *mijo*."

Once we're in the elevator Shy pins me to the wall. I try to push him off of me, but I lose.

"Shy-"

He cuts me off smashing his mouth against mine, in a brutal kiss. We tangle with each other never breaking the kiss. I push at him while he claws at me and we do this until the elevator doors open. Shy breaks the kiss grasping my hand and pulling me down the hall to my apartment. Once the door is unlocked, he shuffles us both inside shutting the door behind him. Before I can protest, he has me pinned against him with my back to his chest. I feel his labored breathing next to me, and when I try to side step away from him, he pushes me up against the wall smashing our bodies together.

Breathing heavy into my ear, Shy grunts, "I'm tired of this shit. You are my girl. Say it."

I don't say anything, but instead try to push away. "You lied to me."

Shy lifts my hands above my head holding them with one hand. "You are my girl. Say it."

I push my hips back connecting with a brick wall. Shy uses his free hand to slip my shirt over my head using it to secure my hands together. My nipples zing against the wall once he has my bra up and around my wrists too.

Stay pissed off. He lied to you.

"You lied to me, *again*." I try to sound mad but it comes out a moan.

Shy thrusts his still clothed cock into my ass with a growl. "You are my girl. Say it."

"No. I'm pissed," I breathe out.

Shy slips my jeans down over my ass and uses his foot to drag them all the way down my legs. I try to fight him, but again with his enormous body pressed against mine I lose. My body becomes alive with his dominance over me.

Reaching around, Shy slips his fingers into my folds and groans when he finds me drenched. "You are my girl. Say it."

Fuck!

My breathing is labored, my face is against the wall and I close my eyes to try to hold onto my anger but fail.

"Say it," he exclaims.

Hearing his jeans fall to the ground and his cock bob up against my bare ass I breathe. "Oh, God."

Shy leans into my ear, sucking on my earlobe. "Not what I want to hear Angel - Don't make me ask again. Are you, my girl?"

Slipping his cock between my legs, he slowly pumps it between my folds lubing his dick with my arousal.

A moan escapes me, and I bite my lip, trying not to come when the tip of his cock teasingly slides over my clit. He repeats his thrust, slow and torturous.

I squirm - causing his dick to almost slide inside my pussy, but he pulls back.

"Angel…"

I break, crying out, "Yes. Fuck Yes, I-" before I can finish Shy slams his cock into me hard and swift and we both cry out, "Fuck."

Shy lets go of my hands to grip my hips, taking a step back from me giving me room to bend a bit. He lifts my ass in the air and starts thrusting harder, slamming my head against the wall. I move my hands to brace myself for his brutal assault.

"Take me," I moan.

Shy hammers into me, hearing our bodies slap together has both of us moaning with each thrust. Shy slaps my ass, and I

moan his name.
"You."
Slap.
"Are."
Slap.
"My."
Slap.
"Girl."

He soothes where he slapped me making the pain turn to pleasure, and I hit my peak shattering all my senses.

"Micah, Oh, God. Yes," I say breathlessly.

Shy's breathing turns erratic while he thrust's faster, moving me up against the wall again, and he bends one of my legs so he can thrust upward into me harder and deeper. Hitting my sensitive spot, I spiral out of control with another orgasm.

"Fuck, yes. Right there. So fucking deep." He chokes out.

I'm so lost in my own pleasurable high that I don't feel his core tighten up, but I hear when he explodes with his release.

"Fu-uck...Ye-ess...Angel!"

Slowing his motions, he sets my leg back down, pressing his body up against mine, squishing me to the wall again.

"Angel, I'm done pussyfooting around with you. You are my girl. There are a few things I have kept from you, but not because I'm hiding them but because I want it to be perfect for you when you find out." He breathes into my ear before kissing my shoulder.

I'm still dazed from my earth shattering orgasm, I can barely stand on my own when he moves away sweeping me up in his arms as we head toward the bathroom.

Once inside I see the bathroom is full of lit candles, with roses scattered everywhere.

Choked up I ask. "It beautiful. How did you?"

"A prospect." Shy says cutting me off. He kisses my cheek before heading over to the bathtub turning on the water.

Oh, my God.
My heart melts.

29

SHY

"Motherfucker!"

Slamming my phone down on the table, I clench my fists, placing them on the table, and lean forward getting everyone's attention. The attention of my brothers. My club, men who look up to me now.

Pull your shit together.

No one has spoken, eyes stare back at me from around the table.

"We just got a call that Snake and his guys are riding south. They just jacked up some bar in North Carolina, for what, who the fuck knows, but we have our sister club looking into it. Dallas, see if you can get any information on the bar and why they fucked it up."

Dallas nods his head and takes notes but doesn't leave. No one leaves. Not until the gavel is dropped and church is over.

"You all know I will be taking off tomorrow with Snow and will be gone for three days. I'll be going back and forth between each of her shows. While I'm gone, Mac here will be in charge to run things. We need to be aware of our surroundings at all times. Word on the street is Snake's looking to build his own club. He wants to try and take us down."

I stand up straight, reaching behind me for my chair at the head of the table and sit down before continuing.

"Snake is a problem, but we need to focus on finalizing the last of the remodel and then Dallas will focus on setting up all the security. We need to make this place a fortress. Not even all of you will know where all the cameras are; it'll be that secure."

I take a breath, placing my forearms on the table and smile.

"Good news. We just closed escrow on the new lounge, so I want Worm and Dallas to review and look into all the staff. We need to have it up and running as long as we can before we close down again for two weeks. We're looking to have the grand opening for Snow's birthday. She doesn't know it yet, but I'm working on it with Luc. The White Wolfe Lounge will be a huge money maker going forward. The sooner we have it running, the faster we make that money. I want to redo all security on that place as well. So our main focuses are on making money, getting our places locked down, and watching each other's backs. We don't want anyone blindsiding us."

The men start talking amongst themselves while Mac gives everyone their orders. Quick walks up with a smirk on his face. "You know…" he hesitates, looking around the room while rubbing his hands together- "I would be the best person to" -he leans in with a cheesy grin- "to… you know- *look into* the staff."

Quick leans back still rubbing his hands together like he just told me some fucking great secret. He's the same height as me, I have more weight on him, but he is fierce. He reminded me of Brad Pitt in fight club or Snatch the first few times I saw him fight. He's even got the sandy blonde hair and cheesy smile like Brad.

Little fucker.

I laugh facing him. "Quick, I wouldn't trust you to" -I make air quotations with my hands- "*look into* anyone. Unless I wanted you to fuck them."

Quick drops his hands looking hurt by my words. "What the fuck, brother?"

I raise an eyebrow challenging him to disagree with me.

He breaks into a smile. "Okay, so I wouldn't fuck *all* of them, but damn a couple of those cocktail bitches are hot as fuck."

We both laugh, knowing damn well he would fuck *all* of them. He's the biggest manwhore I know.

I turn to grab my shit off the table so we can get this fucking meeting over with. But before Quick moves away I say over my shoulder, "Besides, you're coming with me on the road."

"What?" he states, not sounding happy.

I turn back to him raising both brows this time. "What, you have a problem going to clubs, getting free drinks, and having fresh pussy around you every night?"

Quick's face goes from pissed off to looking like he won the lottery. "Is this all business, watch duty and shit too?"

I laugh. "No, it'll be different, *we* will be anywhere Snow is, and there is going to be plenty of Maddox and Luc's men on security duty. I want you with me just in case, and to have one of my own men around. You know the clubs, and you obviously blend in - a little too well, but you've been by my side from the beginning, and you know the routine."

I turn to hand him his airline ticket. "We leave in the morning."

Once I look back over at the table, I see all the men standing, waiting for me to end this meeting. When I bring the gavel down, everyone scatters.

A few minutes later, Mac and I are walking out of the meeting room heading to the bar that's been newly remodeled, and I see my Angel sitting her pretty little ass on one of the new bar stools we just purchased, having a beer with Maze, our bartender.

Maze has been here for years. She's one of the five bitches we kept on after the takeover.

Wondering how the fuck my girl got here, I walk up behind her and hear Snow ask Maze, "Girl, tell me again."

I go to wrap my arms around her when I see Maze flick her long blonde hair over one shoulder, answering in a seductive voice. "Because I am ah-*Maze*-ing," she moans drawing out her name like she's getting off.

Angel throws her head back cracking up laughing, and I catch her around the waist before she falls off the stool.

"That's the best fucking nickname ever!" Snow exclaims.

I'm holding her from behind when she turns to face me, giggling. "Did you know how Maze got her nickname?"

Seeing my Angel so happy warms my heart. Having her in my arms, being here at the club and being able to experience this shit together is even better than I ever imagined. These past few days we've been doing our own thing getting ready to leave, but having her here now has my dick hard as fuck.

"No, Angel I didn't."

Maze slides two beers toward us. Mac, who I forgot was standing next to us, grabs his beer bringing it to his mouth, but says right before taking a drink, "I sure the fuck know how she got her nickname and it's well deserved."

Snow leans sideways hitting him in the shoulder. "Shut the fuck up! No. You. Didn't."

Maze answers with a giggle from behind the bar. "Oh, yes he did. Twice to be exact."

Snow wiggles out of my arms, twirling around to face Maze. Both of them are laughing, and Snow grabs ahold of the bar lifting herself up to reach across it, giving Maze a high-five. "Damn girl! We're going to be good friends, I can tell."

Fuck me.

Trying not to think about bending my girl over this bar and fucking her, I grab my own beer taking a swig before asking, "How did you get here, Angel?"

Snow turns around with a *fuck me* smile. "One of Luc's drivers dropped me off before heading to pick Luc up at the office."

Thank fuck because if she drove here, I would've had to

spank that pretty little ass.

30

GINGER

Having a hangover when you have to travel sucks ass. Hanging out at the clubhouse till almost midnight the night before, *probably* wasn't the best idea. But I was so tired of being in my apartment or Luc's, I had to get out. I was already packed and wanted to have some fun.

Meeting Maze was the highlight of the night. When I first arrived and introduced myself, I was worried she might have been one of the girls Shy fucked while we were apart. But right off the bat, she told me she knew all about me and that I was a lucky girl. Shy hasn't been with any of the girls, new or old, at the club. After that, we hit it off and proceeded to get drunk.

Now I'm waiting at the airport for my luggage to arrive. Quick went to pick up our rental, while Shy manages to get all our luggage. Thankfully our flight was at eight this morning, instead of five AM. We also flew first class, thank God. I had a couple of drinks in between naps, and I feel better, but still lagging.

Shy calls my name drawing my attention to where he's standing. With my sunglasses already on, I smile, pulling myself up off the bench and slowly proceed to follow him. When the automatic doors open the heat hits me, and I want to die. LA is hot as fuck, it's no wonder why Izzy moved to New York.

An hour later due to traffic, we're in our rooms, and just when I'm about to throw myself down on the bed someone starts banging on the door. We have a two room suite, and there is only one other suite on the floor, so I know who it is immediately. Even if I didn't know, I would have figured it out when I heard Izzy and Alex screaming from the other side of the door.

I smile, feeling a burst of energy when I open the door and I'm bombarded with two girls tackling me.

God, I have missed them.

We're all laughing, rolling around on the ground, when I hear, "What the fuck!"

We all roll over to our backs laughing, looking up to find Shy, Maddox, Dominic, and Gus standing over us. Dominic moves into the room looking pissed, along with Gus but Maddox and Shy stand there laughing.

Quick, walks up behind Maddox and Shy, who are still standing in the open doorway. "What the fuck did I miss?"

When he sees us lying on the ground, he smiles down. "Fuck, y'all doing down there?"

Quick points at us on the ground. "Y'all do this shit all the time because next time I want to watch."

Shy smacks him upside the head.

"What? Three girls rolling around is hot as fuck."

Izzy bounces up grabbing my hand and pulling me up into a hug. "Girl, we've missed you so much!"

Maddox helps Alex up before he moves into the suite toward Gus and Dominic, who are in the kitchen in a heated conversation.

Alex grabs me from behind, and I'm sandwiched between my two best friends. I smile feeling whole again with my girls here. My life has been an emotional roller coaster these past few months, but I feel everything is starting to work itself out. Having these girls in my life is one thing I know I need.

While I was getting stuff settled in my room, Alex updated me on who was here and where everyone was. I'm thankful that Brant went with Maddox's guys and Sasha. Sasha wanted to pick something up to wear for tonight, and the boys went with her to get out of the hotel. I guess everyone was feeling cooped up. After we got settled, the eight of us headed out to meet up with the rest of the gang for lunch.

When we get to the restaurant, Sasha rushes up hugging me and rambling in Spanish. Thankfully everyone else is sitting down, so it wasn't too awkward seeing Brant. He acted like himself and said hello to both Shy and I, so maybe I was worrying for nothing.

Shy wasn't bothered either, so we all sat down. After our food came, everyone started talking about the event that we're going to and Izzy being from here she was overly excited. We ran into a couple of people she knew on our way to lunch. She kept telling us all about who was going to be there and how she used to love playing there.

Conversation flows great over lunch, and half way through the waiter walks up with a bottle of Dom Perignon. When he asks if an Isabella Rogers was at the table, Dominic snaps, "Who the fuck is asking."

His thick Russian accent is dripping from each word. The table gets quiet, but the waiter doesn't seem affected by Dominic's rude outburst and instead replies, "Sorry, sir, but is there an Isabella Rogers at this table?"

"Yes, I'm Isabella," Izzy answers.

The waiter turns to her, extending his arms displaying the thousand dollar bottle of champagne. "This is for you, from an old friend."

The table is still quiet. Izzy stretches up extending her already tall torso looking around the room to see if she recognizes anyone as the waiter continues, "He left just a few minutes ago before buying the bottle. He told me to give you this."

The waiter turns, placing the bottle in a canister of ice that I didn't even notice had arrived. We're in a back corner of the restaurant due to the size of our party. He reaches into his pocket and pulls out a piece of paper, but before Izzy can grab it, Dominic snatches it saying, "Who the fuck is buying you a thousand dollar bottle of Dom?

"That's way over a thousand dollar bottle," Alex corrects Dominic.

Izzy's eyes are beaming with excitement, and she's ignoring Dominic's pissy mood. Dominic reads the note while Izzy tells the waiter, "Can you pour us all a glass, please."

"Gu-url... you know I love champagne," Alex squeals.

All the men's eyes are on Dominic, whose face is getting redder by the minute. Izzy turns to him, "So? Who sent the bottle?" Izzy asks like it's nothing and he isn't mad.

Dominic says something in Russian before throwing the paper at her. "Obviously one of your ex's or a very generous admirer, either way, we'll meet him tonight at the club."

Dominic doesn't look at her, but instead stares at the waiter who just placed a half glass in front of him. "I do not want any. We would like the check, please."

Izzy grabs the paper and reads the note. Her face doesn't change, when she's done, she turns to Dominic. "Dom, you can't be mad at me for some guy, who I don't know, buying me a bottle. I'm from here, maybe he recognizes me. This isn't my fault, and I sure as fuck am not letting it go to waste, so get your panties out of your ass and relax."

I hold my breath waiting for the explosion that is brewing in Dominic. But Maddox saves the day, grabbing the note to read it himself. "Dom, we have the girls secured tonight. No one will get by us, and if she doesn't know who he is, then he sure as fuck won't get by us. Don't let it ruin your day."

Dominic closes his eyes, dropping his head, trying to calm himself down. Dominic has a bad temper, and we have all seen him explode more than a hand full of times.

Izzy grabs his drink slamming the champagne, before grabbing her own glass and holding it up. "Cheers bitches. We're all back together!"

Alex, Sasha and I lift our glasses and toast each other. The guys go back to chatting while Dominic just sits there stewing.

This will be an interesting night.

After lunch, most of the men go back to the hotel except our guys and Quick who stays with us girls. We shopped, and Izzy showed us around her old stomping grounds. Shy and Quick were amazing, it was weird having Shy around the girls, he's so attentive to everything. He took a few calls while we were out, one of them being my father who was on the road following a lead on Snake. Shy and Maddox seem to have hit it off really well. Quick and Dominic chatted a lot, but Dominic was never far from Izzy, always pulling her to him and just overall dominating her attention. Around four o'clock, I was exhausted and needed a nap, so we all headed back to the hotel.

Quick and Shy hauled all my shit that I bought up to our room. I plopped my ass down on the couch that was in the middle between the two rooms and when Quick flops down next to me I laugh. "What the fuck, Quick? There's a whole other couch over there, you know."

Quick laughs but doesn't move, just kicks his legs up onto the coffee table.

"So what the fuck is up with that Dom guy and Izzy? They just don't seem like they go together. He's a glass filled with piss and vinegar, while she's like the fucking energizer bunny."

I turn my head towards him and laugh. "Great analogy. I don't know why she stays with him. I guess the sex is good. She likes to be dominated in bed and all that kinky shit."

Quick pops up throwing his feet to the ground and turns to look at me. "Are you fucking kidding me? That fucking tool says he's Dominant? More like a fucking asshole who likes to push his girl around. He's Russian for God's sake. They like their women to obey and shit."

"How would you know? Have you been to Russia?", I ask.

Quick looks away. "No, but I read about it and shit."

I start laughing. Quick snaps his head up giving me a glare. "I'm serious, every single Russian I've ever met are fucking dicks."

I'm still laughing when Shy emerges from our room freshly showered, taking my attention away from Quick and anything he's saying or doing. My body comes alive, but when I see his face I know he's exhausted just as much if not more than I am. I get up, grabbing his hand, ignoring whatever Quick is saying and heading to the bedroom with Shy in tow.

"Let's take a nap, and we can talk about how you didn't invite me to shower with you," I say, kicking my clothes off before climbing into bed in my panties and bra.

Shy laughs. "Angel, I actually needed to shower, and if you were in there, we definitely wouldn't have showered."

Shy drops his towel, pulling on a pair of briefs, before climbing into bed and pulling me next to him so we can spoon and within minutes, we're both asleep.

31

GINGER

"Yes, Auntie. I will call you when we get back to New York. I love you too. Tell the girls hello for me."

When I hang up the phone, I feel good. Auntie and I promised to talk at least every other day and not let weeks or months go by without talking. Being back home and mending that bond we had was something else that is making me feel whole again.

"Are you done?" I ask Izzy who is finishing my makeup. It's been over an hour that I've been in this damn bathroom with her. She came over to get ready with me, saying Dominic was still being an asshole. So she came up to my room, to have some girl time getting ready. Which ended up her taking over and getting us both ready.

Shy left the room a while ago, saying he would get ready in Quick's room to give us privacy.

God, I love him.

I have to say whenever Izzy does my makeup I feel like a rock star. She used to do Alex and my makeup when we were on tour. I loved it and tried to do it myself again, but yeah, that didn't work out too well. She's so good with makeup and shit. I usually just wear jeans, a t-shirt and only put on the bare minimum of makeup like mascara, some eye shadow, eyeliner and some lip gloss.

My hair is down, straight as usual, but she has my bangs hanging to one side instead of their usual split in the middle hanging in my face. She did my eyes in a smokey look with grays, silver, and black shadows, making my eyes look fucking amazing. My lips are lined in a darker maroonish color and red matte lip stain.

I have on my skinny black jeans which I think make my ass look fabulous, where she wanted me to wear these pleather pants that show every dimple to mankind. I told her I don't do pleather only leather. I did let her pick my shoes and shirt. My boobs are nothing to write home about but I definitely have something to work with; she has me wearing a red spaghetti strap low V-cut sheer shirt that hugs what little boobs I have. With matching red heels.

Being around her and Alex, I've gotten used to wearing heels. I've actually bought a few pairs, but I usually pick my Converse or riding boots. Tonight will be the first time I'm on stage and I know Shy is there with me, so I want tonight to be special.

Izzy walks out of the bedroom first, texting Dominic to tell him to come up when he is ready and before I get to the door I hear Gus say, "Jaysus Christ" followed by a whistle.

Approaching the door, I see Izzy stop to look up at whoever spoke and say, "What?"

When I walk through the door, I notice Shy, Quick, and Gus are all in the kitchen with beers in hand.

Shy takes one look at me, puts his beer down and moves toward me with hooded eyes.

Sonovabitch. He looks gorgeous.

Goddamn! He's wearing a gray button-up, and I've never seen him in slacks before. They hang just right, so when he walks, you can see his thigh muscles.

Delicious!

I lick my lips and smile at him prowling towards me.

Quick whistles again, I'm assuming at me, but he doesn't say anything.

Gus takes a sip of his beer and says, "Faaack, you las's don't make it easy for us lads, do you?"

Before Shy reaches me, I look over to Izzy who's staring at Gus funny. I look back over to the guys, and that's when I notice they're dressed up too. Gus isn't in his normal black attire, and Quick isn't in his MC cut, both of them are in slacks with nice button-up shirts too.

Gus is a big man, standing six foot three inches. He's always in black pants, black shirt, and boots. Tonight he has on gray slacks with a red button-down shirt and dress shoes. Gus reminds me of Gerald Butler but with wavy red hair. He always has some kind of facial hair either a beard, a goatee or like tonight he has a five o'clock shadow. When he smiles, which is rare, he has that side smile like Gerald Bulter has and with his Irish accent, he's pretty damn sexy. They all look hot as fuck!

I whistle in return, but my vision is cut off when Shy grabs me. Which reminds me, I have a hottie of my own.

"Angel, you look so fucking good. Half of me wants to keep you here so I can fuck you all night long, but goddamn, the other half wants to show you off."

Shy leans down to kiss me but stops. "Am I going to fuck up your lips and get shit all over me?"

I laugh and use my finger to wipe my lips showing him it doesn't come off.

Shy growls, "Thank fuck." before taking my mouth with his.

Fuck he tastes like mint. Yummy. I moan wanting more.

I hear Izzy say next to us, "What the fuck, Aengus?"

I look over to see she still hasn't moved. "What's wrong?" I ask her.

She starts laughing folding her arms over her chest. "Who knew?"

Lost, I turn toward her breaking Shy's and my embrace. "What?"

She turns to me looking like a fucking model in her short mini skirt that shows off her long as fuck legs. She has on a top like mine, but hers is silver with sequins all over. Izzy is normally five foot nine inches but with her heels on she is a good six foot.

She laughs, pointing toward Gus. "Who knew our brute could actually wear something other than black outfits?"

Gus finishes his beer, placing it on the counter, and turning to face us. "I'm usually babysitting yer arses, breaking up fights or working security. I wear other things besides black; you just don't seem to notice." His Irish accent thick and playful.

Gus moves to the fridge and grabs another beer, which I can see is filled now. Shy or Quick must of gone out while we were getting ready.

Quick hasn't said anything but is still staring at Izzy. She's walking toward the kitchen, and I follow wanting a beer myself.

"Gus, I don't know how the fuck you do it, brother. Fuck, I would have a fucking hard on twenty-four seven with these two around. Goddamn," Quick finally speaks.

Quick adjusts himself before taking another big swig of his beer.

Gus grunts. "Aye, a lot of cold fackin' showers."

Izzy still doesn't let up on Gus. "So what's different about tonight compared to all the other times?"

She grabs the beer he's handing her before he gives Shy and I one too.

Cracking his own beer, he answers, "I'm not working tonight. Between Maddox's guy and us, we're taking turns on who takes the lead on security. Instead of going back to New York, like I usually do, I decided to stay and hang out." He uses his beer to point toward the guys. "I like these wankers." He laughs taking a drink.

Izzy isn't happy I can tell but why I don't understand. "So…

what I'm just a job to you? You don't like to hang out with me? We're always together. I thought we were close."

Gus looks up at the ceiling. "Iz, fer fack-"

Pounding on the door cut Gus off and has everyone jumping. Shy's the first one to move. Gus doesn't finish his sentence, but instead just stares at Izzy who is staring right back. I glance over at Quick who's still studying Izzy.

What the fuck is going on? Is everyone high?

Alex and Sasha bounce through the door giggling about something. When they see Gus, they both stop in their tracks. Alex blurts out, "Jesus Christ, Gus you look fucking hot."

Sasha follows suit. "Fuck yeah."

Gus groans, "G'lawd, it's bloody slacks and a goddamn shirt."

Maddox and Brant walk in but neither of them say anything, they just stand there with their hands on their hips looking irritated. When I hear yelling from the hallway I know why.

Great. Can this night go any weirder?

Dominic, yelling from behind Maddox, has everyone looking. "What the fuck are we waiting on, let's go." When he sees Izzy, his face turns red. "Iz, what the fuck you wearing, girl?"

Okay, this night is definitely starting out wrong.

GINGER

The night went on, getting weirder along the way. I've been gone for close to four months, and I feel everyone is acting differently. Maybe it's just my own insecurities, but I just feel off.

When we first got here, Alex and Sasha seemed to be in their own world with Brant in the corner of the VIP area sitting in the booth, and Dominic sitting on the other side just looking like a dick.

He was eyeballing everyone that came near the entrance of the roped off area like some crazy man. He's probably trying to figure out who gave Izzy that bottle. He just hasn't seemed right since getting that letter.

Quick and Gus brought a couple of girls into the VIP area, and I thought Izzy was going to flip the fuck out, but again she just kept moving around talking to everyone for a few minutes before she moved to the next group. Guess we're all tripping out over Gus's behavior. He's usually way serious and all business.

I used to only care about the music, what the other DJs were playing and dissecting songs, always thinking of what I could do to better myself. Tonight, on the other hand, all I cared about was being next to Shy. When we walked into the club, my heart filled with excitement, like it was going to explode. I'm so happy to be back. I love absorbing the energy of the club, the way the music vibrated off the walls with all the lights flashing around. It was so euphoric. I had electricity spiraling through me, and I swear if Shy would have just touched me I would have come.

Dominic and Izzy are on stage. Izzy is about ready to go on since Sasha is finishing up.

I'm sitting in the VIP booth having a drink when Shy leans over. "Do you always just sit around and watch people?"

I laugh. "You know me, I'm *always* watching people."

Shy pulls me into his side chuckling. "Angel, all these years I've been watching you. You never sit around the VIP this long. You're always on the go, in the DJ booth, on the dance floor, or just moving around. I hope it's not because of me that you're hanging out in VIP."

I turn to look at him and see the worry in his eyes.

"Micah, you being here is everything and before I was just floating around lost. I was trying to fit in, and right now this is the first time I actually just want to sit here and listen to the music and watch people."

Shy leans in to kiss me and I reach up around his neck pulling him closer, but he pulls back slightly to look me in the eyes. "Angel, I want you to be happy. If me being here is too weird-"

I cut him off smashing our mouths together, letting him know in no way is him being here upsetting me. Instead, it's turning me the fuck on.

Breathless, I pull away. "Shy, I've felt so alive these past few weeks, more than I ever have. Each day gets better and better, seeing you in so many different lights, it only makes my love for you grow deeper, if that is possible. I'm starting to feel whole again, like my life is finally where it's supposed to be, with you."

Gus, yelling bloody hell has us both looking to what is wrong. When we turn around, we see a fight has broken out near the stage. Shy instantly stands up blocking me, but I stand up in the booth behind him so I can see and what I see is not good.

Izzy is DJing, but Dominic has some guy on the ground choking him with Maddox's guys trying to get him off the guy.

"Well, I guess we found the guy who gave Izzy her bottle," I say.

Gus left the VIP and is now on stage holding Izzy.

Damn, he's fast.

How he got up there so fast is beyond me, but Gus's blocking her from the fight that seems to be growing in numbers, crowding the stage even more. Security is everywhere trying to break up the fights, but it looks like they're losing. Quick has the two girls behind him but doesn't move to help break the fight up either.

I think about all the fights I've seen and been around. There is usually a fight a weekend, clubs are being closed down early all the time. I wonder how Shy's been able to handle it. "How did you stay away when fights like this broke out back in New York?"

I feel Shy's shoulder tense up under my touch. "It took a lot of men holding me back, but when I would see you were safe, I would calm down."

Quick laughs. "Yeah, one time he was so close to breaking free that I socked him. That is the one and only time I got to sock Prez. It got him to quit fighting us to get to you, that is for sure."

Shy snaps his head to Quick. "You're lucky Mac and Dallas were there, or your ass would've been the one in the hospital, not the other guys."

I laugh but feel sad that we didn't get to experience so much together. When the lights go on, and police come charging in, I know the night's over, and it's only one o'clock, right when I'm supposed to go on, so much for my first night back.

Izzy is crying in Gus's arms, and I feel bad for her. I want to go to her but seeing the mass of bodies between us I know that isn't going to happen. I look for Alex and find her in Maddox's arms and right next to her is Brant holding Sasha.

A sharp pain shoots through me and a jolt of jealousy. I know I should be happy. I want him to move on so we can go back to being friends. It just stings because that used to be me. Sasha seems to be taking my place. She and Alex are all buddy-buddy now, she has been DJing in my place all these months, and now she's in Brant's arms. It just feels weird. Brant isn't and never was my man. He's my friend, *yes,* we have hooked up, but we're still friends.

What the fuck is wrong with me? Jesus Christ, I need to get my head checked.

Once everyone is ushered outside, we were the last to go waiting for the crowd to dissipate. Dominic is arrested and Izzy is a mess. Gus has her in his arms, while we all hustle to get our stuff together to head toward the SUV's that we have waiting for us.

The car ride back to the hotel is quiet and when all three SUV's are emptied, we head up to our rooms. Gus promises us he will stay with Izzy and call one of us if he needs anything. I thought everyone was on the floor below us, so when we drop most of them off, and the doors close, I realize Brant and Sasha are still with us. Our floor is the top floor with only two suites. Alex and Maddox have the one across from us. Both suites have two rooms, Quick is in our other one. Does the mean Sasha and Brant are in their other one? I look over to see Alex looking uncomfortable. When the doors dings, we all shuffle out and I go directly toward our door calling over my shoulder goodnight but Shy stays at the elevator discussing with Maddox our plans for tomorrow. Quick stayed downstairs at the hotel bar with some girls, so I move to our door and notice a small package next to our door.

I bend down and see my name Ms. Wolfe printed on the top. I open it and instantly drop it. "Oh, my God" I scream.

It's another hand with the middle finger placed up flipping

me off.

Shy, Maddox, and Brant are by my side instantly.

"Fuckin' hell!" Maddox roars.

"I got you, Angel." Shy rubs my back holding me to his chest.

Maddox yells, "Alex, Sasha, don't move. Brant call the guys now."

Shy, still holding me, pulls out his phone. "Upstairs now," is all he says before putting it back in his pocket.

Alex and Sasha are freaking out wanting to know what's in the box. Alex keeps repeating over and over. "Maddy, what's in the box. Maddy, what's in the box."

Shy pushes me from his chest, guiding me to the girls. They pull me into their circle. I see Brant open our suite door with his gun out. Maddox right behind him and Shy following.

The elevator door dings, all three of us girls scream, but the rest of the guys come barreling out guns in hand.

Alex points to our suite. "They just went in."

Chad tells Austin to stay with us, and Quick comes to me. "What happened? Are you okay?"

I point to the box. "We got another hand."

Alex gasps, "Santa Maria."

Both Austin and Quick move to the box, careful not to touch it. Quick pulls out a small white piece of paper using his knife.

I move out of the girl's circle to see what the note says but Shy emerges from the suite looking murderous and talking to someone on the phone.

He walks right by me, and I don't bother him. Instead, I turn back to Quick who looks just as scary with his jaw clenched.

"Motherfucker," he seethes.

"What?" All three of us girls ask at the same time.

Austin, who doesn't speak much says, "Fuck. Mad Dog, get out here."

I have to know. I have to see what it says, so I walk the few steps it takes to get to Quick.

> Snow – DJ Gin
> Two faces
> We took from them
> Now I'll take from you
> You GIRLS killed my boy - You will die.
> I'm here

My chest starts to beat uncontrollably, and fear runs deep through me to my bones. "What does that even mean? He's talking crazy. It's like the first message but different."

Maddox walks up putting his phone back in his pocket. "Someone was in your suite and trashed the place. Where did Shy go?"

Right at that moment the elevator door dings and Shy emerges looking grim.

Oh God. Something happened. I know that look.

"Mac just called, Striker is dead along with two of my guys."

Quick drops the note. "What the fuck happened? Who?"

"What guys?" *God, please don't let it be someone I know.*

My phone rings in my pocket when he rattles off two of the Scorpion men that patched over and I feel relieved but sad. I look down and see my father is calling. "Daddy."

"Princess, are you okay?" His voice echoes through the phone.

I start to cry. "Not really but Shy and the guys are here."

"Don't you worry. We'll figure this out. I need to go but wanted to check in with you. I love you, Princess."

"I love you too, Daddy. Always have..."

"Always will, Princess."

When I hang up, all I can think about is the note.

He took from them! Now he'll take from me... Us girls will die...He is here... Shit, Alex!

The rest of the night, and into the morning, was hectic with police and investigators. After the police took pictures and collected evidence, we were able to go back into our room. The girls helped me clean up. Izzy and Gus came up soon after it happened. She was still upset and crying off and on, but no one bothered her or asked what happened, with everything going on it was the last thing on our minds.

After our place was clean and all the police had left, us girls went and curled up on my king size bed while the men walked around, making calls and dealing with the madness.

Alex and Sasha fell asleep first, but I could still hear Izzy's soft crying since she was between Alex and me on the bed. I turned toward her, pulling her into my chest and hugging her until we both fell asleep.

Someone yelling woke me up. Looking over at the clock, I see it's nine in the morning. It's only been a few hours I've been asleep. I roll to my back and listen. I hear Shy telling whoever was just yelling, to shut the fuck up, but other than that I only hear low voices. I climb out of bed and move toward the half-closed door. The room is dark so I can see out into the living area between the two rooms without anyone seeing me.

I see all the guys with now two more of Maddox's men, Ethan and Isaac, his IT guy, the manager and Beau. They must have already been on their way here because it's over a six-hour flight from New York.

I stand there and listen as best I can without being noticed.

All the men are in a big circle, half sitting on the couches the other half have pulled up chairs or are standing. Gus and Beau are pacing around, obviously deep in thought.

"I think we need to pull the girls from the tour and brin'

everyone home." It's Luc's voice speaking, but he isn't here, so he must be on speaker.

"Fuck that," Brant barrels out.

Again Luc's voice rings through the air. "Shy needs to come home and deal with his brothers' deaths, we don't know who this *Cazzo fottuto* is behind this, and we're blind out there. At least here we know our surroundin's and have more backin' with Shy's guys." Luc's Italian accent comes off thick when he is pissed off.

Cazzo, I know is crazy and fottuto sounds like fucker.

Shy stands up. "No, we go to the gig tonight. Then we will come home tomorrow. Snow hasn't been back on stage, and I know what she needs. We have" -he looks around the room counting- "ten guys. I think we can protect two girls. They didn't get to them last night. We'll call the club and set up extra security. Set us up away from everyone. Dominic's still in jail but-"

Luc cuts him off yelling in a string of Italian before saying, "Don't you worry about him, *yeah*. He won't be gettin' out anytime soon. I'm sendin' down our lawyer to deal with that *stronzo*."

Dominic is an asshole.

Shy continues, "Okay, so we just need to get through tonight and head back tomorrow. Luc, can you send your jet to pick us up right after the show? That way we can leave directly from the club?"

Luc replies, "Yeah, I'm on it."

Beau, who is pacing, stops and turns to the guys. "So Snake is down south, but your guys were murdered in New York. Fuck, we're missing something here. How do they know where we all are? Ginger's name hasn't been on any of the production."

Ethan chimes in, "No but Alex's name has, and he said in this last letter, 'two faces - you girls killed' He has to be watching both of them. Like two faces meaning both girls. Maybe the deaths of Shy's men have nothing to do with what we are dealing with but it just a coincidence? What if we are dealing with two different threats? It just doesn't make sense."

My legs get tired and I lean on the door. It squeaks, everyone jumps up and all eyes are on me.

Great...Sonovabitch.

"Sorry, it's just me," I say childishly with a small wave.

Shy comes around the couch. "Angel, how long have you been standing there?"

I push my shoulders back. "Long enough."

Shy reaches me, everyone turns back to what they were doing, and I hear Luc call out to Beau, who picks up the phone.

Shy engulfs me into his body, and the warmth from him sends goose bump across my body. "Angel, you should be sleeping."

I push back. "Shy, I'm not a little kid. It's nine in the morning and you haven't even slept yet. None of you have."

As if they heard me, most of the guys get up, and head towards the door as Chad calls out, "We'll get some sleep and be back up here in six."

Beau gets off the phone and says, "Maddox, the three of us that just got here will head over to my suite downstairs, which is on the same floor as the guys and make some calls and figure out tonight while you guys get some rest."

Maddox agrees.

I turn back to Shy. "You need to rest. We have a long night ahead of us. Let's go lay in Quick's room."

Shy leans down giving me a quick kiss. "Angel, I am far from being tired and have a bunch of calls I need to make. Just go back to bed with the girls. Plus, I'm pretty positive Maddox, Brant, and Gus are not leaving anytime soon. Don't worry about us, just get some rest because tonight is your night. I want to be with you while you're on that stage. I need it just as much as you do. I've been waiting a long time to be able to stand next to my girl while she rocks the house. Now get some rest, and we'll take care of everything else."

I melt into him, and his grip tightens around me, making me feel safe.

Releasing me, he kisses my forehead. "Love you, Angel."

"I love you too, Micah Jenkins."

33

BRANT

"I'm fine," I bark.

"B, you don't look fine. What the fuck, man?" Beau grumbles.

I answer, "This whole thing is fucked up. Can this weekend get any more fucked up?"

I snap my head in his direction. "Don't answer that. We don't need anything else jinxing us."

Beau chuckles but doesn't say anything.

I've known Beau my whole life. He was best friends with my father in high school. My father knocked Mom up right out of high school and then went off to the military to become a Marine. He and Beau stayed close throughout the years. When my father died overseas, Beau was the one who stepped up and helped us out, saying he vowed to take care of us if anything ever happened to my father. I trained all my life to become a Marine, to follow in my father's footsteps, but the day he died that all changed. I was fifteen years old.

"Boy, you listening to me?" he exclaims.

I shake the images of my father out of my head.

"What? And don't call me boy," I grunt.

"Well, then pay attention," Beau replies

Getting irritated, I stand up to move around the room. We're alone in his room; I came down here a while ago to get away from my nightmare that seems to keep getting worse. I thought I could be around them but seeing Shy holding Ginger is gut wrenching.

"What happened at the club? Was that guy a threat to Izzy?" Beau questions.

"I don't know. I was behind them with Sasha, Alex, and Maddox. I didn't see the guy until Dominic had him by the throat."

It's true. I didn't see anything, and I'm usually the first one to see a fight coming. My game has been off since everything happened with Emmett. My mind is so consumed with Ginger and Shy that I've been slipping.

I turn to Beau. "They said he approached Izzy, and when he grabbed her arm Dominic lost his shit, but I don't know."

"Seriously, are you okay? You seem off," Beau asks with concern.

I stop pacing. "You want the truth? I wasn't thinking. I knew Maddox's guys were there doing their job, and Sasha was dancing with her ass up against my dick and I haven't been laid since Ginger and I hooked up. So yeah, I wasn't watching anything. I was trying not to fuck Sasha on stage, while I watched my girl with another guy," I answer truthfully.

Beau stands up coming to stand in front of me. "Jesus. You need to take some time off, get your head straight and get laid. And *not* with another DJ, you work with. Shit goes bad and look where it gets you. She's with Shy. I told you when you first told me you two were hooking up, that it was a bad idea. You've known all along he was there and coming for her. You knew their past." Shaking his head, he turns around and heads to the kitchen.

Goddamnit! I know he's right.

I know it's all my fault, but I can't stay away. A knock at the door pulls me from my thoughts of Ginger. I open the door to find the pain of my existence - Shy.

"What's up?" I ask.

"We need to talk," Shy demands, brushing by me and entering the room.

Fuck this day just got worse!

Shutting the door, I turn around and follow him into the kitchen where Beau is getting a drink.

Shy blurts out, "I feel like this is an inside job."

"What the fuck?" Both of us say in unison.

Shy's pacing stops. "Seriously how can this guy be in two different states at the same time and know what the fuck is going on? He knows where we're staying, the clubs… it just doesn't add up."

Beau leans back against the counter. "So who do you think it is?"

Shy starts pacing again. "Fuck. I don't know, but Emmett was on the inside. Maybe someone at the label? I know that I trust you two and that's why I'm here. I know Maddox and his core group are good too, but it just seems too coincidental to be anything else."

"We could do another sweep of the building at Spin It. Make sure no one has tampered with the system. I've had Ethan monitoring it though, and so far no one has even tried to breach the system. Plus no one knows that Wolfe's clubhouse is where the first box was delivered. None of that's in our system anyway," Beau replies.

"Motherfucker!" Shy roars. "I know it's something right under our nose, I feel it."

"I understand and see where you're coming from but I trust everyone with us except maybe dumbfuck Dominic, but he's in jail right now and to be honest he's so far up Izzy's ass he barely even knows what day it is. You know we looked into him, and he is boring as fuck. He only follows Izzy around. They were fighting or separated until she came back to go on this tour. Again, he's too stupid." I pause thinking who else is with us that could be working against us.

Sasha? No, it couldn't be.

Beau who is looking at me asks, "What B? I know that look."

Shy turns and all eyes are on me.

It can't be.

"This is going to sound crazy, but what about Sasha? I mean she came back from Spain with us but what do we really know about her? Has anyone checked her out?"

Beau laughs. "Little Sasha? No, no way. Plus we did a background search on her when we were in Spain to make sure she wasn't linked to Monico, and she was clean."

Shy looks back and forth between us and says, "Well, now you know what's been eating at me. We need to be on the look out and watch what we say. I'll have Dallas dig deeper into her and see what he comes up with."

Shy heads toward the door and I follow him. He opens the door and turns toward me. "Look, Brant, I know we've had some differences. I know you care about my girl, but we need to get past all that and work together. I might not like it, but I do trust you with my girl." He doesn't wait for me to answer but instead turns and walks out the door.

Jesus Christ. Why does he have to be cool? He's selfless and just stands by and watches his girl grow and make a life for herself from afar. Who does that? I hate that he could be right and it be Sasha all along.

I feel Beau walk up behind me, staring at the closed door.

"Maybe you should get a little closer to her, get a feel for her and see what you think. We really don't know much about her. Maybe get your dick wet along the way. She *technically* isn't one of our DJs. Yet."

Yeah, this day fucking sucks. I need to sleep.

Especially since Shy might be right. Fuck!

GINGER

Waking up with Shy next to me brings a smile to my face. I just lay there, watching him sleep. I know it had to be after one o'clock in the afternoon before he came to bed. Around noon Maddox woke Alex up moving her and Sasha to their room so he could get some sleep. Izzy and I got up to find Gus on the couch and Quick in his room sleeping.

Maddox told me Shy was down talking to the boys and would be back soon. Izzy felt bad having Gus sleeping on a small couch, so she woke him up, and they went down to his room which was across from hers so he could sleep. She was going to call the court and see if she could find anything out about Dominic.

Once everyone was gone, I jumped in the shower and then laid back down, falling back to sleep. Hotel rooms with black out shades are the best. I could sleep all day.

I want to wake him, but I know he needs to sleep. My wolf is protecting his pack, running in all different directions. Laying on his stomach with his arms tucked under the pillow, I can see his back tattoo, and I just lay there thinking how happy I am. Even with all the drama flowing around us again, I feel blessed just having him back in my life.

I move a bit closer and Shy stirs, but doesn't wake up. The covers slip down his body showing he's completely nude with his sculpted ass half on display, just calling to me to touch it. I roll to my back slipping my panties off, then my bra, trying not to move the bed.

I notice his hair is still damp from a shower, so I lean in taking a big whiff of his scent.

God, I love the way he smells.

I'm wet just smelling him for God's sake. I want him - no I need him. I lay on my back, slipping my hand down between my legs, separating my folds, slipping two fingers into my fully aroused pussy. I used to play with myself so many nights, closing my eyes getting myself off thinking of him and here I am doing it with him beside me.

I move my fingers in and out faster. I bring my other hand down to my erect nipples tugging on each one of them before moving my hand down to my clit to double assault myself. Jacking my pussy with my fingers while flicking my clit. I bite my lip, holding back a moan. I look over at Shy's masculine form, his soft silky skin, and his tight ass.

Fuck. Yes!

I close my eyes, imagining Shy fucking me.

Yes. Yes. Yes...

I feel the bed move, my eyes shoot open, and a very sleepy body is moving over mine.

"Shy," I say breathlessly.

"That is the *sexiest* fucking thing I've ever woken up to, but fuck Angel I never want you to come without me again," Shy groans.

Shy moves over my body completely, lifting my fingers from my pussy and I whimper. He moves them up to his own mouth sucking them all the way in. I moan, closing my eyes. "Micah."

Shy slowly slips into me, seating himself all the way in, hitting my cervix. I withdraw my fingers from his mouth sliding them around his neck and into his wet hair.

"Angel, I never want you to pleasure yourself again unless I'm telling you to. This is my pussy to take care of now and if it needs something you come to me. You ask, or you take it, but never do it without me." He pulls out and slams back in followed by a few fast pumps.

"Now this is going to be fast and hard, Angel, because I'm exhausted."

Shy kisses me before moving up and sitting back on his knees. I'm about to pout when he orders me to flip over, and a smile spreads across my face as I do as I'm told.

Flipping over, Shy grabs the globes of my ass and plows into me. I drop my head into a pillow and cry out. I clench the pillow under me and hold on for the pleasurable fucking I'm about to receive.

Slap.

"Yes," I moan.

"I want to be the one making you scream."

Slap.

"Micah."

"That's my girl."

Shy builds both of our climaxes to the brink, pumping vigorously hard and fast.

I moan and cry out his name into the pillow, clenching it for dear life.

"Angel, hold on."

Slap.

"Almost. Fuck," Shy grunts.

He grabs my shoulders as leverage to pound into me deeper.

I feel him tense up, knowing he's about to blow and I push back meeting thrust for thrust until we both explode.

I fall down onto the bed, but Shy holds my hips up slowing his pace until he comes to a complete stop. Exhausted, he falls down next to me.

"Now sleep, Angel. I need sleep."

34

SHY

"Keep close to Snow, no matter what. I don't care if she goes to takes a piss. You have eyes on her unless my arms are around her, even then you don't take your eyes off of her. I want both of us within arm's reach of her tonight," I order Quick.

Quick is standing outside the SUV with me waiting to get the okay to head inside the club.

"Prez, I got it. No one is getting near the girls," Quick replies.

I turn to him. "I don't give a fuck about the girls. There are ten motherfucking guys here to watch over the other girls. I'm worried about our girl."

I'm only worried about my queen. There are enough men here to watch over the other three girls and then some. I want all eyes on my girl, call me a dick.

"Prez, I won't let you down. It's fucking crazy out here. I hope the inside isn't this bad."

"Fat chance. It's crazy as fuck in there too." Brant walks up telling us something we didn't want to hear. I might hate the motherfucker for fucking my girl, but he knows his shit, and I trust him with even my own life. That says a lot about the fucker.

"What's the plan? Did Beau get all the demands met that we

asked for?" I ask.

Brant nods his head in the direction of Beau walking up. "Ask him yourself."

Dick.

All ten of us men circle around to listen to what Beau has to say. The girls are in the SUV hanging out and having some much-needed drinks to calm their nerves.

"All right, the owner is cool and spoke with Luc today. He explained what happened with Dominic and everything that is going on. He's more than willing to help. He added ten more guards tonight. We have the big area that is across from the DJ booth. The DJ will be locked in the booth, and only two at the most can be in there with her. That's good because there's only one way in and one way out. Our roped off area is a level higher than the club. It's eye level with the DJ booth so we can see who is playing at all times. We can also control who comes up to our area. The only bad part is going to the bathroom and getting in and out. We have to use the bathroom in the VIP area and walk through the whole club to get to VIP."

Good shit! Finally good news.

We shuffle the four girls out of the SUV and walk them in, surrounding them as we walk towards the building. As we're escorted through the massive crowd, people are screaming Maddox's DJ name "Mad Max." He is in the middle of all of us with Alex tucked into his side. I have Ginger next to me with Quick behind her. All the other guys crowd around us with the other two girls between them.

Once we're inside the roped area, we spread out. I put Ginger's music bag down and look around the club, checking the exits and getting a feel for the place.

Sasha is the opening set, so Brant is with her at the booth.

Okay, so far so good.

The girls sit down on the couch with a comp bottle already on the table in front of them. Alex grabs the bottle of Vodka and pours the three of them a shot. I walk over and pour myself one. The girls all look up at me, and I smile.

"Cheers, bitches," mimicking them from yesterday.

They all start laughing and cheers me.

I pour another two and walk up to Quick handing him one of the shots. "Nut up, bitch."

Quick downs it laughing. "We are a bunch of bitches. When the girls made their toast yesterday, I thought of us always saying that shit and thought, fuck we're just like these bitches, except we like to nut up," he says, grabbing his crotch.

We both laugh.

I move back over to sit next to Ginger, throwing my arm around the back of her on the couch. The girls are talking music, so I tune them out and look around the club. Sasha is good and has the club moving. I see Brant inside the booth with her, but he doesn't look happy. I hope to fuck that this bitch isn't our leak. It would break my girl.

Quick sits down with a beer and hands one to me. The guys are all set and placed around us. I relax, feeling tonight might not be so bad. Snow goes on in half an hour. My heart races, getting excited to finally experience it with her.

I lean into her and whisper, "Do you want me over here watching you or do you want me in the booth with you?"

Snow turns. "I want you with me in the booth. Quick can come too if he wants."

My heart swells knowing she cares for my brother. I smile. "I'll ask him, but I want to be alone with you some of the time."

She leans in kissing me. "Of course, Micah."

When it's time to head to the booth, Quick grabs her bag, and we shuffle out of the VIP area and make our way over to the booth. It's packed like sardines. Snow is in between us again, but it's hard to maneuver our way through the crowd.

I have to push a couple dudes out of the way, and I worry they will try to start a fight, but when they look over my shoulder, they back down. I turn to see Roc moving along with us. I turn to the other side and see Austin is flanking us, making sure no one can touch my girl.

We make it to the booth, and Brant comes out letting Snow inside. Roc and Austin disappear into the crowd, which is crazy because both of them are six foot four.

Ginger takes a few minutes to get her stuff together, but I know the minute she drops her first song. It's one of her original mixes, and the crowd goes nuts. I puff my chest out feeling proud that she's my girl. She truly is unbelievable on the decks.

Sasha opens the door calling my name. I move up the stairs to enter the booth. Sasha moves out with Brant helping her. Quick shuts the door, and it becomes quiet.

Holy shit!

"Fuck, it's quiet in here. I would've thought it was going to be loud. I mean I can hear the music, but it's not like standing outside," I say, surprised.

Snow laughs, saying, "I can turn up the volume in here as loud as out there or off if I want. I have these to mix with."

She pulls on her headphones and starts preparing her next song. I just sit there and admire her from behind and how fucking amazing she is. Snow starts to shake her ass to the beat of the song in the headphones and my dick jumps to attention. I know she is counting the beats to the song to mix in with the next one. Snow turns the music up so I can hear the mix.

When it drops, I recognize the beat, but it sounds different. Snows head bounces and when the vocal hits I laugh. "Can't Get Enough" by Soul Searcher.

It sounds different though, and when Snow turns around, she is singing to me.

My God, she is beautiful - truly an Angel.

Her smile is beaming, and she's happy.

I pull her to me. "Did you remix this song?"

Her eyes light up. "You noticed?"

I throw my head back and laugh. "Yes, I know my music, Angel. This is good. I like the beat."

Snow dances in front of me, turning to look out at the crowd. I stand up looking out, and you can see everything. I feel high right now with so much excitement and energy pulsing through me.

Fuck yeah.

I can see our group across the way, and the girls are up dancing. I move out of her way but keep standing behind her, looking out at everyone moving to the music. They're all feeling it and moving to their own beat. It's so exhilarating to watch. It's a whole different world being up here compared to being out there looking in.

Snow starts to tweak with the mixer, shaking her head and listening to the new song but keeps bouncing to the song that everyone can hear. When I hear that voice cry through the speakers... 'the night I laid my eyes on you.' I stop moving behind her and watch my girl.

Then "Rapture" by Nadi Ali drops and once it's mixed in Snow moves her arms like an Egyptian up over her head. She turns around moving toward me bringing her hands down around my neck.

"I'll surrender to you," she purrs.

I can't take it, I lean down, taking her mouth with mine, demanding, wanting more with our tongues intertwined together. Snow is moving her body to the music against me, and I'm about to explode in my pants I'm so turned on. I break the kiss, breathless.

"Fuck. I want to fuck you so bad. Do you think we would get kicked out if I fuck you real quick right here?" I ask laughing, but I'm half serious.

Snow giggles, "We will have to put that on our bucket list."

"Bucket list?" I reply.

"Yes, I've started a list of things I want to do with you that we've missed out on these past few years." She turns back around thumbing through her music looking for her next song. I don't reply right away, but think about all the things I want to do with her, and then I ask, "What is on this list of yours? Are you going to share it with me?"

She doesn't turn around but shakes her ass pulling her headphones on to mix.

My little Angel is being secretive.

I'm so in awe of her body that I forget about the fucking list and move up behind her again. Sliding my hands around her waist, I lean down nestling my face into the crevice of her neck and hair. I take a big whiff and inhale her jasmine mist spray that I have craved so much. She starts bouncing to the beat again and I pull away to look out over the crowd. This night has been everything I could have imagined and more. I can see my queen is happy and that is all that matters to me.

When she's done with the mix, she turns around smiling big. "I will tell you a few things on my list. One is right now, you here with me. The second is, waking up to you-"

I cut her off. "Angel those are not things on a bucket list. Those are things we have already done." I laugh pulling her against me.

She smiles looking me in the eyes - eyes that are full of happiness. "This bucket list is from when I was a child, and I'm adding onto it."

My heart skips a beat. I lean down and kiss her, lifting her up off the ground.

The door swings open and Quick walks into the booth with a goofy looking smile.

"All right enough of that. I want to see what all this DJing shit is about." Quick shut the door and when he turns to look out at the crowd he yells, "Holy Fucking Shit, you can see everything. Like you're king of the fucking mountain."

Snow laughs. "Exactly."

35

GINGER

"Hi, Iz," I answer my cell phone in the bathroom.

"What do you wear to a biker funeral? Seriously, I don't know," Izzy asks sounding flustered.

I laugh at my friend, always worried about what to wear.

I answer her, "Well, Shy just bought me some new leathers that I'm going to wear, along with a black Wolfeman shirt."

"That doesn't help me!" she exclaims.

"Iz, just wear some jeans, boots, and a black top. I'm sure you will look fine." I laugh.

"Says the cute little biker bitch," Izzy groans.

"Just get over here." I hang up.

Today's the funeral for Striker and the other two men that were killed. All the chapters are here for the services. This week has been crazy with everyone here including my father. Everyone is still on high alert. Dallas said that he got the video footage from the hotel and they're reviewing it to see if they can figure out who left the box. It's the first lead we've had, and I hope we can figure it out soon. We leave tomorrow for Dallas. We have two shows there, and everyone is pretty antsy and on edge.

My poor Shy is being pulled in so many directions that I don't know how he hasn't had an anxiety attack or flipped the fuck out yet. The club, the lounge, Snake and all my drama on top of that. He's been coming home exhausted each night, but he always finds time for his Angel.

Yesterday when I got back from working on my song with Luc in the studio, I found a big package on the bed. Shy had gone out and bought me new riding leathers. I couldn't believe it. When he got home, I gave him a gift of my own, twice to be exact.

This morning he left early to meet up with my father at the clubhouse, saying he would be back here to pick me up for the service. Izzy and Alex are going to come along with the guys. Gus has been hanging around the clubhouse all week with Quick and Shy.

As I walk out of the bedroom my doorbell rings and I look through the peephole, I see it's Gus. Opening it, I smile. "Hi, Gus. Come on in." Holding the door open for him to come in but he doesn't.

"Shy needs you to come with me," he says in a flat voice.

The first thing I do is panic. "What? Why? What happened?"

Gus does his half smile thing. "Gin, everything's fine. I just need you to come down to the garage with me."

I don't say anything but grab my house keys and follow him.

"Grab everything you will need for tonight. We're not coming back up here."

"What why?"

No answer.

Jesus Christ.

Once I have everything, and we're in the elevator I turn to him. "You sure he's okay? Where is Izzy? I thought you were bringing her?"

Gus just stares straight ahead.

Goddamn him.

"Gus, you're freaking me out."

He tilts his head to me. "Don't be. It'll be fine."

Not helping!

When the elevator dings at the garage level the doors open up, and there are about forty bikers lined up.

I gasp. "What the fuck?"

My father, Mac, Uncle Bear, Hawk, and Stitch are all lined up, and when they move to the side, Auntie, Felicia, Sissy, Gigi and a few of the club girls yell surprise. I knew some of the men would be here for the funeral, but I didn't know my whole family would be here. The men who were killed were Scorpions and only became Wolfeman a few months ago, I had no idea everyone was coming. My heart fills with love and excitement.

"Shy, what's going on?"

Shy pulls me to him with a wicked little smile. "Well, we wanted to surprise you. They rode out here this morning wanting to support us, as family does. Something, we wanted to remind you, that you have."

All the ladies come giving me hugs and kisses. Tears pool in my eyes. This is family. Loyalty beyond words. God, I have missed this.

Bikes start to come alive with everyone mounting their bikes. I hug almost everyone before jumping on the back of Shy's bike. My father, the original chapter president, takes the lead as we all follow, heading toward the funeral home.

Not a lot of outsiders are welcomed into motorcycle clubhouses, but my girls and the guys have become part of my life. My father and Shy have let them into my life to protect me all these years, so having them at the funeral and after-party wasn't even questioned. Maddox and Gus have become really close with Shy, and I see a close bond forming. Maddox and his men ride as well, so they have a lot in common. It is rare for a brotherhood to depend on an outsider for support. They usually only depend on their club, but I guess we're one of those rare clubs that make the exception.

I introduce the girls to Maze at the bar while the three of us get a drink, then move toward the DJ that the club hired. The three of us girls decide it would be fun to tag team DJing.

The three of us play a couple songs and then switch. We have everyone up dancing and laughing. Maze even gets my father up shaking his ass. Everyone looks happy and not sad or stressed out. We wanted to get everyone in a good mood. Music can always change someone's mood. The boys are all huddled around watching us, smiling, laughing, talking amongst themselves. My auntie has Uncle Bear dancing and I move to dance with them when I see Maze walking up again.

Maze walks up. "Another shot?"

Izzy tilts her half empty drink toward Maze. "Fuck, I like her. She always knows when we need a drink."

Alex is laughing her ass off on the other side of me and says, "Yes, please and another round of drinks too."

I drop my head.

It's going to be a long night.

The next morning, all three of us were so hungover, that we took turns puking in the plane bathroom. After the Los Angeles incidents, Luc booked his plane for all our travels. At least we could move around on the plane.

Since I was back on tour, Sasha stayed back this weekend, so Brant stayed with her. With Dominic out we all extended our time slot.

The good thing about being sick was that we were so hungover we didn't even worry about someone being after us. We were just praying we could make it through our sets without throwing up.

The guys were high strung, but we made it through both

nights without throwing up or someone trying to kill us. We joked about it all weekend, but the guys weren't too happy with us.

Overall, our weekend in Dallas was uneventful. Thank God. I don't think our group could have handled any more bad stuff.

We're back home, and I've been busting my ass with Luc to finish my song, that I named "My Life." Alex, Luc, and I have been in the studio all week. The label plans to release the song right before we head to Miami, so we are putting the final touches on it.

Shy, Mac, and the boys have been over for dinner, or I go to the clubhouse. I feel so complete with them in my life now. I feel like things are finally falling into place.

We're headed to New Orleans this weekend where we rented a house instead of staying at the hotel. I guess the guys wanted to switch up our plans, hoping to throw whoever off.

We have three days that we all can be normal before we gear up for the weekend travels. I wish it could just be fun for us, but I understand the threat is real and is out there. It comes with both my lifestyles, just now I have it more often than not.

Sasha and Brant are not going this weekend either, but they will be joining us in Miami. I told them she could still come, we could share time slots, especially since Dominic wasn't returning. But, they had other things they needed to attend to.

GINGER

My song hit the top hundred the first day. Everyone was ecstatic for me making our first night in Miami unbelievable. I was so high on life that nothing and no one could have ruined it. The night went off with no drama and no problems. It was just about my song release. When I dropped the song, the crowd went ballistic, and the best part was I had my love there with me, sharing in this unforgettable memory in my life.

He teases me about my stupid bucket list telling me we need to add stuff like this moment. My first ever song release. I was a love sick girl when I wrote the damn list but have kept it all these years. Things like ol' lady, kids, having our own clubhouse, were on it. I never knew the things we were doing today would even be possible when we were together back then.

Being able to travel around with him these past few weeks is something I never thought about. Tonight, walking into the club, people were screaming out my name. It was the first time I heard the crowd call out any of our names besides Maddox's. It was surreal, and I felt lucky to have Shy by my side. I squeezed him tighter, and I felt like I was on top of the world. Things between us are better than ever, and I feel stupid for not believing in myself and that these two lives could coincide.

We fly out tomorrow, and I can't wait to get home. I like this stuff, but now that I have Shy and the club, I'm never really comfortable. Especially knowing it's hard too for Shy being away from his club and brothers with the threat still out there. I'm always the happiest when we're at home.

It's the last night in Miami, towards the end of the night with Maddox and Alex mixing. This place has a booth which is great for us to watch them. The only bad thing about the VIP is we are far away from the booth and across the dance floor. I told the guys it reminded me of Los Angeles, and they yelled at me, but thank goodness we had no problems last night. The crowd down here is good, and everyone is having a good time.

Us girls start dancing with all of our guys around us when Shy yells, "Snake."

I see three men moving toward us, and these guys don't look like they belong. No… they look like bikers.

Sonovabitch.

Everyone jumps into action. Quick throws me up against the wall, while everyone else huddles around.

"Get those guys. They're with Snake. Snake is here," Shy yells out. Our guys start shoving people, and Brant gets around the crowd moving swiftly with Roc and Austin.

Shy jumps over the ropes. I try to see if I can see Beau or Isaac who were up at the booth with Maddox. Fights start to break out with all the shoving and pushing. Quick completely shoves me down into the booth trapping me so no one can get near me and I can't see anything but his ass.

Goddamn it.

When I hear my father's voice yelling my name, I'm pushing at Quick and trying to stand up. Is my father here? He can't be… When I see Mac running toward us, I yell for him. "Mac, I'm up here."

When he sees me, he stops, and I see he is talking to Brant

who has someone down on the ground. My father yells my name again, and both Mac and I yell for him. He comes barreling across the dance floor as Shy emerges from the other side.

Security is everywhere, and luckily there aren't too many fights, it's more like a stampede than anything else. Gus has Izzy pinned in a corner. I look to the booth where Maddox, Isaac, and Alex are waiting. Beau is outside the door. I ask Quick, "Where is Sasha?"

I look around the VIP area. "Quick, Sasha isn't up there, where is she?"

Holy Shit.

Brant jumps up. "Where's Sasha?"

They all look up to the booth and yell, "Is Sasha with you?"

Knowing they probably can't hear us, I yell to Beau, "We're missing Sasha."

Beau moves from the door making his way over to us.

"Are you fucking serious? Where's Austin?"

"Lost him chasing the bikers," Roc answers.

My father comes up and hugs me. "Princess, I'm so glad you are safe."

Shy walks up. "How did you get here?"

My father answers, "We've been tracking Snake the last two days. I didn't want to alarm you if they weren't here."

"Yeah, I lost Snake at the door and didn't want to get stuck outside, so I turned around," Shy says.

The place starts to empty out. Security is forming a circle around us and the biker who is knocked out on the floor. Chad's been dealing with security keeping them off of us and getting them to help us instead of making things worse.

"You knocked him the fuck out," someone tells Brant.

Brant doesn't smile just looks down.

"I need to go find Sasha!" Brant exclaims.

Beau steps forward. "Let's spread out, search the place and I'll head outside, see if she's with Austin. We need to deal with the cops and get this guy out without being arrested; we need answers."

Brant takes off in search of Sasha. Roc moves with Beau. "I'll go with you. We need to get the car so we can dump him in it." I throw Roc my keys. "Let us know when it's okay to come out."

My phone chirps with a notification. I hurry and grab it hoping it's Sasha telling us where she is but when I see the text, I yell for Shy. My father also turns around.

Shy looks around for the immediate threat and moves toward me. Quick and Ethan looking at my phone with my father. Ethan yells, "Fuck, Austin," as he takes off running for the front door. Quick hands Shy my phone.

He looks down and sees the text. "Motherfucker."

My father follows Ethan, yelling at my cousin and the other men who were with him. As everyone runs outside.

I look back down to my phone again.

UNKNOWN
I like Sasha. Sorry about the bald guy. I take from you. I take from them.

Oh, God!

"What the fuck happened? What's wrong," Maddox yells.

I hand him the phone. "They got Sasha, and something's happened to Austin. We need to find him."

It's all my fault. They should have pulled us from the tour.

SHY

It's been a week. A week since we got back from Miami. Everyone is still pretty devastated over the death of Austin and losing Sasha. Brant, Ethan, and Roc are still in Miami, hopefully returning next week. Wolfe and the men went searching for Snake and his men. Roc stayed to deal with Austin's body and make arrangements to get him home. Brant and Ethan stayed to keep looking for any leads on Sasha or who killed Austin. Luc pulled all the girls from the tour, replacing them with a few other DJs from the label.

It was a shit show trying to get everyone on Luc's plane that night. If anyone says money doesn't talk they're full of shit because... that night it sure as fuck did. Not one person questioned Chad carrying an unconscious biker over his shoulder. My Angel went into shock and closed herself off, not speaking. The two other girls were hysterically crying and being carried by the men. It was a complete disaster. Isaac and Beau handled most of the negotiations with the police and the club owner, while we herded everyone into the cars, trying to get to the plane to get us out of the state.

When Ethan and Roc found Austin, shot dead in the parking lot, they wreaked havoc on a few cars nearby until Maddox and Chad calmed them down. Maddox and Chad held it together, but you could see the pain in their eyes at losing such a close friend.

Brant losing Sasha pushed him over the edge, freaking the girls out even more. He kept saying it was his fault she was taken and that he should've made sure she was safe before running after the guys. We all told him that was crazy, that it wasn't his fault, but he didn't listen. He refused to leave and hasn't returned anyone's calls. Roc has been informing us of what he's doing.

Once we got back, things didn't get much better. Snow retreated to her apartment, as did Alex. I haven't seen Izzy, but Gus says she's doing the same, holed up in her apartment. Izzy doesn't live in the building owned by Luc. Her parents have cash and lots of it, so they put her up in an apartment closer to the label downtown.

We have Dallas, Hawk, and Ethan doing everything they can to find out any information on the whereabouts of Sasha. We've been interrogating the biker, one of my guy's ID'd as Ball Z, a former Scorpion member.

All we've been able to get out of him so far is that they wanted me that night. He says he doesn't know anything about taking any girls, that he was coming for me. We know Snake had gotten himself in with some bad guys, making deals he couldn't keep, all because he wants revenge for us killing his father. The guy confirmed that all Snake cared about was killing me for taking his father's life and destroying our club for taking over.

My phone rings, interrupting my thoughts.

"Yeah," I bark into the phone.

"How is she?" Wolfe's voice echoes through the phone.

I let out a long breath. "Same. Hasn't gone out of the apartment since you last saw her a week ago."

"Should I come there and see if I can get her to come out? Or maybe bring Storm?" he asks sounding concerned.

"Nah, I'm headed there now. I'm going to join forces with Maddox in getting both girls together for dinner. I'll keep you posted. Any news from your guy down South about Snake?"

"Hawk has an inside connection at the Devils, and he's looking into finding him, so we should hopefully have something soon."

Fucking finally something.

"Okay, let's connect soon for updates."

Wolfe hangs up after saying goodbye.

Now all I have to do is break that fucking wall down around my girl.

I need my Angel.

GINGER

When I hear the lock turn on the front door, I know it's Shy. I'm on the couch, sitting in the corner with my legs pulled up under me. I'd been on the phone with Alex a few minutes ago. She called to see how I was doing. The three of us girls have been calling each other daily when the guys weren't around.

Izzy has been holed up at her place dealing with Dominic who still hasn't returned but instead has been calling and harassing her about everything. Gus finally took her phone one day when he found her curled up in her bathroom crying. He told her she needed to get some rest and took her phone. She called us on her house phone letting us know what happened and to call her at the house.

"Angel?" Shy's voice pulls me from thoughts of my friends.

I look up at my amazingly good-looking man. He has been so unbelievably good to me, just giving me my space, only coming home and holding me. He has always been good at helping me heal. I just feel so responsible for Austin and Sasha. If this guy wasn't coming for me, everyone would still be here and alive.

When I don't answer, Shy moves to the couch and sits next to me, pulling me onto his lap. He smiles down at me. "Hi."

I can't help it but smile back. "Hey."

Shy leans down, placing a kiss on my nose. "Maze says hello and that she misses you."

I don't say anything, but just look off toward the kitchen. I don't want to be around anyone. I don't feel like having fun when Sasha is somewhere probably hurt, scared or even dead. I can't just act as if *nothing* happened, plus if I stay inside, the crazy fucker can't hurt anyone else.

Shy grabs my chin, turning my head to face him, "I miss my Angel. Tell me what I can do to fix this?"

I shrug because I really don't know. I can't tell him it's because of *me* that they're gone because he will flip out. Tears pool in my eyes, and I fight trying to hold them back from falling.

"Angel, you need to get out of this house. You can't hide here forever. I know you, and you think it's because of you that they're gone, and that's bullshit."

My brows go up in shock that he can read me so well, but I try to mask it. Of course, he would know, it's Shy.

"Angel. Look at me," he demands.

Irritation starts to bubble up inside of me, not wanting to talk about it, hoping he will let it go.

"Angel, don't make me drag your ass out of here."

My temper wins, and I can't take it.

"Just leave it be, Shy. I'm not leaving here. Not until we find Snake," I huff out.

"The fuck you will. Look I'm sorry about Austin and Sasha but you, my girl, are not a quitter or a coward." Shy's voice sounds pissed off.

My own fire boils, deciding it's time to fight back.

I jump off Shy's lap. "Fuck that, Shy. I'm no coward, but fuck you. They're gone because of *my* situation."

Shy gets up coming to face off with me. "*Our* situation."

Sonovabitch.

"Shy, I don't want to fight with you. There is nowhere I want to be right now, except here, so drop it."

Shy spreads his legs wide making himself shorter, becoming eye level with me and folds his arms across his chest. He states with a wicked grin, "Well, I don't want to fight with you either, but damn, at least I got to see that fire in your eyes again."

This little fucker just played me.

"Shy…"

"Angel, all I ask is that we head upstairs and have dinner with Luc, Mia, Alex, and Maddox." The sparkle in his eye has mischief written all over it. I fold my arms over my chest. It would be nice to get out of here and see my friends.

"It technically isn't leaving the building," he pleads with me.

I stand there holding out as long as I can with a straight face. I make him wait for my answer since he pushed my buttons earlier.

Frustration gets to him. "Angel…"

I huff, "Only if Izzy comes too."

Shy stands, dropping his arms and smiles. "Done. Get dressed. They'll be here in thirty minutes." Shy heads to the kitchen with his back to me.

Shocked I answer, "Wait. What? Who will be here? And you haven't even called Izzy."

Shy pulls a beer from the refrigerator, twisting the lid off and smiles at me again. "Already talked to Gus and Maddox. They'll be at Luc's in thirty minutes," he finishes, taking a big long swig of the beer.

Jesus Christ.

I fold my arms looking amused. "What if I didn't agree to go."

Shy walks by me plopping back down on the couch and taking another drink of his beer. "I would have thrown you over my shoulder and carried you up there. No matter what, you were getting out of this fucking apartment tonight," he ends with a smart ass grin plastered across his face.

"Now, quit stewing and get ready."

𝄞

Walking up to Luc and Mia's penthouse thirty minutes later, I have knots in my stomach. I know that no one blames me, but *I* blame myself. Austin was one of Maddox's best friends. I'm worried he'll be upset.

"Angel, whatever you're thinking in that pretty little head of yours, you need to stop. What happened was not your fault. Everyone in there loves you."

Shy pulls me to his side kissing the top of my head. "I love you, Angel."

My heart warms, taking away some of the knots in my stomach.

The door flies open with an energetic Mia behind it. "*Hola*, come in."

Mia grabs me, pulling me into a hug before either of us can say hello.

"*Cariño*, how are you?"

I squeeze her back and whisper, "Been better."

"I know *bebé*, I know," she replies.

Shy shuts the door behind us and says hello to Mia. She pulls away, moving to give Shy a hug. We follow her into the living room where everyone is hanging out. We are the last to arrive, so everyone gets up to greet us. Alex and Izzy beeline it straight for me while the guys all shake hands with Shy and Luc hands him a beer. Once us three girls finally release each other, Mia walks up handing me a glass of wine.

When I finally turn around to greet the men, Maddox is the first, and he's not smiling. My heart starts racing and tears pool up, there is no stopping them. Alex grabs my glass of wine and Maddox pulls me into an embrace.

"Gin, it's okay. They wouldn't want you to blame yourself. It wasn't your fault."

"I'm so sorry, Maddox."

He pulls back looking down at me. "Ginger, listen to me. You got shot protecting Alexandria. She tried to blame herself for that too. You both need to quit blaming yourselves for crazy motherfuckers. This is *not* either of your faults."

I hear Alex sniffling next to me and reach out to grab her hand. Maddox pulls both of us into his massive chest. God, he's huge, a good foot and a half taller than Alex and myself.

"Ok - Okay, no more sad talk. Let's have some dinner," Luc announces from behind all of us.

Maddox releases me only for Gus to replace him, giving me a hug too. My heart fills with so much love for these people that all the knots in my stomach are gone now. I just feel so much love from my second family. I would do anything for any of these people.

Shy moves up behind me, bending down to kiss my neck. "See Angel, nothing but love. You all need to be together during this time, not alone in your rooms." Shy walks by smacking me on my ass. "Now let's eat."

Dinner was filled with great conversation and lots of laughter. We discussed my new song that includes Alex's vocals, and her and Maddox's album that will be coming out in six months. Luc wants me to release another one of my songs in three months.

Once we moved on from music talk, we jumped into the topic of Shy and the lounge that he purchased. I've only been over there once since he became the owner. I could tell Shy didn't want to talk about it, but he answered all of Luc's questions.

Izzy was quiet most of the dinner, she talked and laughed, but she wasn't her bubbly self. I know she is upset and concerned for Dominic, but she won't talk about it. When we've talked this past week, she always changes the subject, saying she doesn't know what's going on with him. All he does is yell at her, and since Gus took her phone, she's trying to not think about it.

I look over at Izzy and smile. She smiles back and says, "So Gin, what are we going to do for your birthday?"

Goddamnit. I was hoping no one would remember.

I shrug. "Haven't thought about it. That's the last thing I want to think about right now."

Everyone gets quiet at the table, and to my surprise, Luc speaks, "Ginger, I think it would be a good thin' to have everybody here for a party. Have your father and everyone at Spin. We could do a big celebration for your birthday and showcase your song."

I haven't been back to Club Spin since the night Alex was taken. I look toward Alex, who's smiling at me, not showing any signs that it would bother her. But I wonder how she'll feel being back there.

I smile. "I'll think about it."

After dinner, we migrated back into the living room to hang out for a while just drinking and laughing. Watching Shy smile and laugh so freely has me tingling all over. He truly is my soulmate. He always seems to know what I need. This past week all he's done is be there for me, holding me, telling me everything will be okay, not pushing me but instead making me feel safe. We haven't had sex in a week, and my wolf needs some love. It's time for me to take care of him.

We're sitting on one side of the couch with his arm around my shoulders. I'm leaning half way over him with my arm between his legs. I run my fingers over his thigh, moving my elbow up and down over his massive erection. Shy groans low enough for just me to hear him.

I lean back onto his chest, turning my head back, I whisper, "I'm hungry for some dessert, are you?"

"Angel..." Shy warns.

I smile.

"Yes, Micah?"

"It's time to go, Angel, unless you want me to fuck you here,"

Shy whispers to me, pushing me to get up off the couch.

"Mia, Luc, thank you for dinner, but I need to get this girl home before she passes out or turns into a pumpkin."

I giggle. The last thing I want is sleep, and he can eat my pie all night long.

38

BRANT

"How are you doing?" Beau asks concerned.
Not fucking good!
"I'm good. We'll be at the office in thirty," my reply dead of any emotion.

I know everyone means well, but I'm fucking sick and tired of everyone asking me if *I'm okay*. I quit taking calls and let the guys deal with everyone. But, I can't ignore Beau's calls, he's my boss, and he's been like a father figure since I was a kid.

"Good. Everyone is just now arriving. We'll see you guys when you get here," Beau exclaims.

I reply with a short, "okay" sounding annoyed.

Roc, Ethan and I have been in Miami for close to two weeks dealing with all the bullshit from that horrific night. I tried to pick up the pieces, figuring out where I went wrong, how they got to her, but each tip we got ran dry. The security footage didn't show us anything. We couldn't find her anywhere on camera; it's like she just vanished.

We also stayed to follow through with Austin's last wishes, which were to be cremated. I guess Austin paid for a national cremation, saying he never knew where he was going to be and he didn't have any family, just the guys, so he took care of everything. Said he didn't want anyone to deal with it just in case something did happen to him. So here we are bringing the box of Austin's remains back to New York. We definitely paid a few people off to get it expedited so we could get back sooner rather than later.

"Are all the guys meeting at Beau's office?" Ethan asks from the front seat, where he and Roc are sitting.

"Yeah," again, I reply sounding very annoyed.

They get it though. They haven't pushed or asked me every fucking two minutes if I'm okay because they get it. They lost one of their best friends. I lost the girl I was supposed to be protecting. The girl I just started fucking around with in hopes of getting over Ginger. But I fucked up. I was so hell bent on getting the guys who were threatening Ginger, the girl I love, that I lost sight of what I was supposed to do, and that left Sasha unprotected.

Fucking hell.

I lost it. I want to find out who took her and kill them. The video shows Snake running out the front door, but he doesn't have her. It also shows Snake shooting Austin, who was holding one of his guys down in the parking lot, but no signs of Sasha.

We pull up to the building where we have our main security office, and it is also where the Spin It label is located. We all fold out of the SUV and head inside with Austin in Roc's hands.

Jesus Christ.

It's so fucked up to be carrying around someone's ashes. Hanging out with these two I can see the bond they all have with one another. Over these past few months, with everything that has gone down with Alex and now Ginger, these dudes have really come through, and I consider them friends.

We walk into the main conference room where everyone is mulling around, but once the door opens and they see us walk in, all eyes are on us.

Fucking beautiful.

Just what I want, to speak to these motherfuckers about that night. Announcing to everyone that I fucked up letting Sasha get taken while trying to be the hero for another woman who is definitely in love with another man. A man who is standing across the room.

"Whaddup," Ethan breaks the ice moving to hug Maddox. Roc follows Ethan handing Austin's box over to Maddox.

I've come to appreciate Roc and how he barely fucking speaks, but everyone gets him. I've learned from him these past few weeks that words are not really needed. I just wonder what fucked him up in the head for him to not want to speak to people.

A hand on my shoulder pulls me from my thoughts. "Brant, good to have you home."

I turn, and both Beau and Luc are standing in front of me. I half hug both of them and give them a head nod, hoping they won't press me to speak. I know I look like shit and they are probably treading water around me to see what emotional state I am in.

When I turn to the rest of the men in the room, I notice we have doubled in number with Shy being here with his men. It looks like both chapters' officers are here, but Wolfe isn't present. Beau has all our men here as well. I wonder if they have new information.

"What's going on? Do we have new information?" I say looking at Beau.

Beau, Luc, and Maddox make their way to the front of the conference room.

Fuck this can't be good.

"We had a tip, or should we say sighting, of Snake and five guys in Knoxville, Tennessee. Wolfe and a group of men have gone in search of them."

I become enraged just thinking about that motherfucker. Seeing him on tape shooting Austin will forever be embedded into my brain. I glance over to Roc, who is now standing next to Chad, and I can see by his expression he feels the exact same way.

Beau continues. "The guy we brought back, he goes by Ball Z, seems to be just a front man, meaning he knows nothing. It seems Snake isn't telling all his guys the truth or at least what he has planned. Which is smart - if they go down they don't know shit, either way, both my team and Shy's team have tortured and interrogated him, but he doesn't know anything except Snake wants revenge on the MC, and to be precise, Shy."

Ethan interjects, "Can we see the fucker?"

Shy steps forward. "He's gone. No one will be seeing him anytime soon."

"Our three groups have been working together for almost a year now. I, myself have worked with Wolfe for several years now, but we all need to trust each other. This fight with Snake is not just the MC's problem but all of ours. He killed one of Maddox's men, took one of our DJs, and is after Ginger who is linked to all of us in some way. We need to join forces and expand our resources to catch this guy. We have all been huddled in a circle, trying to protect what we think he is after, instead of stretching out and building a stronger force so they can't even get near the center."

What the fuck is he talking about?

All the men look lost, not understanding what Beau is trying to get at because we have all *been* working together and sharing our resources.

I rub my face, irritated and ask, "What are you saying? We *have* been working together."

Maddox steps forward. "What he's saying is we are going to draw them out. Our girls have been hiding thinking if they come out, something will happen to someone else they care about. I don't want Alexandria living like this. We need to outsmart this motherfucker."

"What he's also saying is, we're going to promote and plan a huge event in celebration of Ginger's birthday, drawing this son of a bitch out."

I blow the fuck up. "Are you fucking insane? What if they get her?"

"They won't, not in our own club," Shy growls.

Are they fucking for real? "Have you all forgotten they *took* Alex right in front of all of us? In. Our. Own. Club." I am seething.

Beau takes a step toward me but stops. "Brant, you know there was a lot of things we did wrong in Alex's situation. It won't happen again. We will have the backing of the MC, all of Maddox's men and our guys."

Maddox steps forward. "I've called in a couple of sleepers, or like you guys call them, ghosts. The plan is to start acting normal, and we go back to our usual routines with our usual security. It will make them think they can outsmart us, but if we have undercover guys, sleepers, and half of the MC without cuts, they won't know who all's with us."

"What sleepers?" Chad shoots off.

Before Maddox can answer, one of Beau's new guys speaks up, "How do you know they will even come? They know we'll have people at the door. It won't be like in Miami where no one knew who they were except us. It will all be for nothing."

"Okay, look. We have a bunch of events comin' up. The party for Ginger is just goin' to be the first big event. It will be publicized and promoted. Everythin' we do will be here in New York, where we can control it. The girls are not on tour anymore. We all are goin' back to our normal lives. Work. DJing... If we put this into play and plan out each event, they won't see us, and we will be prepared," Luc answers.

Fuck this shit. Ginger will be a sitting duck.

Maddox continues after Luc pauses, "I already have two ghosts watching both Ginger and Alex at all times. They both live in the same building. If either of them leaves, I will have eyes on them. No one knows what these people look like but my team, and believe me when I say you will not see them."

I look over to Shy to see how he feels about two people he doesn't know watching his girl, because I would be fucking pissed.

Folding my arms over my chest, trying to control my rage, I ask Shy, "Are you okay with this? You're okay with dangling Ginger out there like bait?"

Shy turns to face me looking pissed as ever. "*My* girl can handle herself. She *will* be strapped, aware of *all* our plans, and what is going on. I can not and will not let her sit in our apartment like some caged animal. *I will* be there to protect her."

It's like a blow to my gut, the undertone and meaning in each of his words, letting me know he believes I fucked up with Sasha. I didn't protect her. Instead, I was blinded by my own need to win Ginger back.

Goddamnit!

GINGER

When Shy comes home and tells me about the meeting they all had in regards to Alex and my safety, I was pissed. It's like they are putting us on display and just hoping that this stupid fucker will show his face. Plus, I have people watching me, and no one knows who they are or what they look like beside Maddox.

I was pissed off and called Alex to discuss it with her. She was pissed too. She told me that Maddox's team and Brant are pissed off at him because he won't tell anyone who he has watching over us. Maddox said the less we know, the better. He promised his men that if they saw them, they would know who they were immediately.

The three of us girls have gone into work a couple days this week to work on music. My birthday celebration is in three days at Club Spin. I'm not looking forward to it because I feel like we're all just on display. I'd rather spend my birthday at the clubhouse with my family and close friends. Somewhere I would feel safe. All my family is coming to be with me no matter what, and that puts too much pressure on me. What if something happens and my auntie or one of the other girls gets hurt.

Tonight I'm DJing at Club Touch. It's a smaller club and one that we don't have control over. We won't have eyes at the door or on the cameras. Shy has me strapped with a knife just in case. I'm wearing skinny jeans, and instead of heels, I have on boots to hide my knife inside. With a flowy shirt and my black leather jacket.

I told Shy I didn't have a good feeling about tonight. Alex and Maddox aren't even DJing, only Izzy and myself. They have some new rookie DJs playing before and after us.

"You ready Angel?"

I look up in the mirror while finishing putting on my lips stain. Shy has insisted that I wear it all the time, now that he found out he can kiss me as much as he wants and it stays on.

I smile. "Ah-ha."

I walk by him, giving him a quick kiss.

"Damn you woman and that *fuck me* lipstick," Shy groans

I giggle, making my way to the front door.

The VIP area is full with all our friends and people from the label. Tonight everyone has congratulated me and told me how good my song is. The night has been fun, and I have tried to relax with everyone here.

Us girls have been taking shots and trying to relax. I don't know how anyone would be able to get through our wall of men. Izzy has been quiet all night, and I've wanted to get her alone to see what's wrong. She was fine earlier when I called to see what she was wearing, but now it looks like she is upset.

"Iz, want to hit the bathroom before we go on stage?"

Izzy looks up from her phone to reply. "Sure, let me get my stuff."

I walk up to Shy, who's looking out over the crowd with Mac and Quick standing at his side. It's the first time Mac's been to the club with us. He's had me cracking up dancing around. I grab Shy's ass, rising up on my tiptoes to speak to him in his ear. "I'm going to the bathroom with Izzy before we go up on stage.

Something is wrong, and I want to talk to her alone."

Shy turns around throwing his arm over my shoulder, kissing the top of my head. "You got it, Angel. Let me tell the others while you grab your stuff."

Shy walks off toward Maddox and the guys. I walk over to where we put all of our music stuff and see Gus speaking to Izzy, who looks like she is going to cry. When he sees me coming, he steps back from her picking up her and my stuff.

"Gus, you don't have to do that, I can carry my stuff." I laugh.

Gus gives me one of his scary looks. "Not happening. I'll go with you girls and hold it while you go to the bathroom."

I smile. "Okay, thanks."

Izzy still hasn't said anything, and I link my arm with hers, pulling her toward the exit of the VIP area. Shy, Quick, Gus, and Chad are all waiting for us. The guys box us in, and we all head to the bathroom. We have a special bathroom for DJs and VIP guests, but tonight there are two women ahead of us. It's a small hallway with one door at the end, which is the girl's bathroom, so the guys stand to watch at the entrance of the hall, but Shy heads down the hall with us. I give him a look, knowing he knows I want to talk to her. Shy slows but is still near us.

"Iz, what's going on?"

Before I can even finish, she is crying. "Dom just won't let up. He's back and wants to see me, but I've told him not right now. I told him everything that's going on and that he is too possessive of me. We don't need to fight right now. I miss him, but I'm so tired of fighting. He's just so aggressive and verbally demanding."

I stand there rubbing her arms to comfort her while she vents.

I want to smack the shit out of Dominic myself. I don't know how she puts up with it, but I think he plays on her insecurities. He verbally wears her down, getting his way in the end. Luckily she has us girls and Gus protecting her, but he still gets to her.

"Iz, do you want one of the guys to talk to him?"

Her head snaps up, and I see she is terrified. "No! I don't want anyone to talk to him. It will only upset him more. I'll handle it. I'm just upset right now and needed to vent."

I see the look in her eye though and know she is scared shitless of him. My blood boils. I make a mental note to have a discussion with Shy about this and maybe have the guys pay a visit to Dominic. This can't keep going on, and you can see she wants out but she's scared.

The hallway light is dim, but you can see well enough, so when the door to the bathroom opens, the bright light shines out blinding us, while a group of girls come out. The girls in front of us head in, and we all move to the side. When the girls are passing us, I notice the red hair.

It can't be...

I'm not so lucky, because I come face to face with Raven. I look over to see Shy is down the hall talking to the guys and not paying attention.

"Look who it is. The little princess. You don't have your auntie or the club to back you up tonight, bitch," Raven teases.

Izzy stands up straighter, pulling herself together, and just like that she is back to my Izzy-full-of-hell.

"The fuck she doesn't. Who the fuck are you?" Izzy threatens.

I move forward, not backing down, and putting myself in front of Izzy. The girls form a circle blocking the guys from us, making it look like girls are in line for the bathroom. No matter though, I don't need Shy to fight my battles, this cunt needs her ass beat.

"Rave, you need to be moving along. I don't want trouble in here tonight."

She gets in my face. "You should have thought of that before you broke my nose."

Rave pushes me back against the wall, but my right hand is already coming up to meet her face. Izzy moves to grab one of the other girls. Rave and I are tangled together. I have my hands full of her hair when I hear Shy yell, "What the fuck?"

Shy and Gus break up Rave and I while Quick handles the other girls. Once Shy has us apart, he moves to stand in front of me looking at Rave. "Cunt, you better start stepping before I put my hands on you. I think it's time you leave this club and don't come back. If you lay another hand on my girl, there will be a fucking price to pay. Do. You. Hear. Me. Bitch?"

Rave fixes her hair, pulling her shoulders back and laughing, not even fazed by Shy's threat. "Yeah, I hear you."

Izzy and I are amped up when the guys turn to us asking questions. The door to the bathroom opens, and we go in to pull ourselves together. By the time we come out of the bathroom, we're laughing and talking shit about what just happened. Gus and Shy haven't moved from outside the door.

Izzy and I have our arms linked together following them out. Once we hit the crowded area on the dance floor it gets tight, and we have to squeeze together. Shy and Quick are in front of us, and when they stop abruptly, we run into them laughing.

Shy's voice sobers me up. "What the fuck do you want? I told your ass to leave."

I look around Shy, seeing Raven with her girls and the group of men behind them.

This isn't good.

Chad and Gus move us out of the way to stand next to Shy and Quick. Raven starts mouthing off, and one of the other girls tells the men they're with Shy put his hands on them.

Rage consumes me, and I bust through launching myself at Raven. "You fucking whore. That is a bunch of fucking lies."

All hell breaks loose from there, with people trying to pull us apart, but when Raven's group of men rush our guys, I lose track of everyone. All I care about is beating this bitch's ass. I have Raven in a headlock, and I'm about to throw an uppercut to her face, when I'm hit on the back of my head with something hard, knocking me out.

BRANT

All I see from the VIP area is Ginger launch herself toward some redheaded girl, following a bunch of guys jumping in all around them. I yell at Maddox, and we all jump into action. I make my way over, but I can't see Ginger. Shy has two guys on him, but I turn to look around, and Ginger is not there.

Oh, God. No.no.no.no...

Panic sets in and I start shoving people out of the way when I see him. Snake is dragging a lifeless Ginger toward the exit with the redheaded bitch. If you didn't know it, you would think they were trying to help get her out of the circle of fighting. I'm about fifteen feet away, and I see the back of another woman with crazy brown curly hair approach them asking them something. I yell Snake's name. When he looks up, the woman throat punches him before knocking the redhead out with one punch. She turns, grabbing Snake flipping him over, body-slamming him to the ground.

Holy fucking shit. What the fuck!

I'm just feet away, and the woman has him down on the ground, clutching his throat. This girl is like a buck twenty, and she just immobilized Snake, who is well over a hundred and eighty pounds and the redheaded lady. I'm stunned and about to say something when another biker approaches from behind her. Before I can warn her, she kicks out knocking him back on his ass. She jumps on him throwing a couple punches, knocking him out.

Jesus Christ.

Who is this girl, Jackie Chan? Obviously, this chick can take care of herself, so I move over to Ginger to see if she's breathing when the woman jumps up and moves to strike me.

I put my hands up. "Relax. I'm Brant, her security." She stops to blow her hair out of her face and just stares at me for a minute. I feel Ginger's neck for a pulse.

The nameless girl relaxes, grabs all of her wild hair, and puts it on top of her head in a bun before placing her hands on her hips. "She's alive, but he hit her in the back of her head."

She's beautiful. "Who the fuck are you?"

I hear Chad growl from behind me. "Andy, what the fuck are you doing here?"

I look over my shoulder to see a pissed off looking Chad with bloody knuckles and lip.

What the fuck is going on? Who is this chick?

GINGER

I wake up not knowing where I am, with my head pounding. I try to sit up, but pain shoots through my temple.
"Fuck." I hiss in pain closing my eyes and falling back onto the bed.
"Don't try to move, you were hit pretty hard on your head. The doctor thinks you have a concussion," Izzy says from somewhere next to me.
I'm relieved to hear her voice. "Where are we?" I ask.
"They brought all of us girls back to Luc and Mia's house. You're in Alex's old room. Here, take these."
Izzy hands me some pills and helps me lift my head to drink the water.
"Where is everyone? Where's Shy? What happened?" I ramble off questions trying to remember.
"Alex and Mia are in the kitchen making food and drinks for everyone. The guys all left with Shy, and they headed over to the clubhouse."
"My head's fuzzy, what happened?"
"Ginger, you need to relax. Don't try to sit up." Alex's voice rings through the room.

"Iz, what happened?" I ask.

"We were all at Club Touch. That redheaded whore and her group instigated a fight with us distracting everyone and giving Snake the opportunity to grab you."

"Oh, God. I remember. Izzy are you okay?" I rush out worried someone hurt her in the fight.

"You're worried about me? It was you that got knocked out by Snake."

"So what happened?" I panic. "I need to sit up and see you girls. Help me sit up, please."

They gently pull me up into a sitting position before I open my eyes slowly. My head feels like it's splitting open from the back. Izzy looks fine, with no marks or any sign that she was in a fight.

They're okay. Thank God.

"Okay, now tell me what happened after I was hit."

Alex fills me in on what she saw. Then she tells me what Shy told them about some girl saving me. I'm shocked, and she laughs, saying everyone was. After that, they got me out and back here. Now all the guys are interrogating Snake and that redhead at the clubhouse, in hopes of finding out where Sasha was taken.

"Please let them find her. Can one of you text Shy that I am awake."

Alex agrees, jumping up from the bed and heading out of the room. I look over at Izzy and can see she is struggling.

"Iz, I'm sorry you were pulled into that shit. That bitch is from the clubhouse and used to fuck around with Shy," I say in a calm voice.

"Don't be sorry. Shit, that was like the highlight of my week, shit maybe my month. It felt good to hit someone." Iz laughs.

I reach my hand out to her. When she takes it, I pull her into me for a hug.

"Iz, I love you. Thank you."

Izzy leans forward hugging me. "Girl, you know I have your back. You're one of my best friends. I wouldn't let anything happen to you."

A warm feeling settles over me. I hear Faith's voice saying that same thing to me years ago. Love for these girls has become my life, and I will do everything in my power to keep them safe.

Around mid afternoon the next day, with still no word from the guys, Izzy and I are on my couch watching movies. Luc came home last night telling us we all needed to stay the night. I texted Shy, and the only response I got was that he loved me and to stay with Luc. I was okay with that. But the next morning my head hurt and I want to change my clothes. Izzy and I talked Luc into letting us go to my place and clean up. Which led to us laying on my couch. I know they're doing horrible things to Snake, so I don't bother Shy.

Izzy leans forward grabbing her phone off the coffee table for the millionth time.

"Iz, who are you hoping is going to call or text?" I wonder if Dominic is still in the picture.

She puts the phone back on the coffee table. "Gus. He hasn't replied to any of my texts. He has *never* not replied. It's freaking me out."

"Is something going on with you and Gus?" I ask without even thinking.

She sits up. "No, we're like best friends. Like you and Brant were."

I laugh. "I was messing around with Brant for over a year."

Izzy throws herself back down onto the couch saying, "I've been with Dominic. I'm his job. He's my security detail. We're just really close, it's nothing like that."

"Would you want it to be more if he did?" I question.

Izzy is quiet for a moment, and I hear the front door lock open. We both sit up on the couch, and I grab my head that is still hurting.

Shy and Gus come walking in looking really tired. Izzy is off of the couch, rushing up to Gus and pushing him.

Holy shit!

"What the bloody hell, Iz." Gus grabs her arms before she can hit him again.

"You didn't call or text me back. I've been worried sick," she states.

Shy navigates around them, getting out of their way, and over to me.

"Angel," Shy says exhausted.

I smile. "Micah."

I'm in his arms kissing him, thanking God he is home and okay.

Gus and Izzy yell goodbye, but neither of us acknowledge them as we make our way to the bedroom.

Before he places me on the bed, Shy stops to look at me. "It's over Angel. We have nothing to worry about; the threat is gone. It's all over."

A feeling of relief runs through my body. "Sasha? What about Sasha?"

Shy's face falters. "She's gone, or at least that's what Snake said. He said she was gone for good. Brant and the boys are going to look into what we found out, but it doesn't look good."

My heart breaks. I know Brant is still dealing with her being taken. Shy grabs my chin, lifting my face to look at him again. "You and me. We're all safe now, and that's all that matters."

Shy kisses me deeply, but pulls back breathless. "I'm going to take a shower and let you think about everything I just told you. When I come out, I want to make love to you, long, deep and slow. I want to feel every inch of you, Angel, so relax and get all this negative shit out of the way, because when I get out of that shower, there will be no more negative shit around us, you hear me?"

"I hear you," I whisper.

Shy kisses my forehead and walks into the bathroom shutting the door behind him.

We're all safe. Finally.

41

GINGER

I'm on stage mixing at Club Spin where it all began, but this time I have both my families here. It's my birthday celebration, and the place is packed. Everyone from the label and both MC chapters are here.

Seeing my father watch me on stage is one of the most fulfilling things I've ever felt, bringing tears to my eyes. I felt my momma and Faith with me too. Living the life of an international DJ, and being part of the MC is who I am, I just needed to embrace it and love all the things that I have in my life. No matter what life I live, there will always be drama, but I'm a Wolfeman and can deal with anything as long as I have my friends and family. That's what my song is about "My Life." It's moved up on the Billboard chart making the top twenty.

I laugh, watching the girls pull my auntie out onto the dance floor. I jump around behind the decks, pumping the crowd up and it hits me - I need to play my girls' song that I know everyone will love. Well all of us girls, maybe not so much the men.

Fuck them. It's my birthday!

We started playing this song when we were on tour, and I swear Brant wanted to kill us for playing it on repeat, but this song was made for us. It's our song, and I still listen to it on repeat, but at least Shy laughs at us, not like Brant who would turn it off.

I look over and see Shy's on stage next to me bobbing his head to the music. I laugh thinking of all the times us girls sang how bad-ass we were or how he would love us. Each time he would laugh and say yes 'you are, bitches.'

I turn back to the decks and listen, waiting for the right moment and beat to drop it in…once I hit the button, I wait for the reaction. I just wanna have fun screams through the speakers, and I start bouncing on my tippy toes with my arms pumping in the air, "Bitch, I'm Madonna" by Madonna and Nicki Minaj plays out.

The crowd, along with my girls, screams throwing their hands in the air. All my girls look to each other mouthing "Bitch" and pointing at each other, hopping around.

When I feel him behind me, I laugh, knowing what he will say, "Who do you think you are?" Shy growls into my ear from behind.

I swirl around to face the love of my life. Shy is wearing his cut tonight, Luc said it was my party, and all the MC's could wear their colors. He looks so fucking powerful wearing it. His hair is down and hanging around his face. My hands instantly go up, running them through it, tugging at the end.

"Bitch, I'm your Angel," I sass back.

Shy throws his head back, laughing.

I smile seductively. "I'm done in twenty minutes. Want to check another thing off my bucket list?"

Shy's head snaps back with eager eyes looking straight at me, and a huge smile. "There are quite a few we could knock off that list tonight."

I push him away, turning to the mixer, but looking back over my shoulder. "Bathroom in twenty."

I turn, laughing, knowing I just made his night. I put my

headphones back on. I love teasing him.

I'm mixing another song when a hand touches my shoulder. I'm thinking it's Shy, still turned on, waiting impatiently for my set to be over so we can have a quickie in the bathroom, but I turn to face my father.

I pull my headphones off. "Daddy."

He hugs me, telling me in my ear, "Princess, they told me to come up here and see what all the fuss is about, but Jesus Christ that's a lot of fucking people watching you. I'm good."

He pulls away with a smile.

"You don't like people watching you?" I say jokingly.

He looks out over the crowd."Yeah, I'm good with small crowds and no one watching me, but baby girl I am so proud of you. I love you!"

I hug him, "I love you too, Daddy, always have..."

"Always will, Princess."

It's close to the end of the night, and everyone is still going strong. The VIP area is full of my family and friends. Shy fully fucked the shit out of me in the bathroom for a good ten minutes. It was not a quickie. Thankfully, Quick was outside the door making sure we weren't bothered. He was going to ask Mac to do it, but I said hell no, that he was my cousin and that I wouldn't be able to concentrate.

Since Snake is gone, along with the threat, everyone has relaxed some, letting the girls go on the dance floor and dance. We can all move around without being boxed in by security. It's been by far the best night of my life.

I see my auntie and Gigi walking up to me, and I smile. "Are you having fun?"

Gigi throws her hands in the air. "Fuck yes. Now I know why you want to live here."

My auntie smacks her. "Don't you even think about leaving me, girl."

We all laugh, but Shy grabs me around the waist, and I squeal.

I turn in his arms laughing, but when I see the look in his eyes I sober. "What is it? What's wrong?"

"Angel, there was a vote a long fucking time ago, but we just made it official this morning, and I wanted to give you this." Shy turns and that is when I notice my father, and all the original officers, are standing there. When my father steps forward, he hands Shy a small petite cut. My eyes start to pool with tears.

"Snow, I've waited years for this moment, and I think today is the perfect day to give this to you. With both of your lives becoming one, I need to make it official, and with everyone here, I thought it would be perfect."

Shy hands me a Wolfeman cut, "Property of Shy Jenkins."

The entire VIP erupts with cheers, whistles, and people yelling my name.

I launch myself at him, and of course, he catches me with ease.

"I love you, Micah Jenkins."

"I love you too, Angel."

When I hear my song, "My Life" drop, Alex who's DJing yells over the crowd, "This is for you Gin!" The crowd goes crazy, and I am crying, crying happy tears.

I put on my cut and go around hugging all the members, starting with my aunt who pushes my father out of the way.

I'm so proud of you, my girl. You look so much like your momma. I know that my Foxy's looking down on you today with so much pride and love. I love you, Snow."

My father grabs his sister. "Move woman."

I laugh. "Daddy."

He looks at me with a straight face. "What? She was

monopolizing you." He pulls me into a tight hug. "Now you're Shy's queen. Just like your momma was to me. She would be so happy for you."

"Thank you, Daddy. I love you."

Once I am finally passed back to Shy, he pulls me close, kissing my forehead.

"See, we checked two things off your bucket list off tonight. We could try for three."

I throw my head back laughing.

I love my life.

Epilogue

GINGER

(Four months later)

It's the grand opening of the White Wolfe Lounge, and everyone is here. Life has been good. Balancing both lifestyles has actually been easier than I thought. After my birthday, I was back in the studio working on my second original song. With "My Life" still rising up the charts, pushing me into the top ten, I've been pushing myself to make this next one even better.

Shy threw himself into his club and fixing up the lounge. When he told me they were going to name it after the MC and me, I laughed. But when Mac said White Wolfe, I fell in love with the name instantly.

Alex and Maddox have been touring Europe for the last month with a new couple the label is looking to bring onto the label. They DJ together just like Maddox and Alex do. They call themselves X-Ray, but their names are Dex and Raydene. They're really good and super nice. Maddox said he wanted to have some time with just the two of them and travel.

Of course, his team went with them, along with Brant. He said he was going to follow Alex and that he needed some time away. We talk, but it's not like it used to be. He still hasn't given up on looking for Sasha. He's changed since she was taken. Plus I think losing me, pushed him over the edge and he just needed some time to sort his shit out.

Brant told me he would always have a place in his heart for me, and I said the same, but as a friend. When he told me I had a good man and that he was happy for me, I cried. I think Roc's helping Brant deal with whatever he has going on, because they have become inseparable since they came back from Miami.

Tonight we're also celebrating Gus becoming a prospect for the Wolfeman, along with two other guys. He has been hanging around the clubhouse, and going on rides with the guys, so when they told us girls Quick sponsored him to become a prospect, it wasn't a big surprise to us. Gus said it just feels right. He still works for Beau, but only watches over Izzy and me.

I have been talking about maybe doing another tour myself, but I told Luc only one weekend a month. I don't want to be away that much. I love DJing, but I love my life as an ol' lady more. I will be playing at the White Wolfe one night a week.

Overall, everyone is happy and moving forward in their lives. Shy and I keep checking things off my bucket list and of course adding new things. Shy thought it would be fun to make one of his own, but when he showed me his list, I fell over laughing, because it was all sexual things. We finished his list in a week.

Izzy is probably the only one that is still dealing with drama. She has been trying to get rid of Dominic, but he is one crazy fucker. After my birthday he was non-stop calling, texting and trying to see her, but she has told him it's over. I tell her to quit answering the phone, but she still answers.

He showed up at the club last week where she was DJing and was arrested for assaulting some guy that Izzy was talking to. The next night some Russians came in asking where he was and they weren't happy he was in jail. Once he got out of jail, Gus and the guys tried strong-arming him, but that didn't stop him. It only made it worse.

With all the shit he got into down in LA and then last week's incident, he went back to Russia to deal with some family stuff, and we think to get away from his court stuff. Luc says it's a fucking mess. We're just glad he is gone for now, and all I can do is be here for her and help her along the way. The three of us girls' bond is tighter than ever.

"Bitch, you ready?" Izzy yells from behind me, scaring the shit out of me.

"Jesus, Iz. You scared me."

Izzy laughs. "We're heading back to the clubhouse, and it's you and me on the pole. We need to show these *little girls* what's up."

I smile. "Okay, go tell the guys we're ready."

I turn and watch my auntie and uncle dancing around the small dance floor. If a year ago you would have told me that I would be Shy's ol' lady or be seeing my family on a regular basis, mixing and producing, I would have thought you were crazy. But, this year changed me, and it was all for the better. Relationships were mended, some even blossomed.

The best thing that ever happened to me is walking toward me right now like a man on a mission- that mission being me.

"Angel, you ready to ride?"

I smile. "Always."

THE END

ABOUT THE AUTHOR

Crazy, outgoing, adventurous, full of energy and talks faster than an auctioneer with a heart as big as the ocean... that is Angera. A born and raised California native, Angera is currently living and working in the Bay Area. Mom of a smart and sassy little girl, an English bulldog, and two Siamese Cats. She spends her days running a successful law firm but in her spare time enjoys writing, reading, dancing, playing softball, spending time with family and making friends wherever she goes. She started writing after the birth of her daughter in 2012 and hasn't been able to turn the voices off yet. The Spin It series is inspired by the several years Angera spent married into the world of underground music and her undeniable love of dirty and gritty romance novels.

ALSO BY ANGERA ALLEN

Alexandria – Book One – Spin It Series

COMING SOON…

Izzy – Book Three – Spin It Series

FOLLOW AND CONNECT

Email ~ authorangeraallen@gmail.com
Website ~ authorangeraallen.com
Facebook ~ /authorangeraallen
Instagram ~ @angeraallen
Twitter ~ @angeraallen

Available ~ Amazon – iBooks – Nook – Kobo

ACKNOWLEDGEMENTS

Wow... It has been a crazy six months since my first book Alexandria was published.

First and foremost, I want to thank my family but most importantly my parents. They are my biggest fans and supporters. My father for all his love and support, especially his hugs. My mom has and will always be my biggest cheerleader and my best friend. My auntie Debbie for always being there for me. You always put a smile on my face no matter what is going on. I can't wait for our next girl's trip.

To my baby girl: Thank you for understanding Momma has to work on her computer at night. Your daily smiles, hugs and I love you's are priceless. The love and support you give to me is the strength I need to keep going. I love you, my little sunshine.

To my die-hard beta readers: Marlena S., Andy B., Jeriann O., Jennifer G., Kim H., Dawn B., Nicole F., Jennifer R., and Angie D. All of you ladies have been with me each step of the way, giving me honest advice and unwavering support. Thank you for always dropping what you are doing to read the newest chapters, and respond with your honest advice. I love each and every one of you.

Marlena Salinas, I know I said this in the first book, but you are my partner in crime and soul sister. I could be here all day listing all the things you have done for me throughout the years. You are my spiritual ground, and you always help me lighten my soul when it is full. You've been my main support throughout writing BOTH of my books, helping me develop each character's story, keeping me on track when I start to wander from the story. After Alexandria, I have learned no decisions are made without your final approval. I am so thankful for your true friendship. I love you Mar.

Kim Holtz, Gu-url… where do I start? We met at Book Splash 2016, instantly becoming friends to Book Splash 2017 where we were roommates to friends for life. Thank you for listening to me ramble non-stop day and night about this damn book and giving me your honest opinion. Most importantly for coming to my office during crunch time helping me edit this damn book. It was priceless to hear us on the phone going over last minute stuff and the screenshot texting with more edits. You always know what I am thinking, so thank you for fixing my mixed up words! I love that you can understand me even when I don't make sense. I look forward to all our upcoming book endeavors including another round of Book Splash in 2018. Love yah girl!

Angie Davis: Thank you for keeping my Angels group going strong with all the planning, building, scheduling of takeovers and daily devotion to the group. I love you girl, you've been my rock, and I couldn't do it without you. Thank you for all you do.

Andy Barba: Thank you for pushing me each step of the way. I just want you to know how much it means to me you are calling and texting me asking for more. You have been a huge factor in both of my books being published when they did. I love your opinion, the ideas, and advice you give me. I really love how you get so excited or even mad at me with each character. I promise his story is coming and yes, I used your name.

Heather Coker & Jennifer Ramsey: Thank you, ladies, for designing and making my swag. I love them! Both of you have been by my side through both my books, and I am so grateful to have each of you in my life.

Roche Family: Thank you for all the love and support. Sonya, my sister, thank you for the Nut Up Industries promotional box that you sent me. Sweet Heat Almonds will be one of my swag from here on out. Nut up, bitches.

To all my guy friends who helped in making this book by giving me advice, doing "research" or stating the facts: N. Llama, S. Rhib, N. Northrop, Worm, Baby J.

Tawnya & Steve Rhib: My daughter's Godparents and two of my closest friends. Thank you two for putting in all those long nights of "research." You're welcome, Steve! The Sleep Number bed will be forever a part of our life now. I wish I could have put the stick figure picture that Steve made you, describing a sex scene that you didn't understand. Tawnya, I added this character (Lolli-Tawnya) because it reminded me of your bachelorette party in Tahoe with the stripper poles. And the endless nights dancing at the clubs. Thank you for all the "research" pictures and demonstrations. I love you both so much.

Photographer-Model-Cover Design: Eric Battershell, I want to thank you for a few things. First, for doing two photo shoots in order to get the right shot I was looking for. Second, for putting up with me changing the cover photo at the last minute and asking you to edit it during a crazy time in your life. I will forever be indebted to you. The third is for referring CT Cover Creations to me for the cover design. Clarise Tan, thank you for being patient with me. You were brilliant, and I love the cover designs you made. Kaitlin Hughes, thank you for shooting twice for me to get the right shot I was looking for. I love the cover and can't wait to have you by my side at book signings.

To my editor, Ellie McLove: It all started with me Facebook stalking you. Then I went to your LoveNVegas 2016 where we first met. The fact that you say, "Fuck" all the time won me over, and I knew I had to have you as my editor. Thank you for reading my words and making my story shine. I thank God you pushed my book through getting it finished in time. I can't wait to work together again soon.

My bloggers: Book Happiness, Romance Book Worm, Jam Book Blog for pushing my cover and book release.

Give Me Books Promotions: Thank you for doing all the promotional giveaways, release blitz and boosts. I look forward to working with you more.

To my Angels, thank you for all your support and helping

me build my dream. I love my group, and it just keeps getting bigger… let's keep it going!

Thank you to all my author friends who have helped me through this process with so much love, lots of patience and much needed support: S.R. Watson, Leela Lou Dahl, Chelle Bliss, Felicia Fox, Chelsea Camaron, Kathy Coopmans, Harper Sloan, Felicia Lynn, AD Justice, and Vicki Green.

To all my friends and family that have pushed me and supported me through these past six months, I just want you all to know I love you and thank God every day for you. Without your love and support, I wouldn't have been able to finish this book. I know I'm forgetting people, and I am sorry for that, but just know I am so thankful for everyone that had a part in making this dream a reality.

Last but definitely not least, to my fans. It has been CRAZY these past six months with all the emails and reviews from my first book. I can't wait to see what you all think of Ginger. I love each and every one of you.

With Love, Angera

Made in the USA
San Bernardino, CA
02 September 2017